THE
LEGEND
OF AUNTIE PO

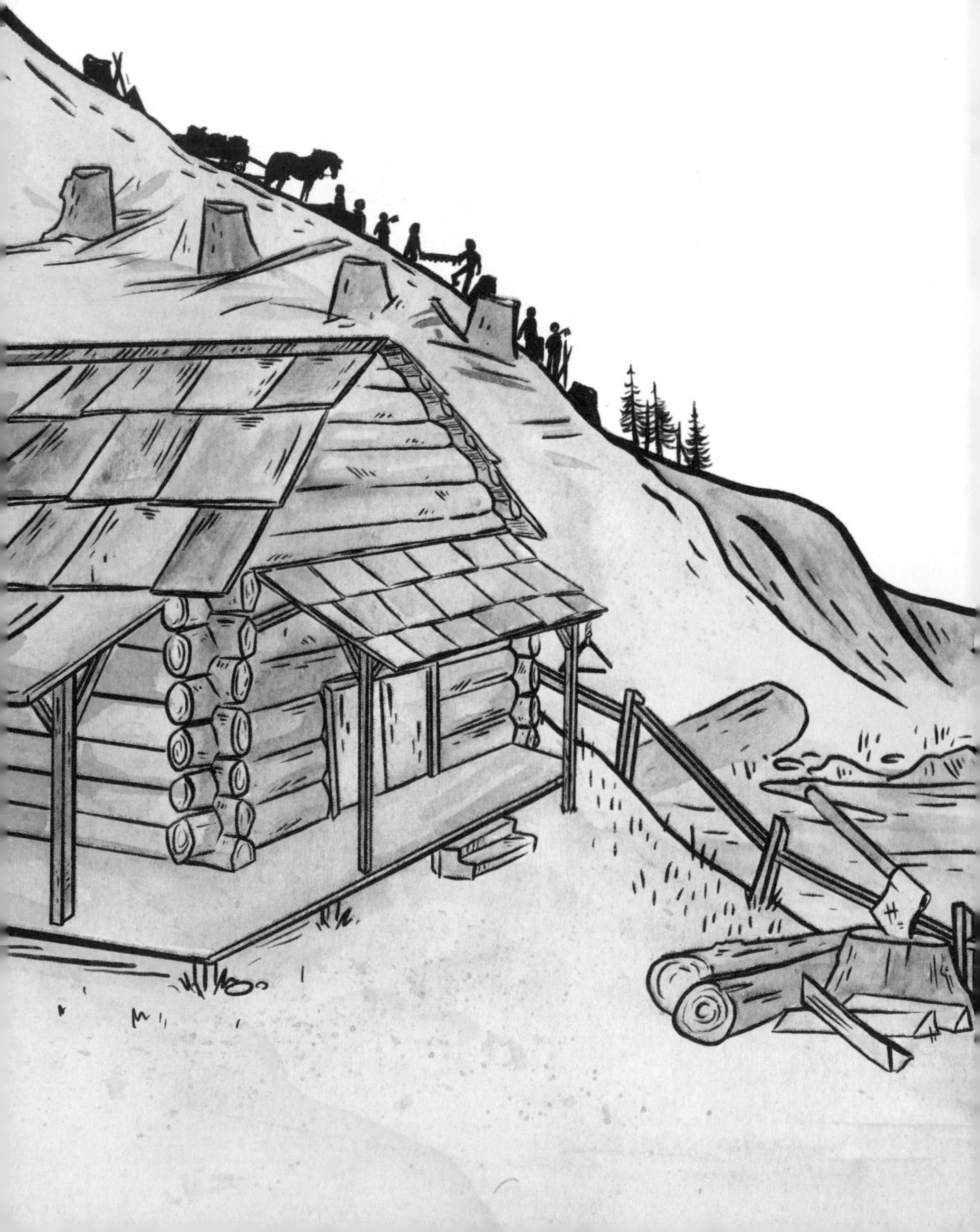

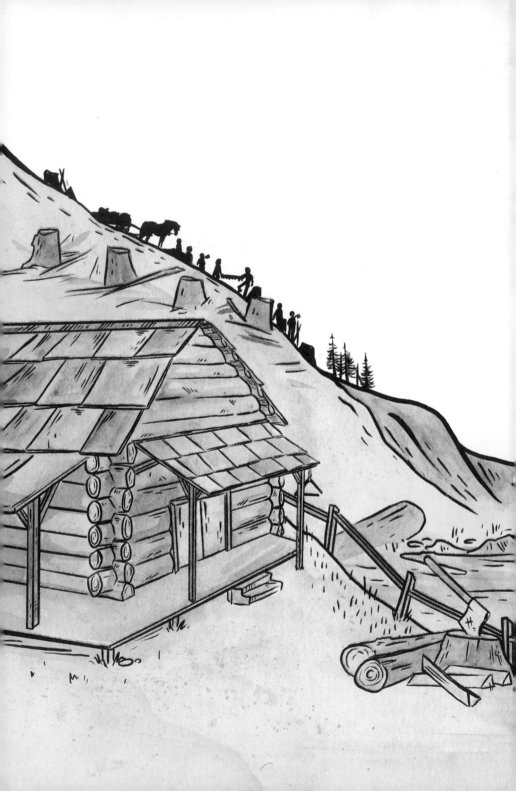

THE LEGEND OF AUNTIE PO

SHING YIN KHOR

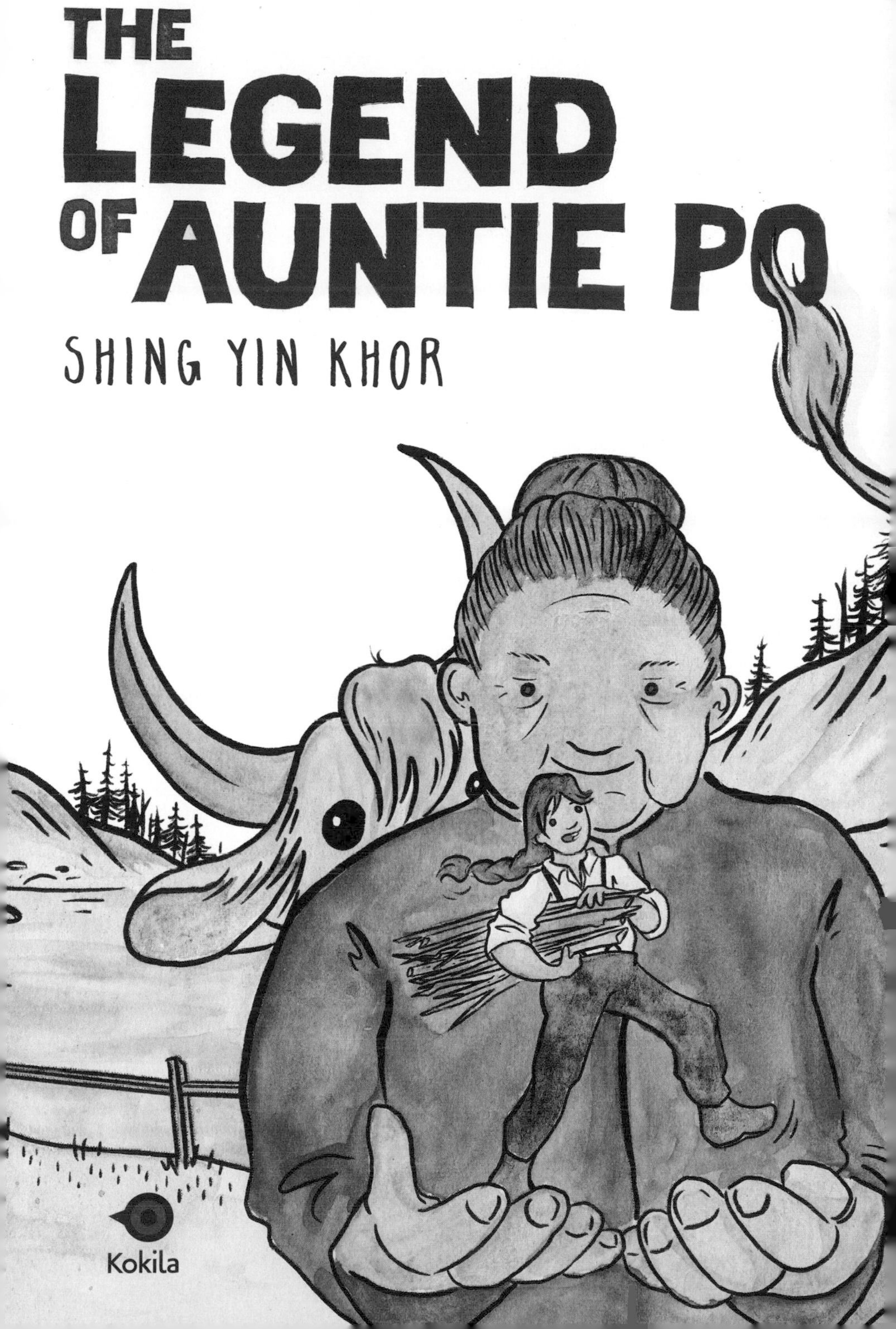

Kokila

KOKILA
An imprint of Penguin Random House LLC, New York

First published in the United States of America by Kokila,
an imprint of Penguin Random House LLC, 2021

Kokila & colophon are registered trademarks of Penguin Random House LLC.
Visit us online at penguinrandomhouse.com.
Library of Congress Cataloging-in-Publication Data is available.

Manufactured in China

ISBN 9780525554899 (PBK)   10 9 8 7 6 5 4 3 2
ISBN 9780525554882 (HC)   10 9 8 7 6 5 4 3 2

Design by Jasmin Rubero
Hand lettering by Shing Yin Khor

Heather L. Gilbraith assisted with pencils
Language consultant and translation by Chai Hiong Ng

*The art for this book was created using digital pencils and
hand-painted watercolor.*

For my dad, who worked so I could paint.

CHAPTER ONE

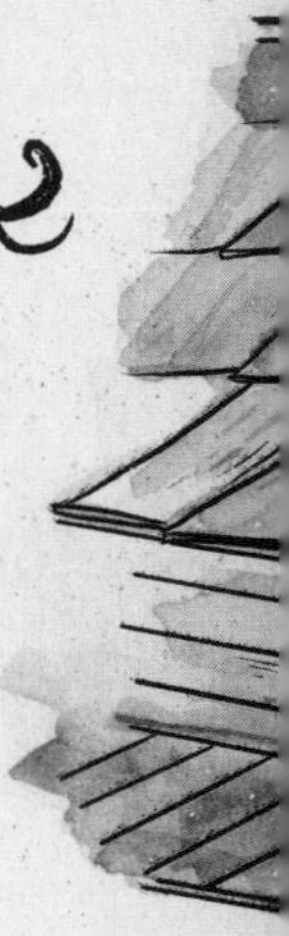

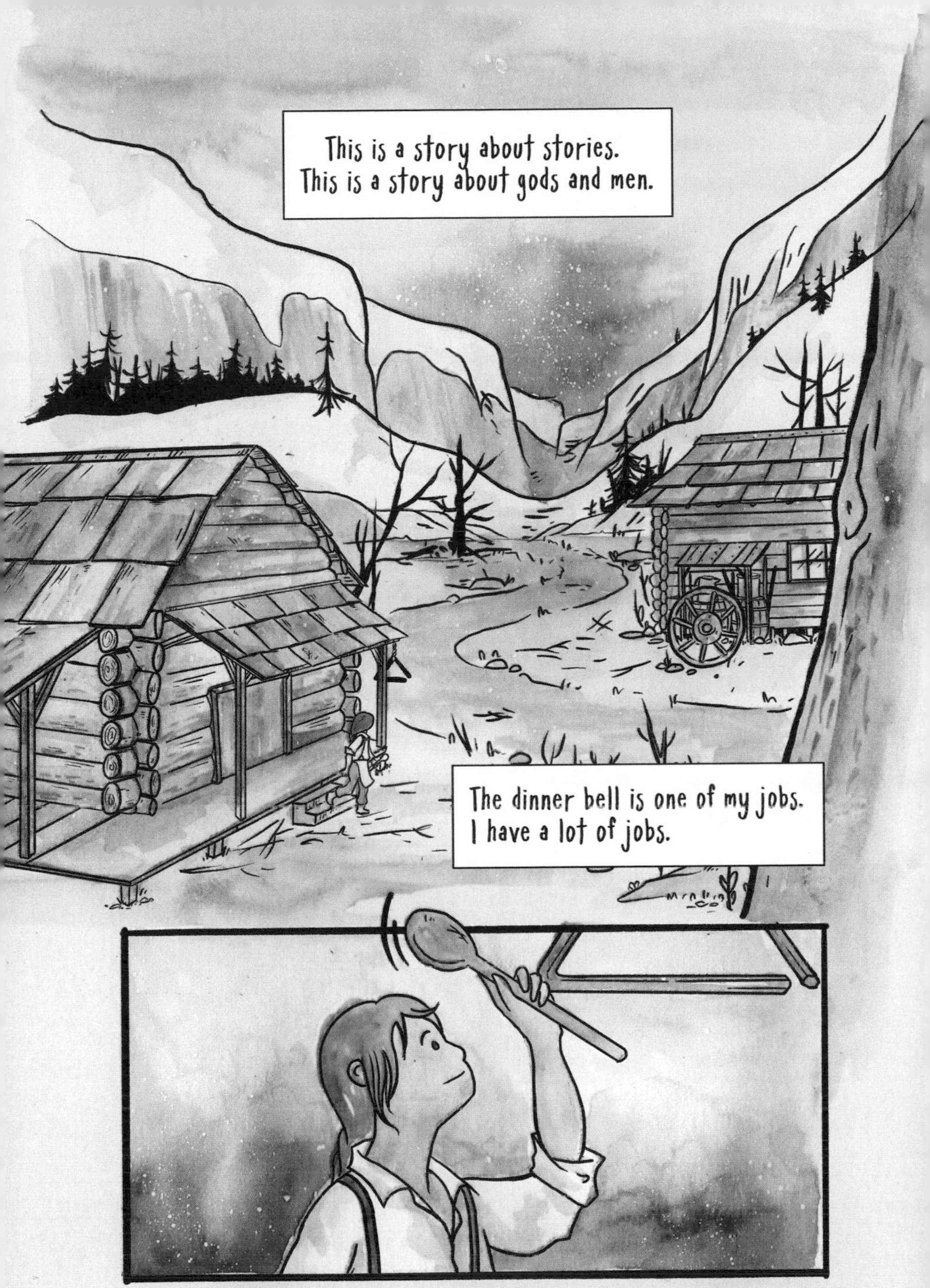
This is a story about stories.
This is a story about gods and men.
The dinner bell is one of my jobs.
I have a lot of jobs.

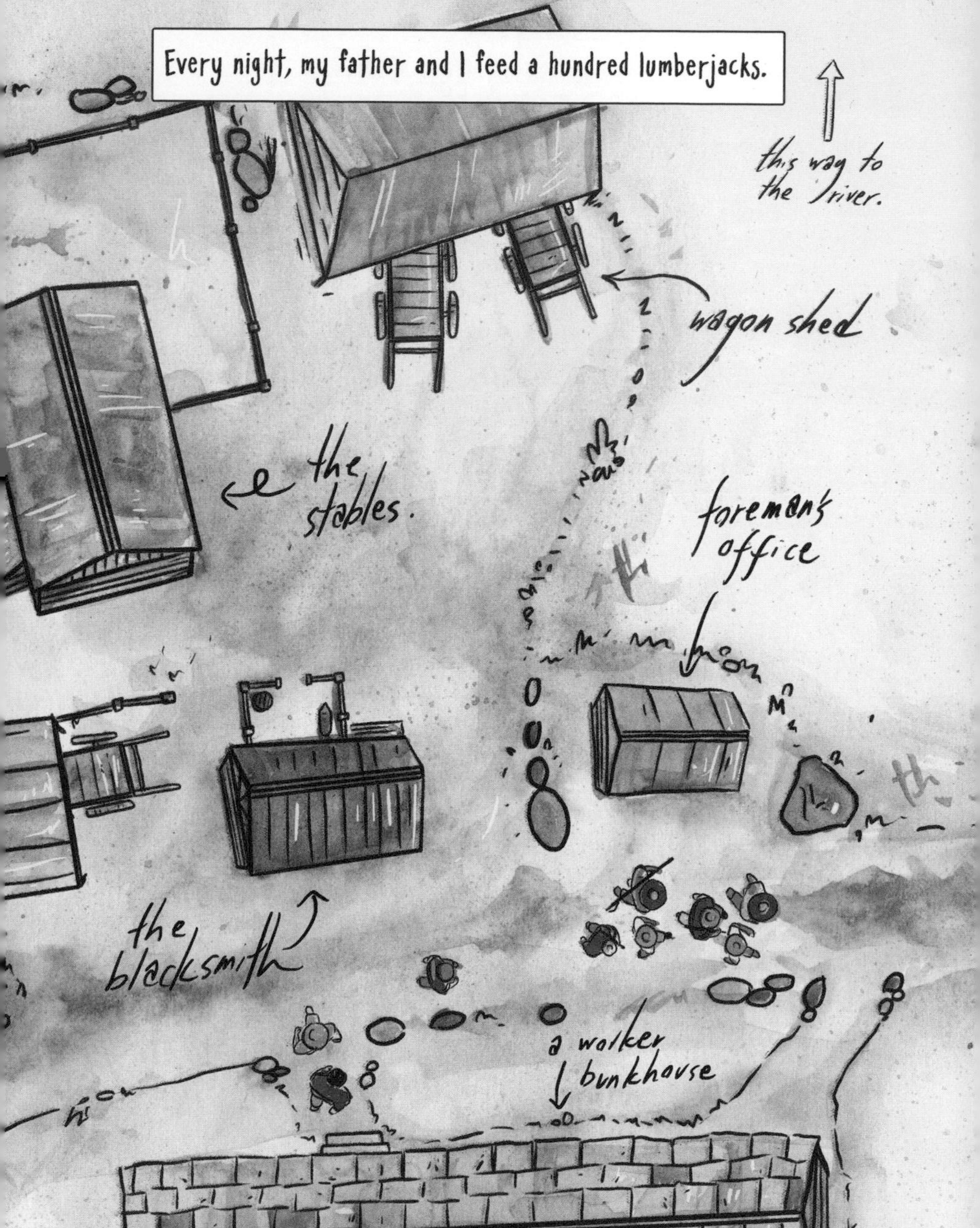
Every night, my father and I feed a hundred lumberjacks.
this way to the river.
wagon shed
the stables.
foreman's office
the blacksmith
a walker bunkhouse

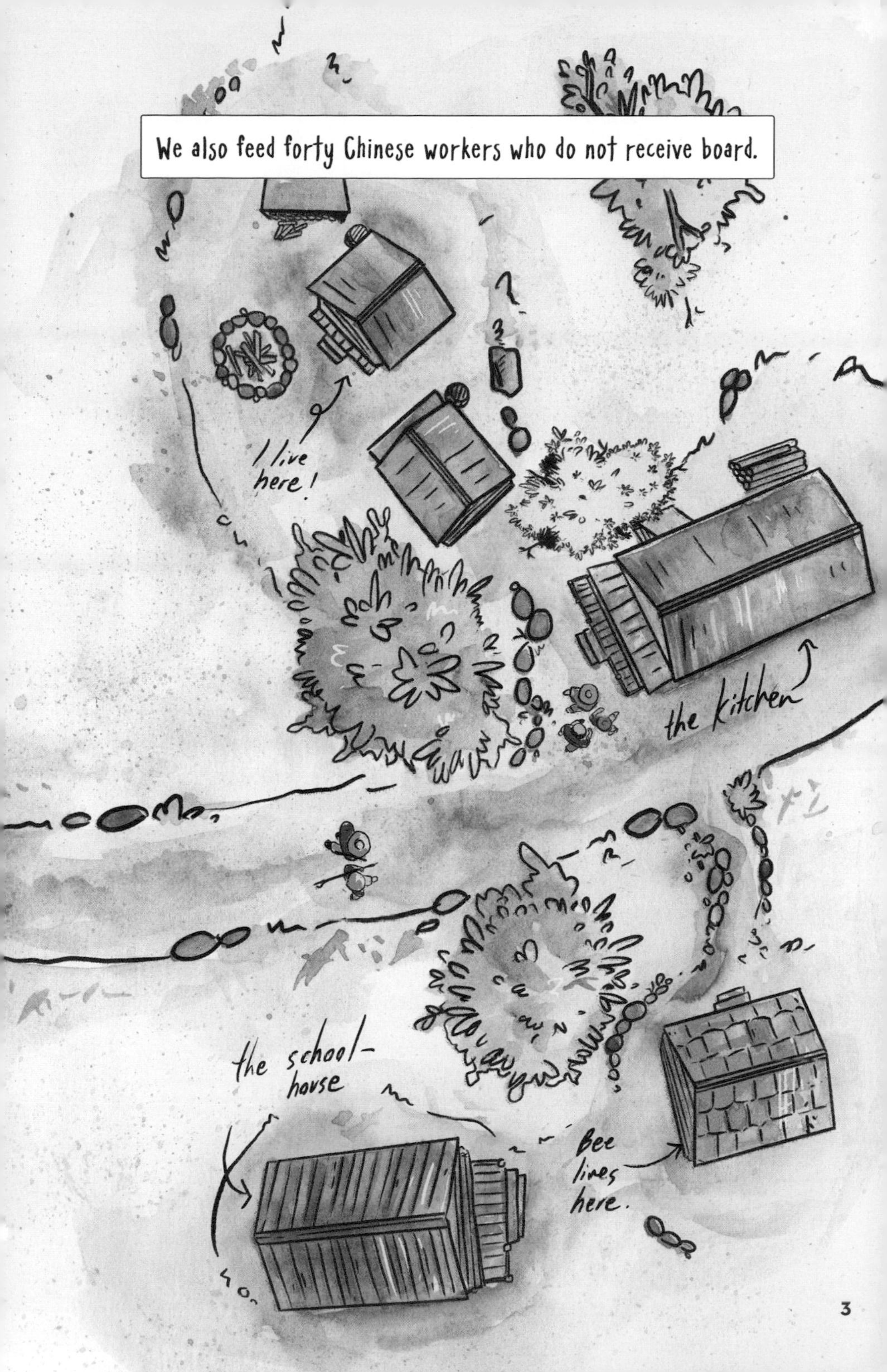
We also feed forty Chinese workers who do not receive board.
I live here!
the kitchen
the school-house
Bee lives here.

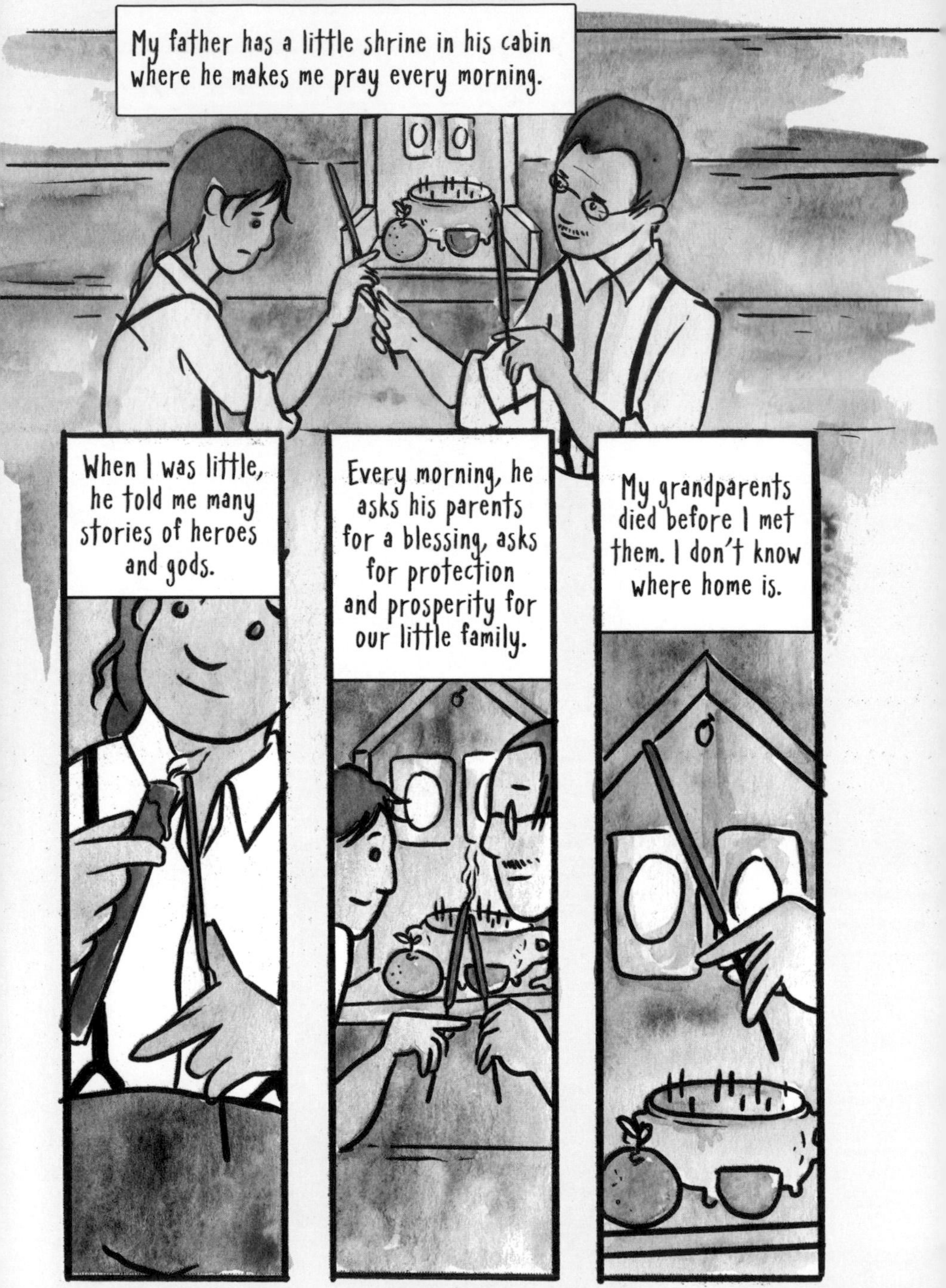
My father has a little shrine in his cabin where he makes me pray every morning.
When I was little, he told me many stories of heroes and gods.
Every morning, he asks his parents for a blessing, asks for protection and prosperity for our little family.
My grandparents died before I met them. I don't know where home is.

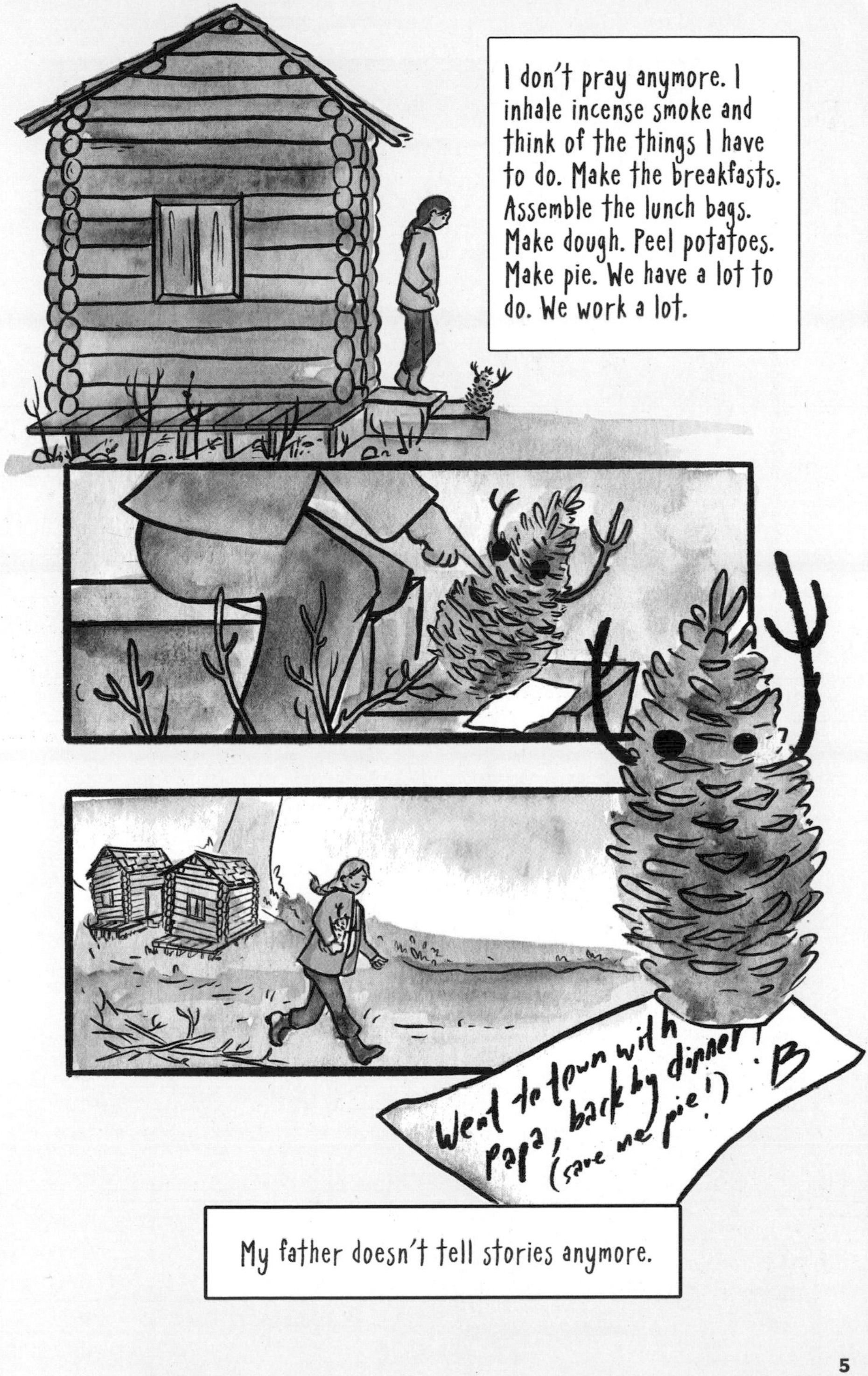

I don't pray anymore. I inhale incense smoke and think of the things I have to do. Make the breakfasts. Assemble the lunch bags. Make dough. Peel potatoes. Make pie. We have a lot to do. We work a lot.
Went to town with papa, back by dinner! (save me pie!) B
My father doesn't tell stories anymore.

A logging camp in the Sierra Nevadas, 1885

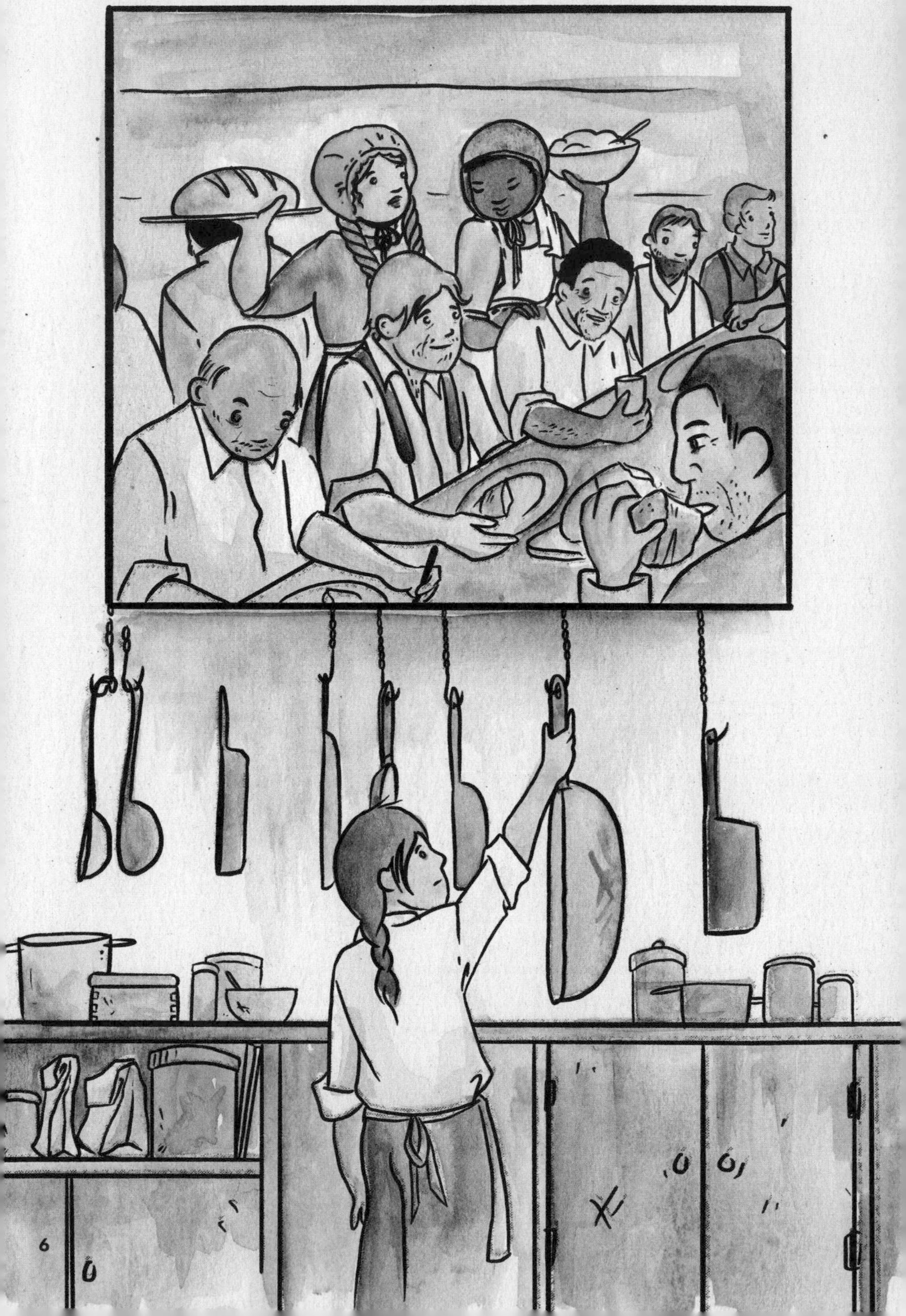

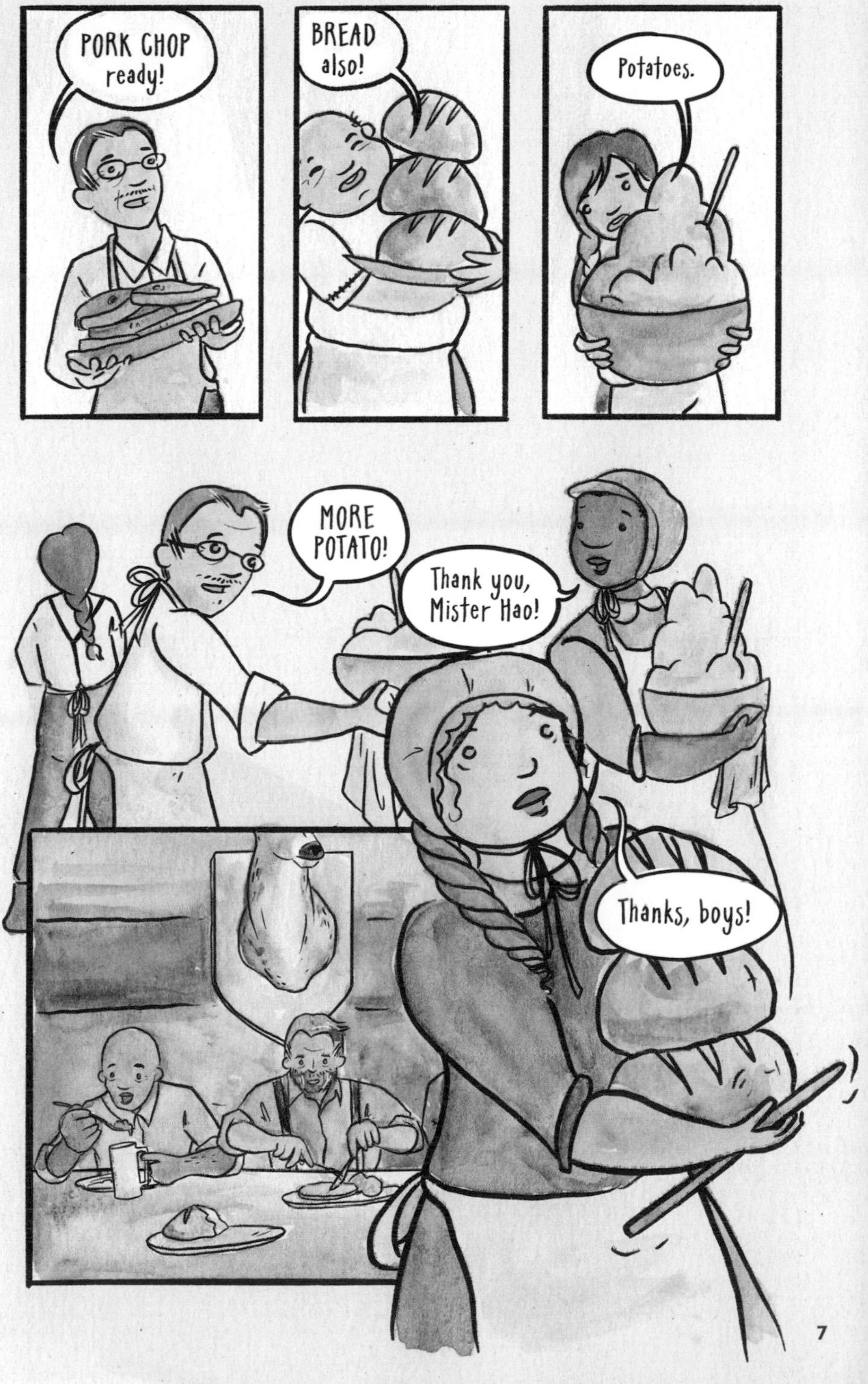
PORK CHOP ready!
BREAD also!
Potatoes.
MORE POTATO!
Thank you, Mister Hao!
Thanks, boys!

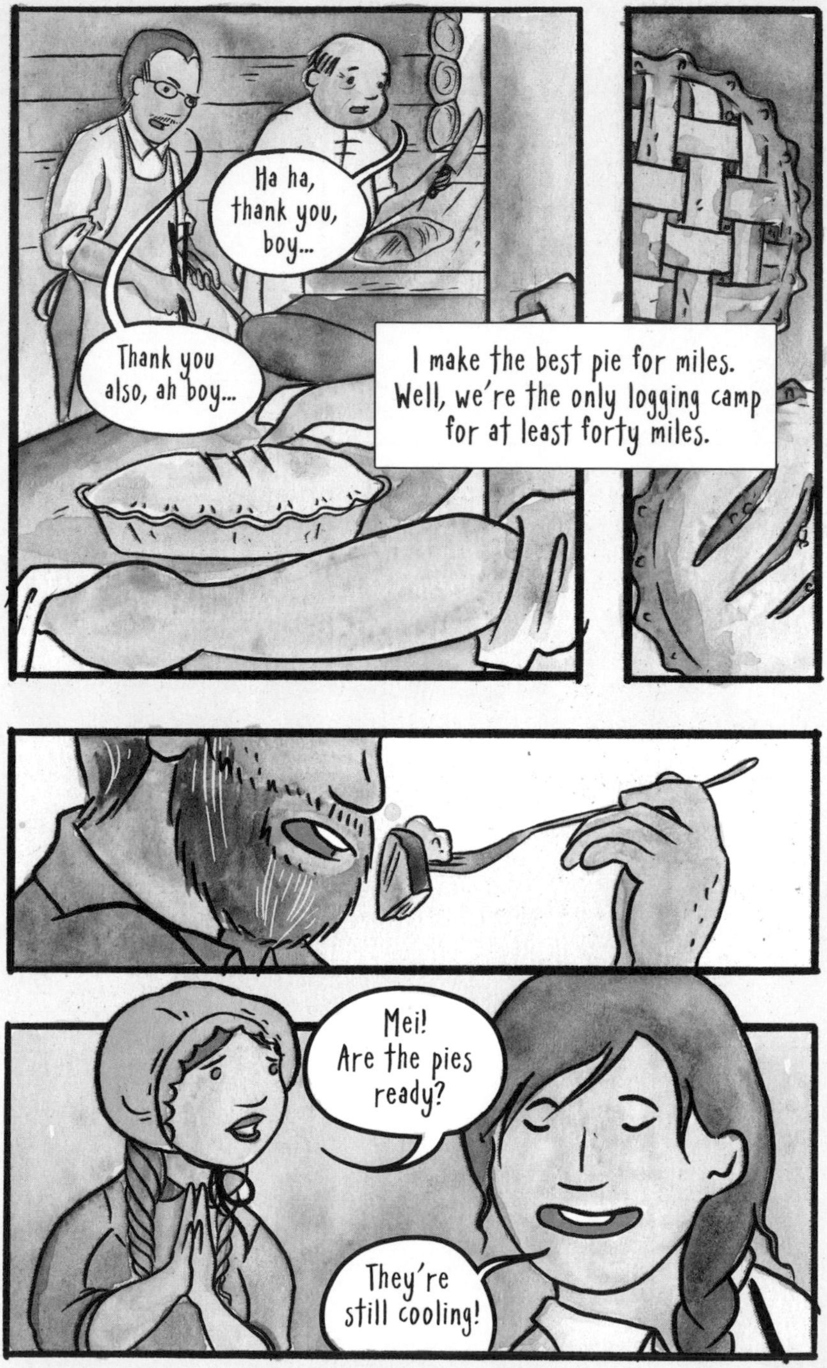
Ha ha, thank you, boy...
Thank you also, ah boy...
I make the best pie for miles. Well, we're the only logging camp for at least forty miles.
Mei! Are the pies ready?
They're still cooling!

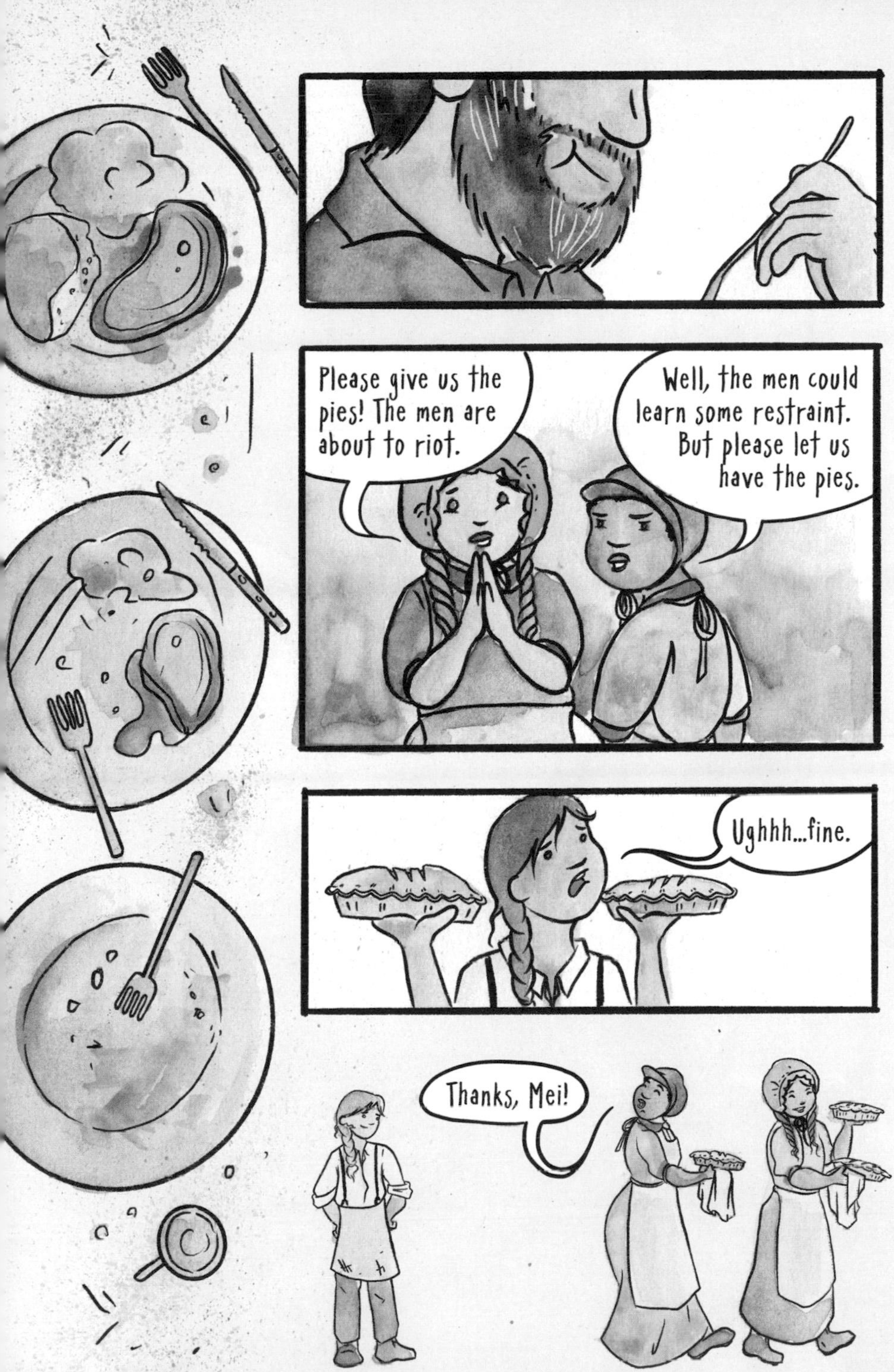
Please give us the pies! The men are about to riot.
Well, the men could learn some restraint. But please let us have the pies.
Ughhh...fine.
Thanks, Mei!

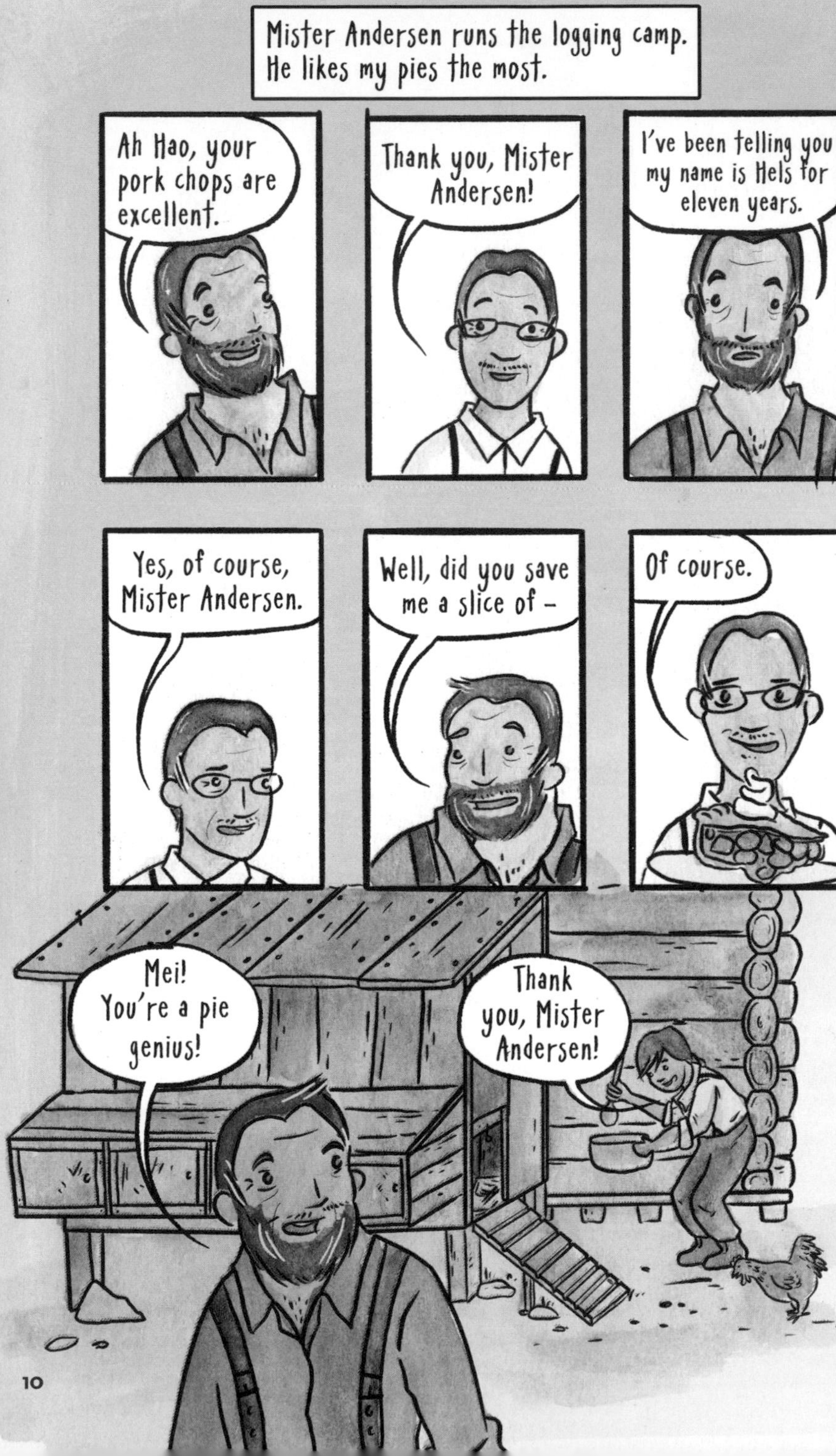
Mister Andersen runs the logging camp.
He likes my pies the most.
Ah Hao, your pork chops are excellent.
Thank you, Mister Andersen!
I've been telling you my name is Hels for eleven years.
Yes, of course, Mister Andersen.
Well, did you save me a slice of –
Of course.
Mei! You're a pie genius!
Thank you, Mister Andersen!

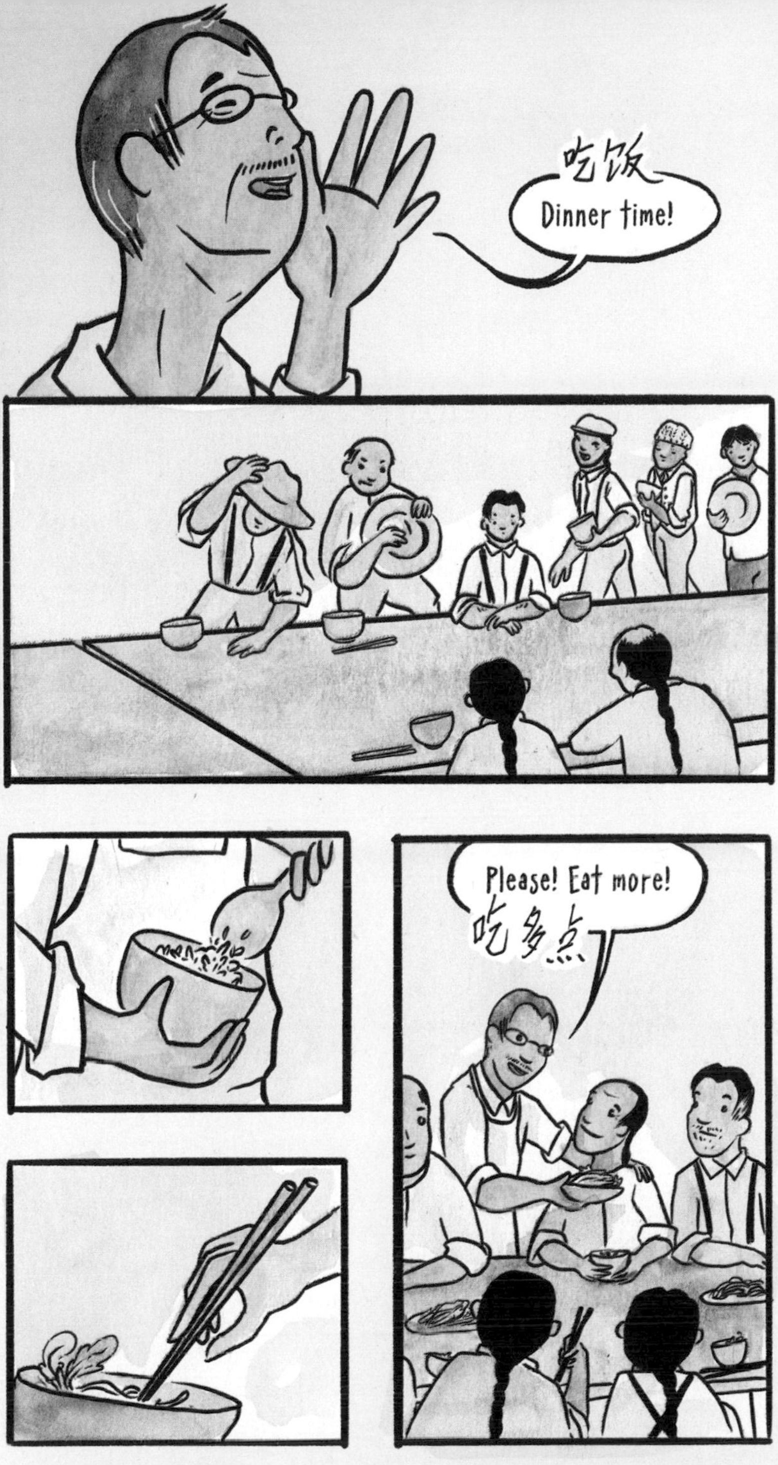
吃饭
Dinner time!
Please! Eat more!
吃多点

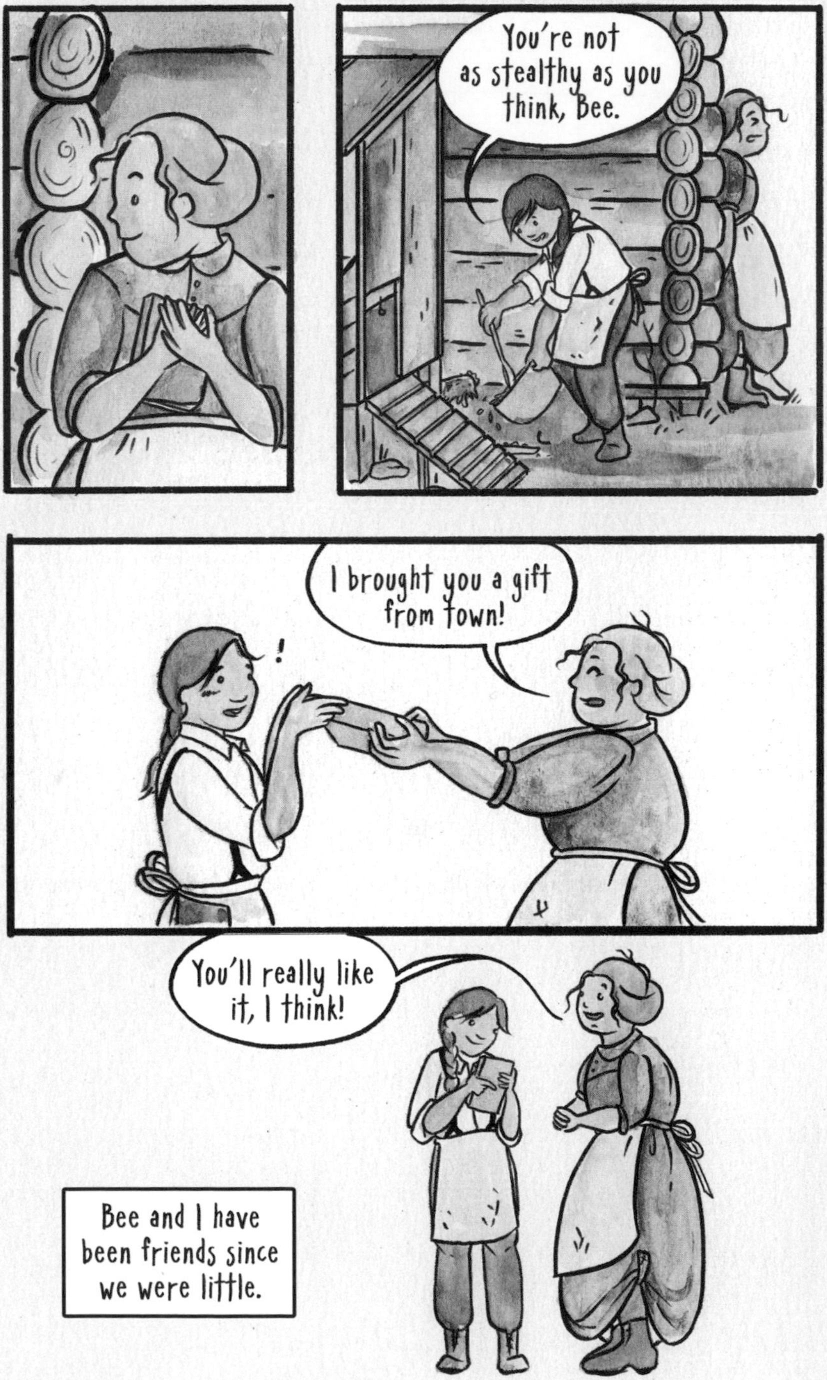
You're not as stealthy as you think, Bee.
I brought you a gift from town!
!
You'll really like it, I think!
Bee and I have been friends since we were little.

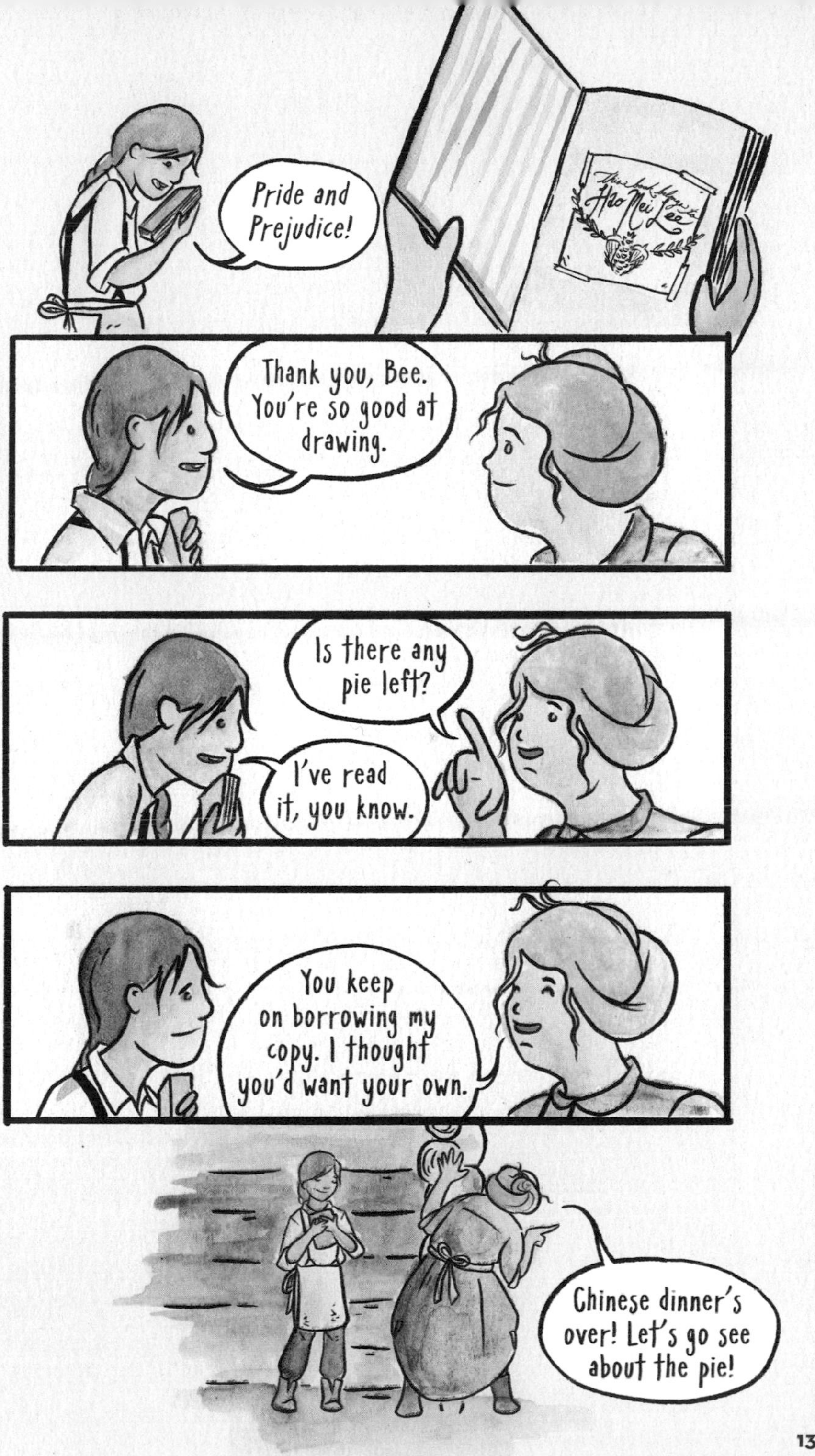
Pride and Prejudice!
Thank you, Bee. You're so good at drawing.
Is there any pie left?
I've read it, you know.
You keep on borrowing my copy. I thought you'd want your own.
Chinese dinner's over! Let's go see about the pie!

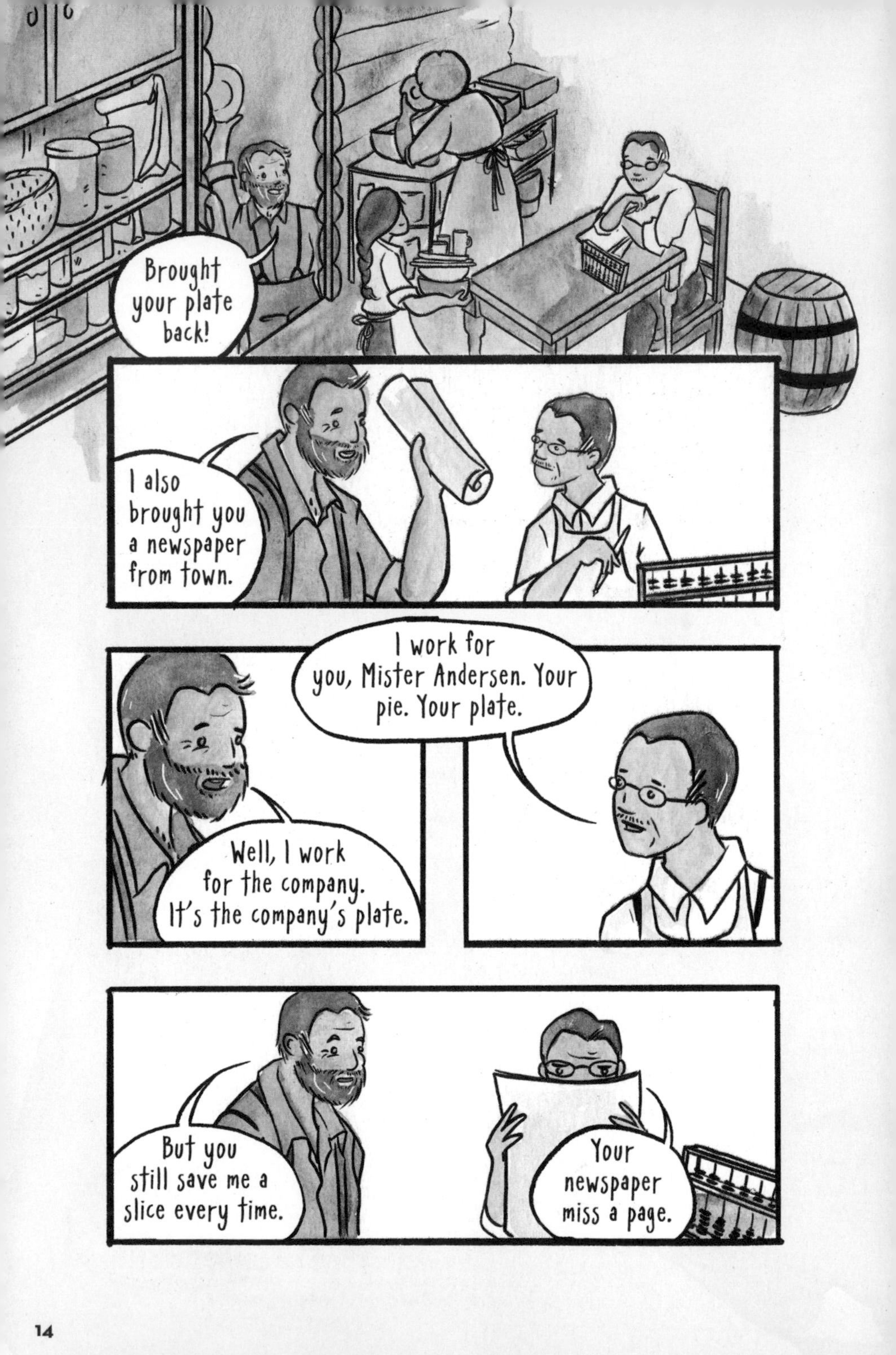
Brought your plate back!
I also brought you a newspaper from town.
I work for you, Mister Andersen. Your pie. Your plate.
Well, I work for the company. It's the company's plate.
But you still save me a slice every time.
Your newspaper miss a page.

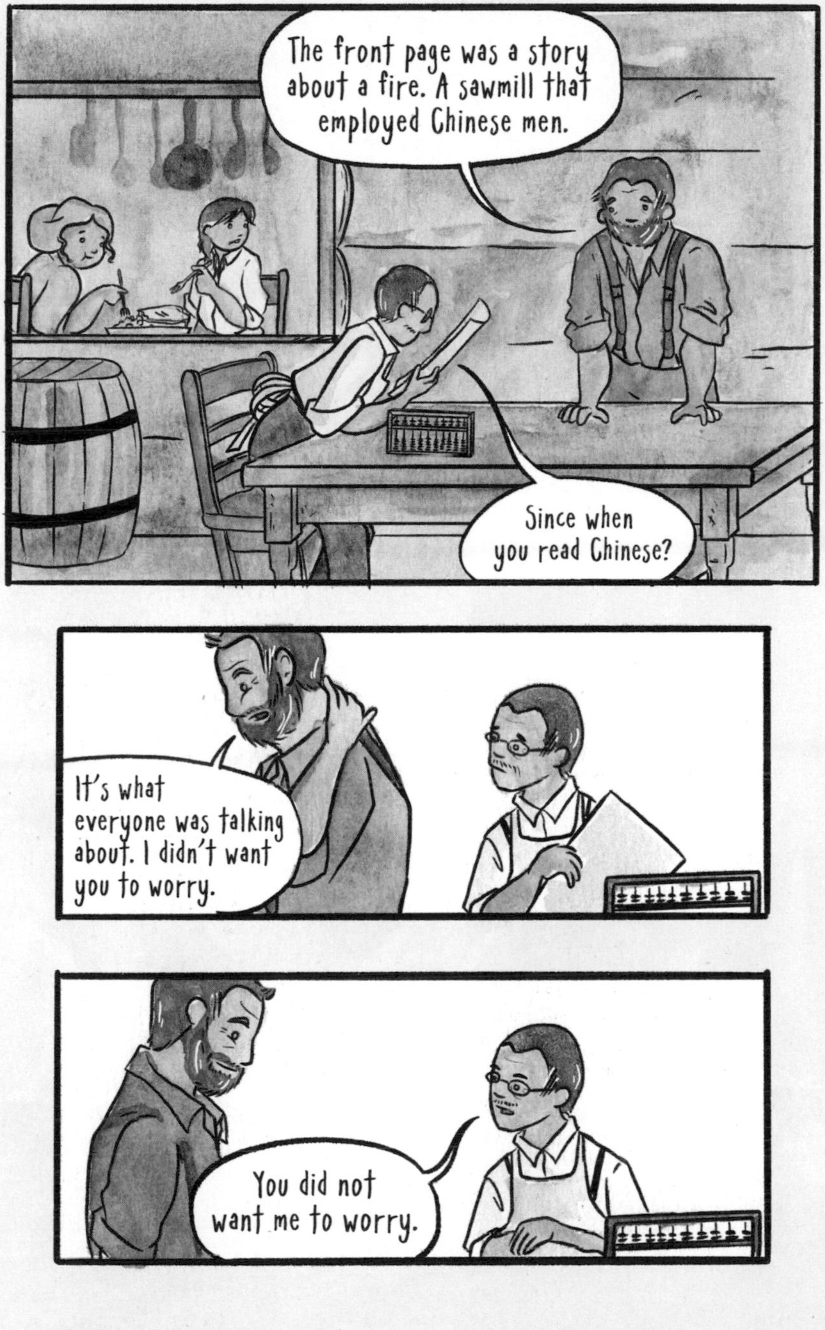
The front page was a story about a fire. A sawmill that employed Chinese men.
Since when you read Chinese?
It's what everyone was talking about. I didn't want you to worry.
You did not want me to worry.

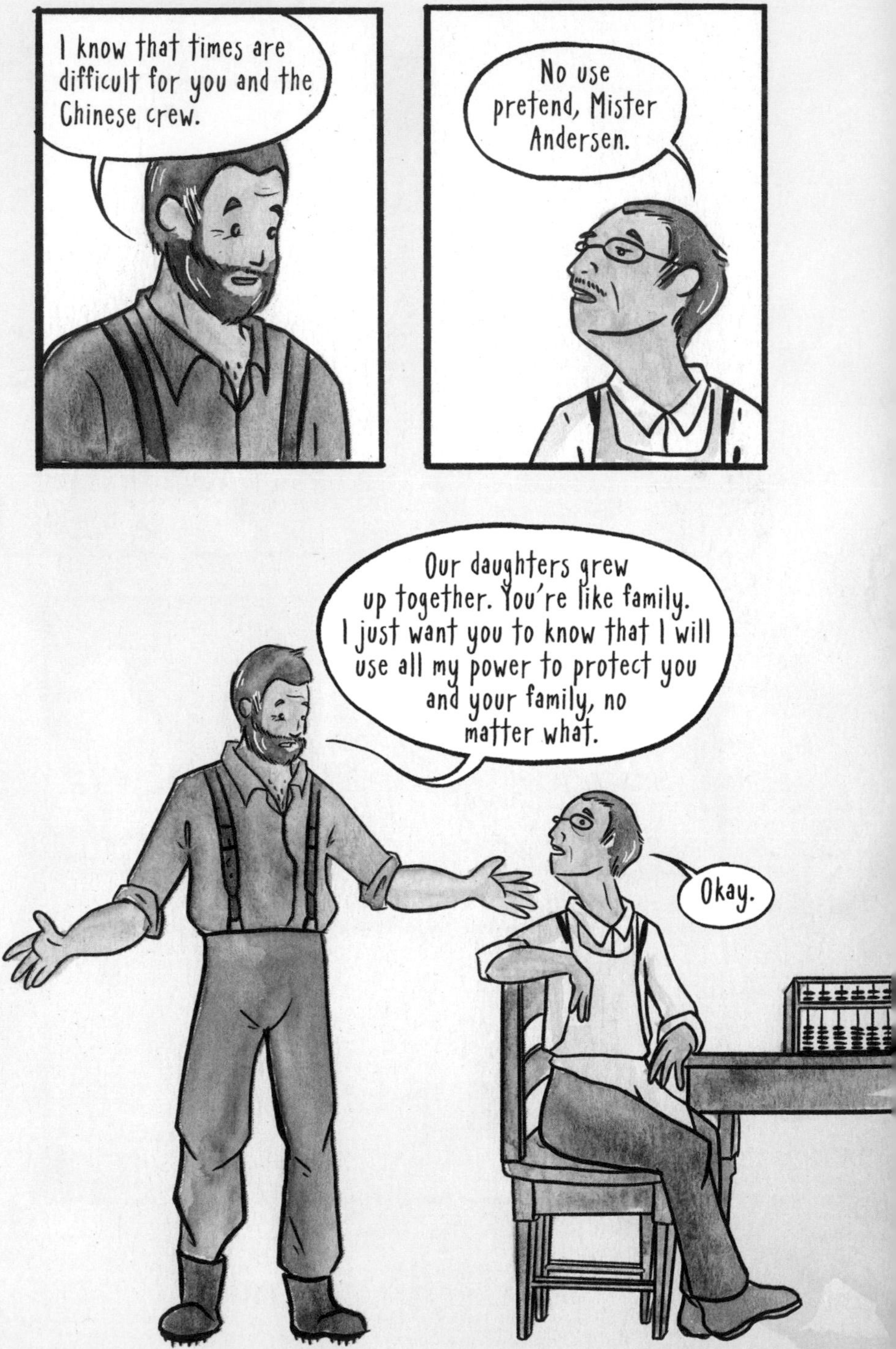
I know that times are difficult for you and the Chinese crew.
No use pretend, Mister Andersen.
Our daughters grew up together. You're like family. I just want you to know that I will use all my power to protect you and your family, no matter what.
Okay.

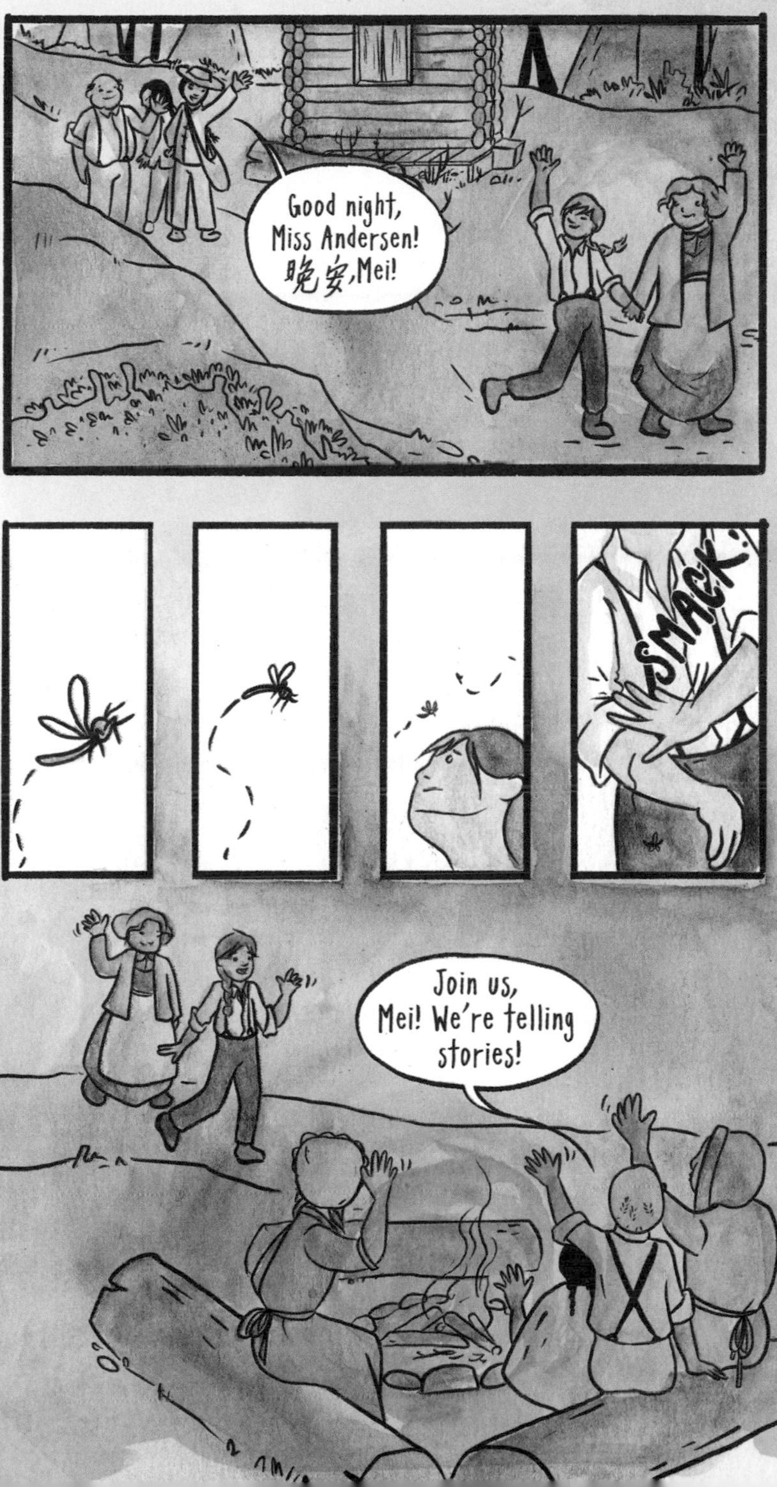
Good night,
Miss Andersen!
晚安,Mei!
SMACK!
Join us,
Mei! We're telling
stories!

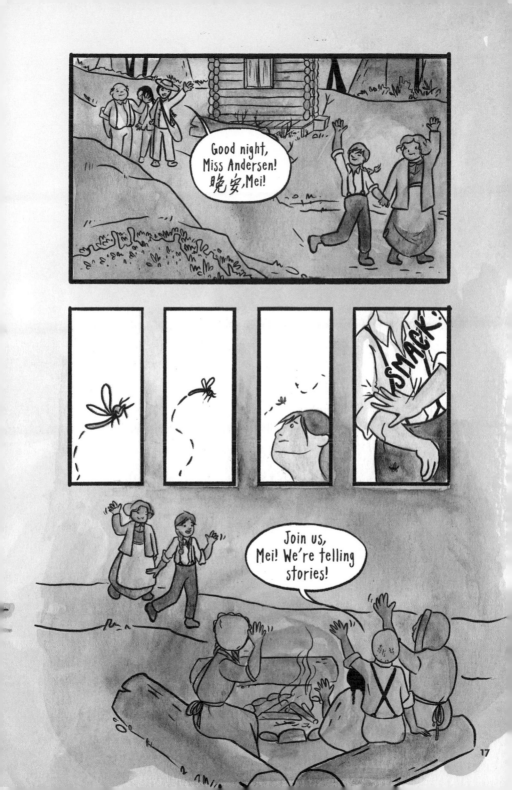

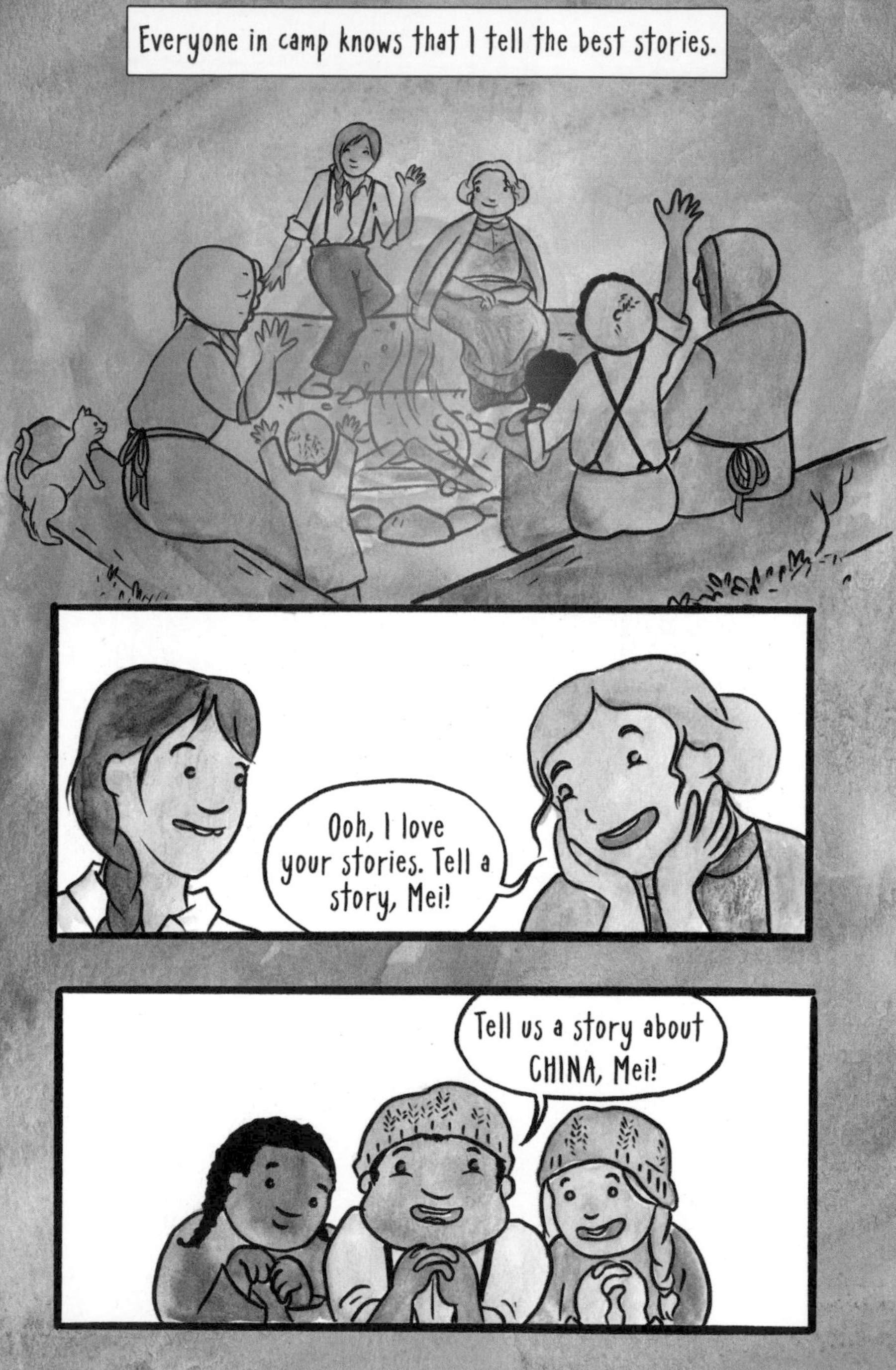
Everyone in camp knows that I tell the best stories.
Ooh, I love your stories. Tell a story, Mei!
Tell us a story about CHINA, Mei!

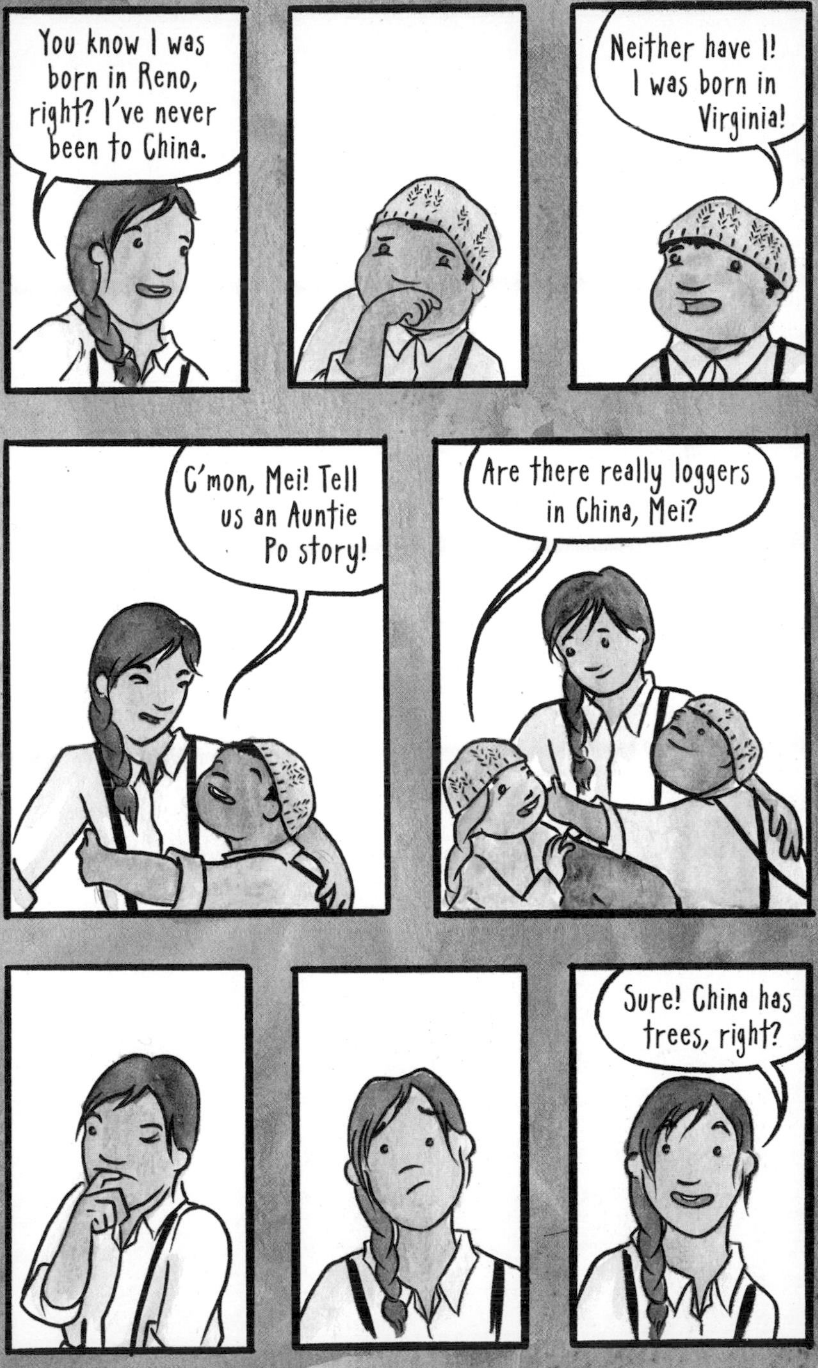

You know I was born in Reno, right? I've never been to China.
Neither have I! I was born in Virginia!
C'mon, Mei! Tell us an Auntie Po story!
Are there really loggers in China, Mei?
Sure! China has trees, right?

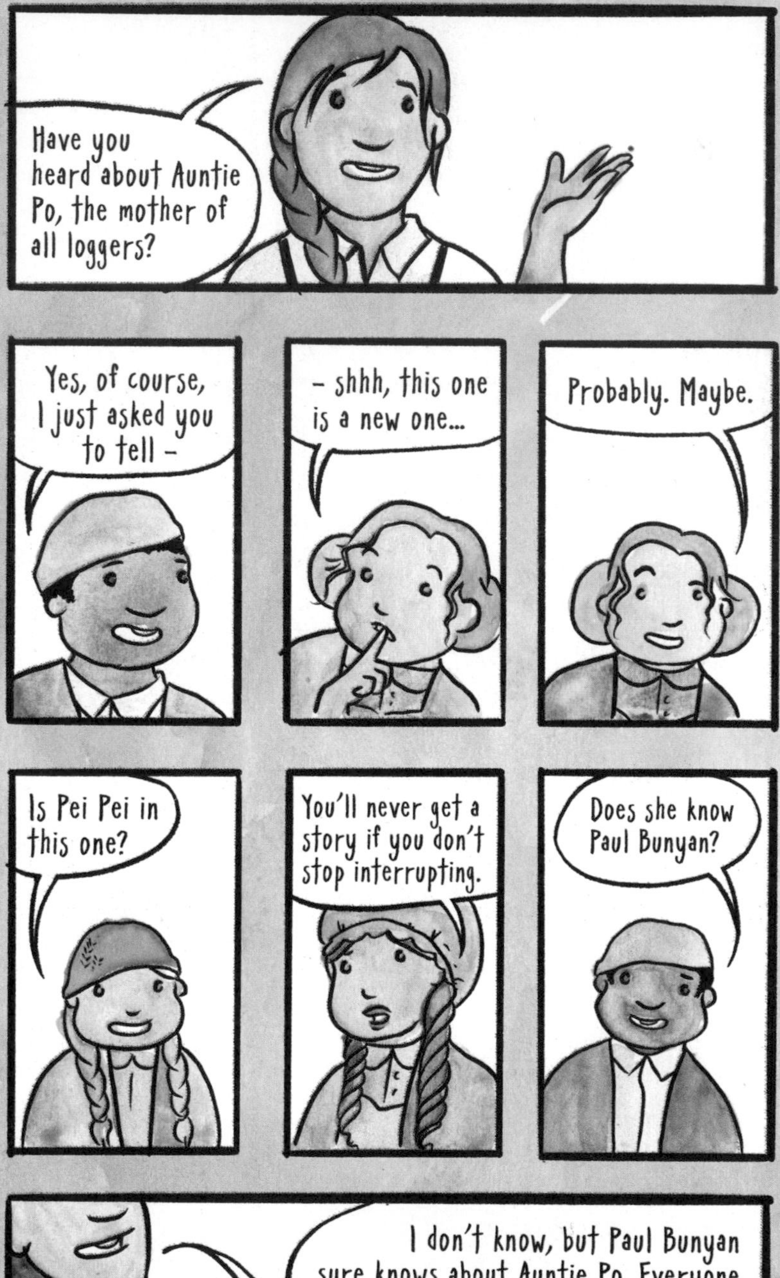
Have you heard about Auntie Po, the mother of all loggers?
Yes, of course, I just asked you to tell –
– shhh, this one is a new one...
Probably. Maybe.
Is Pei Pei in this one?
You'll never get a story if you don't stop interrupting.
Does she know Paul Bunyan?
I don't know, but Paul Bunyan sure knows about Auntie Po. Everyone knows about Po Pan Yin.

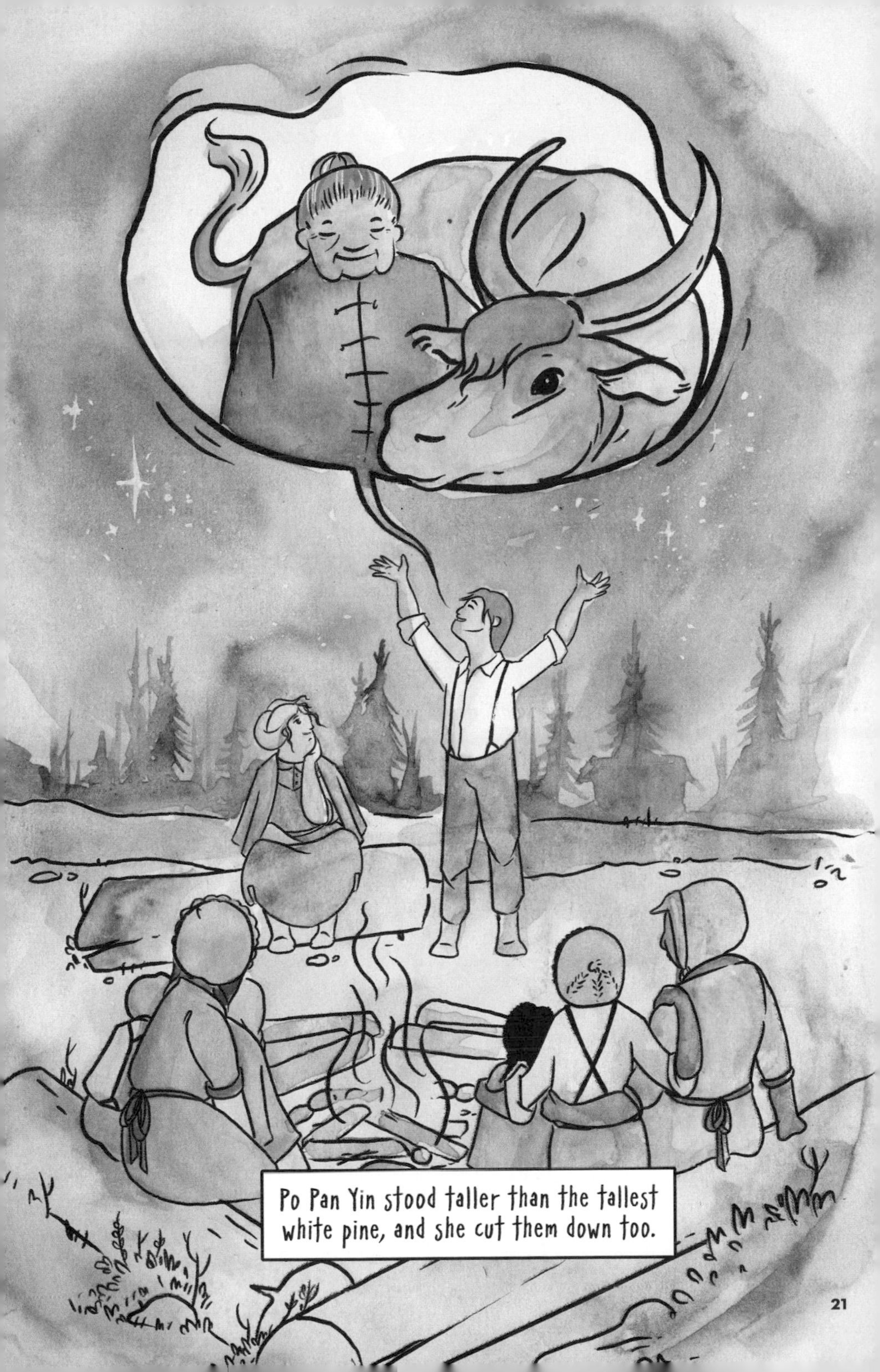
Po Pan Yin stood taller than the tallest white pine, and she cut them down too.

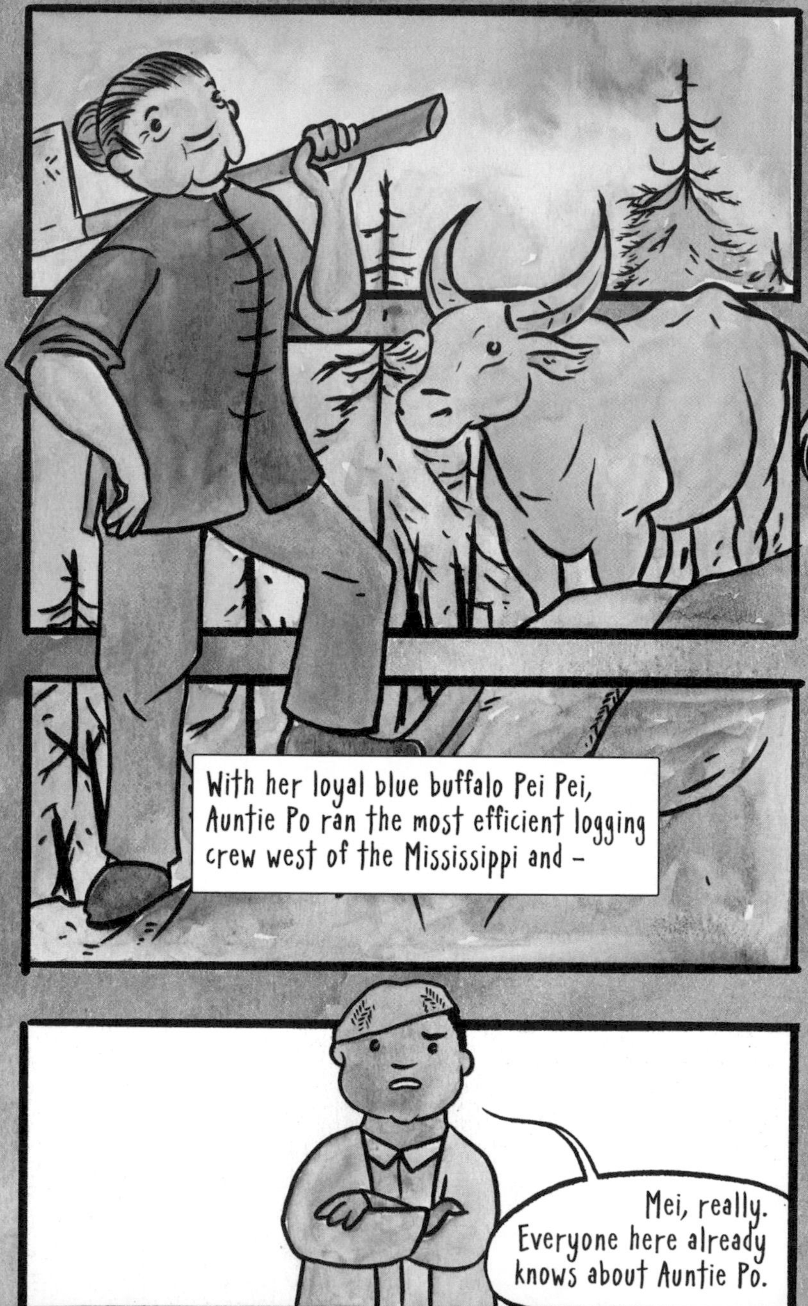
With her loyal blue buffalo Pei Pei, Auntie Po ran the most efficient logging crew west of the Mississippi and –
Mei, really. Everyone here already knows about Auntie Po.

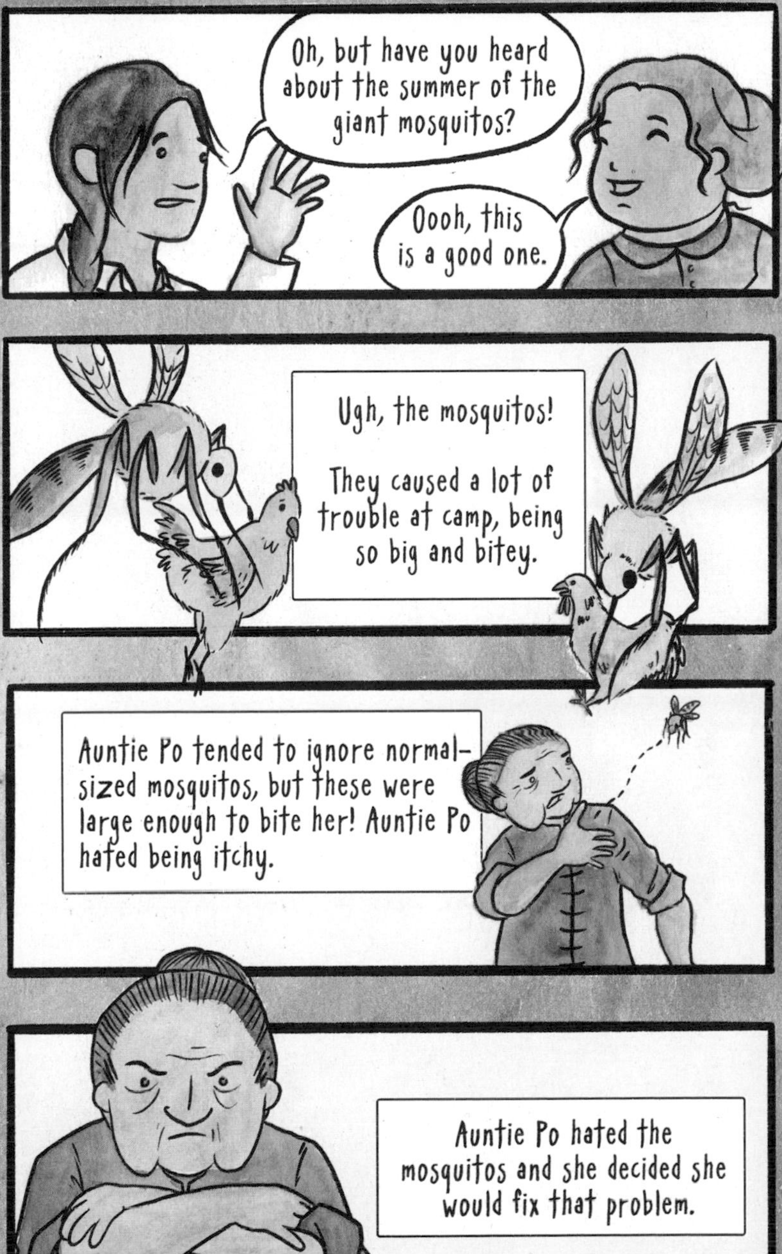

Oh, but have you heard about the summer of the giant mosquitos?
Oooh, this is a good one.
Ugh, the mosquitos!
They caused a lot of trouble at camp, being so big and bitey.
Auntie Po tended to ignore normal-sized mosquitos, but these were large enough to bite her! Auntie Po hated being itchy.
Auntie Po hated the mosquitos and she decided she would fix that problem.

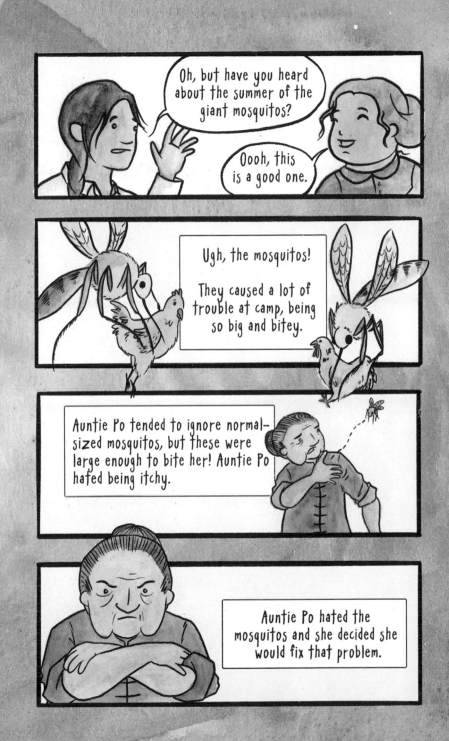

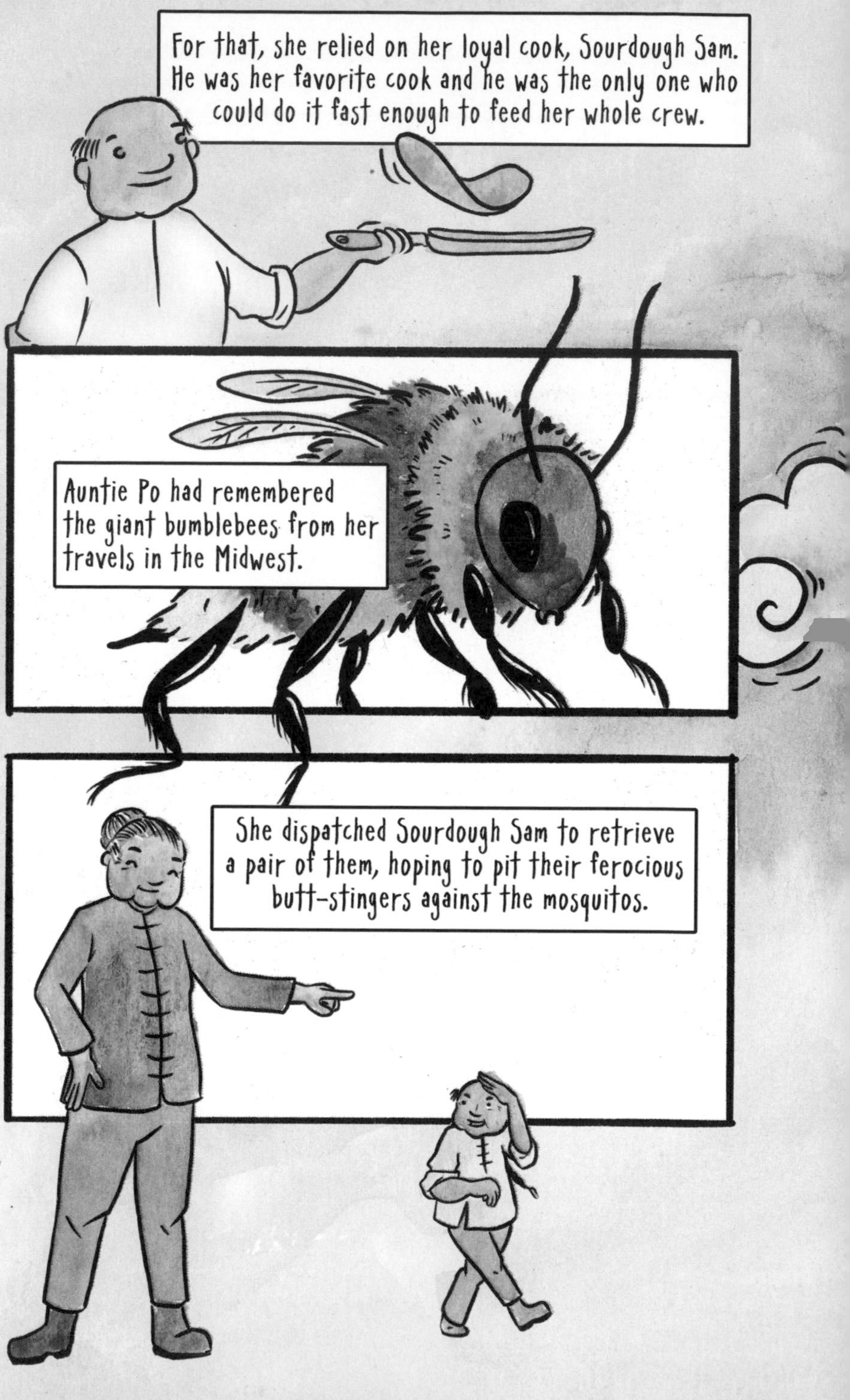
For that, she relied on her loyal cook, Sourdough Sam. He was her favorite cook and he was the only one who could do it fast enough to feed her whole crew.
Auntie Po had remembered the giant bumblebees from her travels in the Midwest.
She dispatched Sourdough Sam to retrieve a pair of them, hoping to pit their ferocious butt-stingers against the mosquitos.

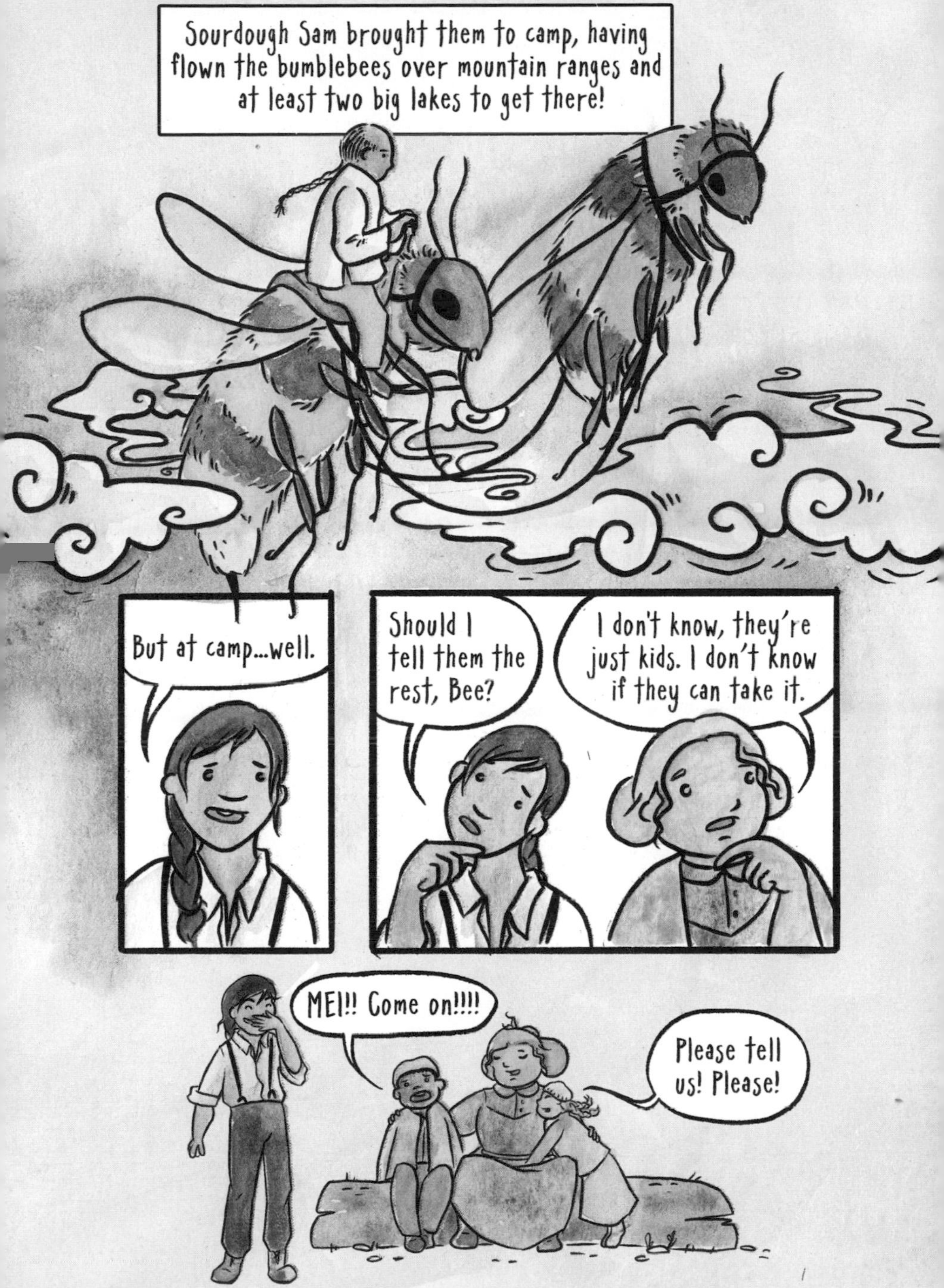
Sourdough Sam brought them to camp, having flown the bumblebees over mountain ranges and at least two big lakes to get there!
But at camp...well.
Should I tell them the rest, Bee?
I don't know, they're just kids. I don't know if they can take it.
MEI!! Come on!!!!
Please tell us! Please!

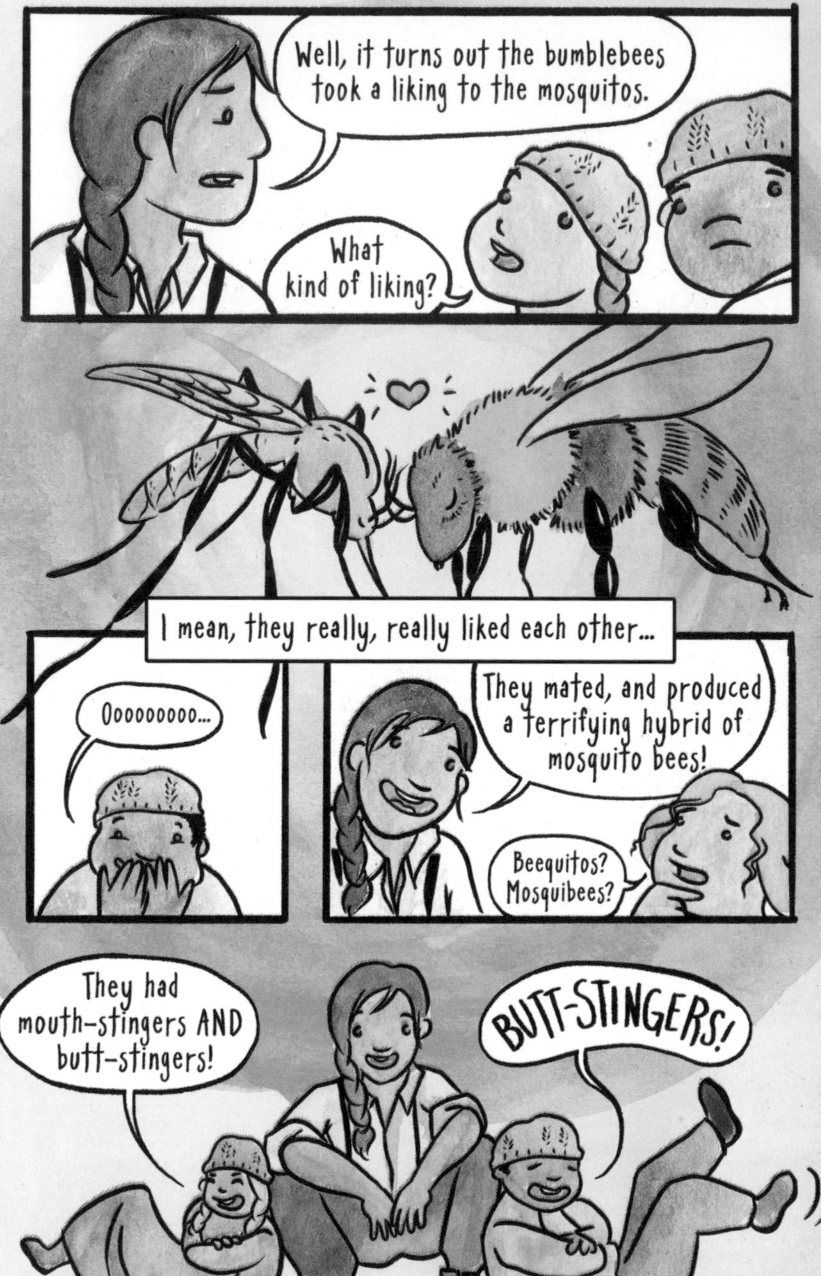
Well, it turns out the bumblebees took a liking to the mosquitos.
What kind of liking?
I mean, they really, really liked each other...
Oooooooo...
They mated, and produced a terrifying hybrid of mosquito bees!
Beequitos? Mosquibees?
They had mouth-stingers AND butt-stingers!
BUTT-STINGERS!

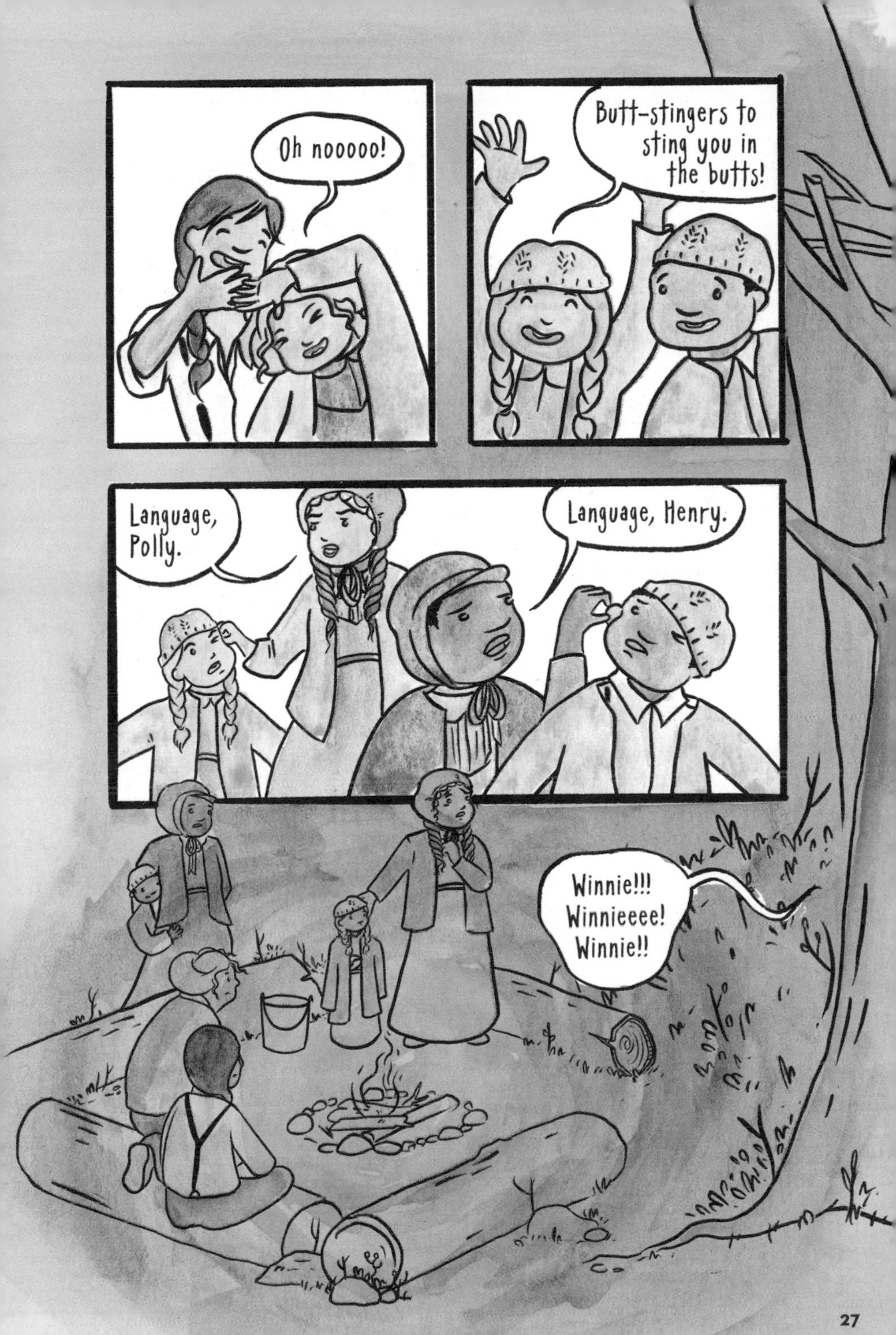
Oh nooooo!
Butt-stingers to sting you in the butts!
Language, Polly.
Language, Henry.
Winnie!!! Winnieeee! Winnie!!

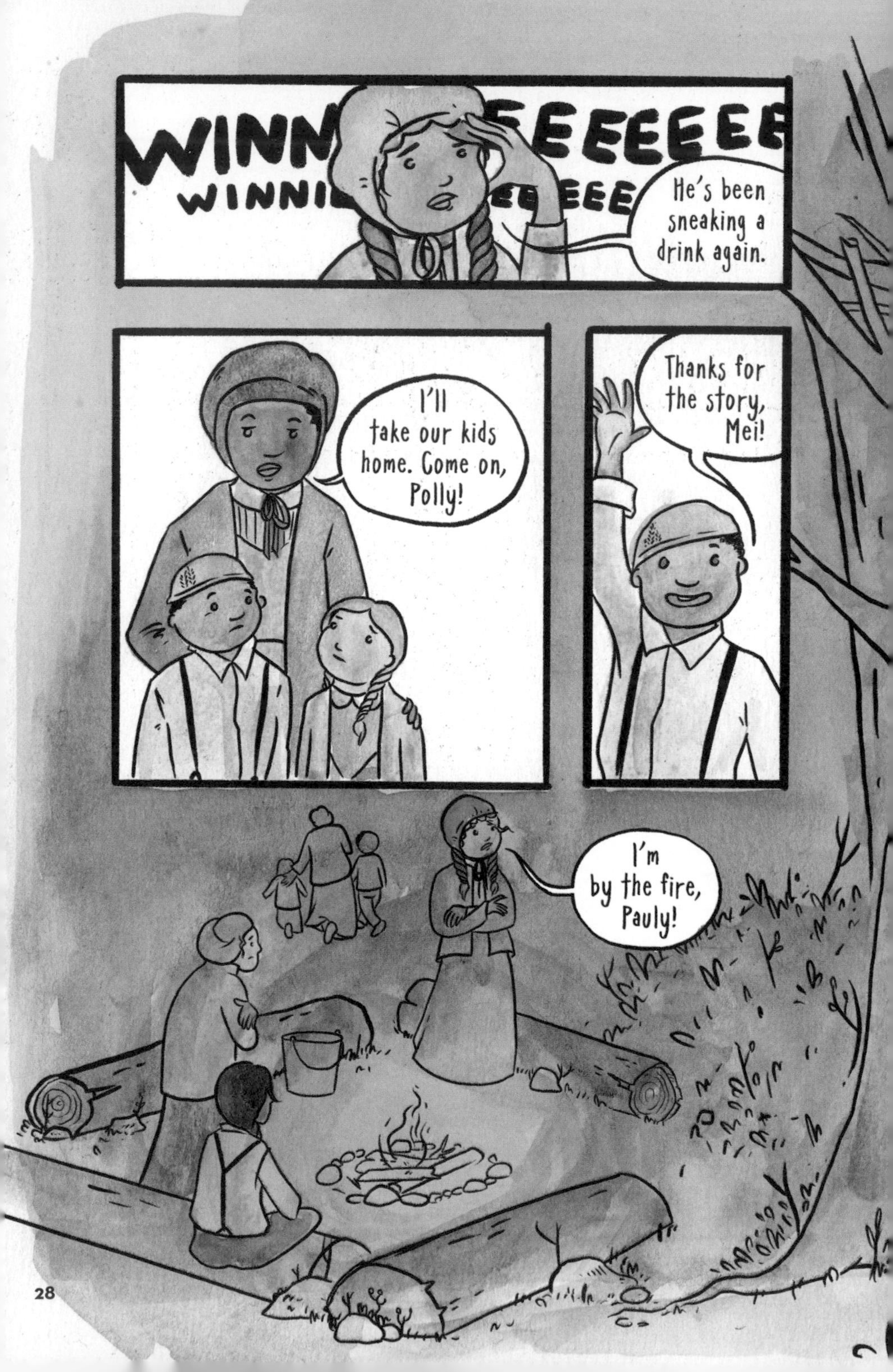
WINNIEEEEEEE
WINNIEEEEE
He's been sneaking a drink again.
I'll take our kids home. Come on, Polly!
Thanks for the story, Mei!
I'm by the fire, Pauly!

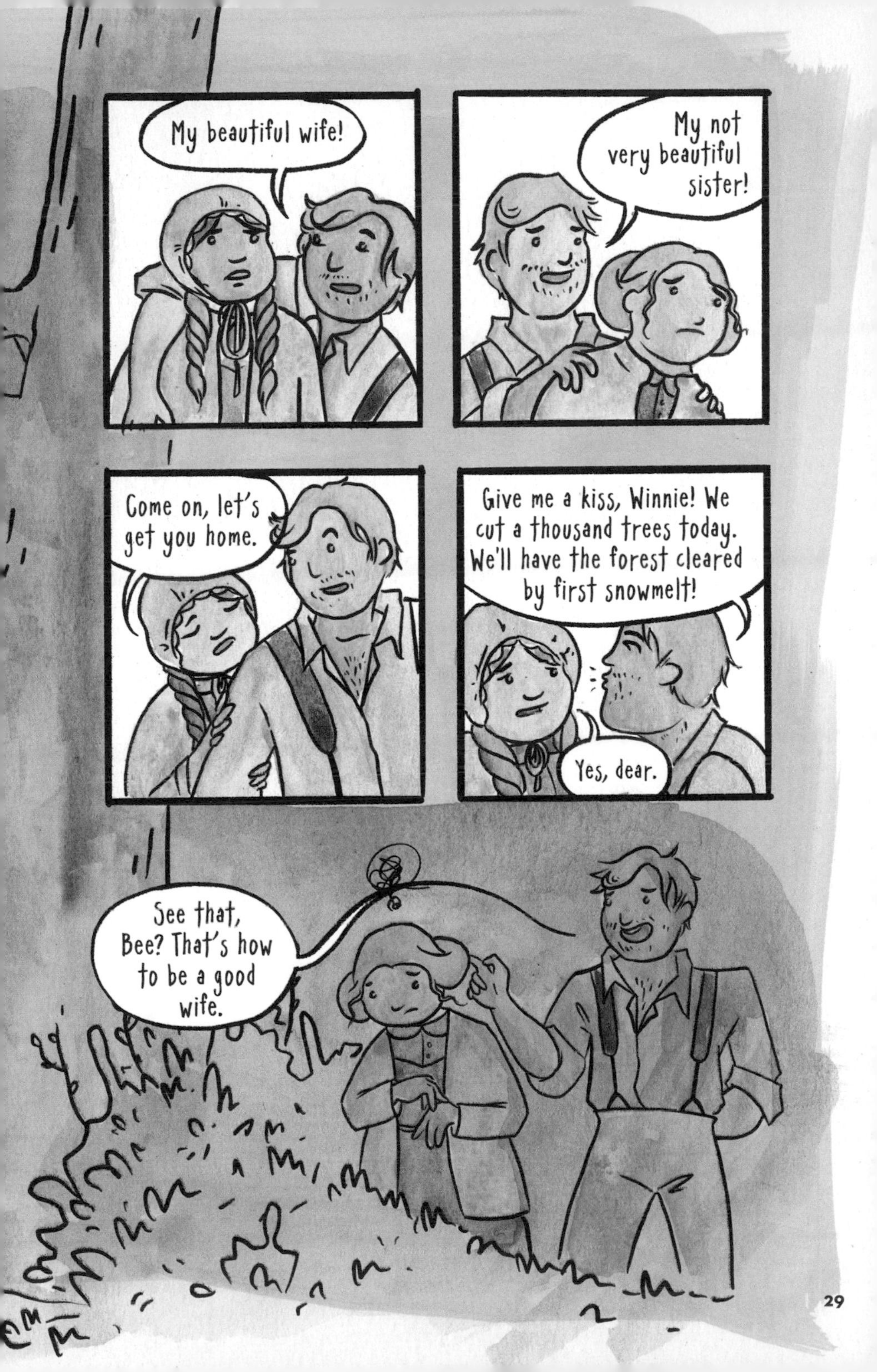
My beautiful wife!
My not very beautiful sister!
Come on, let's get you home.
Give me a kiss, Winnie! We cut a thousand trees today. We'll have the forest cleared by first snowmelt!
Yes, dear.
See that, Bee? That's how to be a good wife.

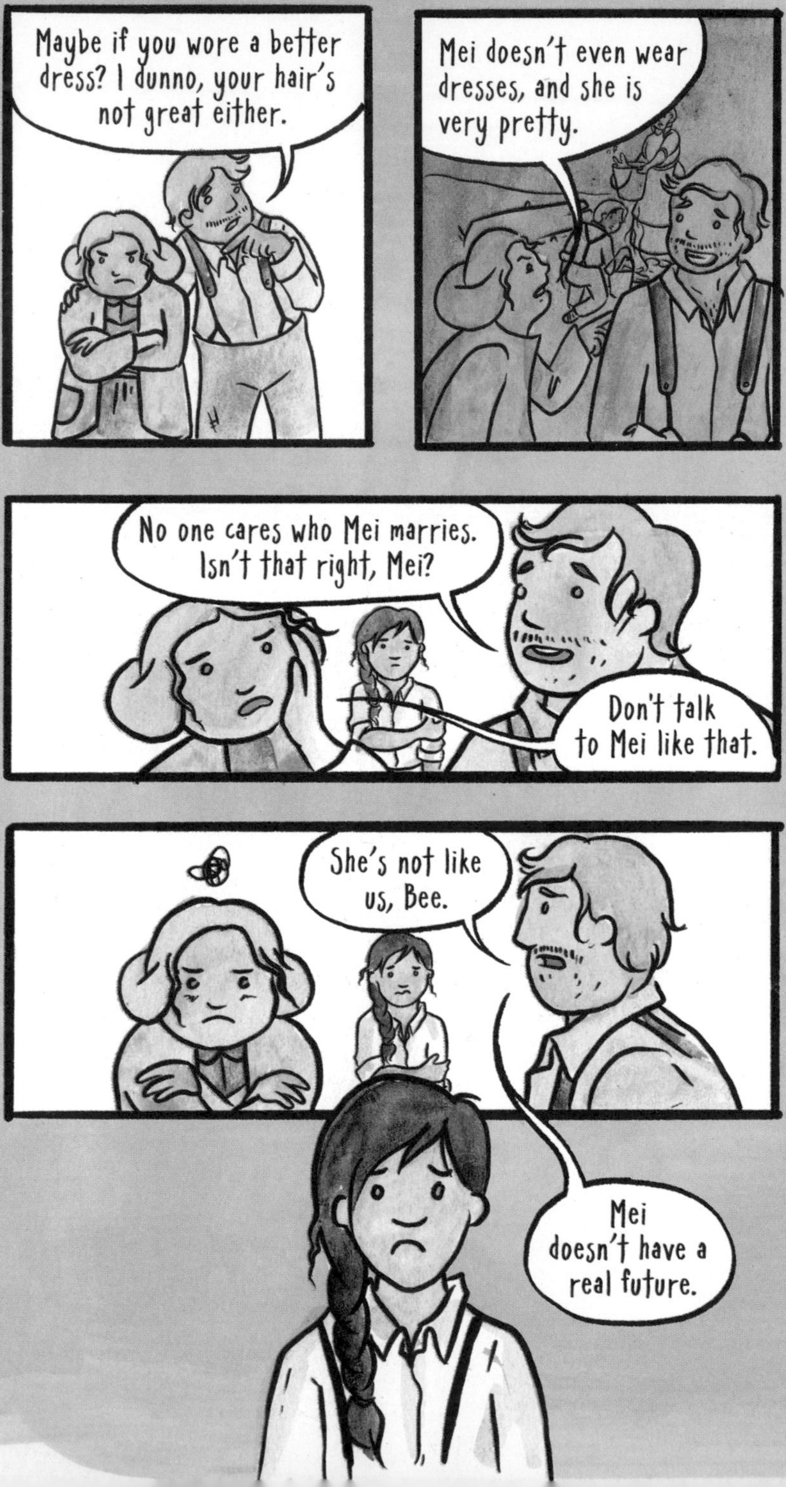
Maybe if you wore a better dress? I dunno, your hair's not great either.
Mei doesn't even wear dresses, and she is very pretty.
No one cares who Mei marries. Isn't that right, Mei?
Don't talk to Mei like that.
She's not like us, Bee.
Mei doesn't have a real future.

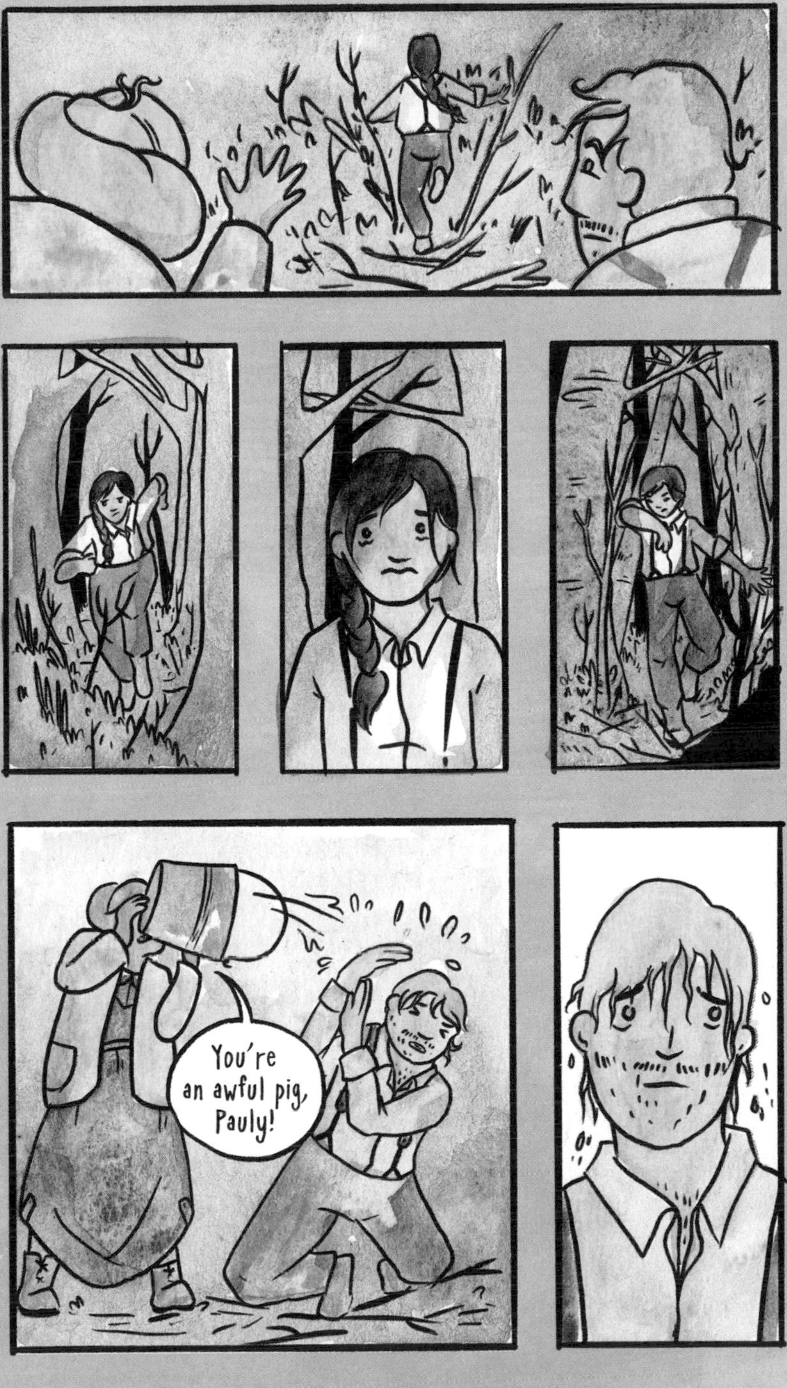

You're an awful pig, Pauly!

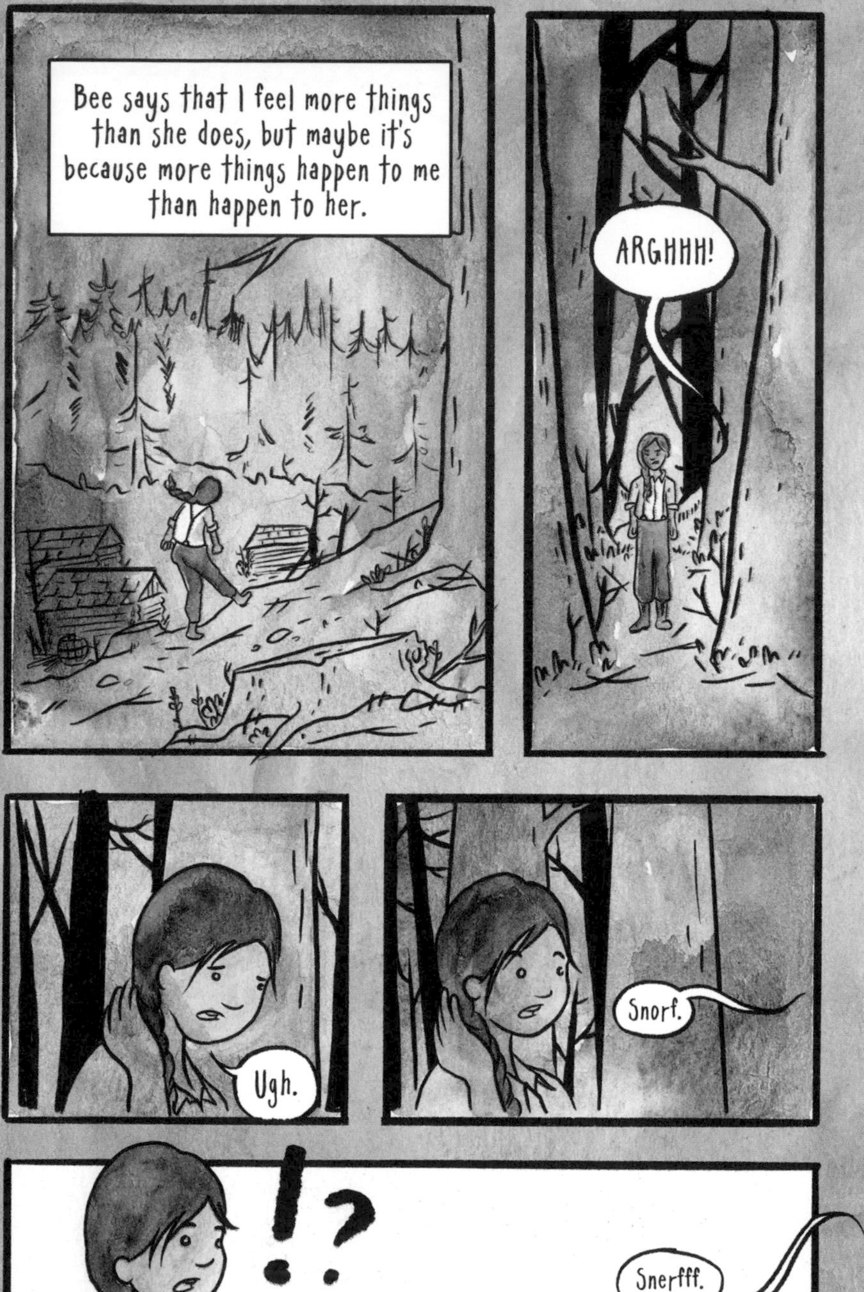
Bee says that I feel more things than she does, but maybe it's because more things happen to me than happen to her.
ARGHHH!
Ugh.
Snorf.
!?
Snerfff.

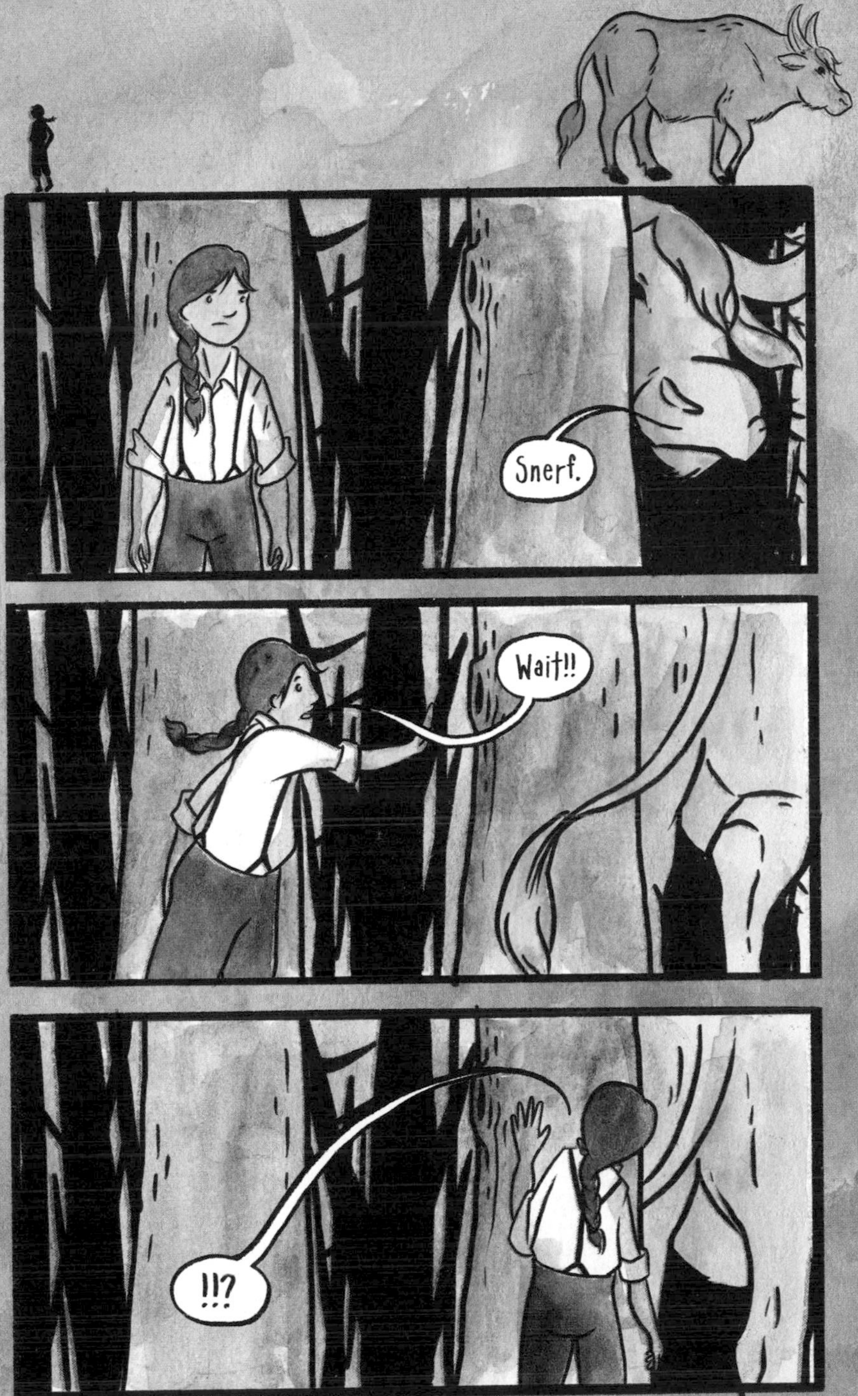
Snerf.
Wait!!
!!?

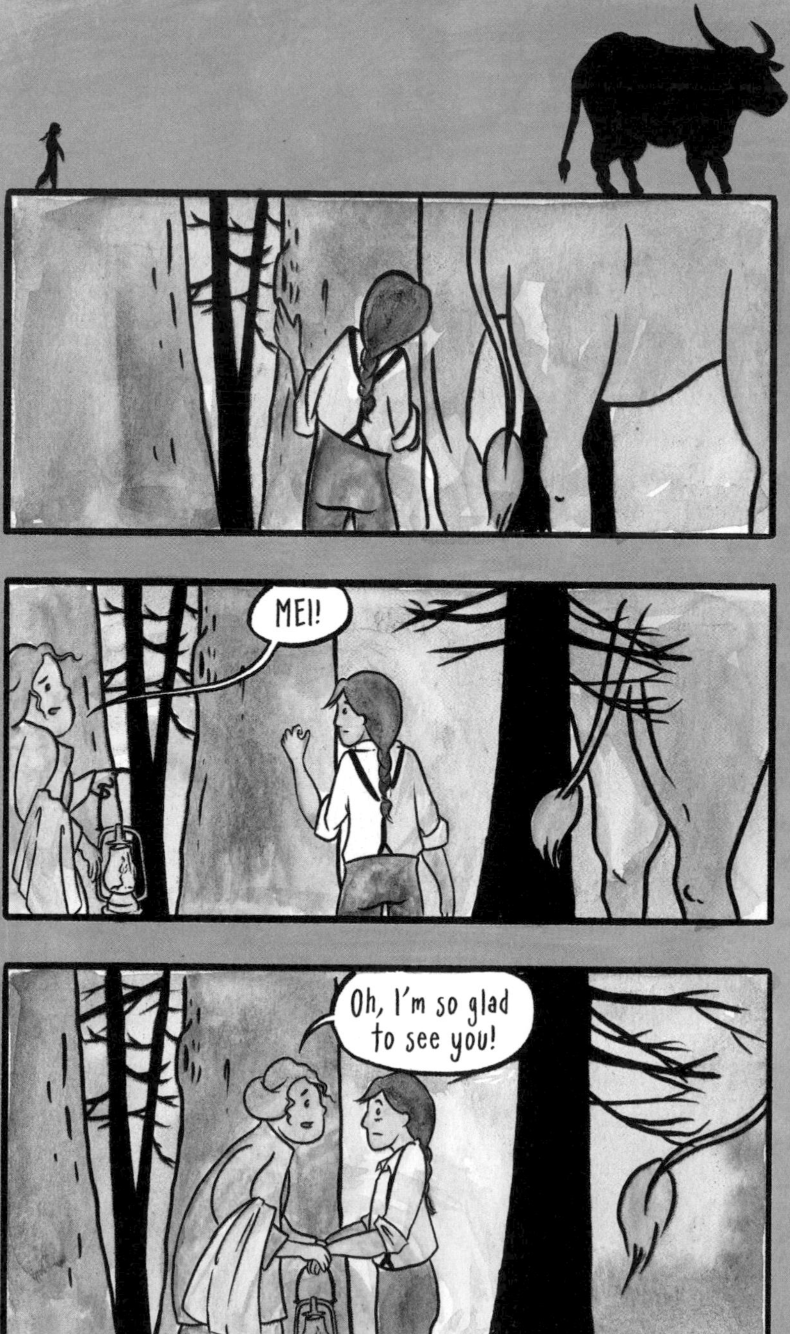
MEI!
Oh, I'm so glad to see you!

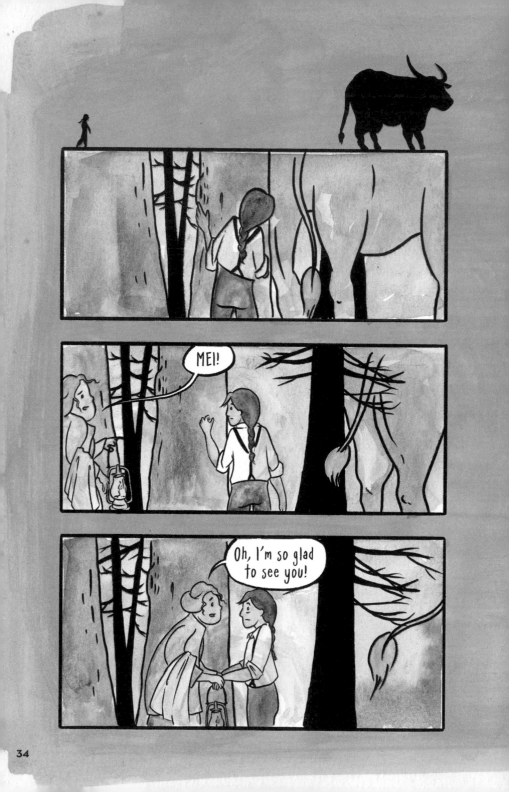

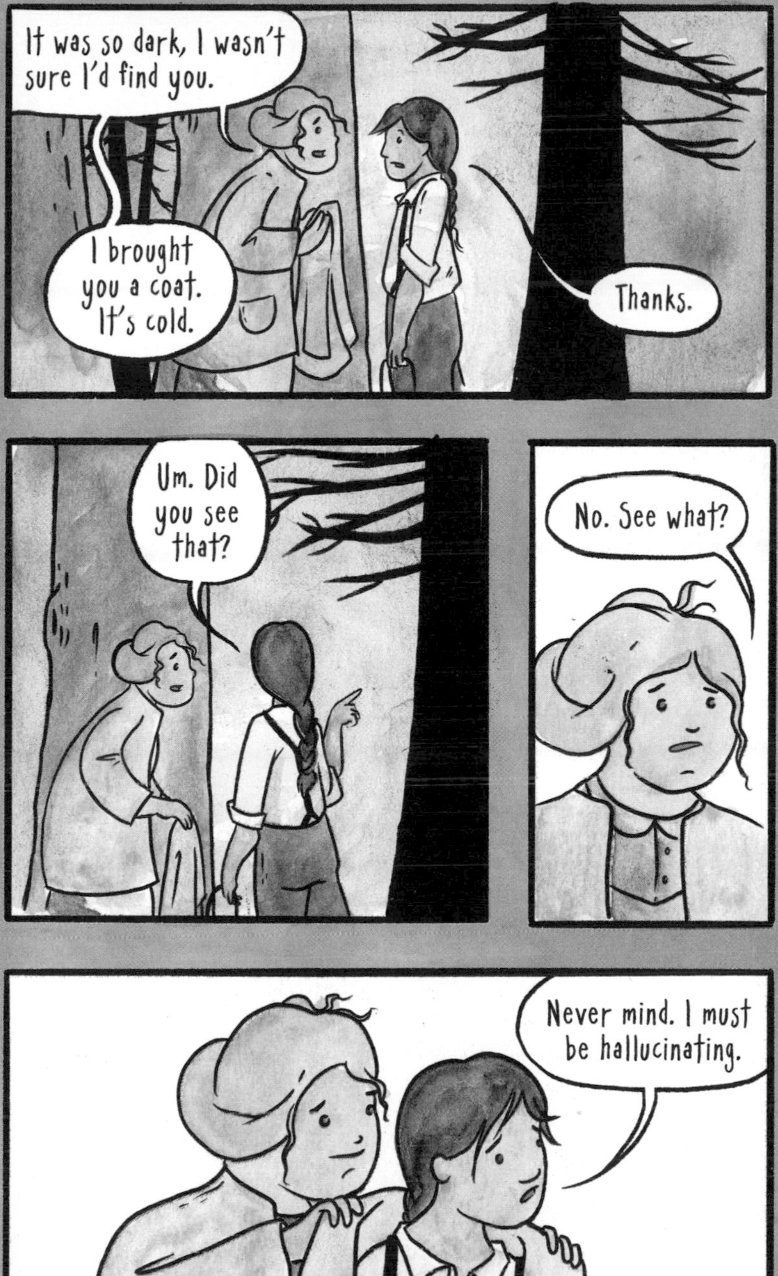
It was so dark, I wasn't sure I'd find you.
I brought you a coat. It's cold.
Thanks.
Um. Did you see that?
No. See what?
Never mind. I must be hallucinating.

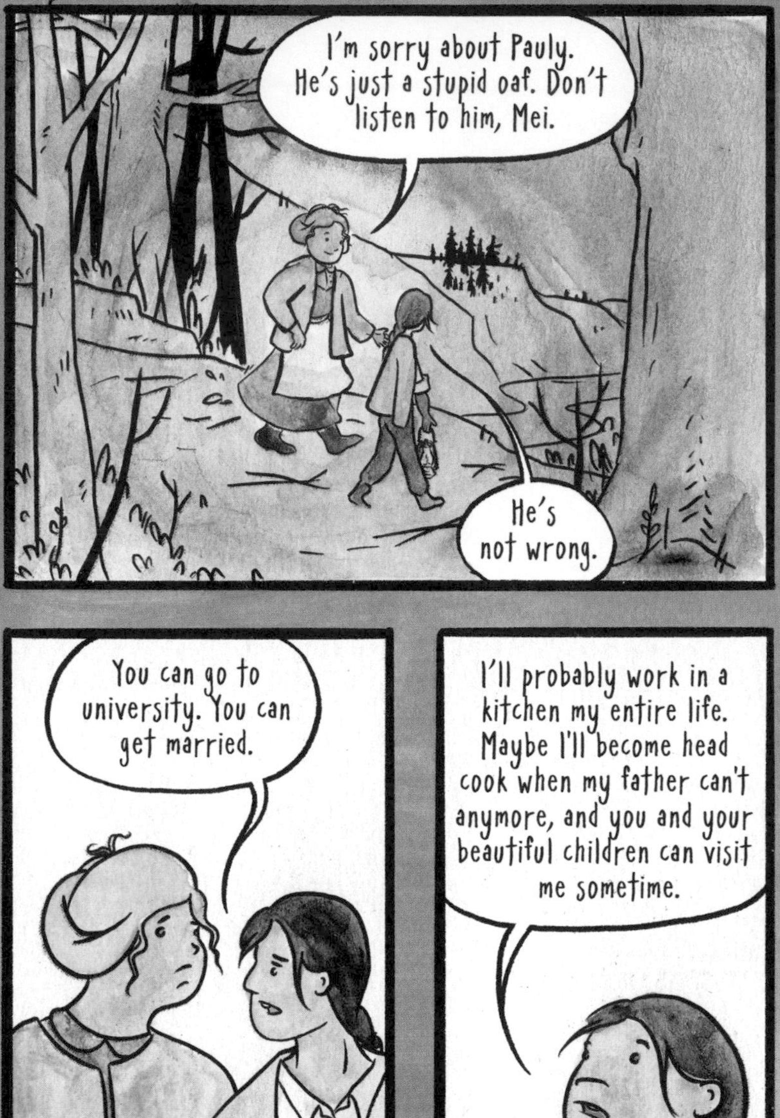
I'm sorry about Pauly. He's just a stupid oaf. Don't listen to him, Mei.
He's not wrong.
You can go to university. You can get married.
I'll probably work in a kitchen my entire life. Maybe I'll become head cook when my father can't anymore, and you and your beautiful children can visit me sometime.

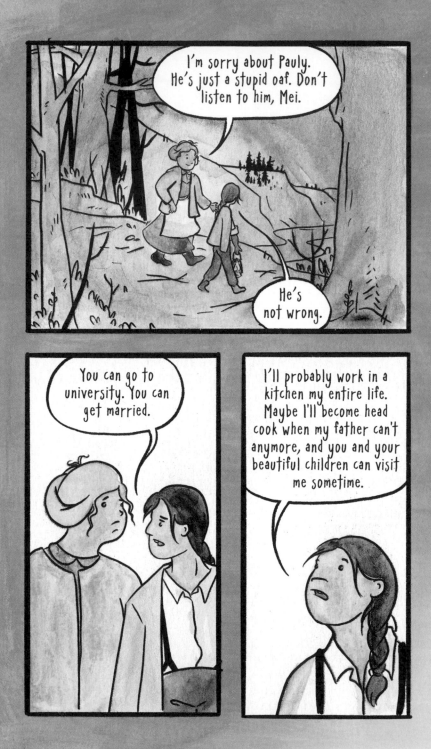

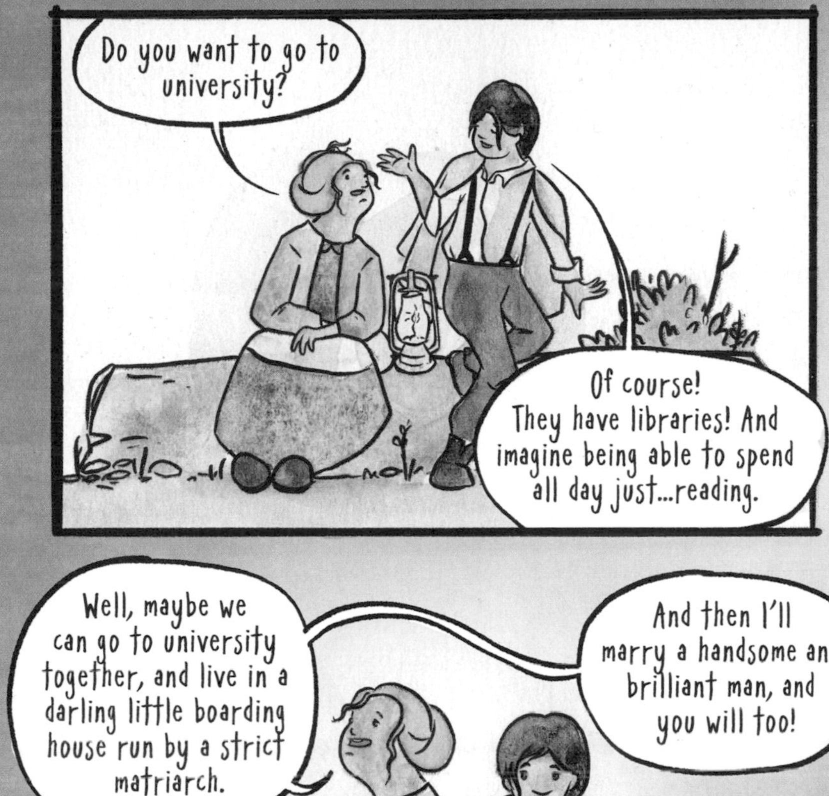
Do you want to go to university?
Of course! They have libraries! And imagine being able to spend all day just...reading.
Well, maybe we can go to university together, and live in a darling little boarding house run by a strict matriarch.
And then I'll marry a handsome and brilliant man, and you will too!
This is Bee's story. Bee will go to university, and marry a man.

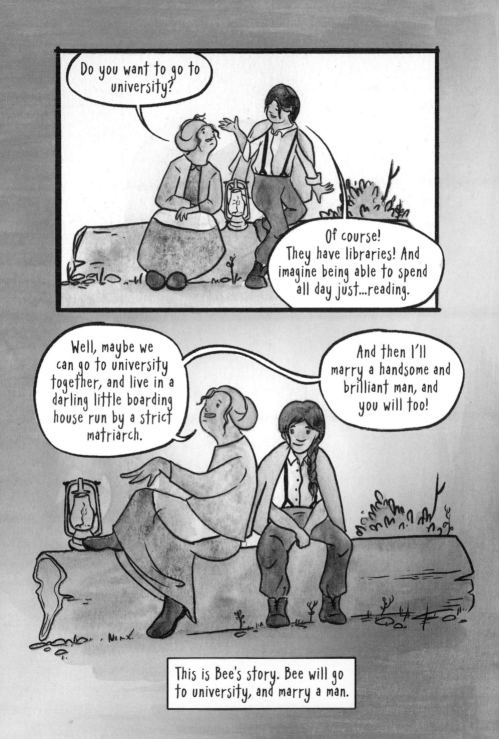

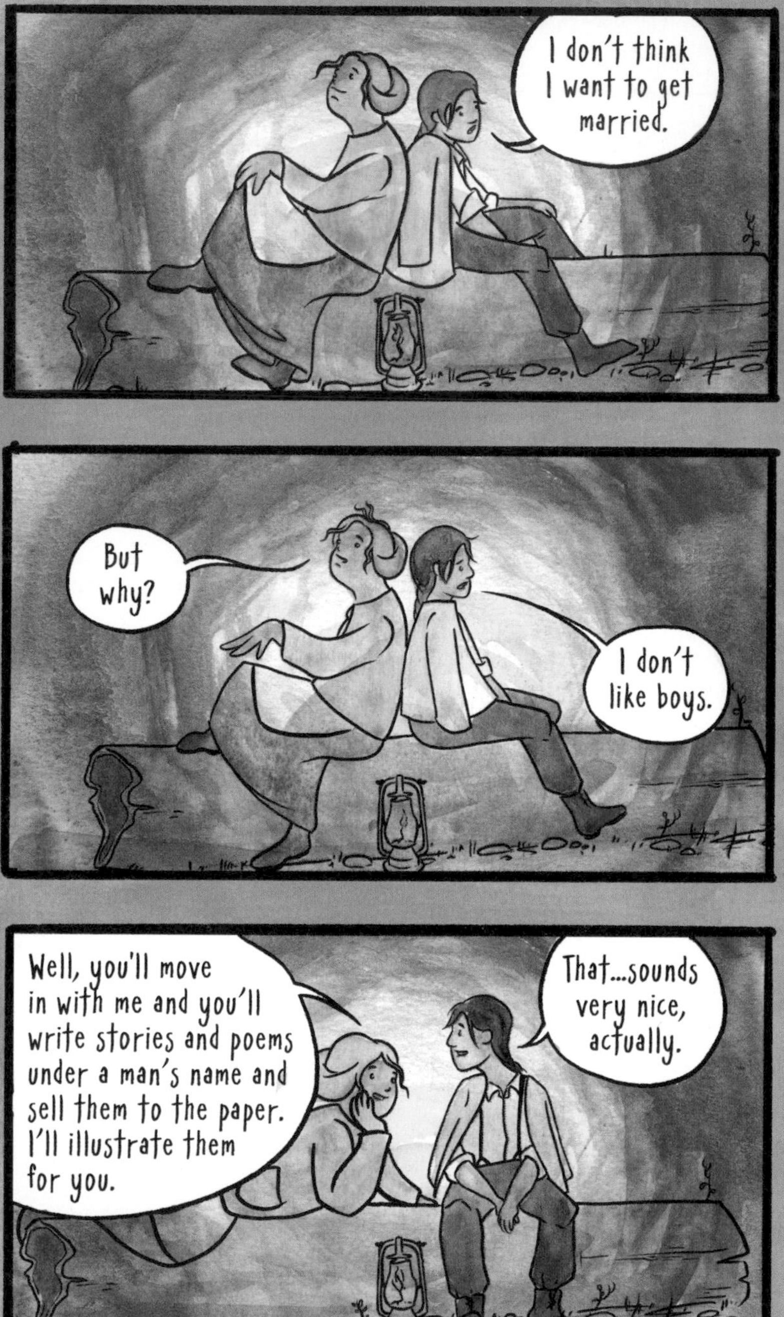
I don't think I want to get married.
But why?
I don't like boys.
Well, you'll move in with me and you'll write stories and poems under a man's name and sell them to the paper. I'll illustrate them for you.
That...sounds very nice, actually.

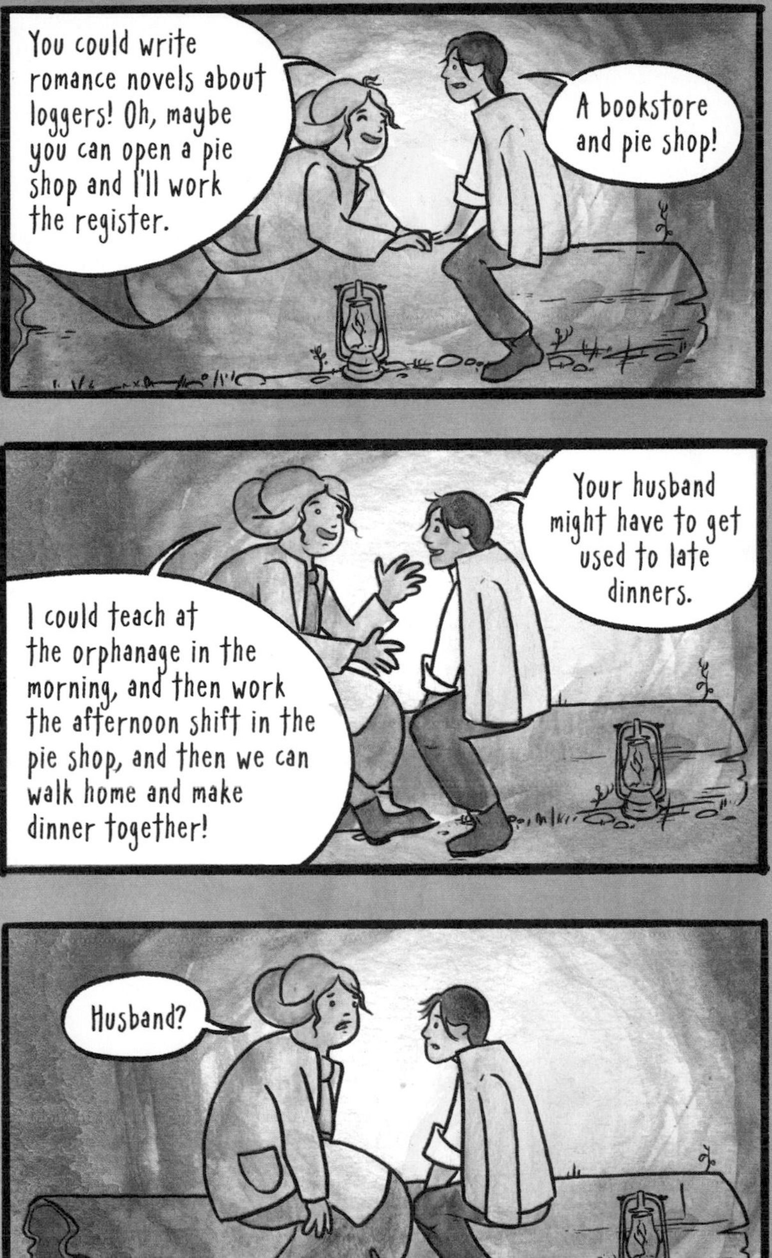
You could write romance novels about loggers! Oh, maybe you can open a pie shop and I'll work the register.
A bookstore and pie shop!
I could teach at the orphanage in the morning, and then work the afternoon shift in the pie shop, and then we can walk home and make dinner together!
Your husband might have to get used to late dinners.
Husband?

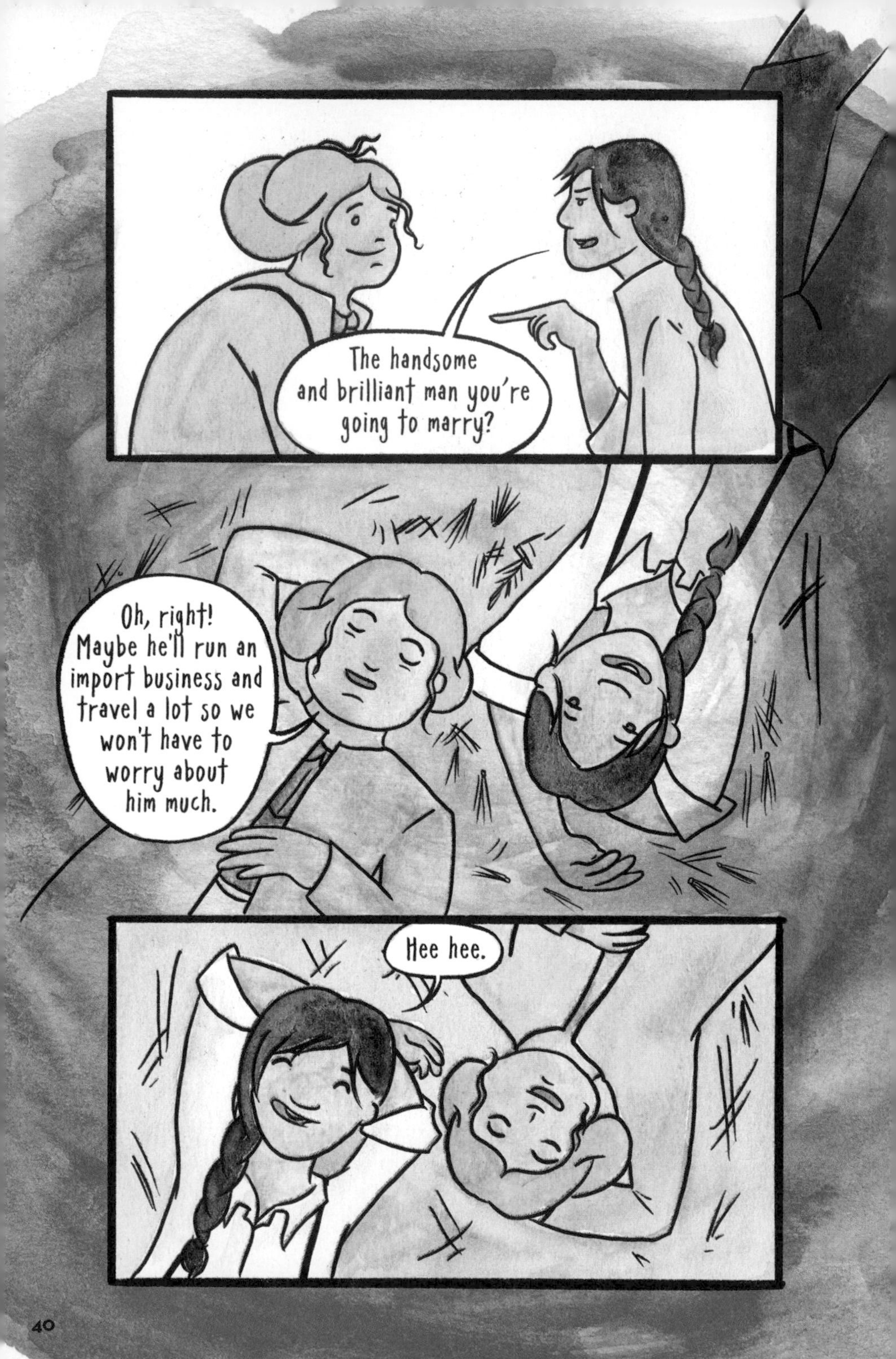
The handsome and brilliant man you're going to marry?
Oh, right! Maybe he'll run an import business and travel a lot so we won't have to worry about him much.
Hee hee.

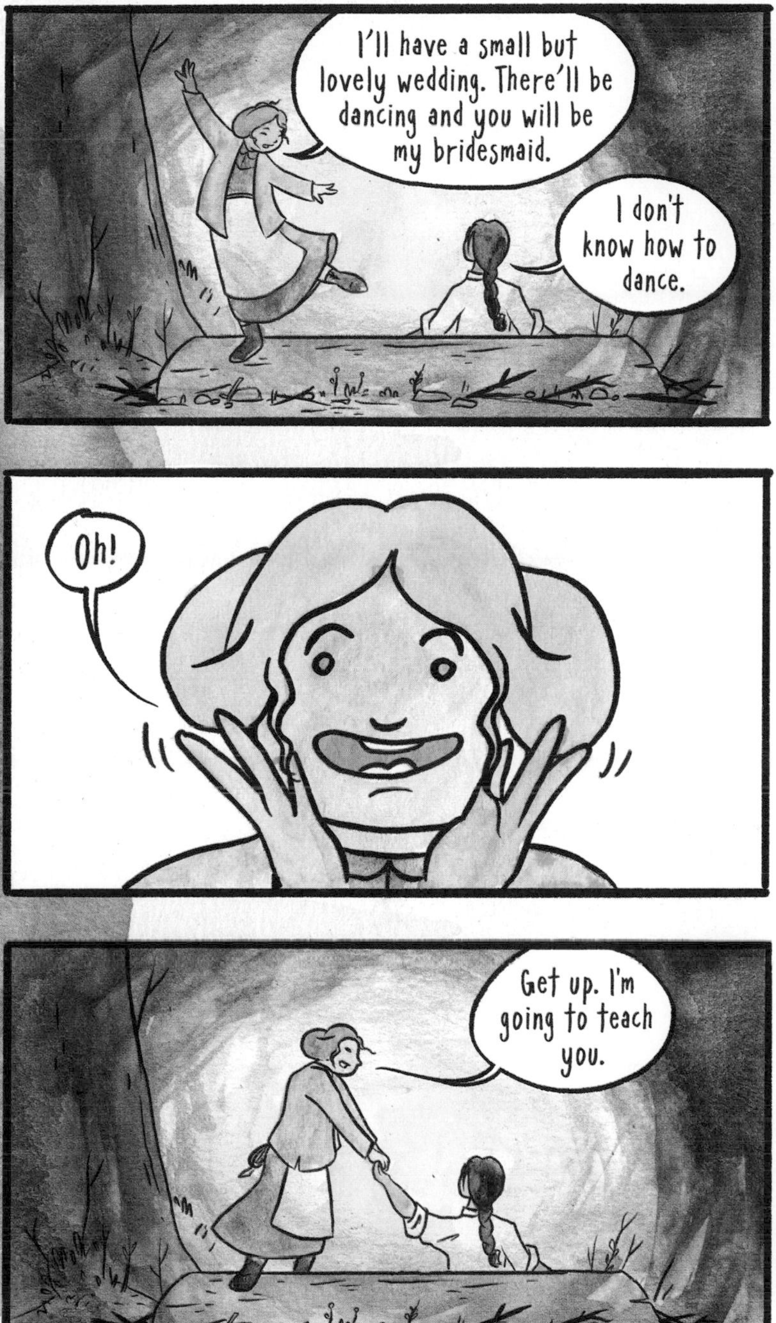
I'll have a small but lovely wedding. There'll be dancing and you will be my bridesmaid.
I don't know how to dance.
Oh!
Get up. I'm going to teach you.

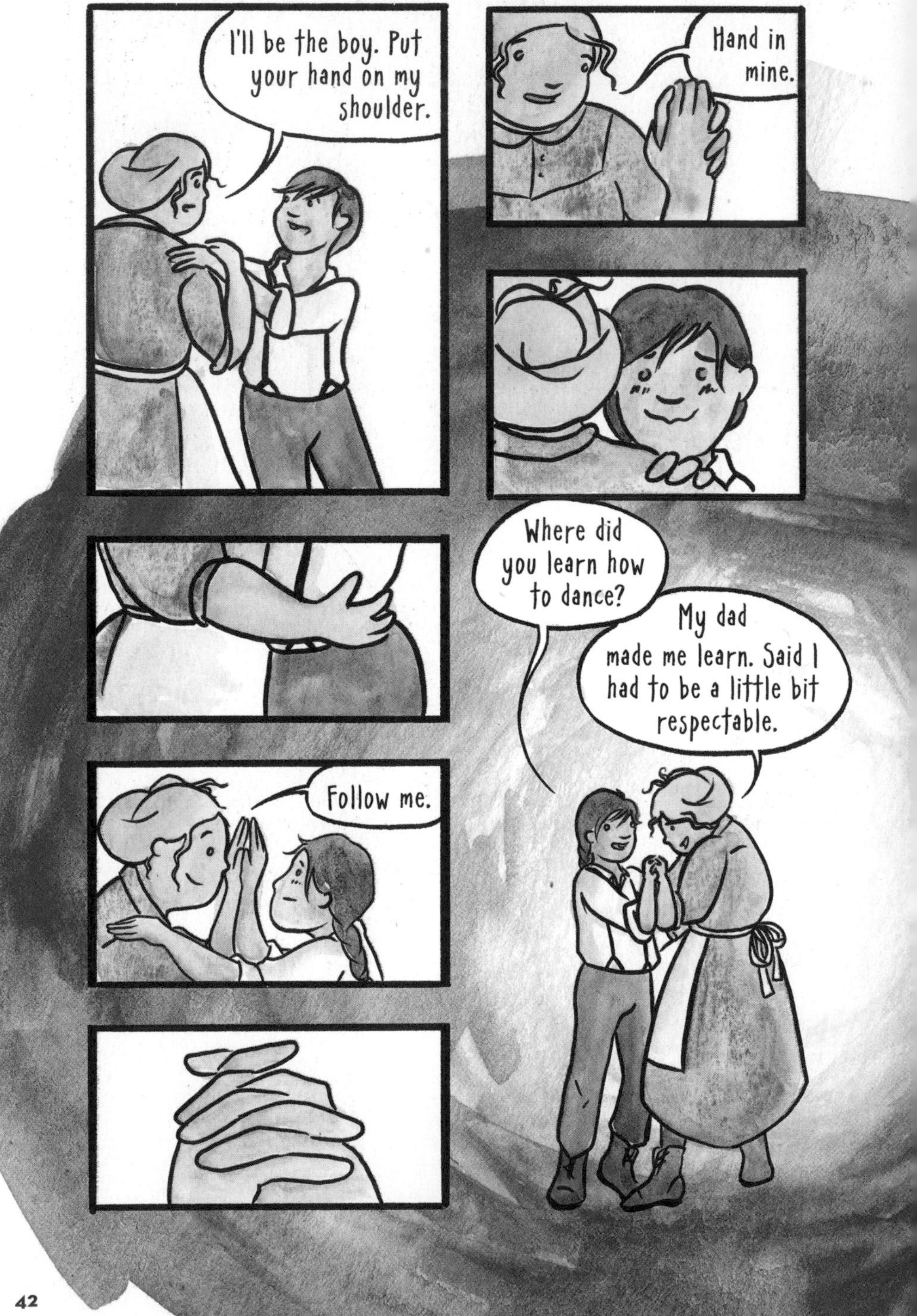
I'll be the boy. Put your hand on my shoulder.
Hand in mine.
Follow me.
Where did you learn how to dance?
My dad made me learn. Said I had to be a little bit respectable.

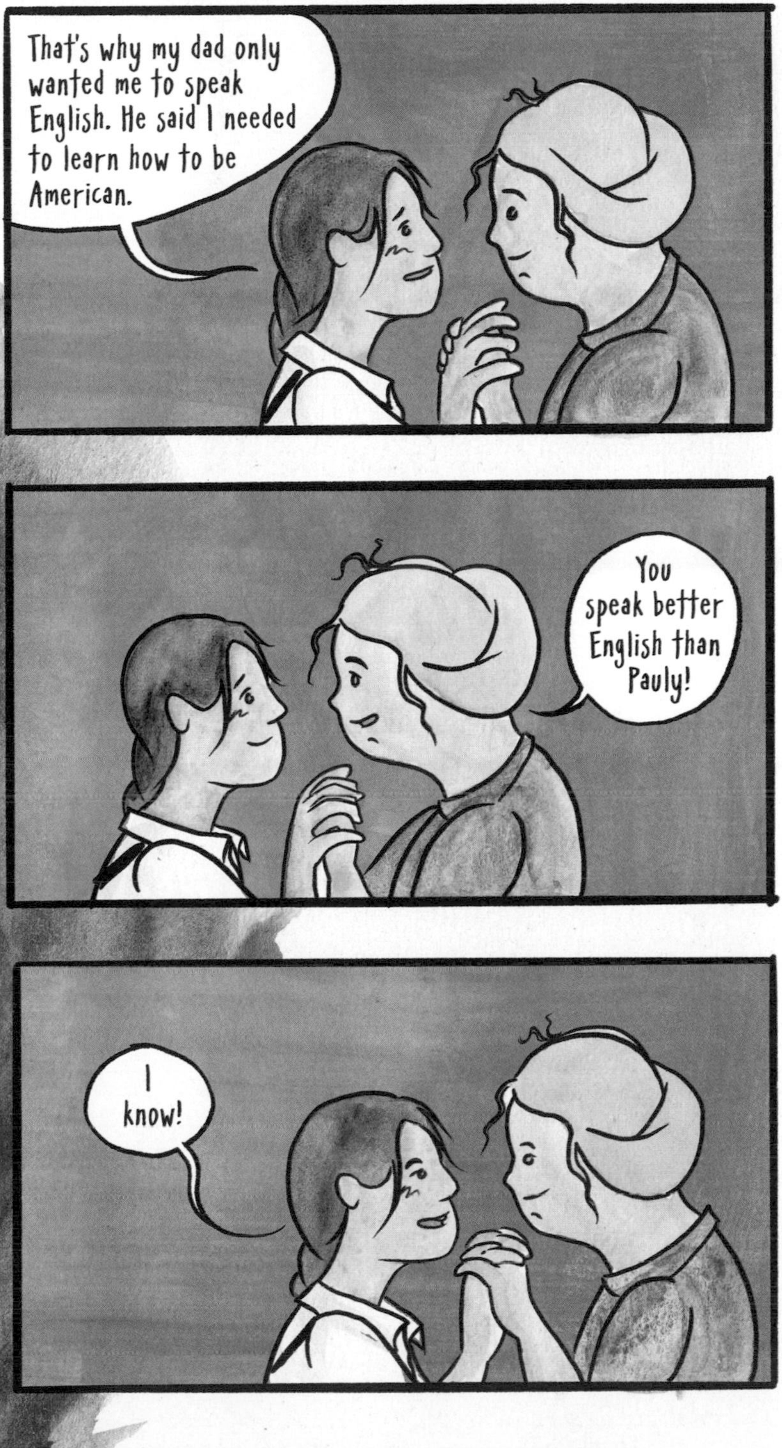
That's why my dad only wanted me to speak English. He said I needed to learn how to be American.
You speak better English than Pauly!
I know!

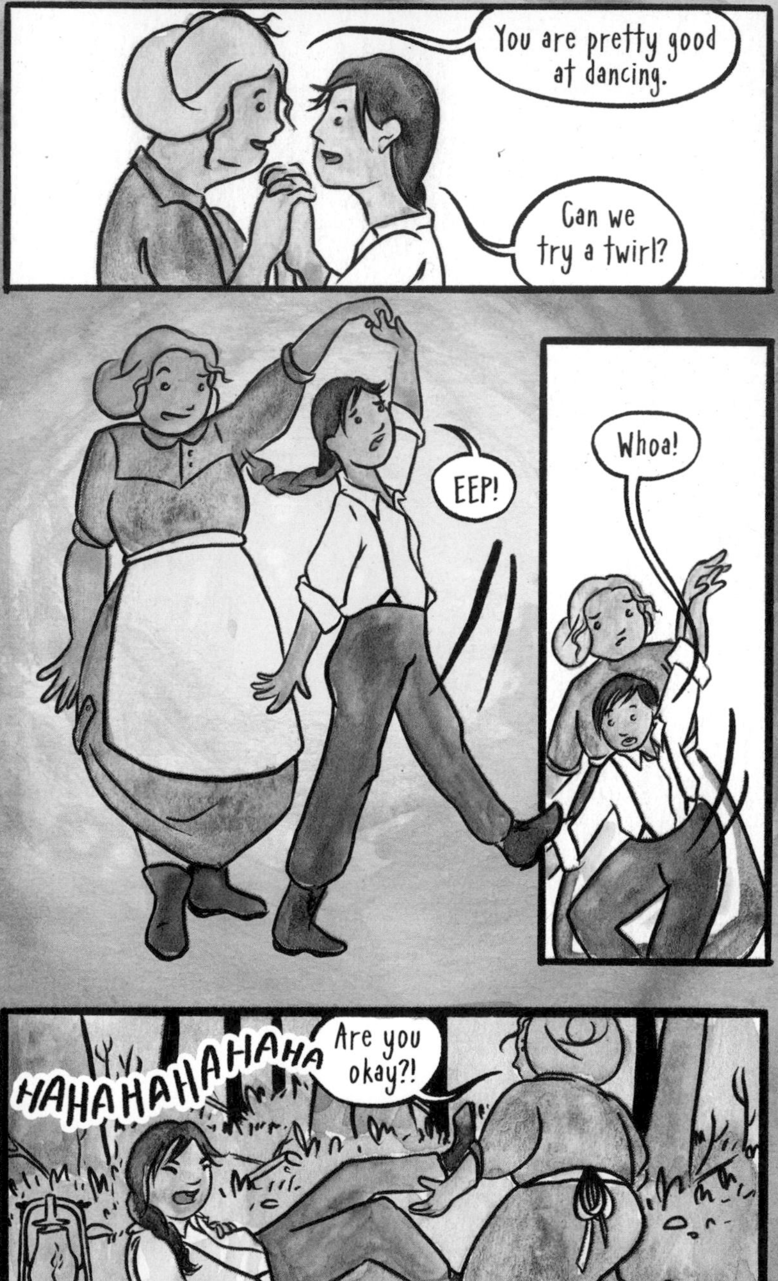
You are pretty good at dancing.
Can we try a twirl?
EEP!
Whoa!
HAHAHAHAHAHA
Are you okay?!

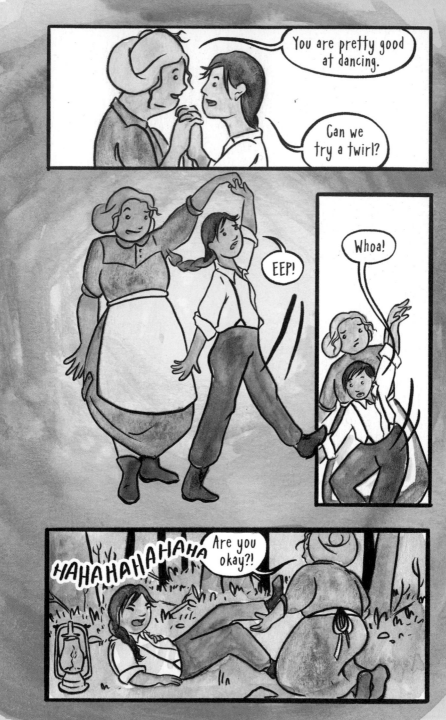

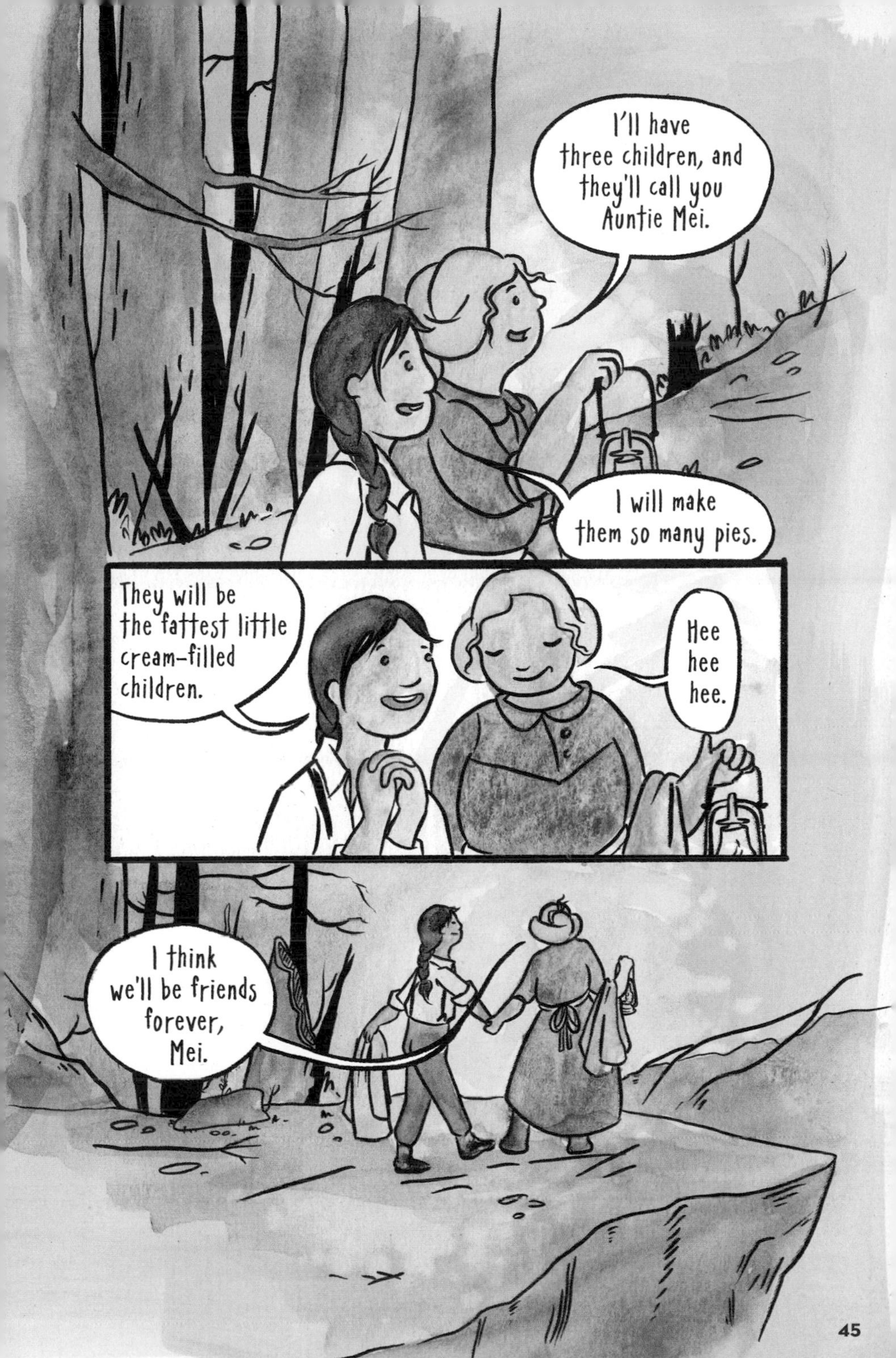
I'll have three children, and they'll call you Auntie Mei.
I will make them so many pies.
They will be the fattest little cream-filled children.
Hee hee hee.
I think we'll be friends forever, Mei.

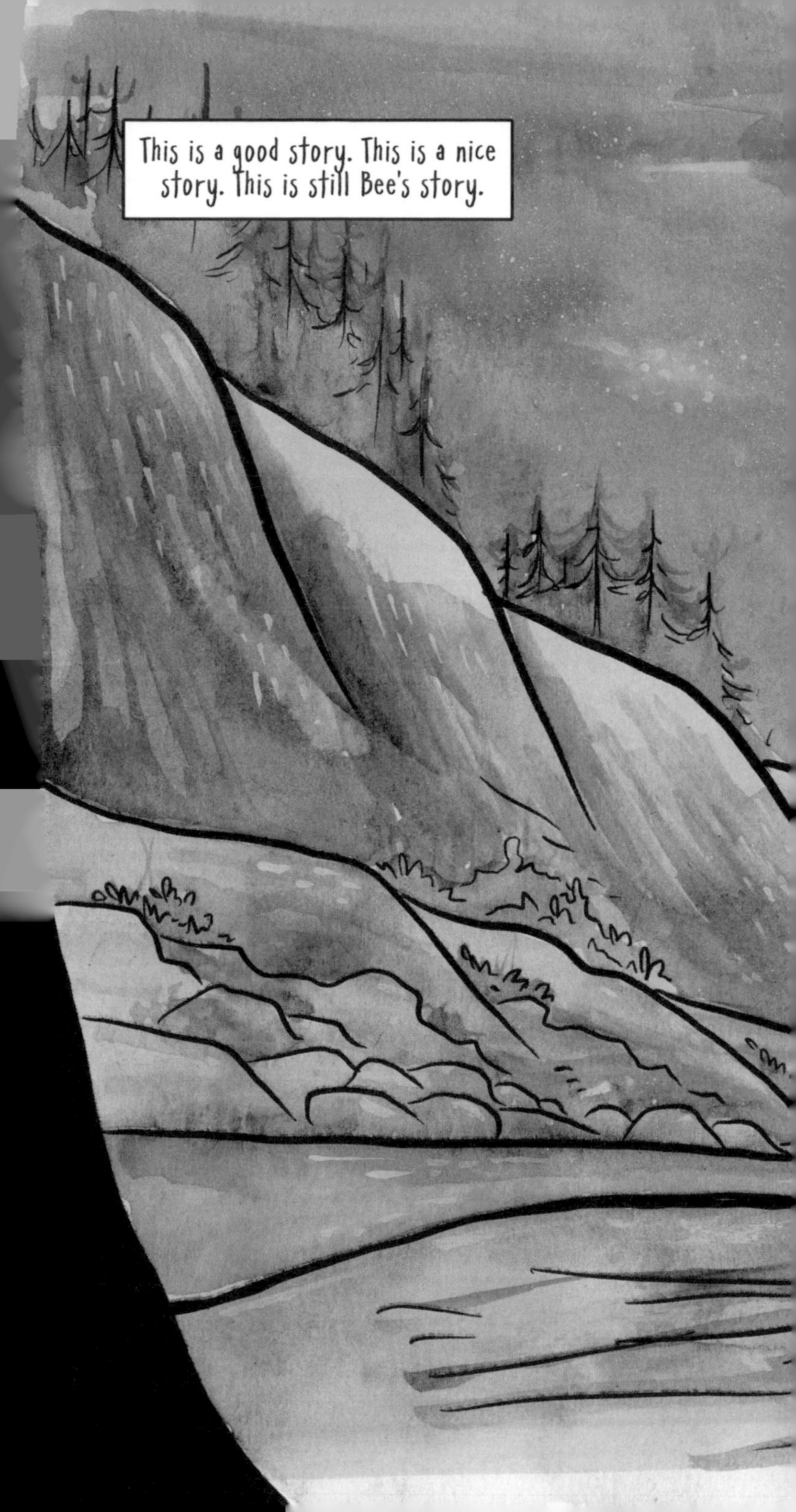
This is a good story. This is a nice story. This is still Bee's story.

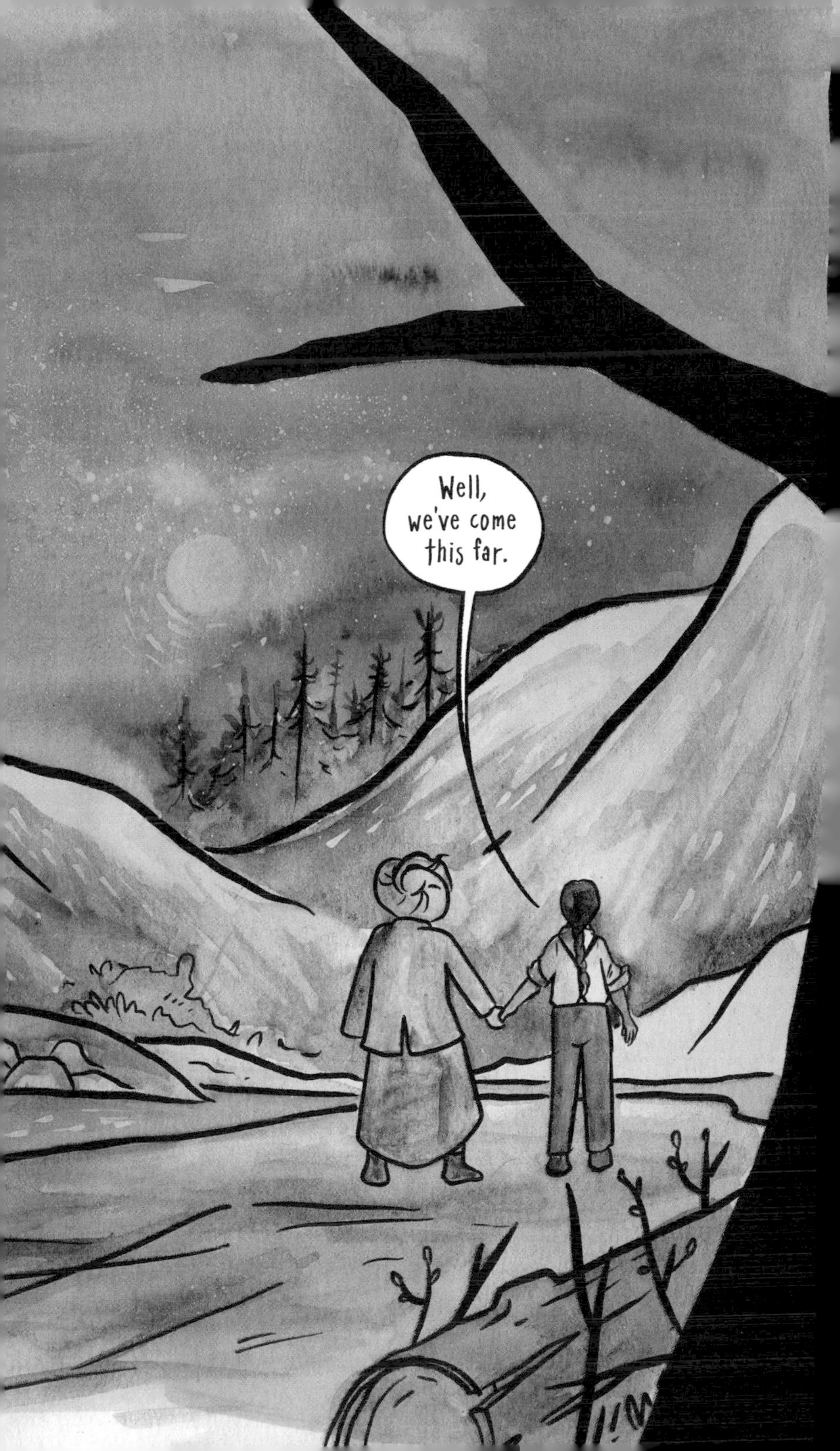
Well, we've come this far.

CHAPTER two

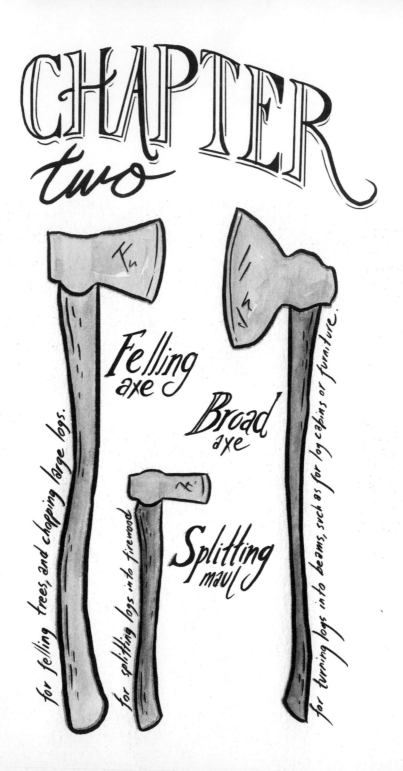

Felling axe

for felling trees, and chopping large logs.

Broad axe

for turning logs into beams, such as for log cabins or furniture.

Splitting maul

for splitting logs into firewood

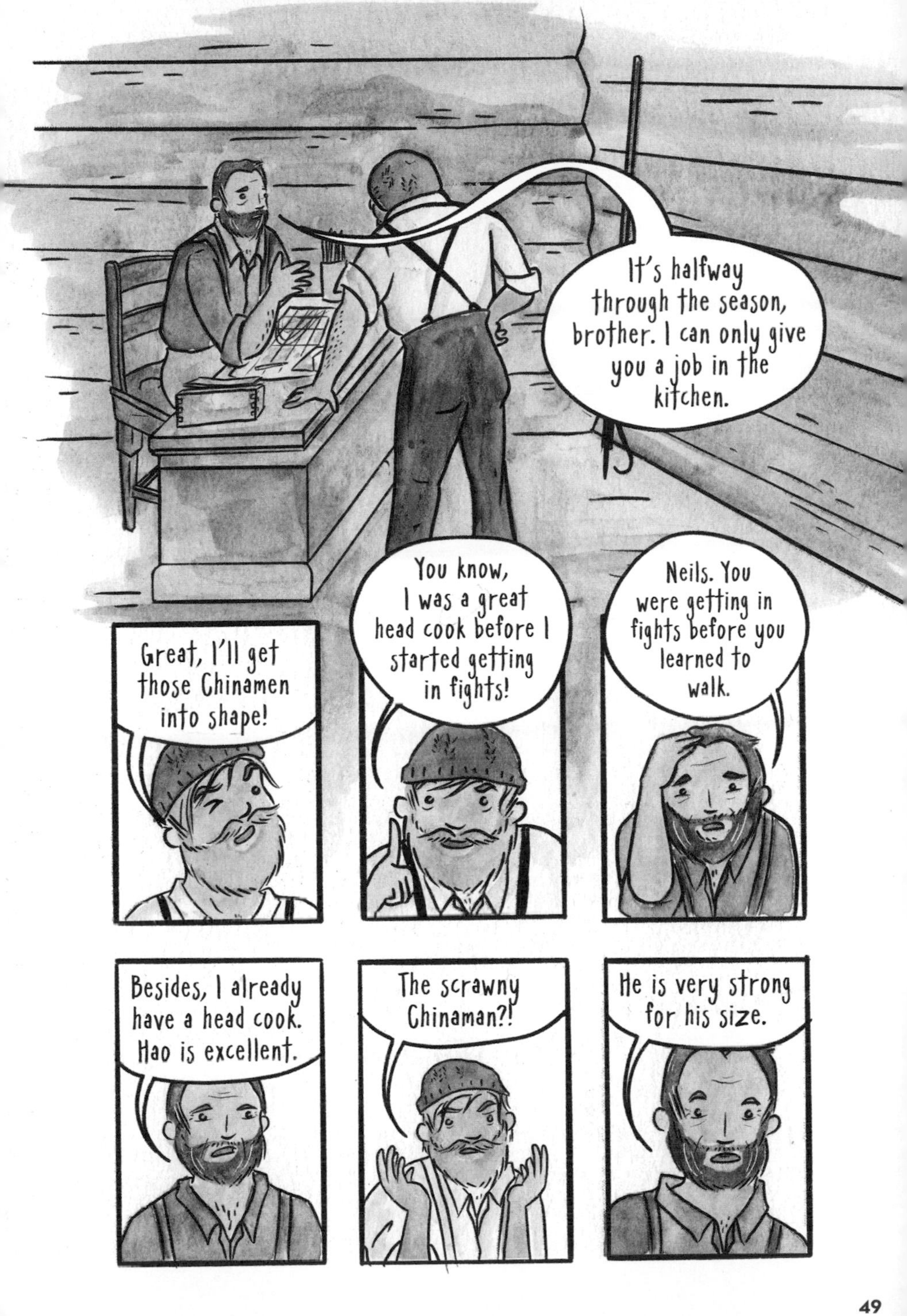

It's halfway through the season, brother. I can only give you a job in the kitchen.
Great, I'll get those Chinamen into shape!
You know, I was a great head cook before I started getting in fights!
Neils. You were getting in fights before you learned to walk.
Besides, I already have a head cook. Hao is excellent.
The scrawny Chinaman?!
He is very strong for his size.

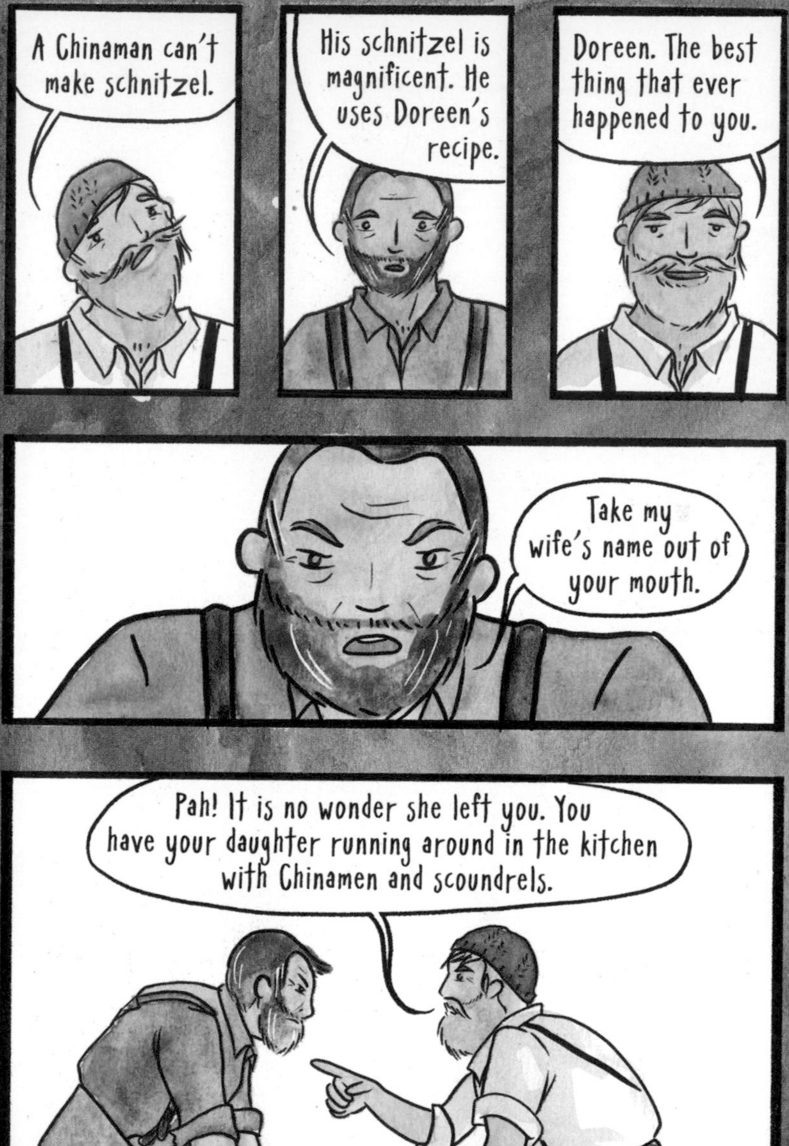
A Chinaman can't make schnitzel.
His schnitzel is magnificent. He uses Doreen's recipe.
Doreen. The best thing that ever happened to you.
Take my wife's name out of your mouth.
Pah! It is no wonder she left you. You have your daughter running around in the kitchen with Chinamen and scoundrels.

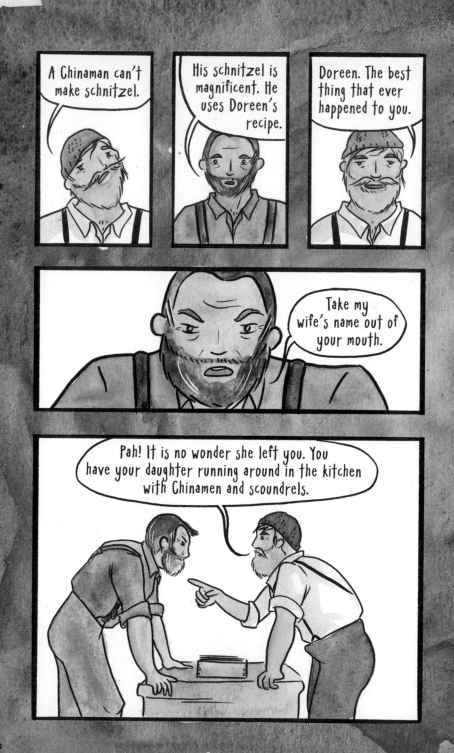

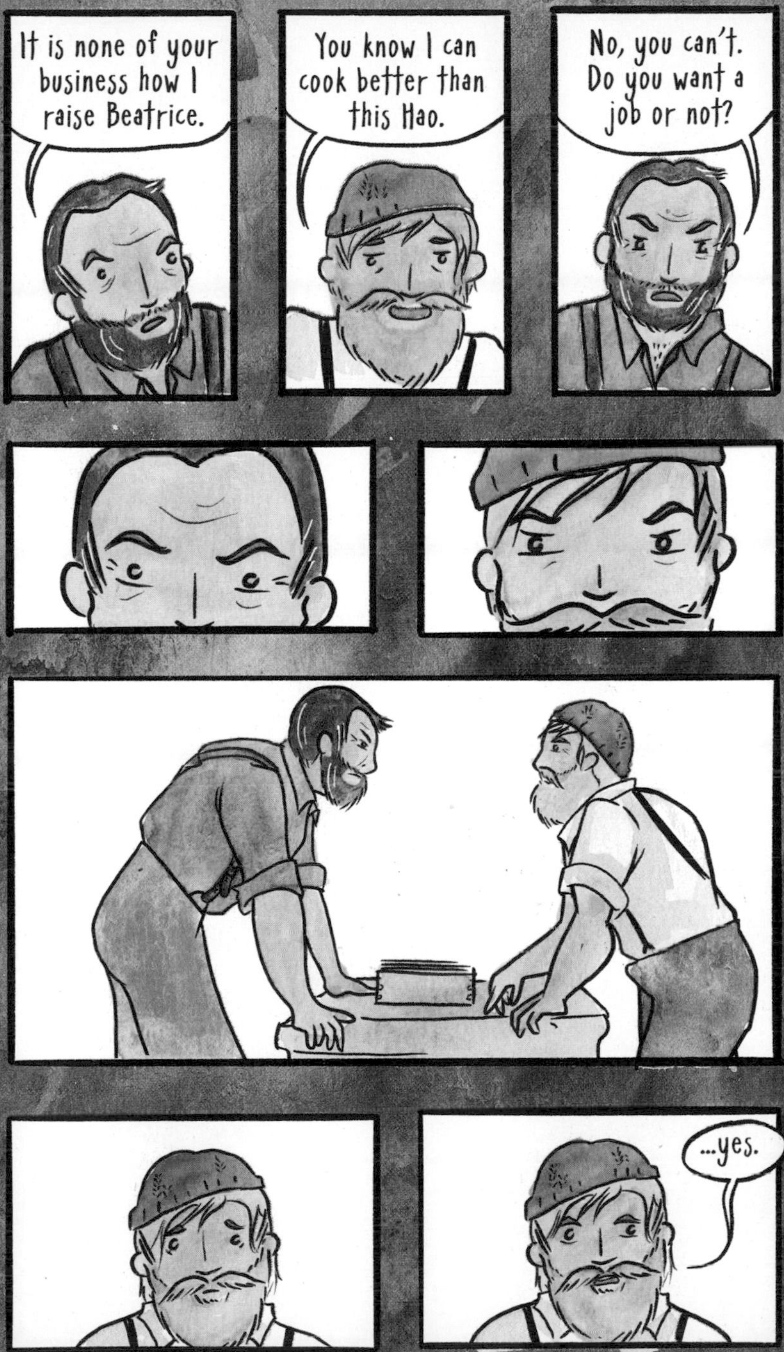
It is none of your business how I raise Beatrice.
You know I can cook better than this Hao.
No, you can't. Do you want a job or not?
...yes.

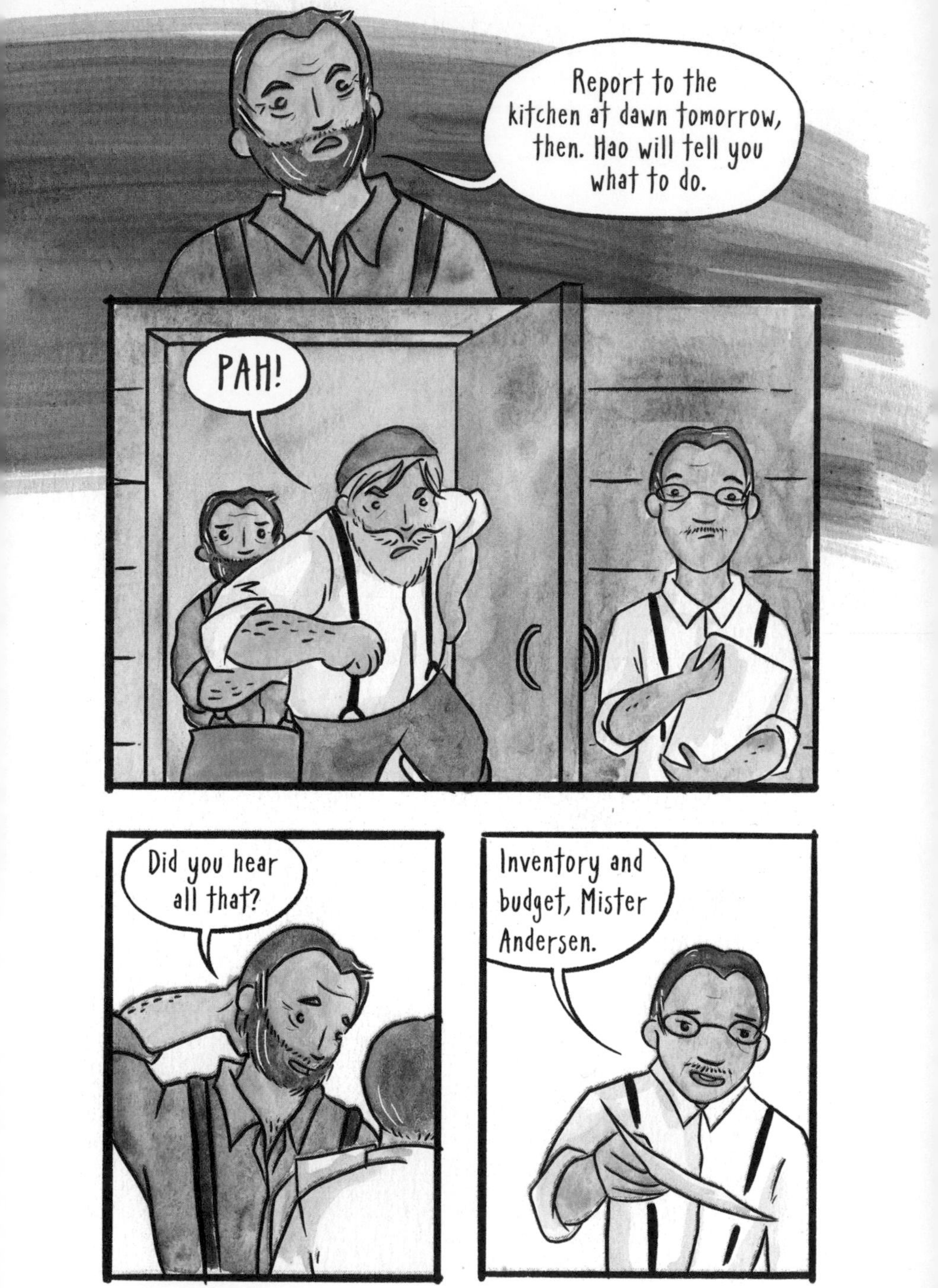
Report to the kitchen at dawn tomorrow, then. Hao will tell you what to do.
PAH!
Did you hear all that?
Inventory and budget, Mister Andersen.

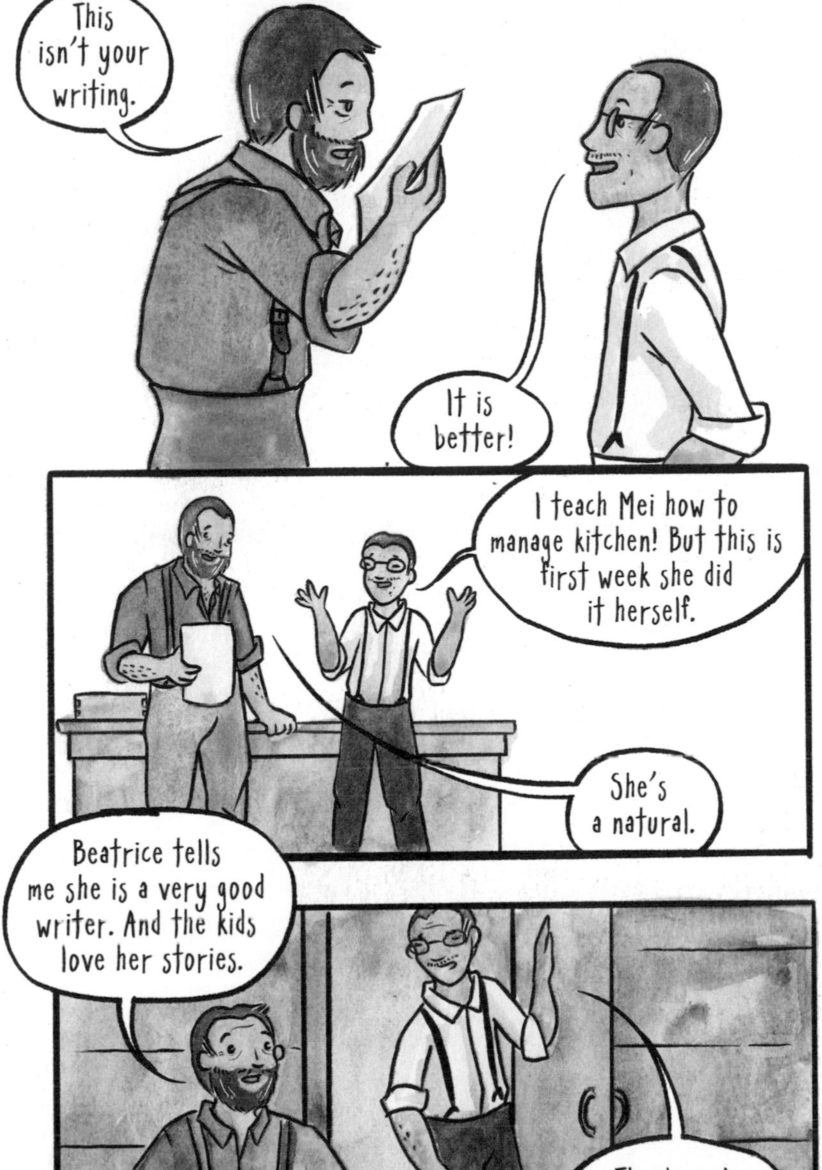
This isn't your writing.
It is better!
I teach Mei how to manage kitchen! But this is first week she did it herself.
She's a natural.
Beatrice tells me she is a very good writer. And the kids love her stories.
Thank you! Miss Andersen has help with her reading.

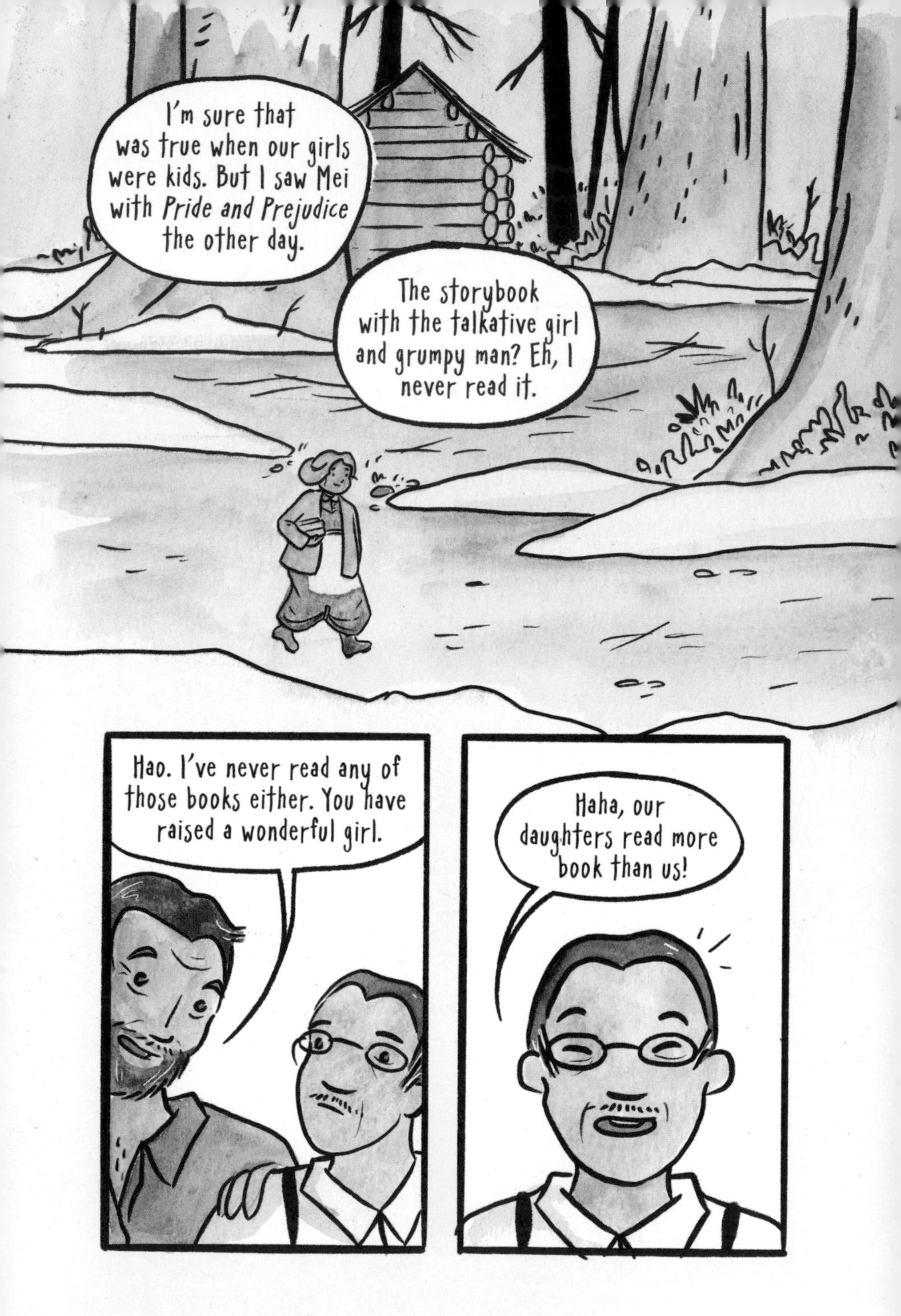
I'm sure that was true when our girls were kids. But I saw Mei with *Pride and Prejudice* the other day.
The storybook with the talkative girl and grumpy man? Eh, I never read it.
Hao. I've never read any of those books either. You have raised a wonderful girl.
Haha, our daughters read more book than us!

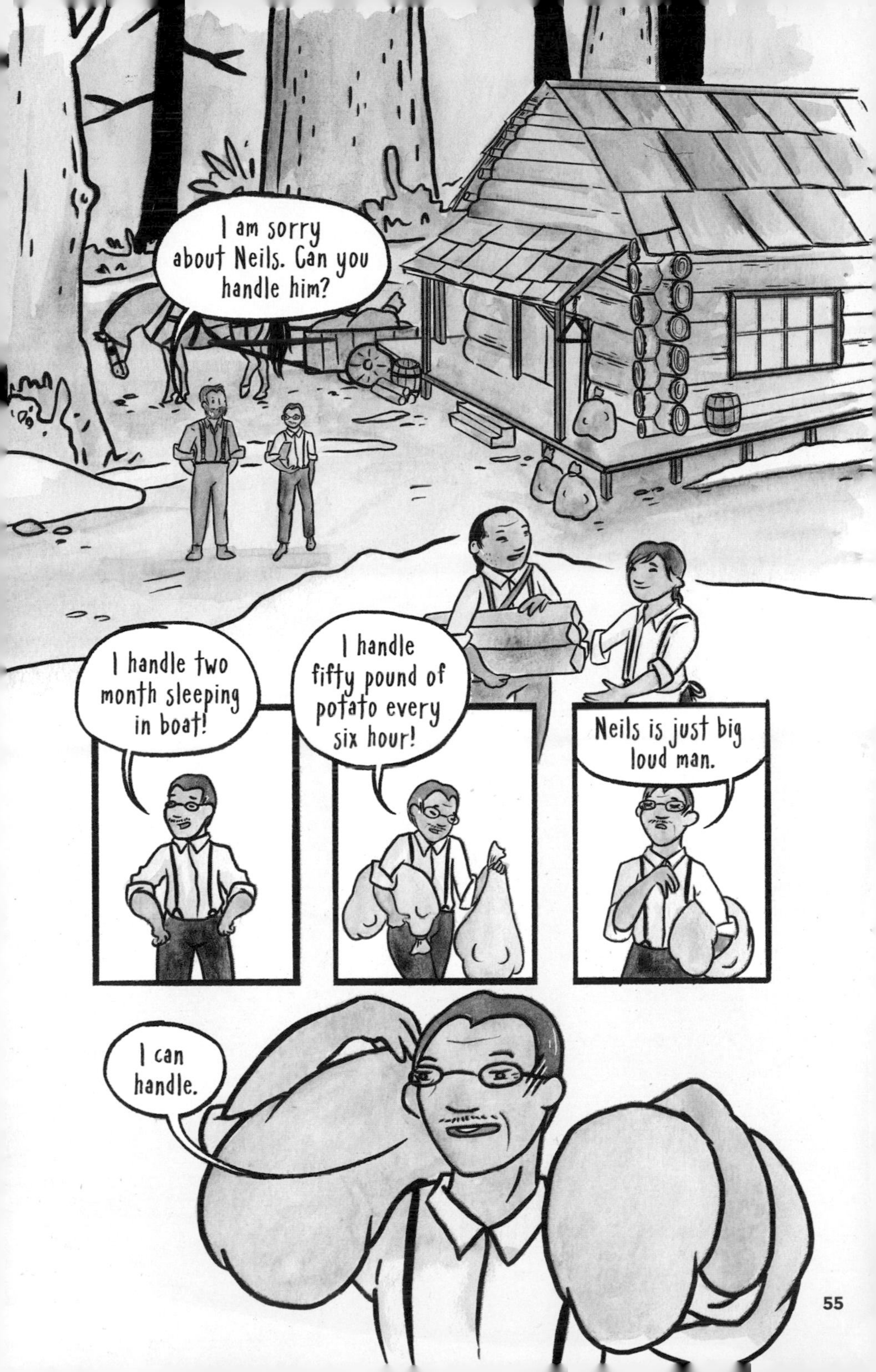
I am sorry about Neils. Can you handle him?
I handle two month sleeping in boat!
I handle fifty pound of potato every six hour!
Neils is just big loud man.
I can handle.

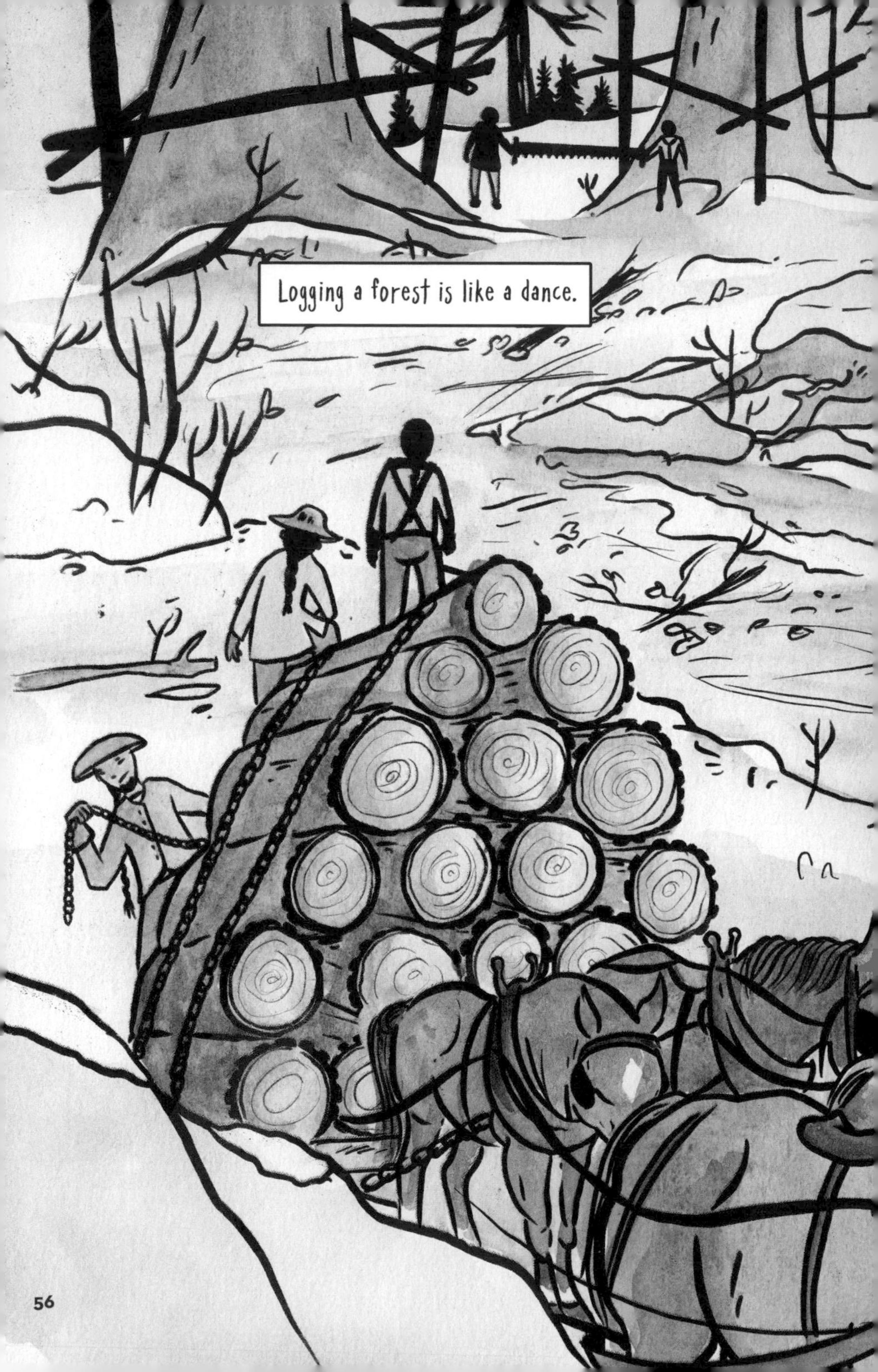
Logging a forest is like a dance.

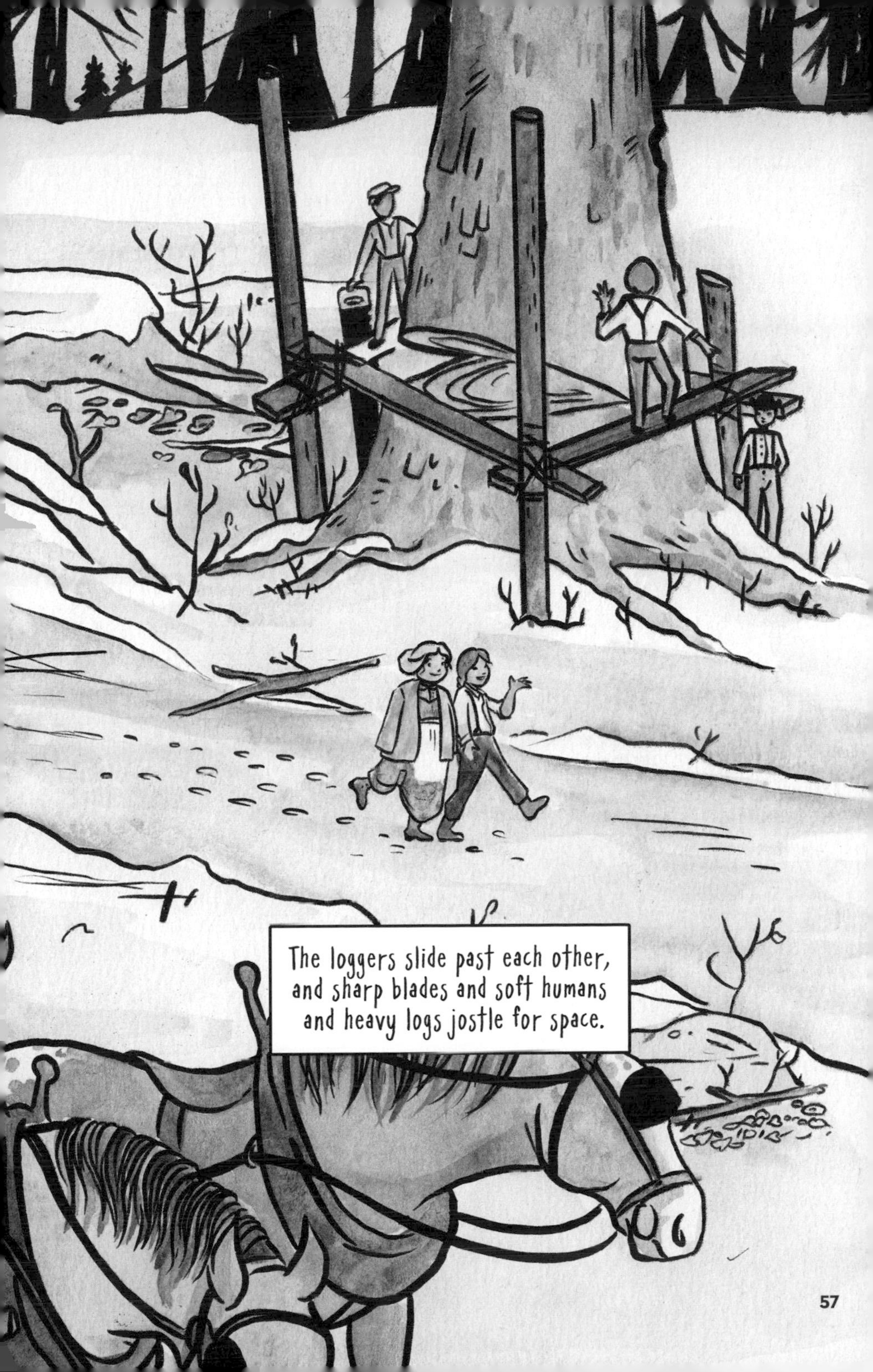
The loggers slide past each other, and sharp blades and soft humans and heavy logs jostle for space.

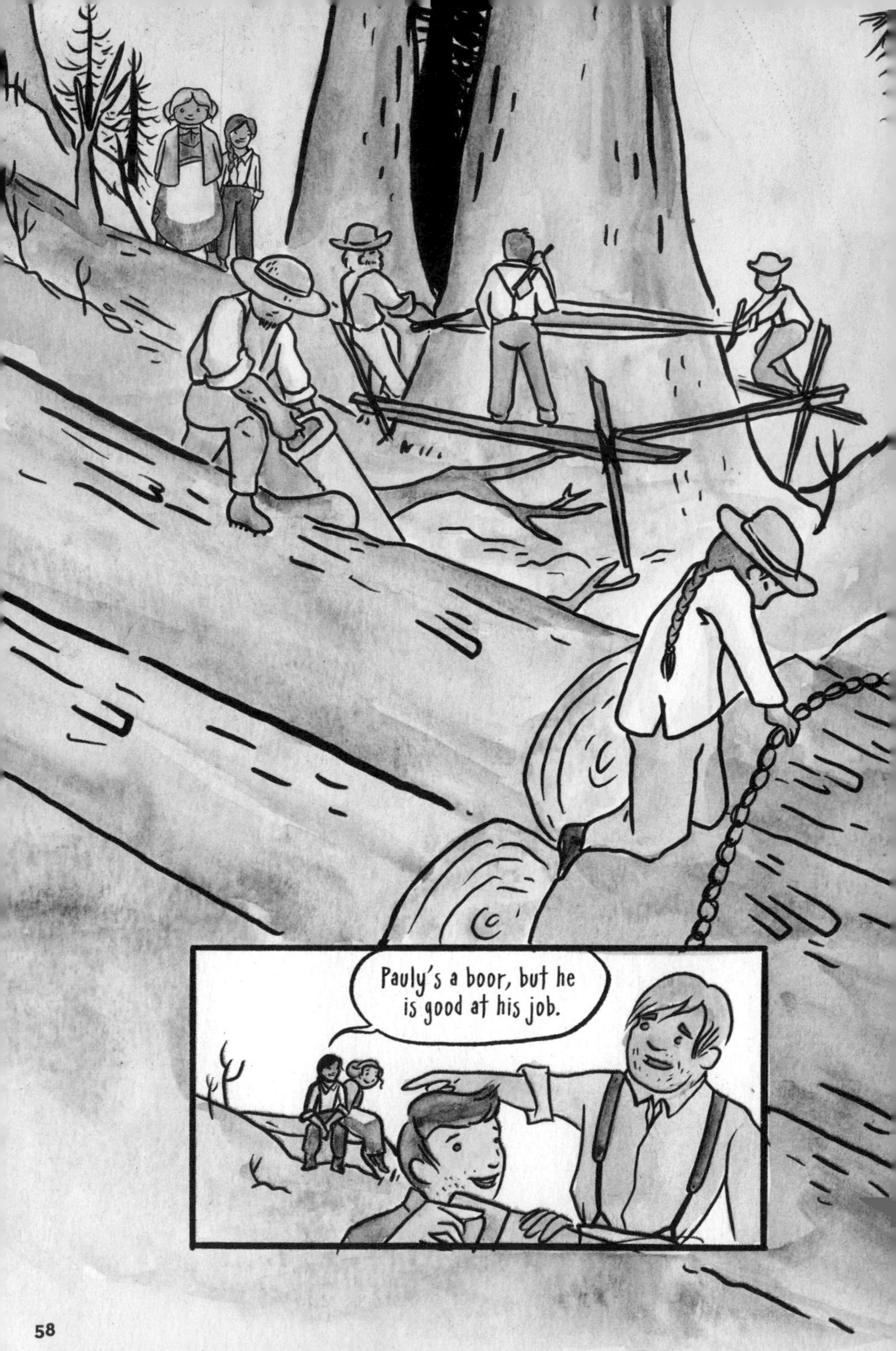
Pauly's a boor, but he is good at his job.

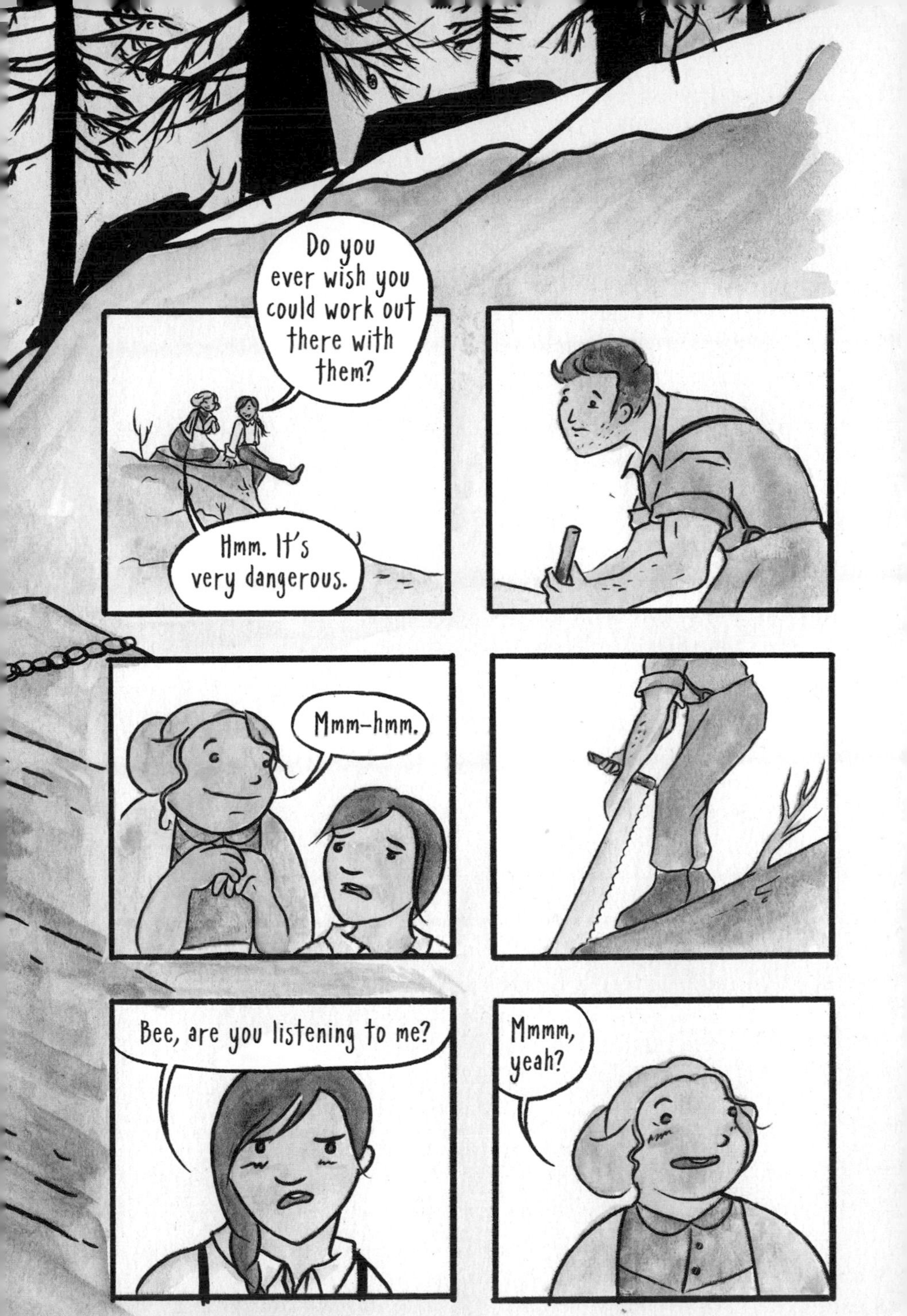
Do you ever wish you could work out there with them?
Hmm. It's very dangerous.
Mmm-hmm.
Bee, are you listening to me?
Mmmm, yeah?

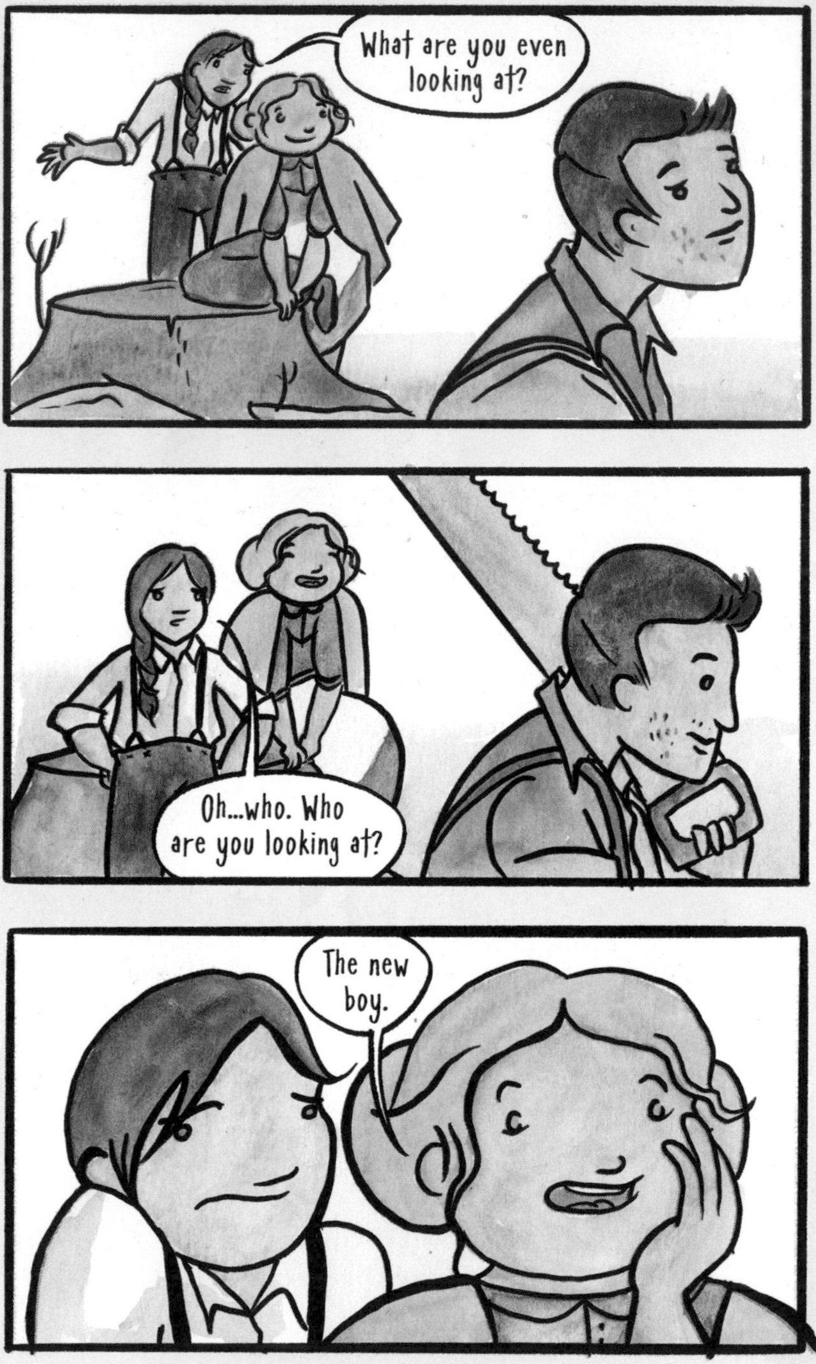
What are you even looking at?
Oh...who. Who are you looking at?
The new boy.

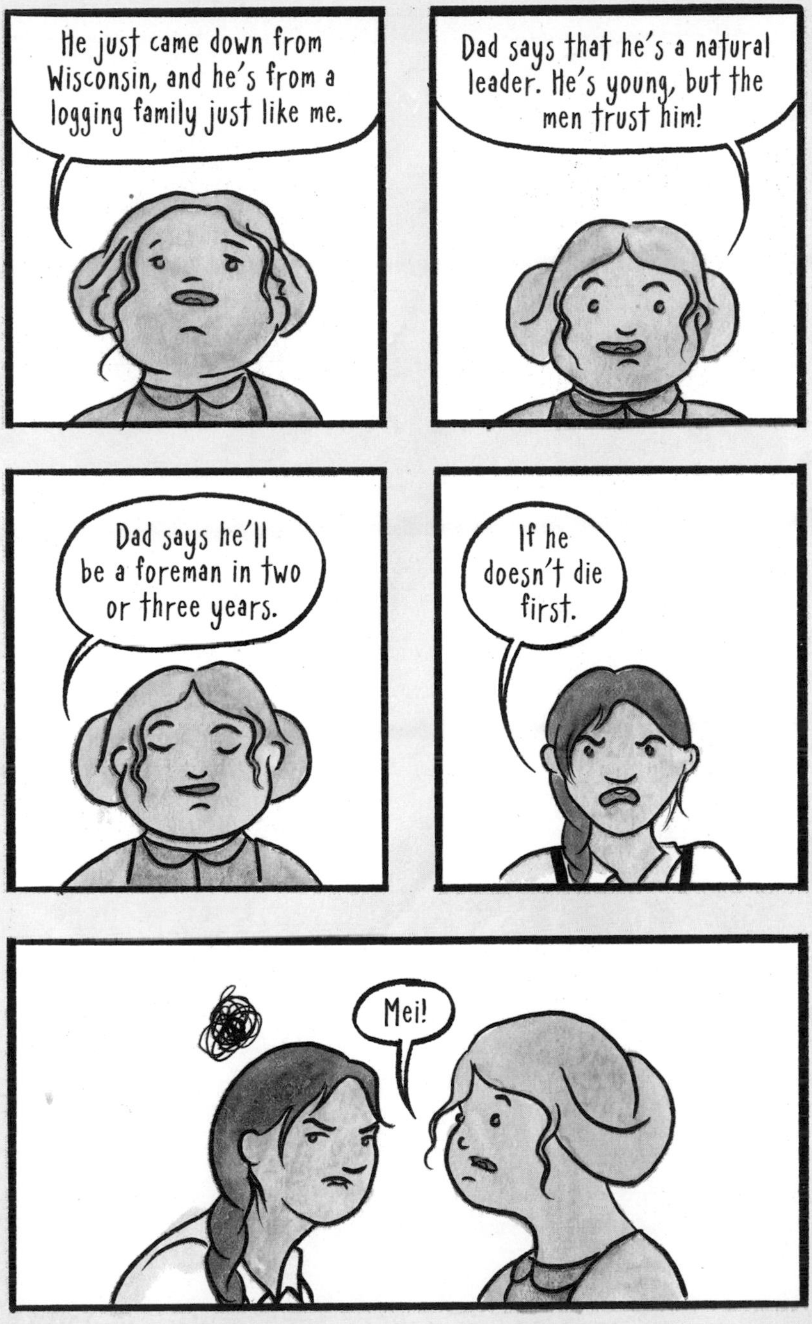
He just came down from Wisconsin, and he's from a logging family just like me.
Dad says that he's a natural leader. He's young, but the men trust him!
Dad says he'll be a foreman in two or three years.
If he doesn't die first.
Mei!

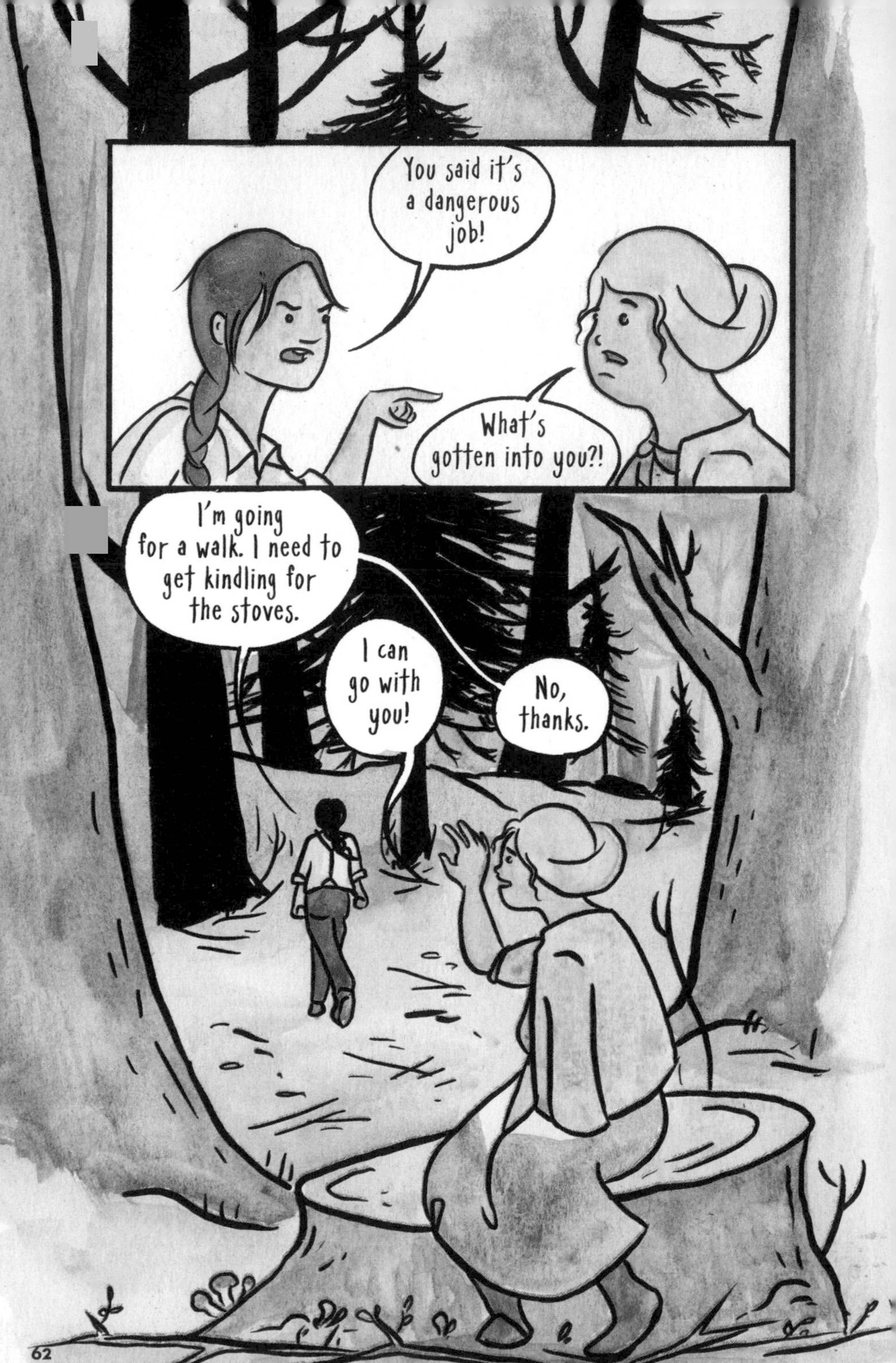
You said it's a dangerous job!
What's gotten into you?!
I'm going for a walk. I need to get kindling for the stoves.
I can go with you!
No, thanks.

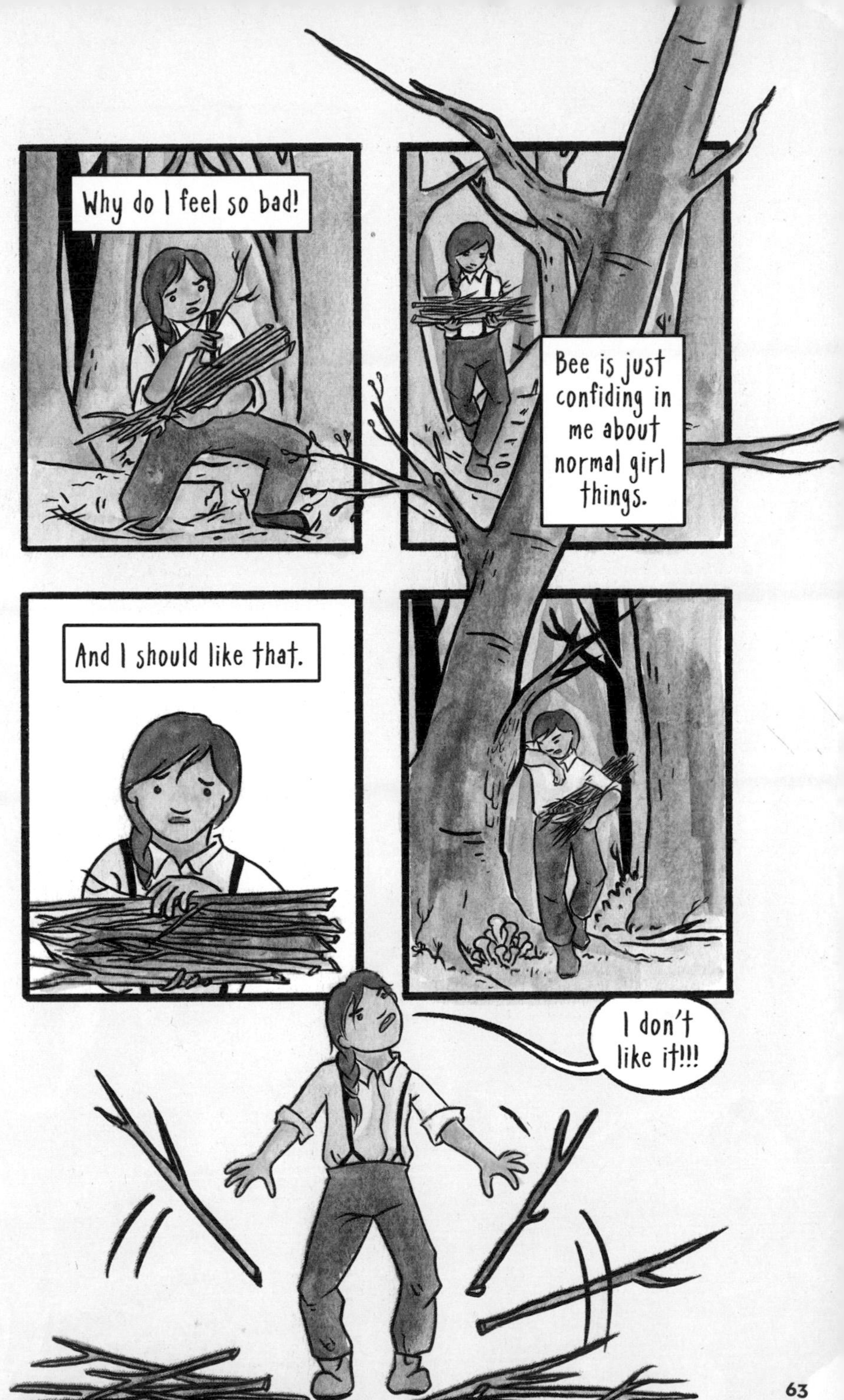
Why do I feel so bad!
Bee is just confiding in me about normal girl things.
And I should like that.
I don't like it!!!

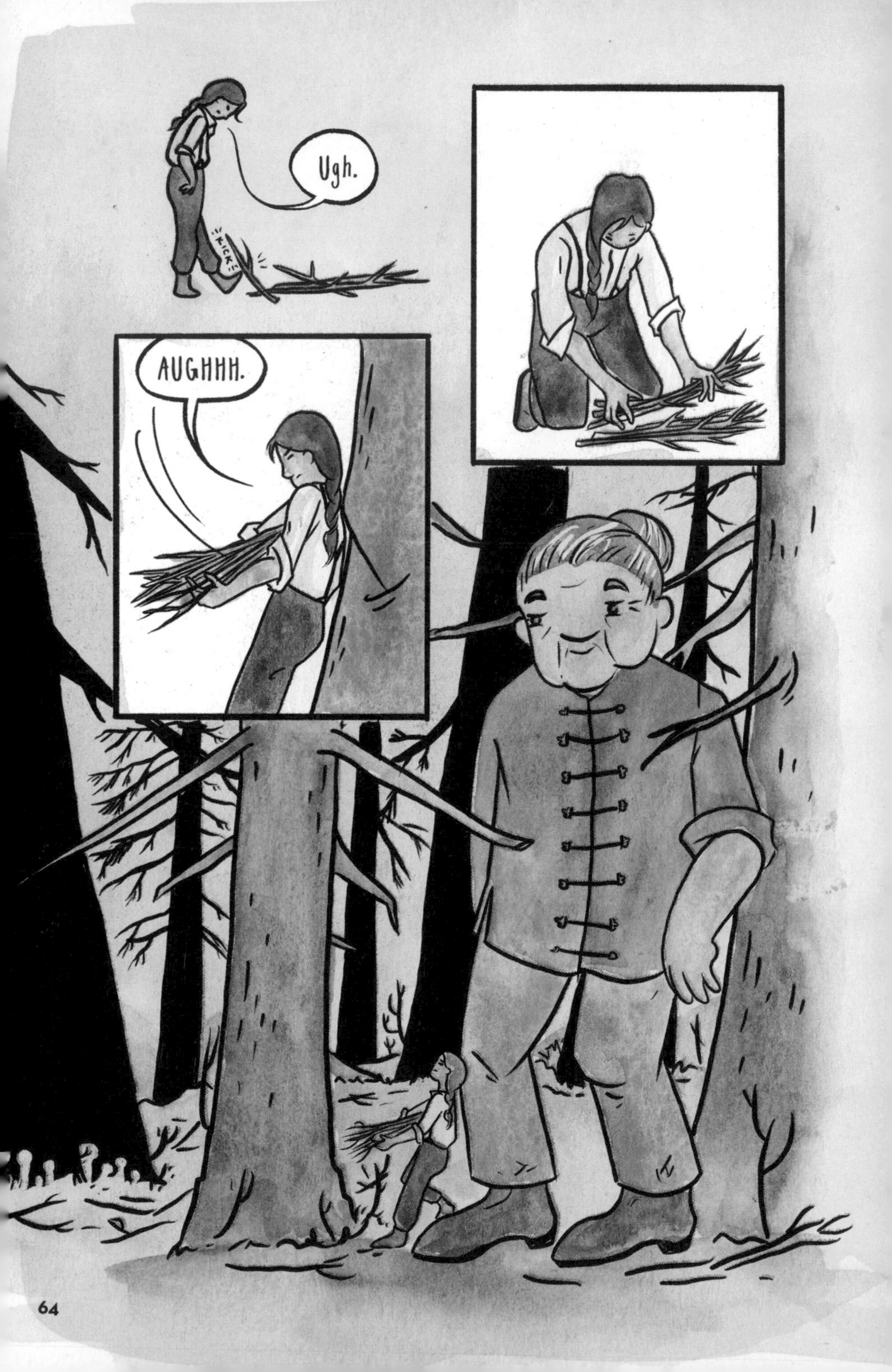
Ugh.
KICK
AUGHHH.

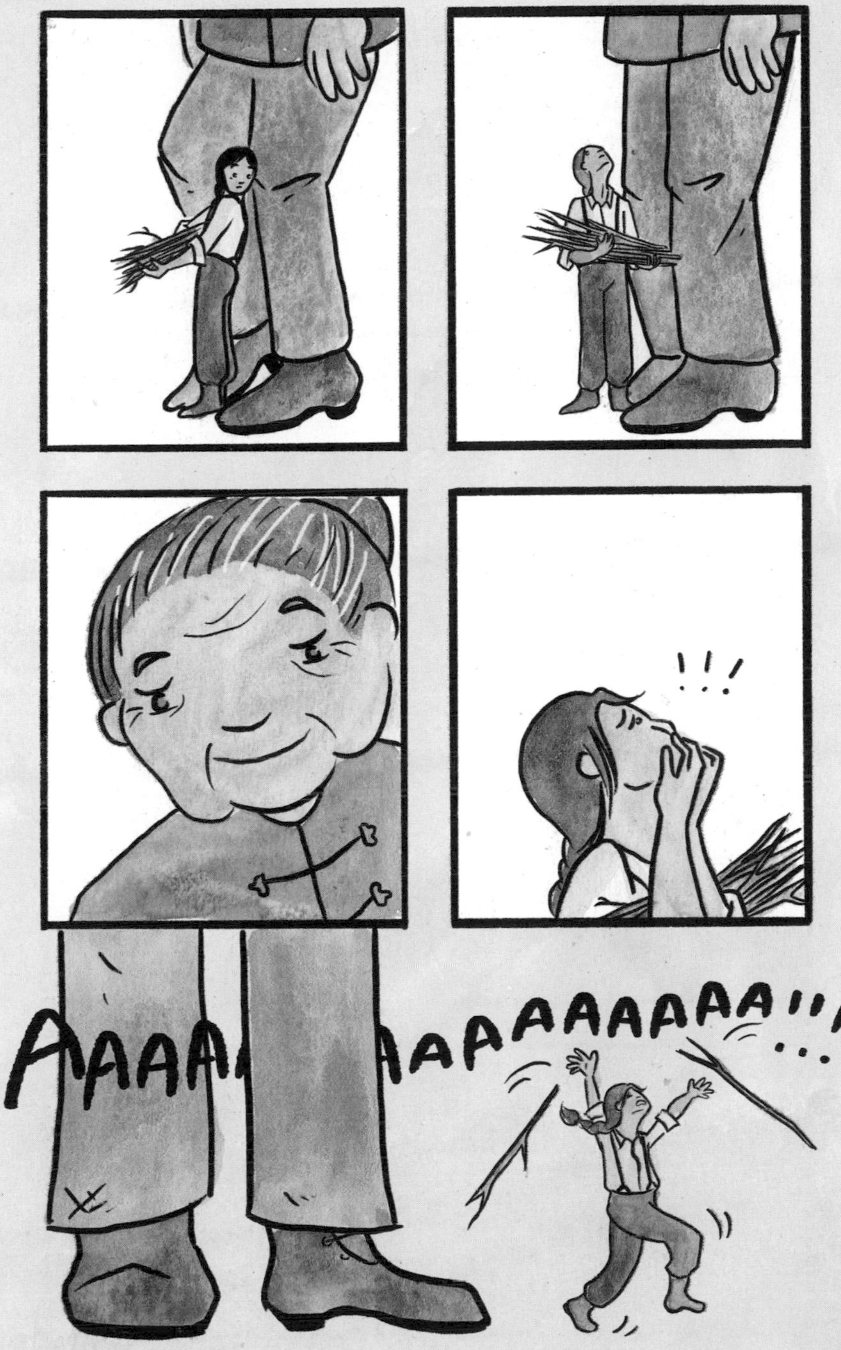
!!!
AAAAAAAAAAAAA!!!
...

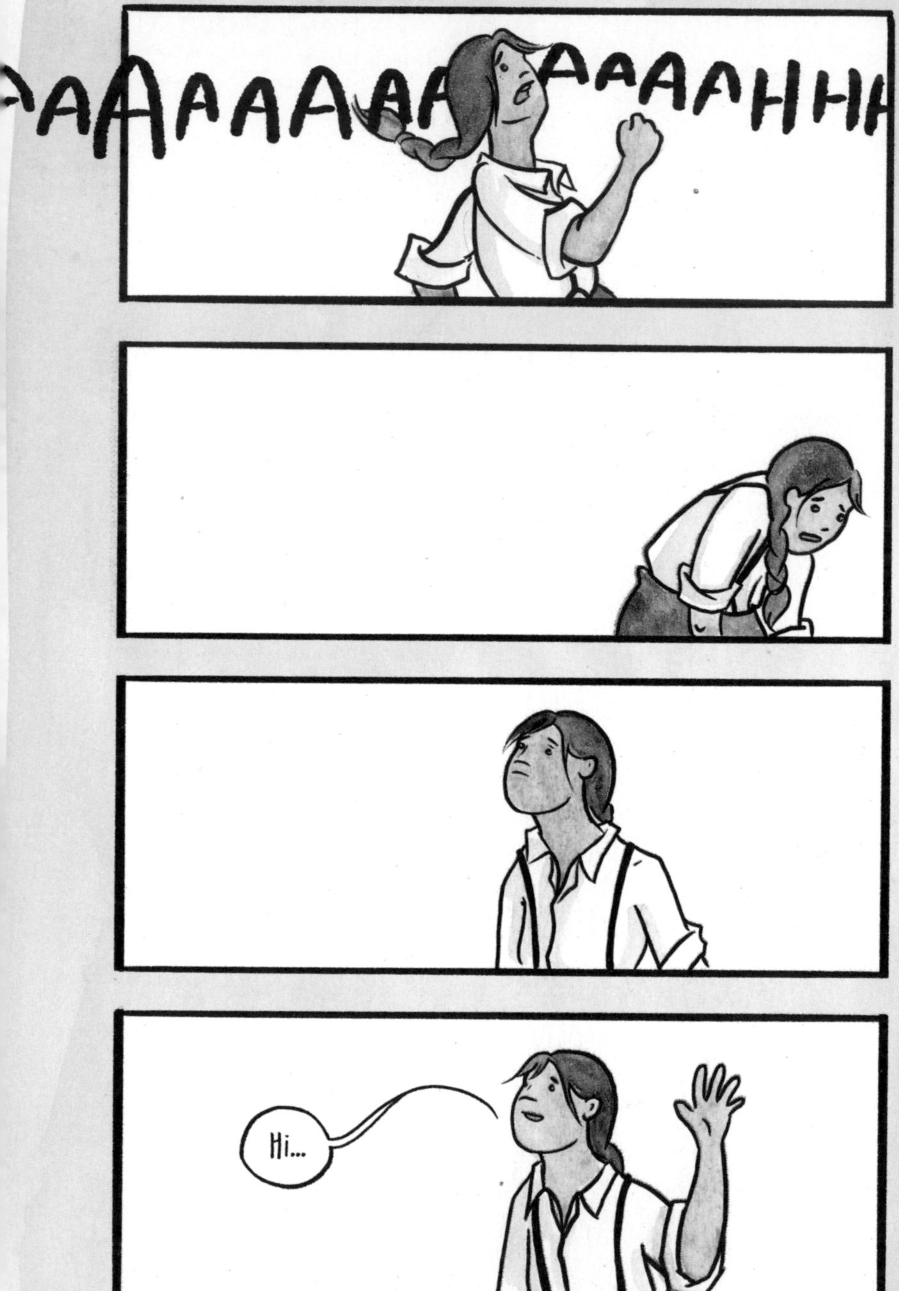
AAAAAAAAAAAAAAAHH
Hi...

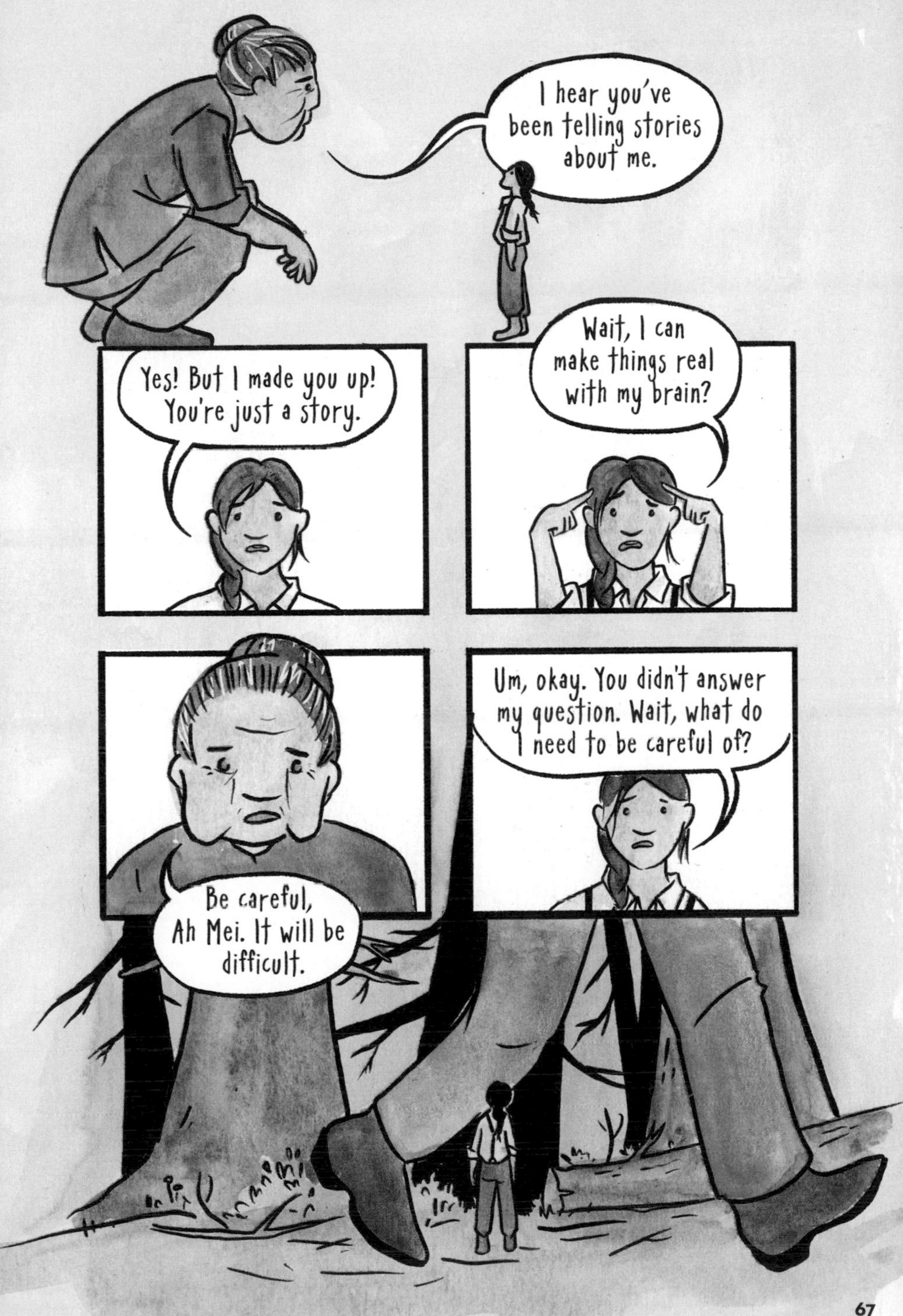
I hear you've been telling stories about me.
Yes! But I made you up! You're just a story.
Wait, I can make things real with my brain?
Be careful, Ah Mei. It will be difficult.
Um, okay. You didn't answer my question. Wait, what do I need to be careful of?

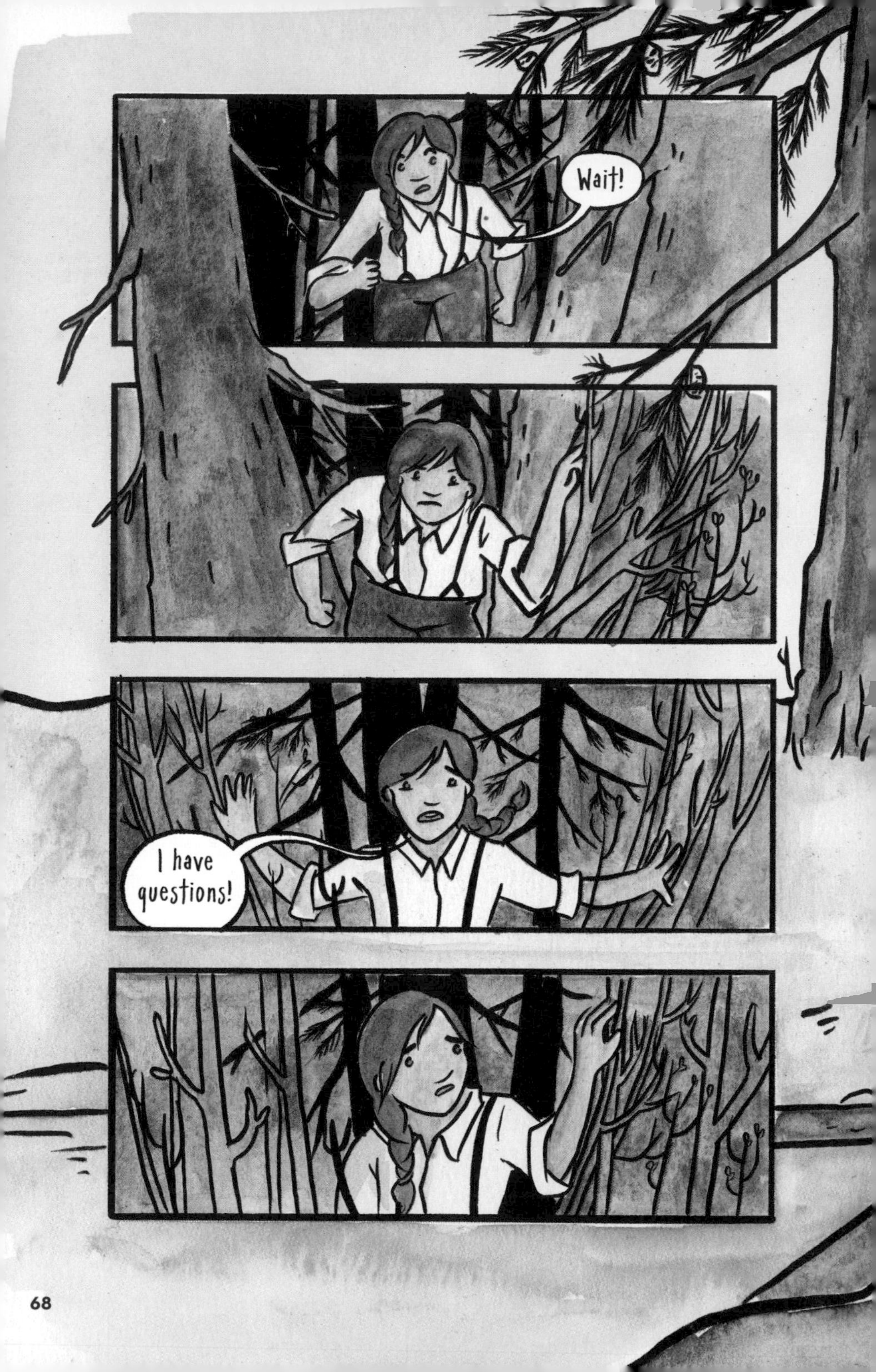
Wait!
I have questions!

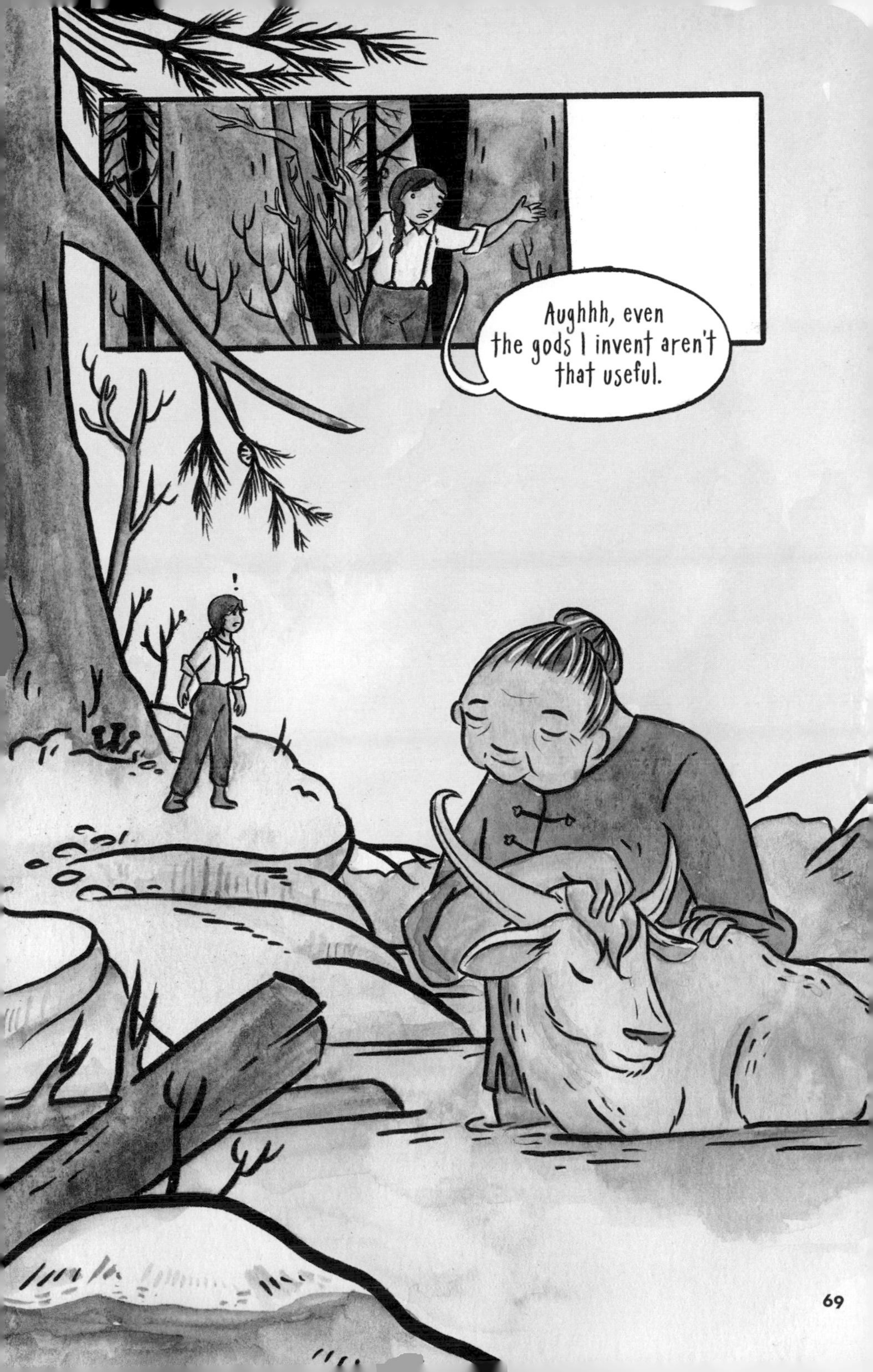
Aughhh, even the gods I invent aren't that useful.
!

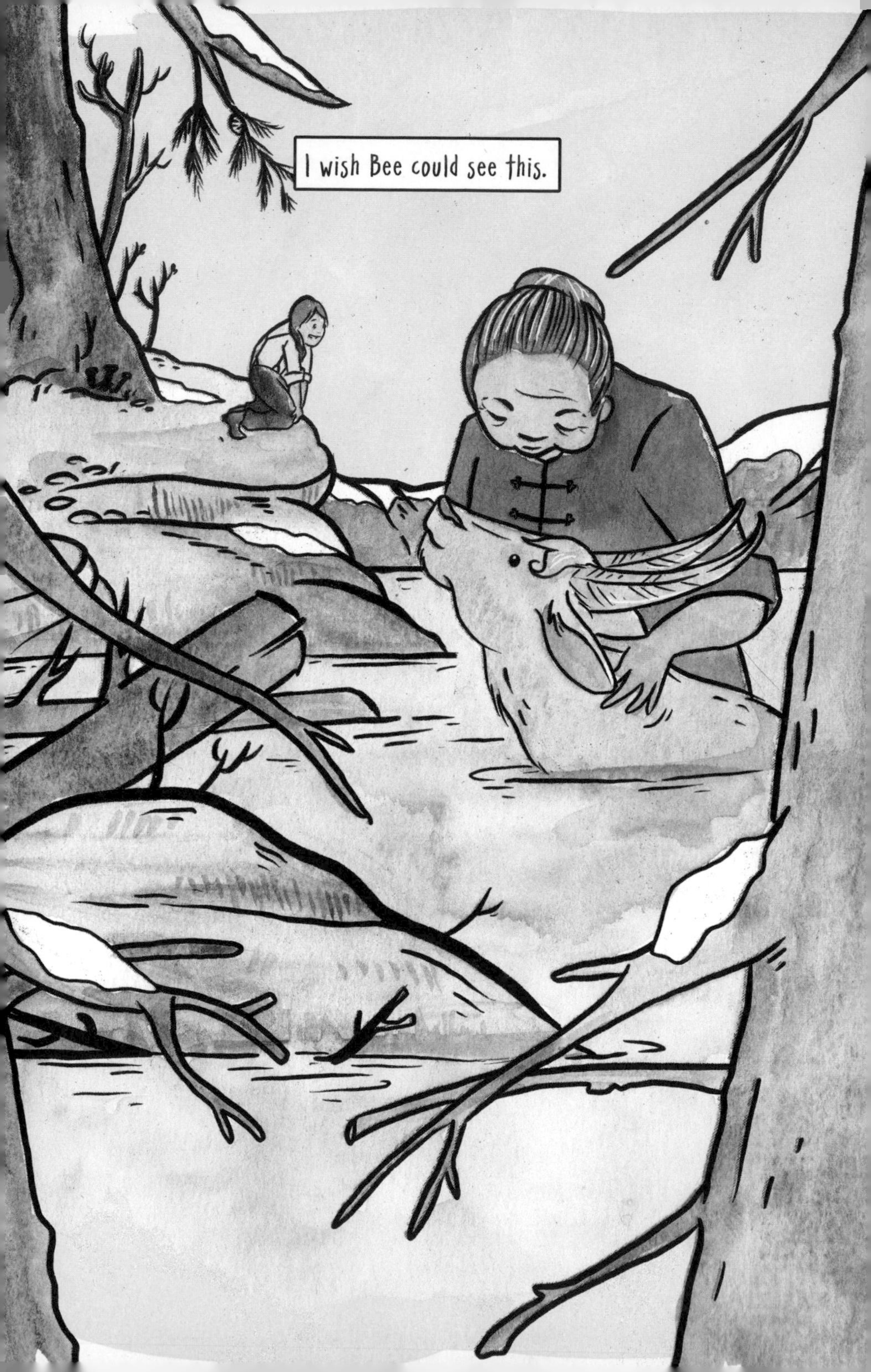
I wish Bee could see this.

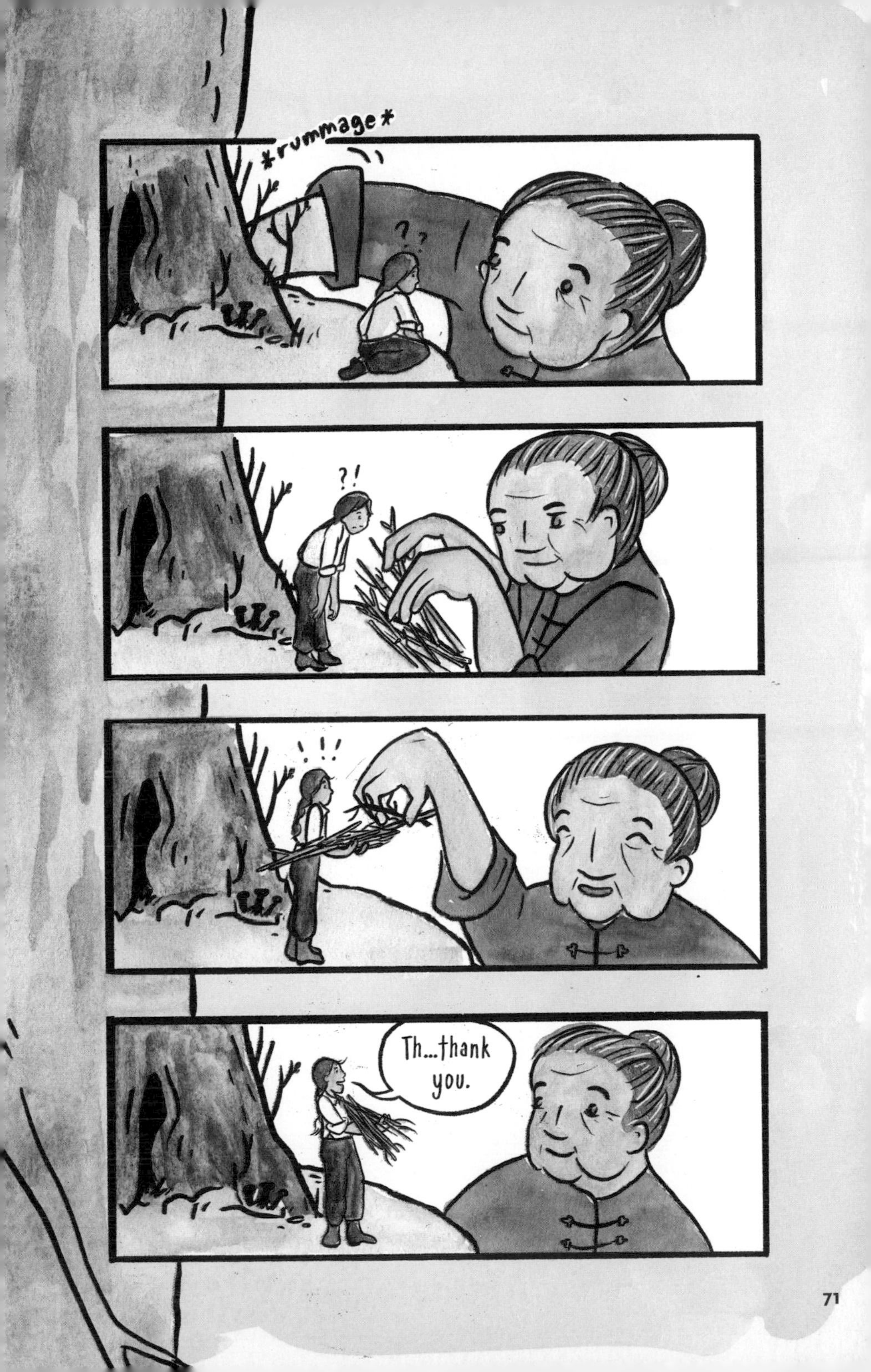

rummage
? ?
?!
! ! !
Th...thank you.

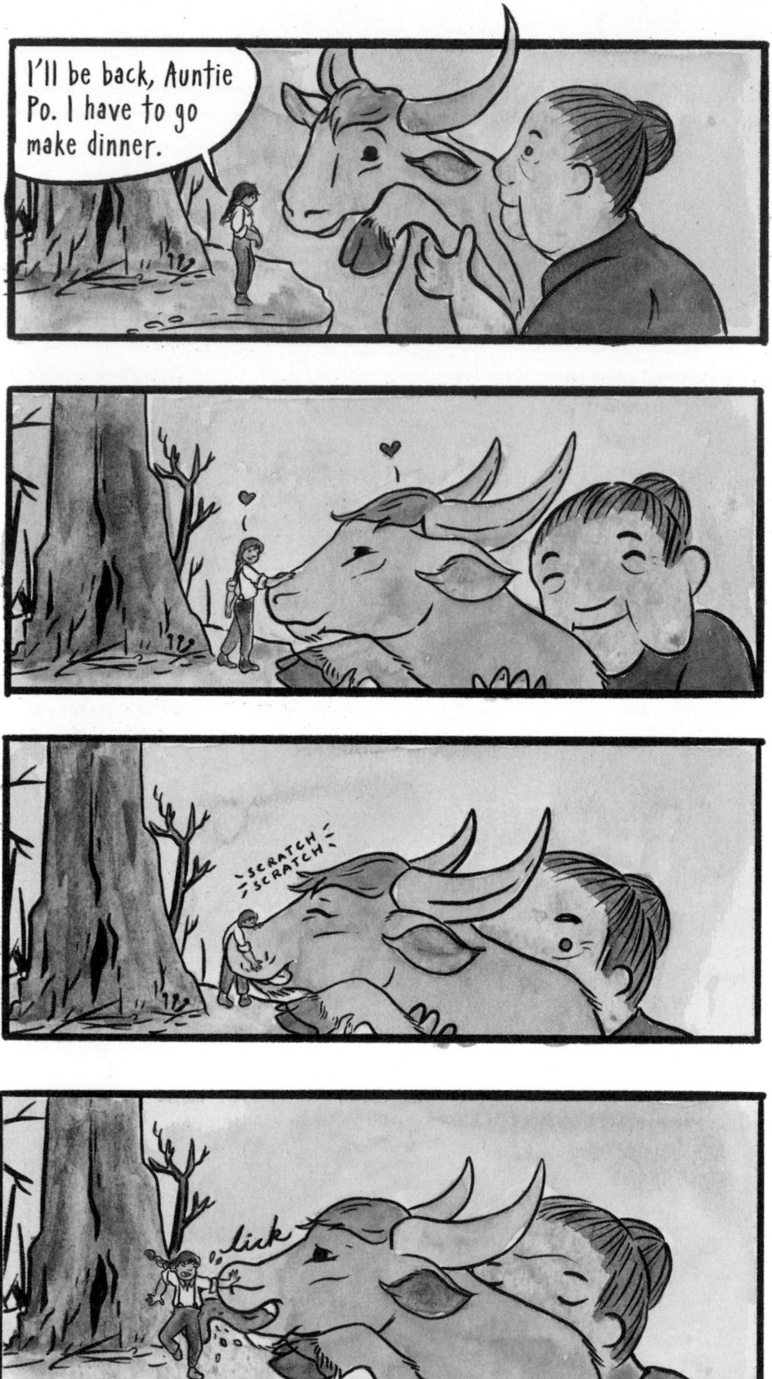
I'll be back, Auntie Po. I have to go make dinner.
SCRATCH SCRATCH
lick

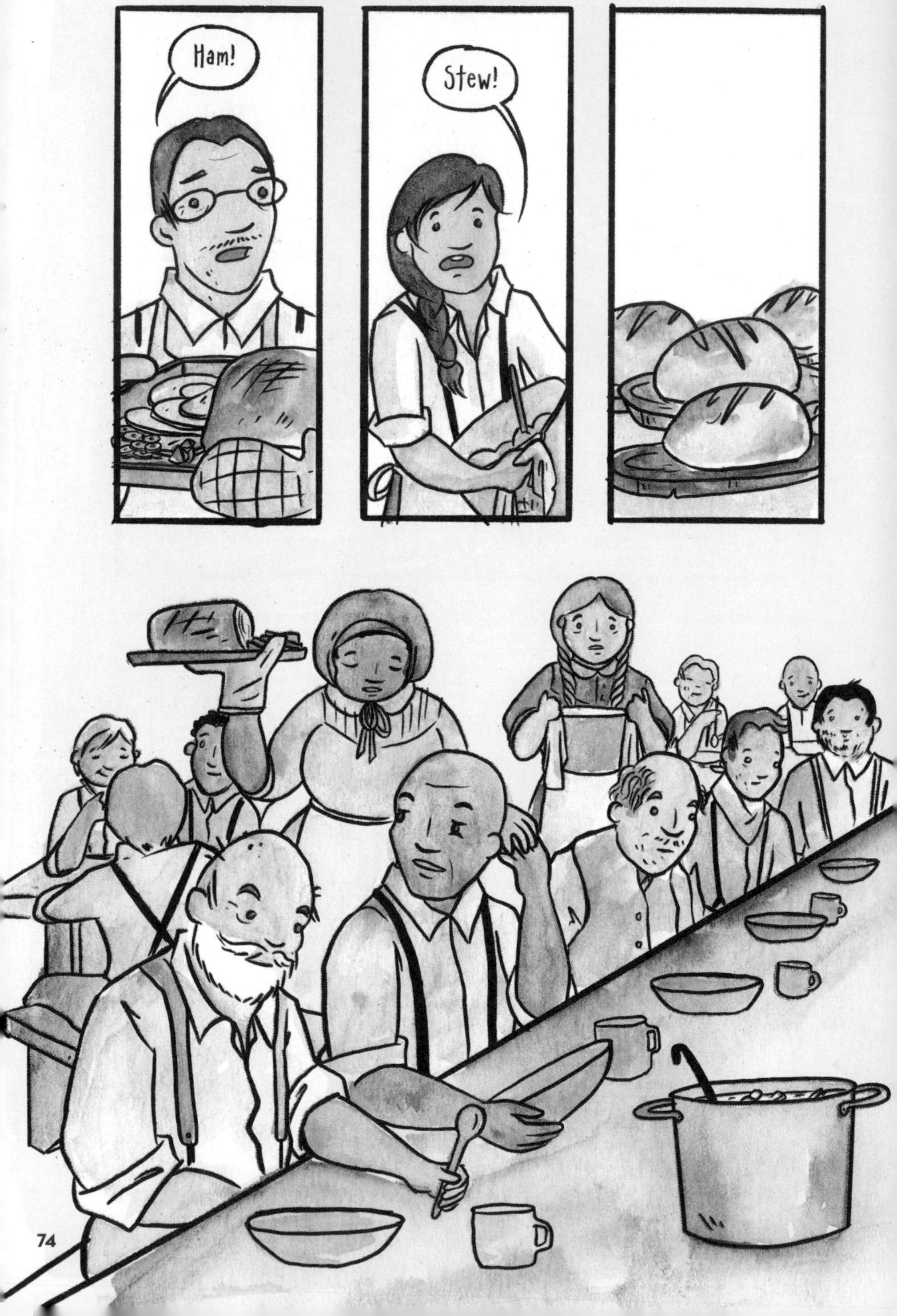
Ham!
Stew!

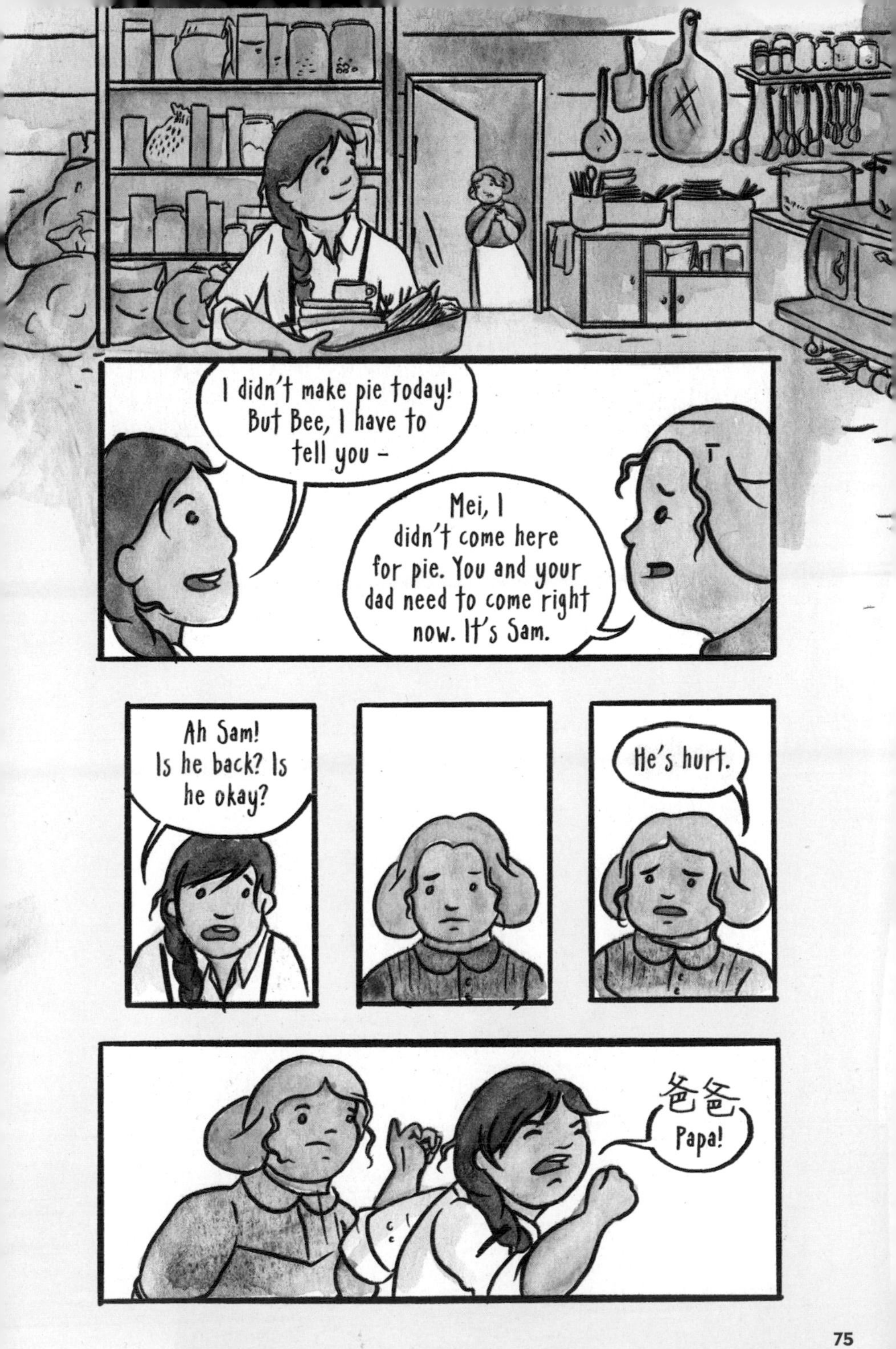
I didn't make pie today! But Bee, I have to tell you –
Mei, I didn't come here for pie. You and your dad need to come right now. It's Sam.
Ah Sam! Is he back? Is he okay?
He's hurt.
爸爸
Papa!

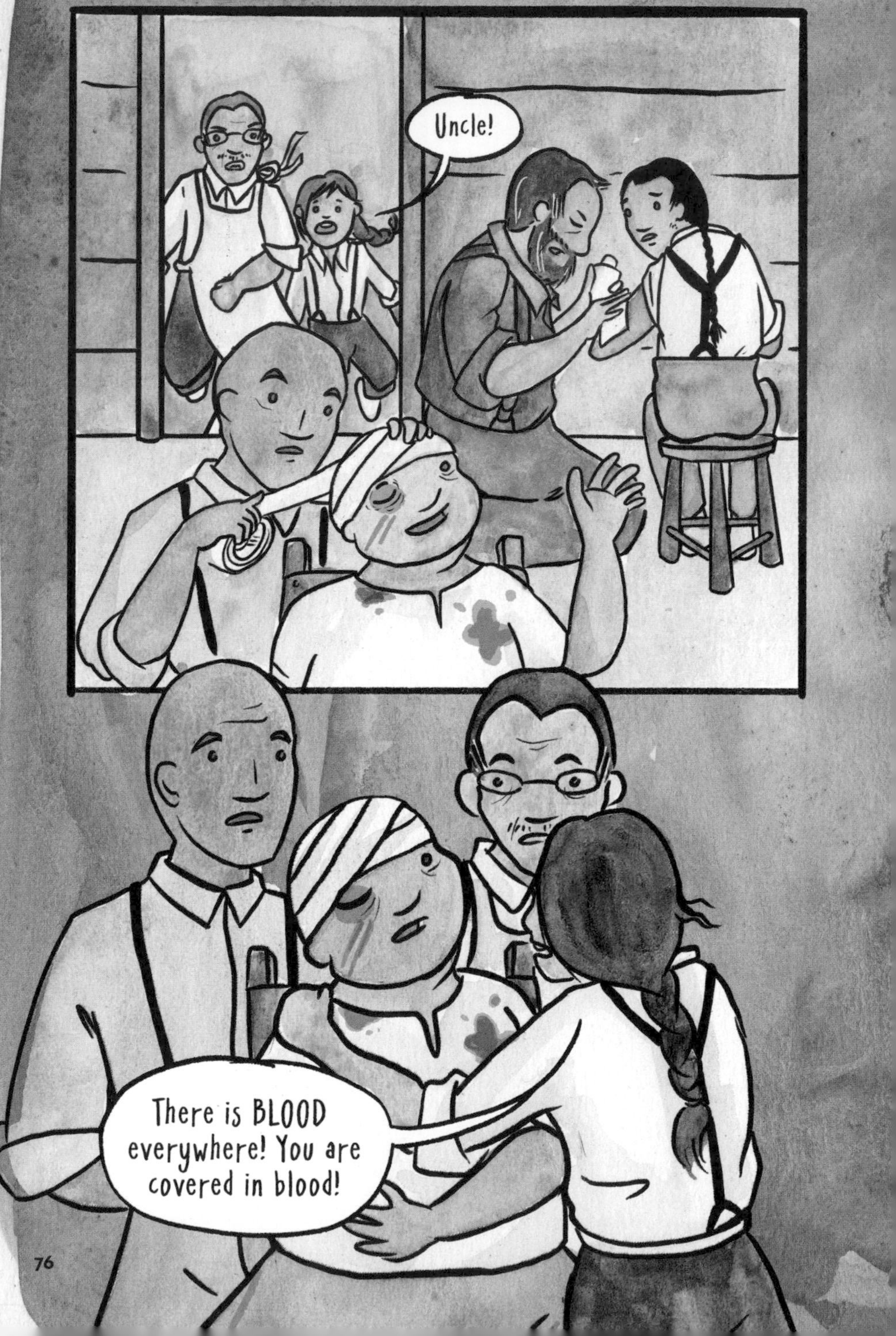
Uncle!
There is BLOOD everywhere! You are covered in blood!

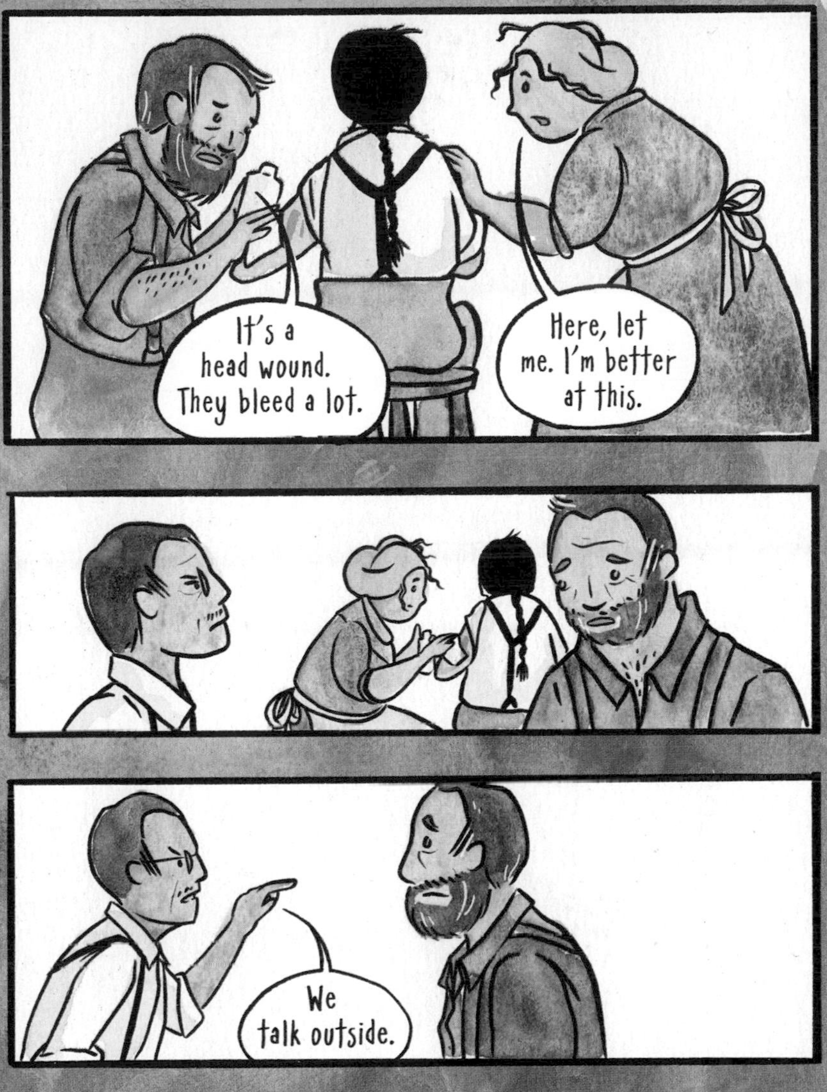
It's a head wound. They bleed a lot.
Here, let me. I'm better at this.
We talk outside.

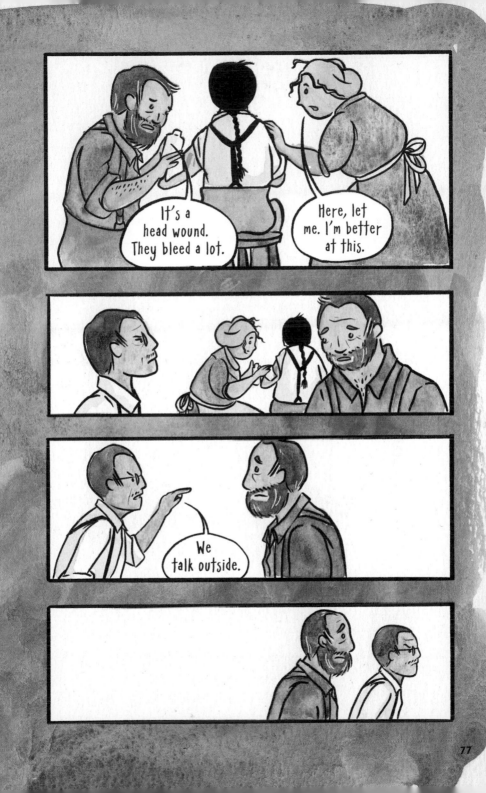

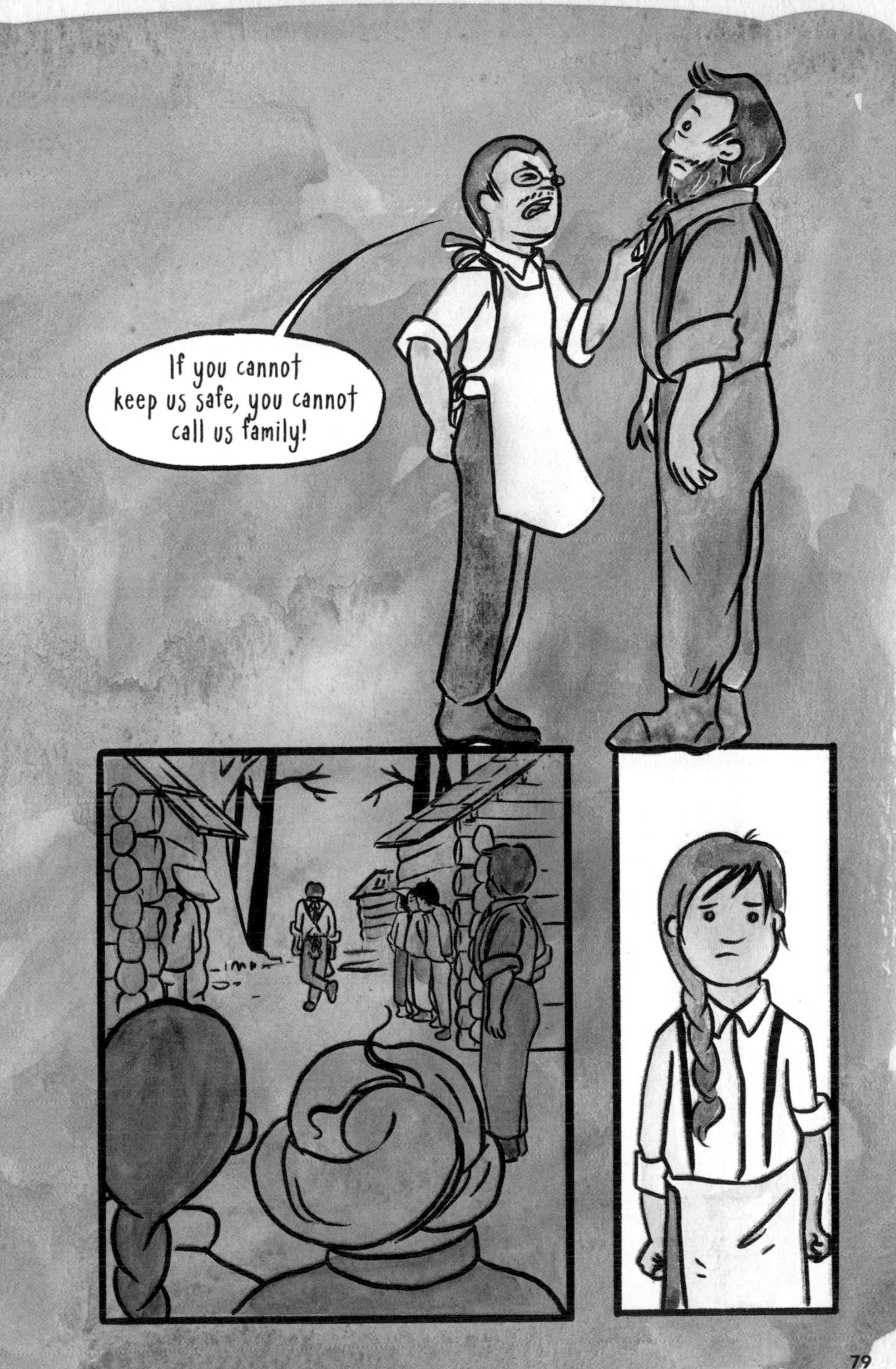
If you cannot keep us safe, you cannot call us family!

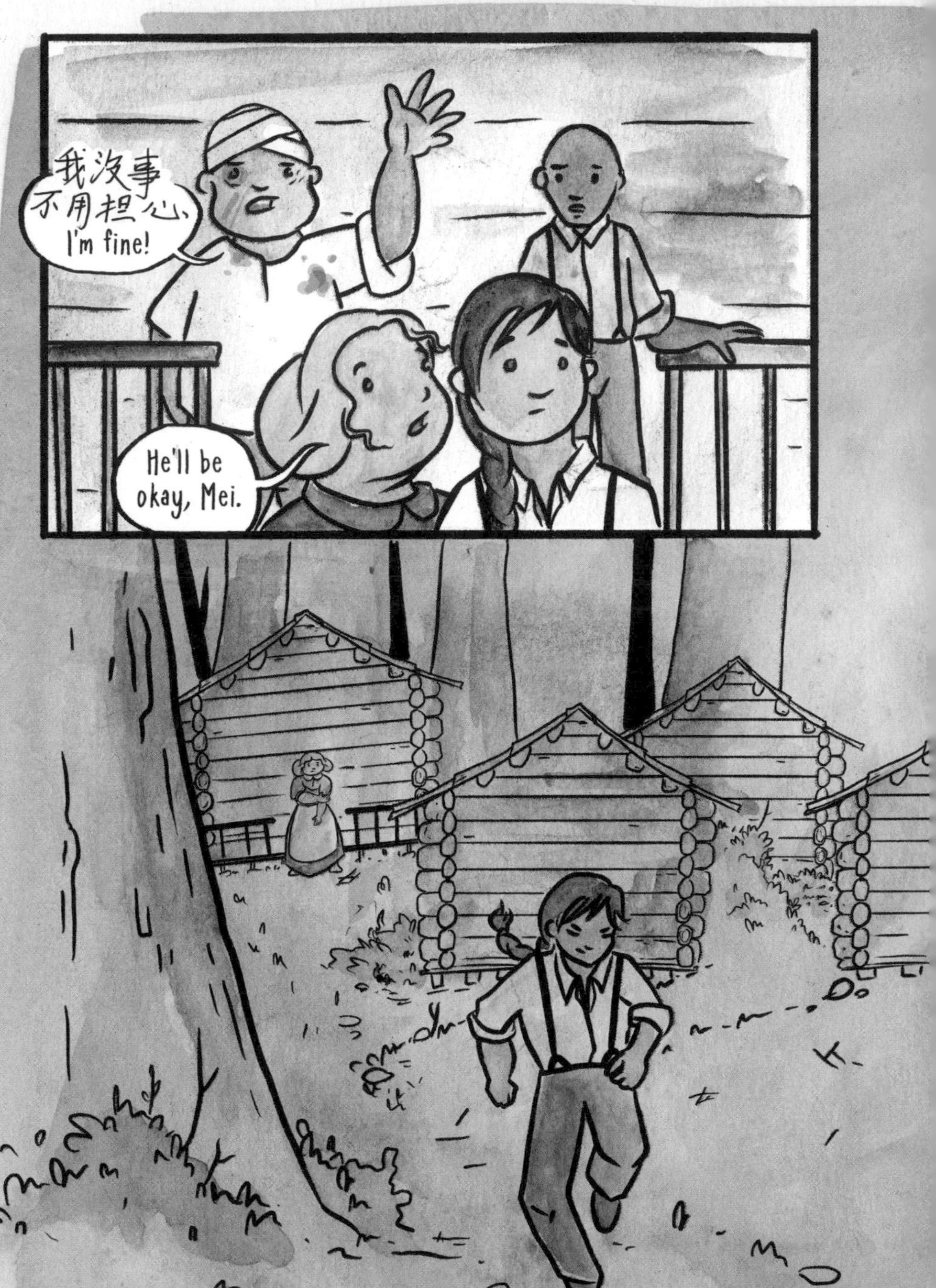
我沒事
不用担心
I'm fine!
He'll be okay, Mei.

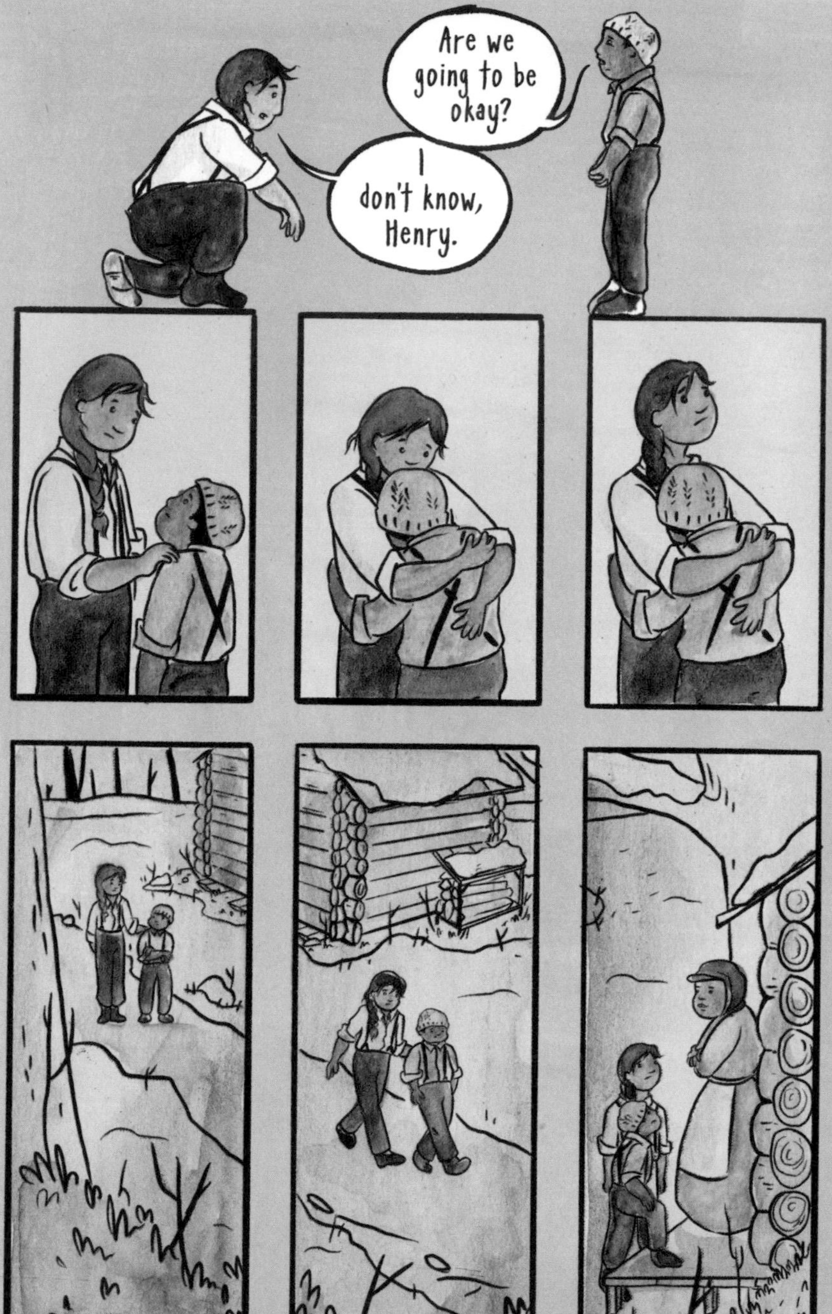
Are we going to be okay?
I don't know, Henry.

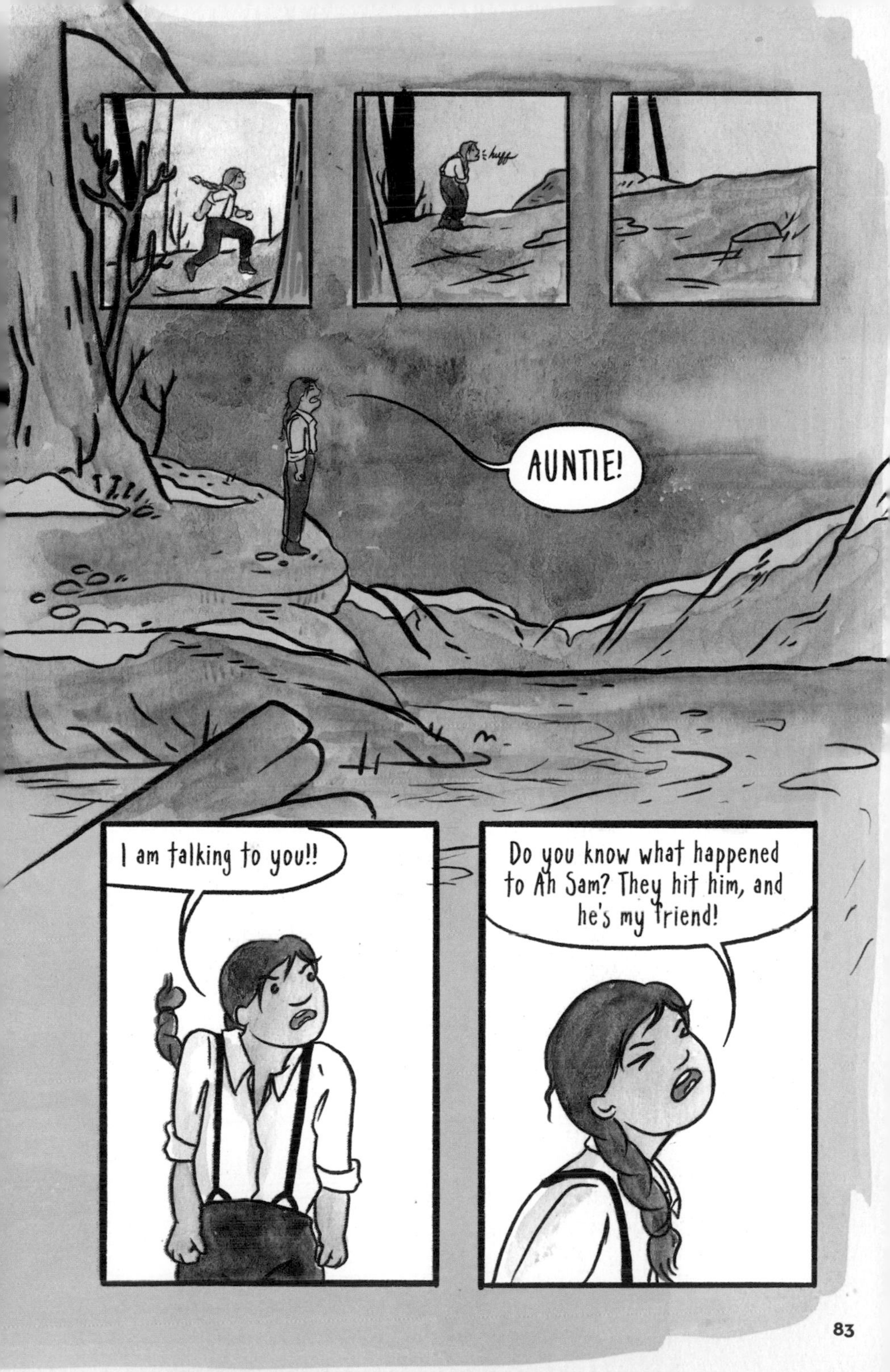

huff
AUNTIE!
I am talking to you!!
Do you know what happened to Ah Sam? They hit him, and he's my friend!

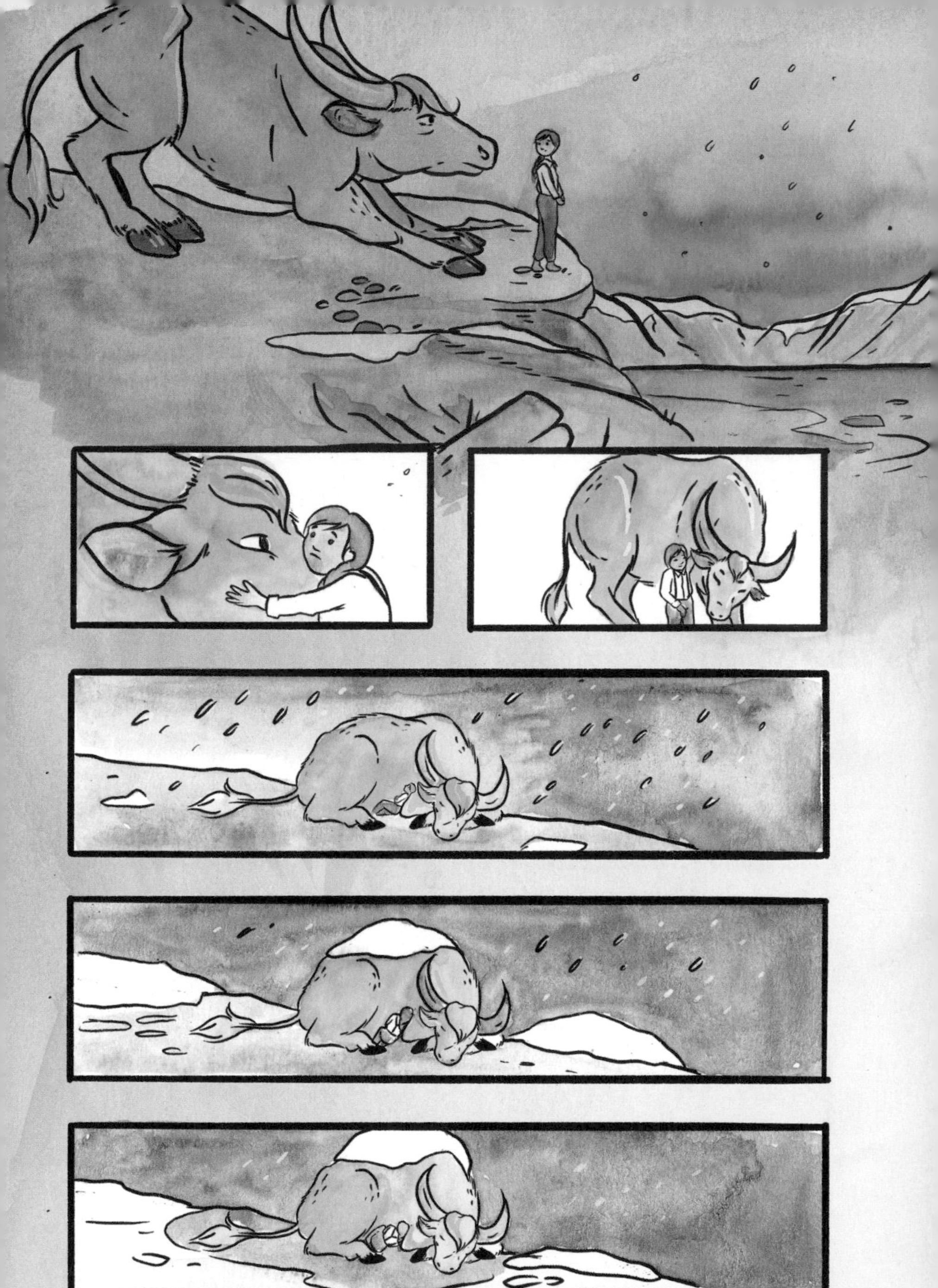

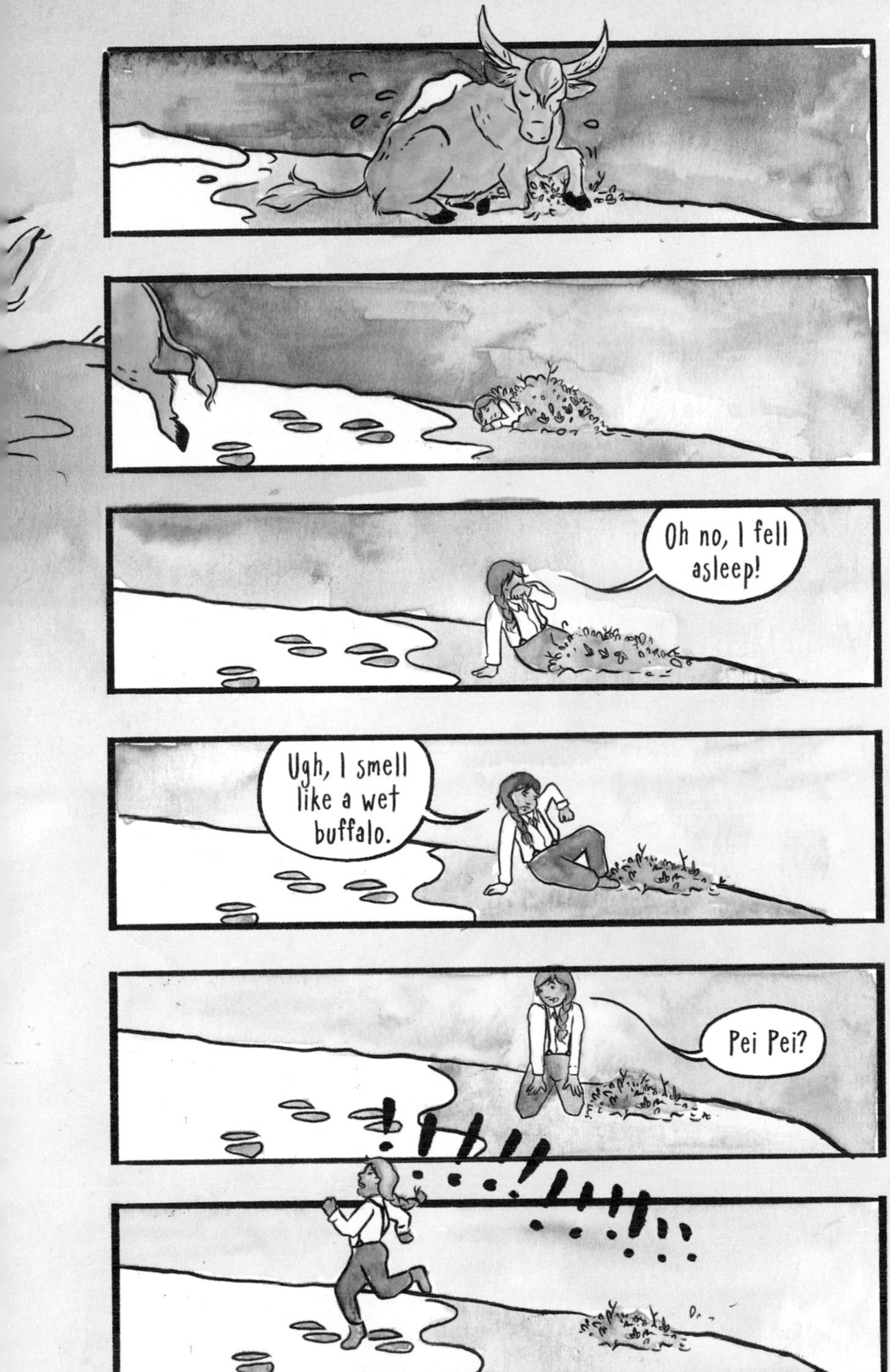

Oh no, I fell asleep!
Ugh, I smell like a wet buffalo.
Pei Pei?

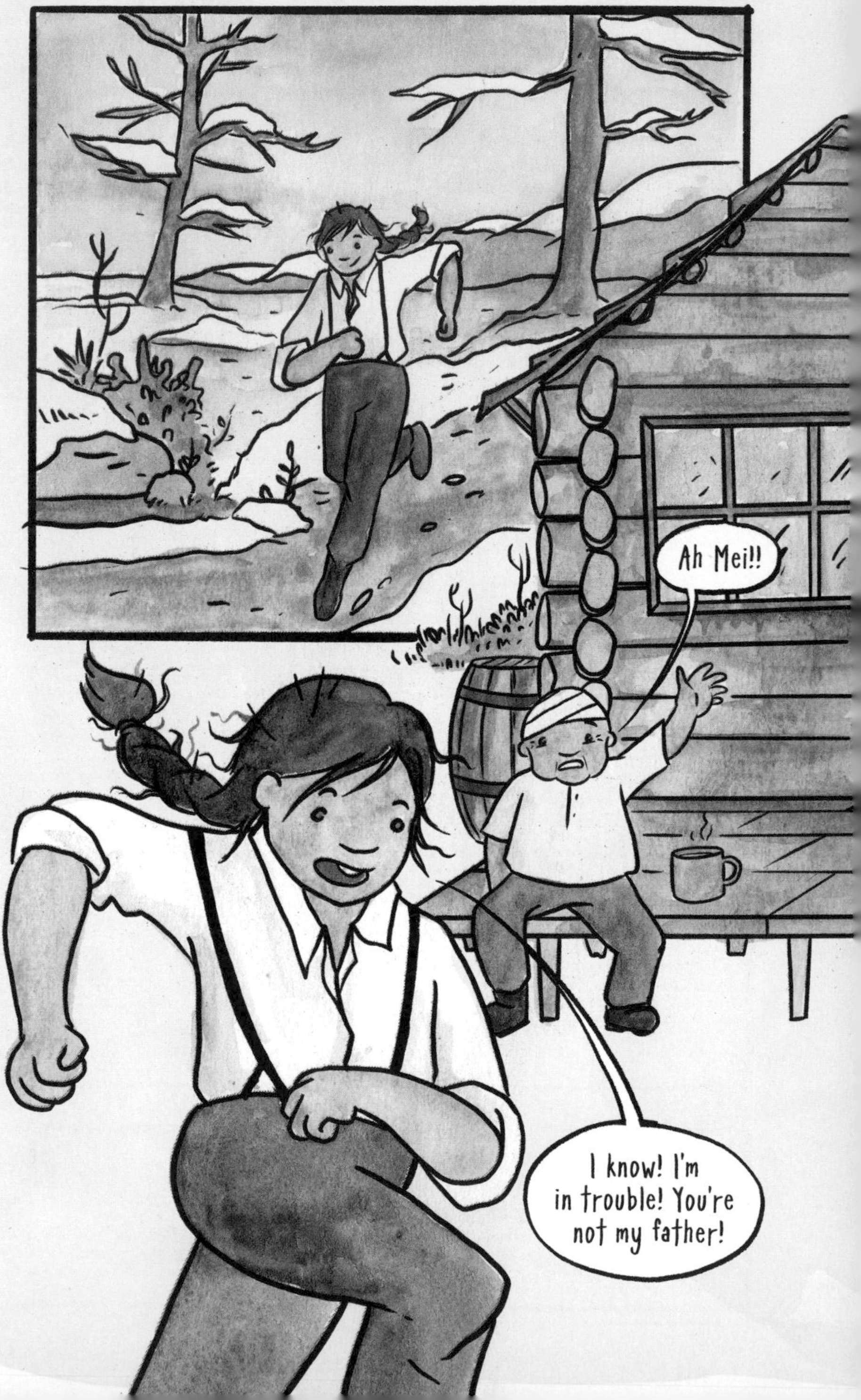
Ah Mei!!
I know! I'm in trouble! You're not my father!

88

89

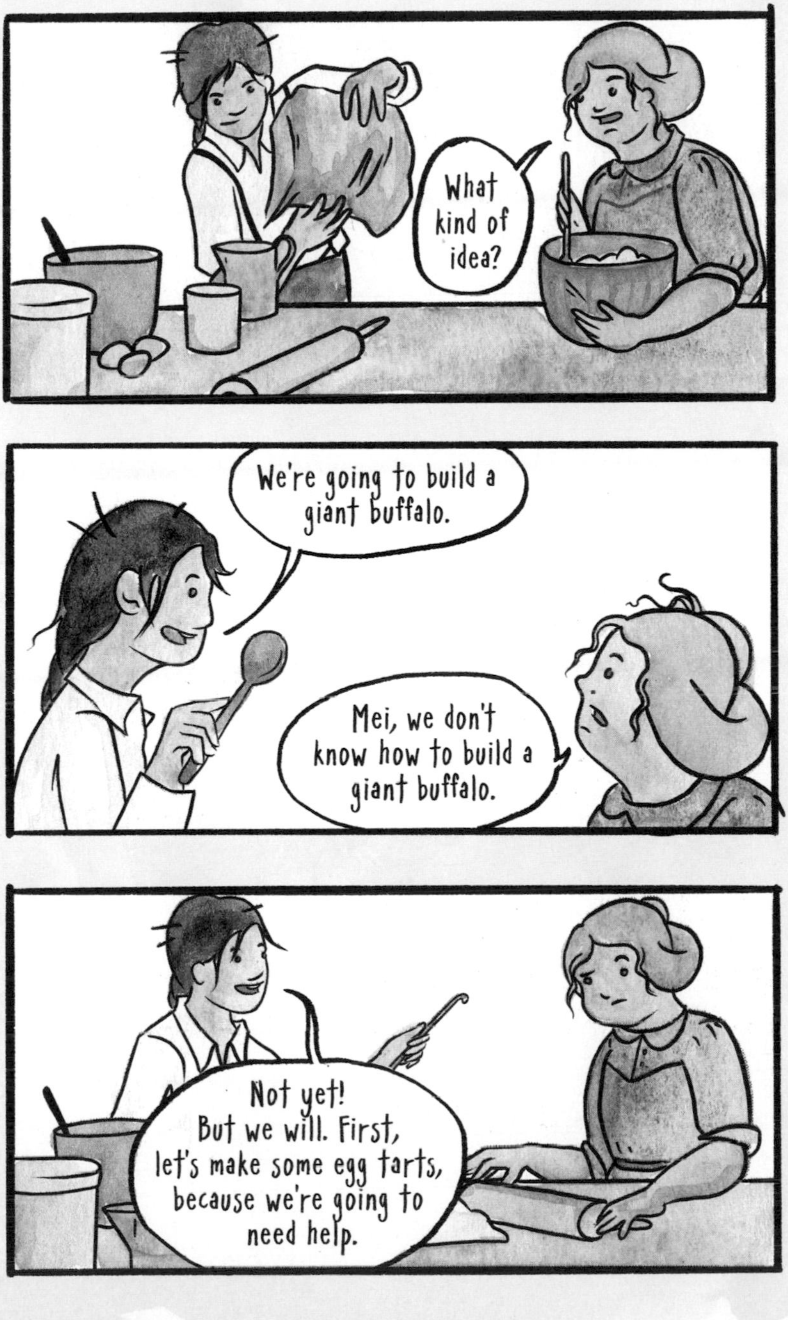
What kind of idea?
We're going to build a giant buffalo.
Mei, we don't know how to build a giant buffalo.
Not yet! But we will. First, let's make some egg tarts, because we're going to need help.

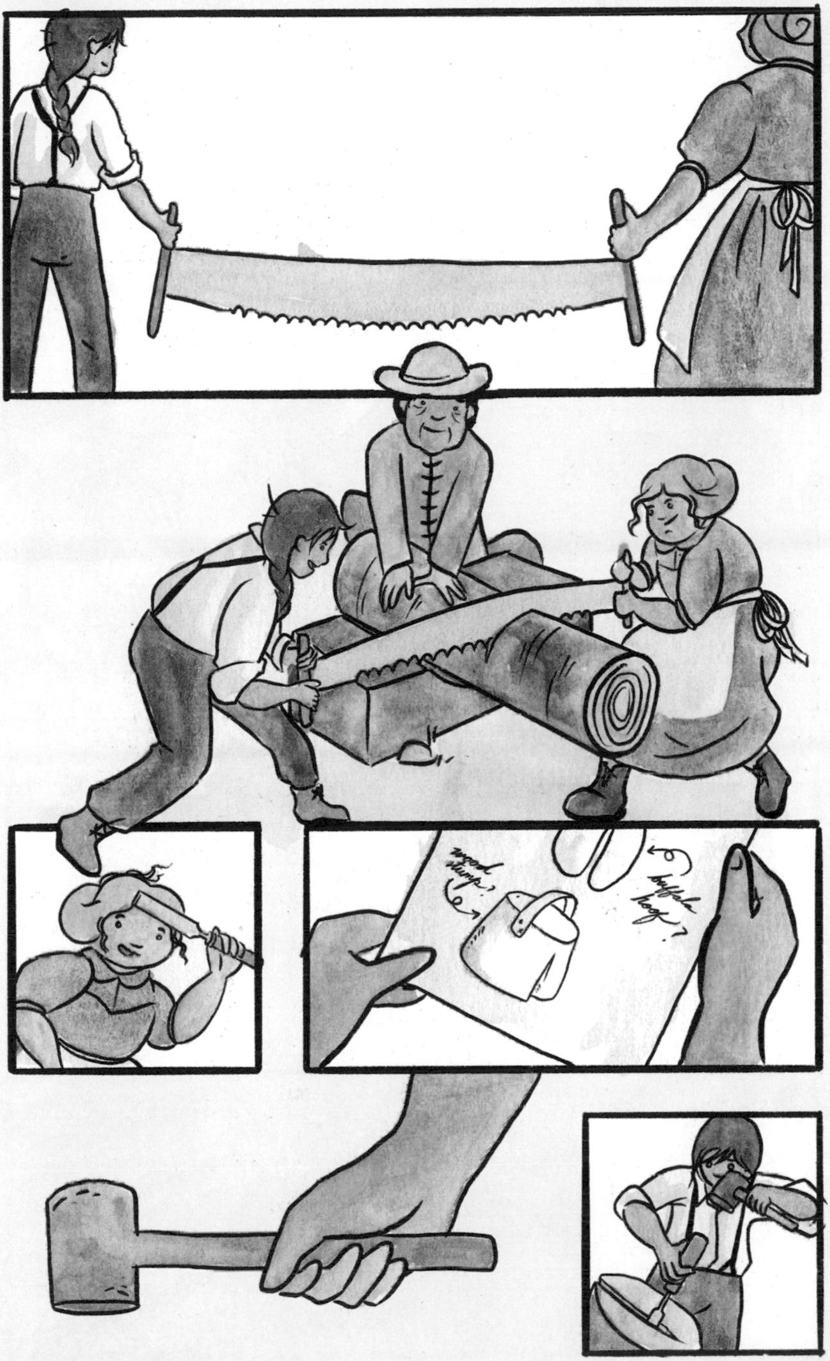
wood stump?
buffalo hoof?

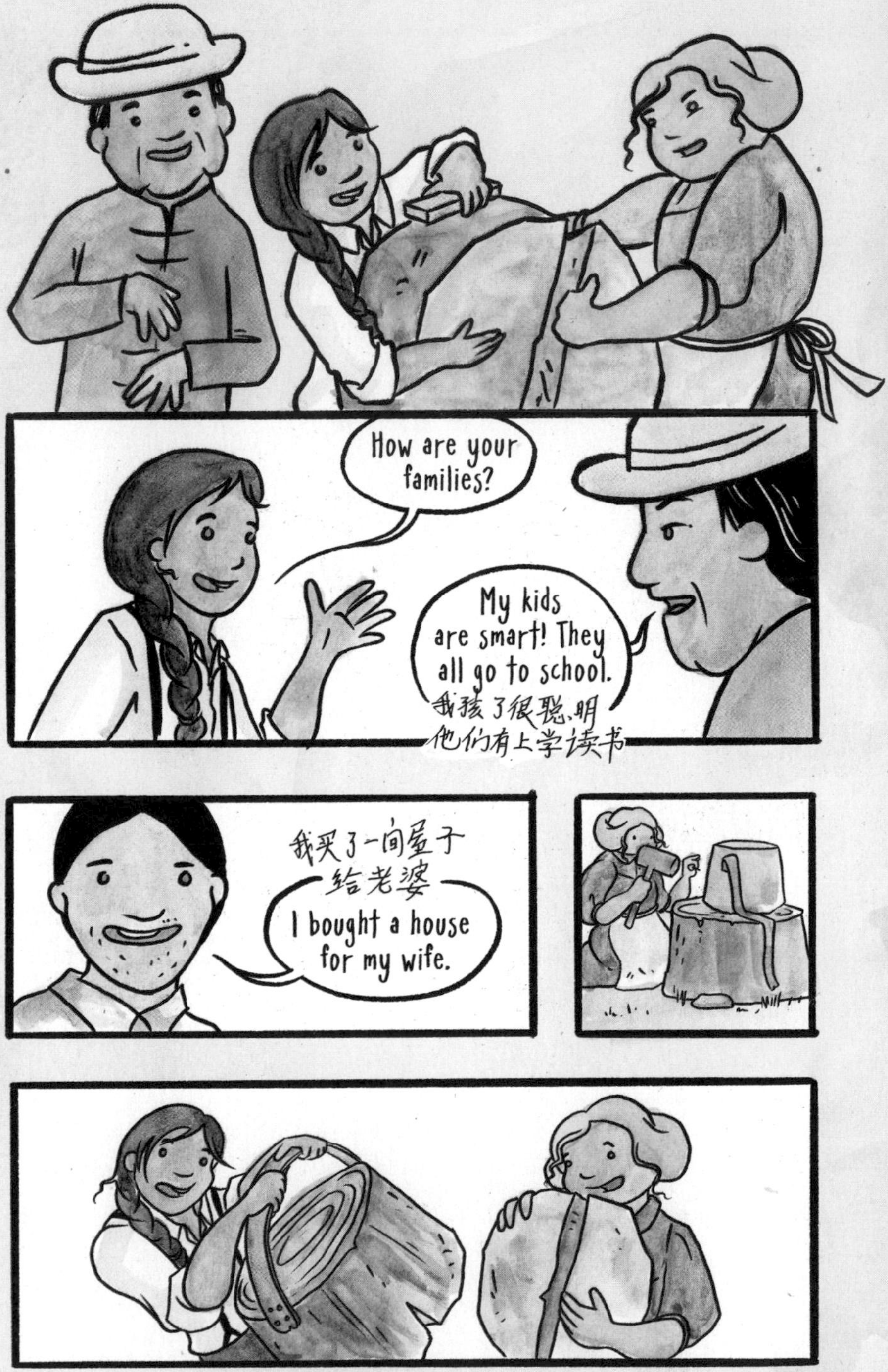
How are your families?
My kids are smart! They all go to school.
我孩了很聪、明
他们有上学读书
我买了一间屋子
给老婆
I bought a house for my wife.

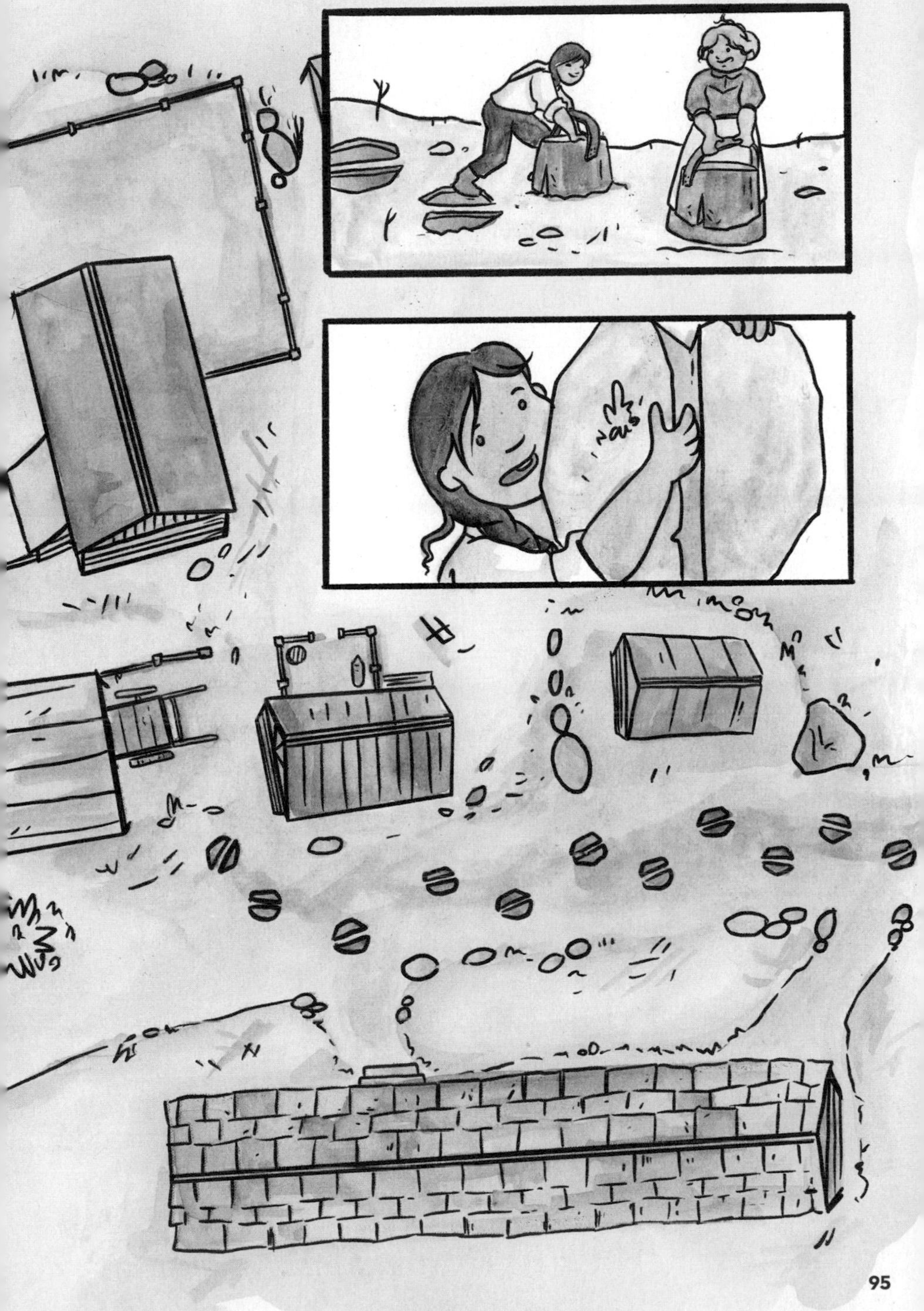

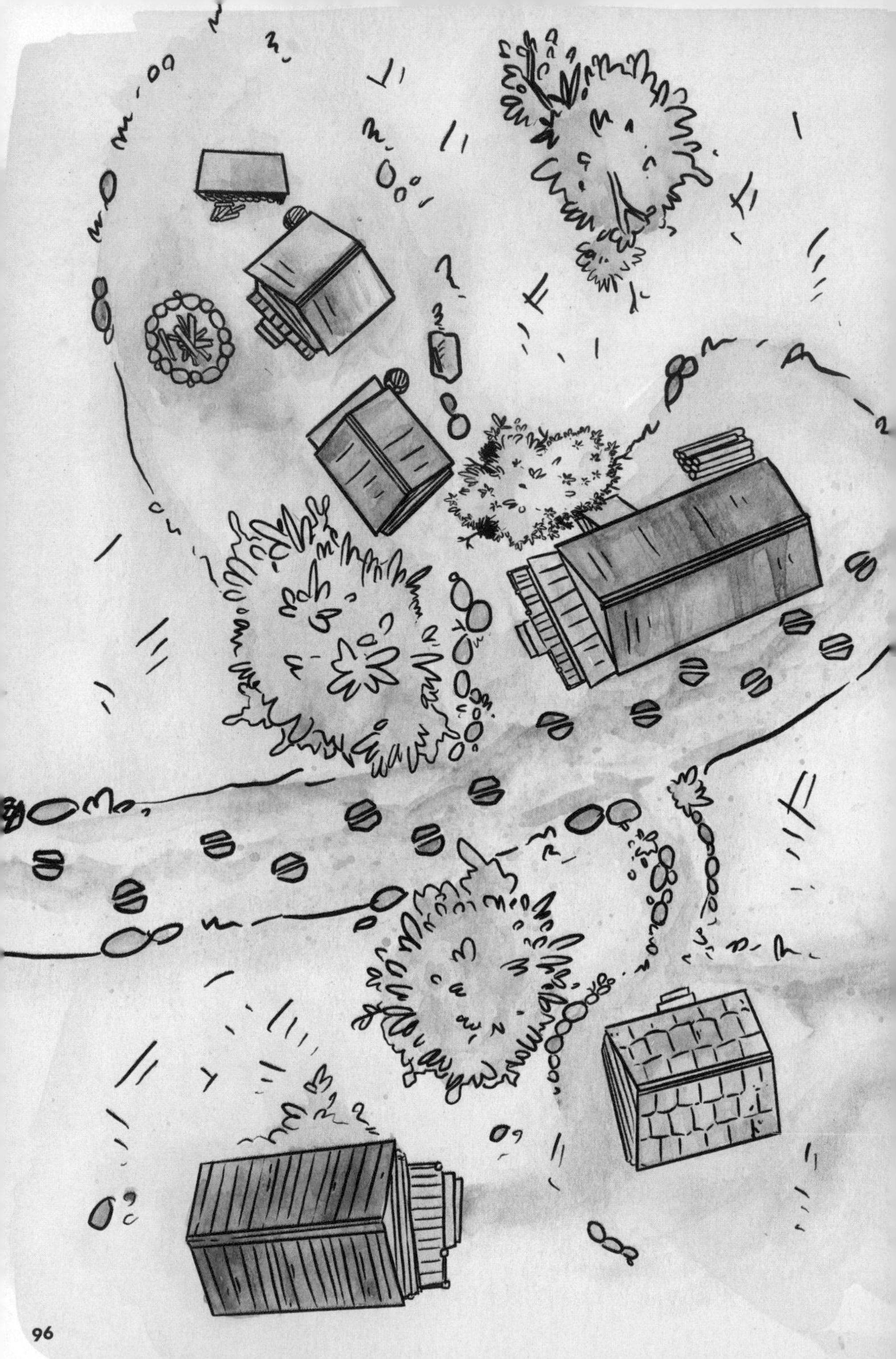

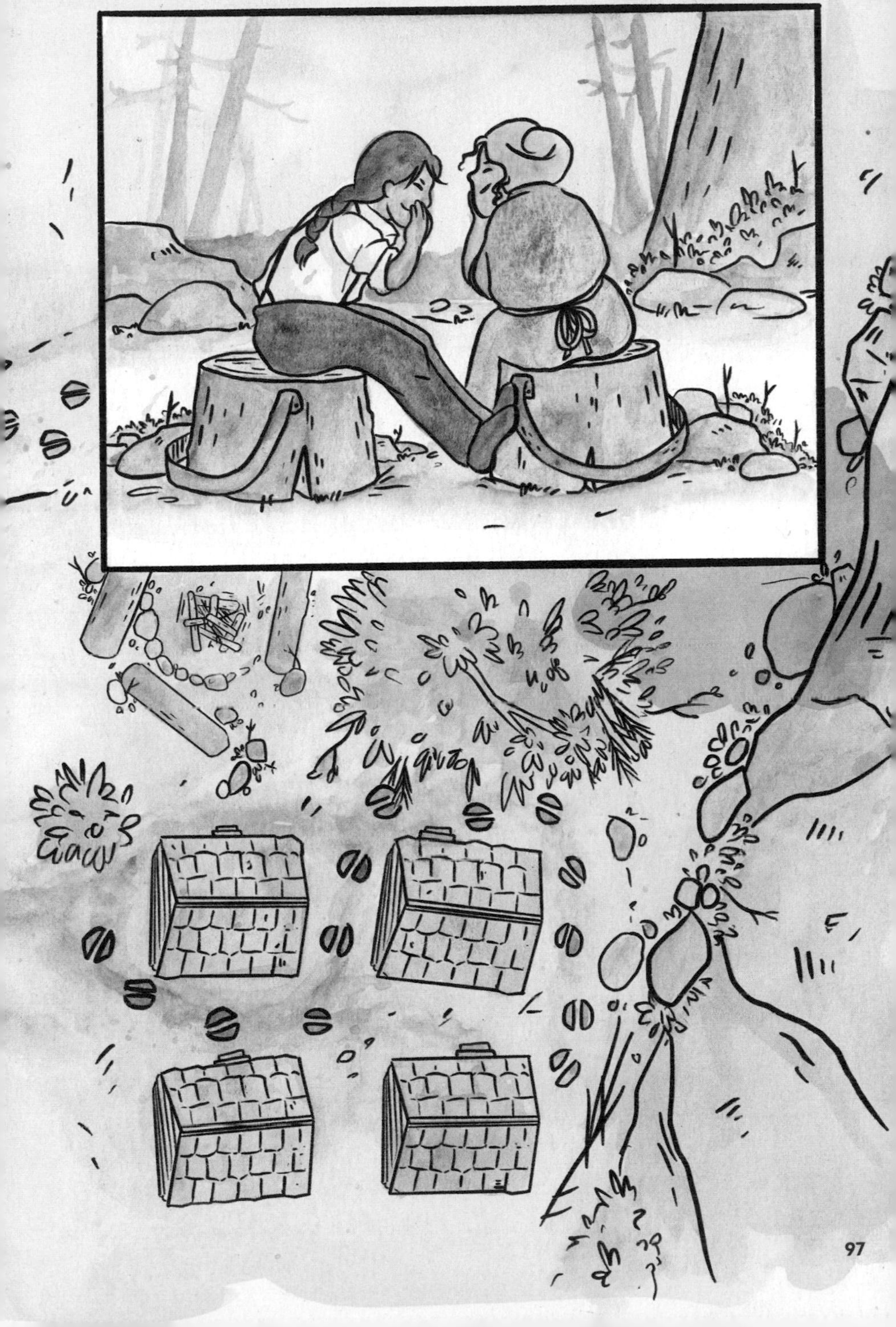

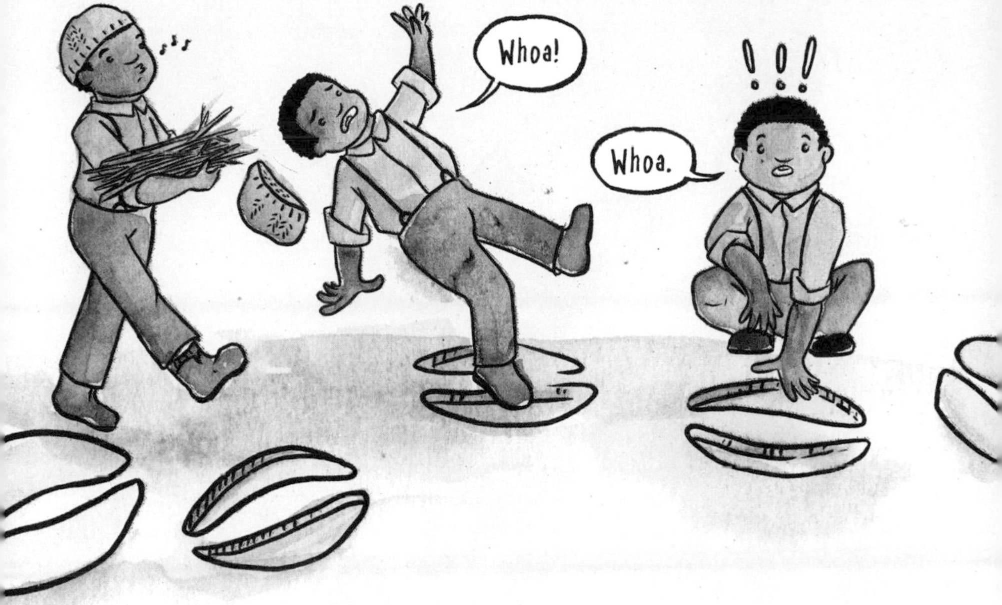

Whoa!
!!!
Whoa.

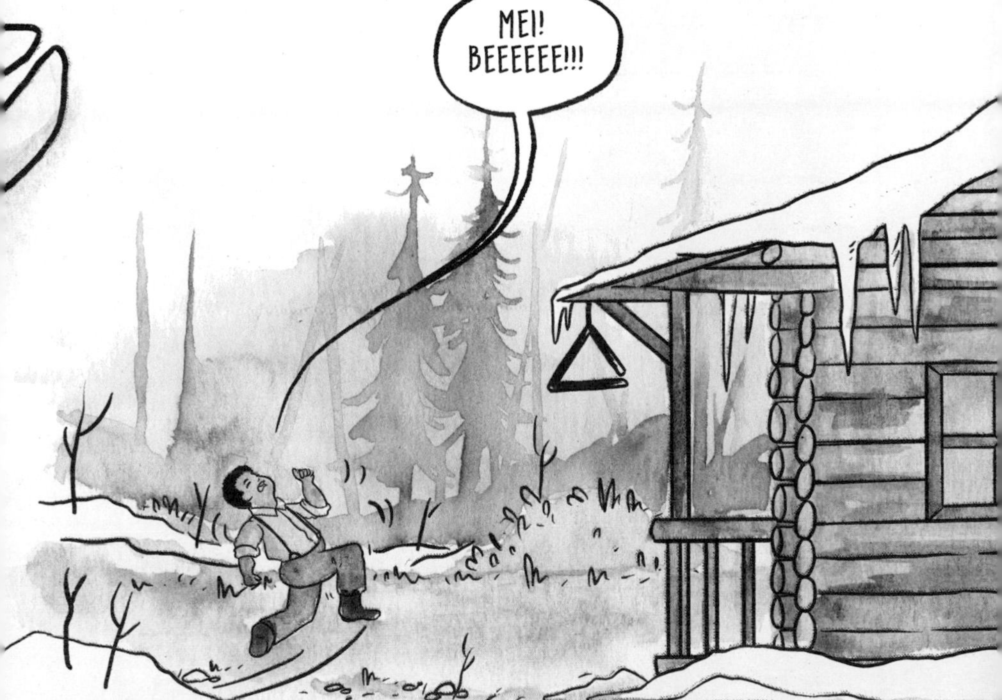

MEI!
BEEEEEE!!!

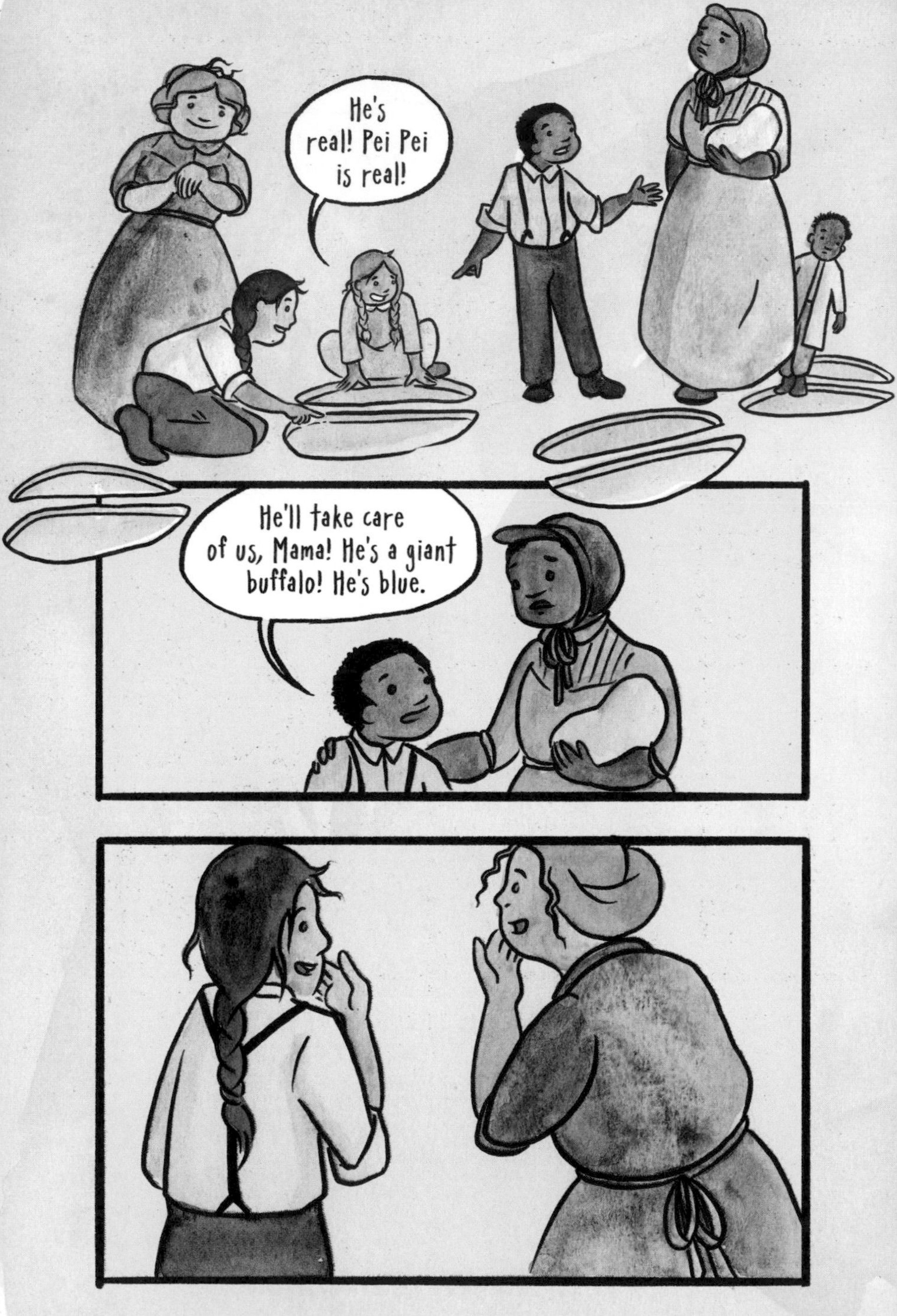
He's real! Pei Pei is real!
He'll take care of us, Mama! He's a giant buffalo! He's blue.

CHAPTER THREE

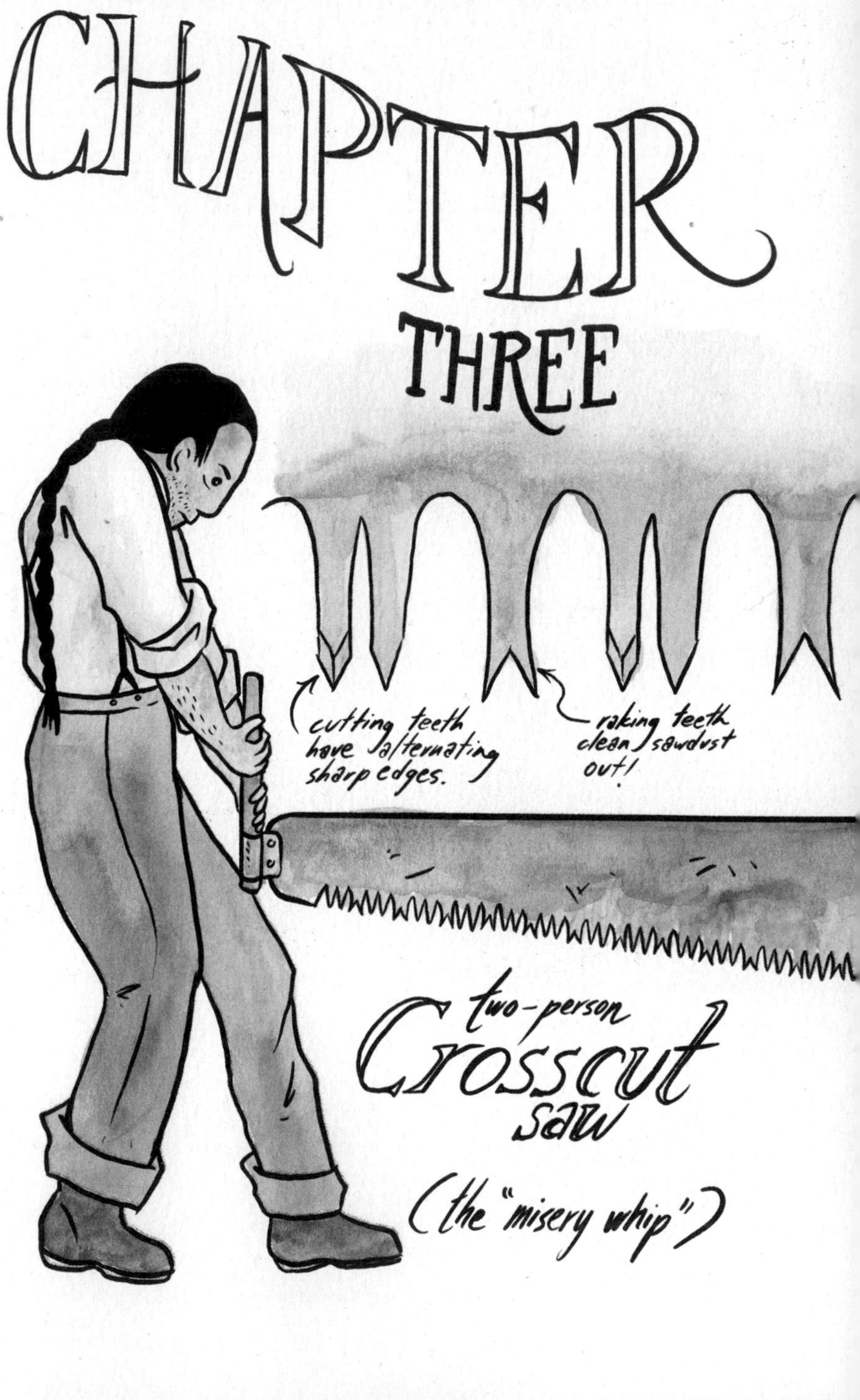

cutting teeth have alternating sharp edges.
raking teeth clean sawdust out!
two-person Crosscut saw
(the "misery whip")

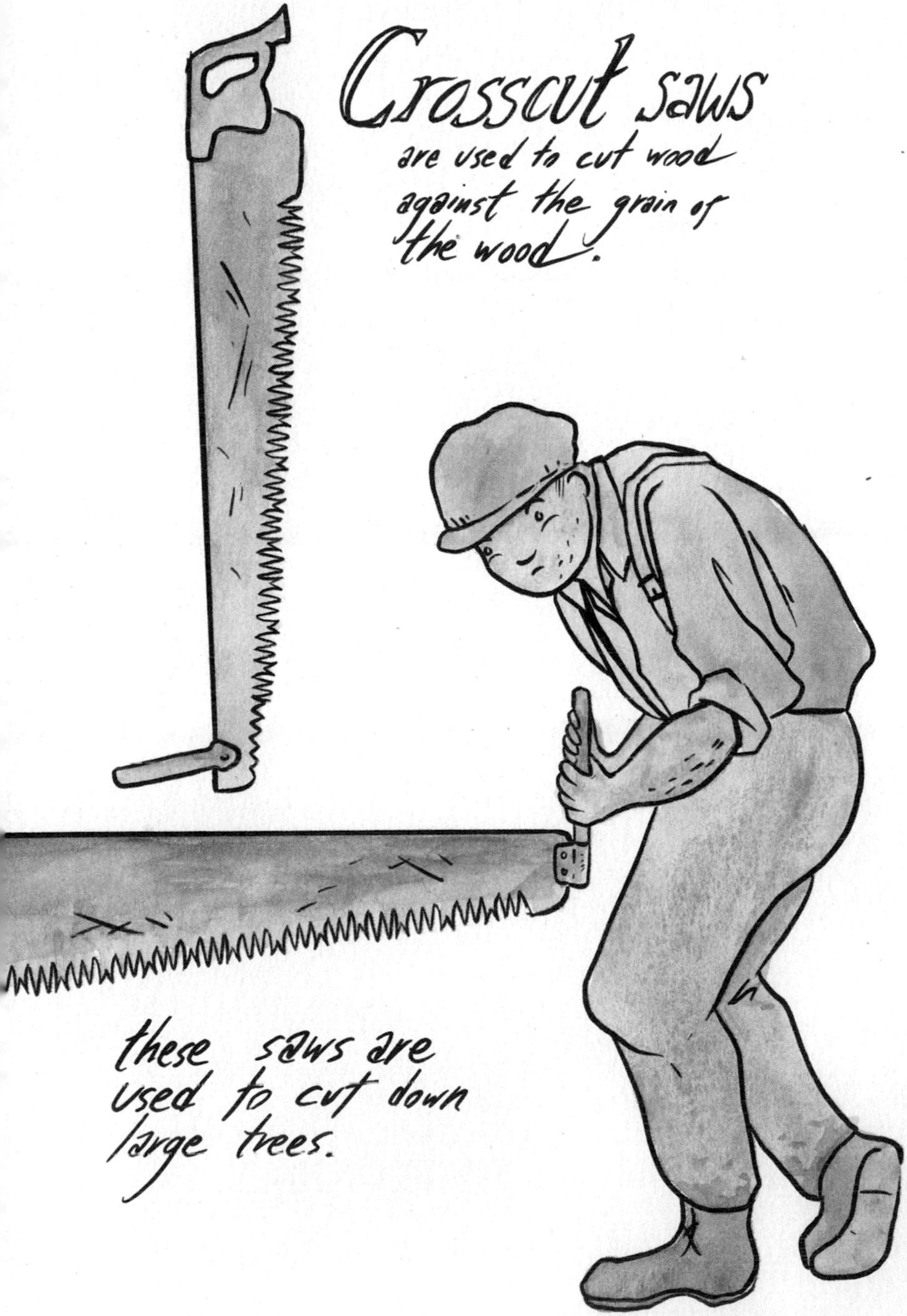
Crosscut saws
are used to cut wood against the grain of the wood.
these saws are used to cut down large trees.

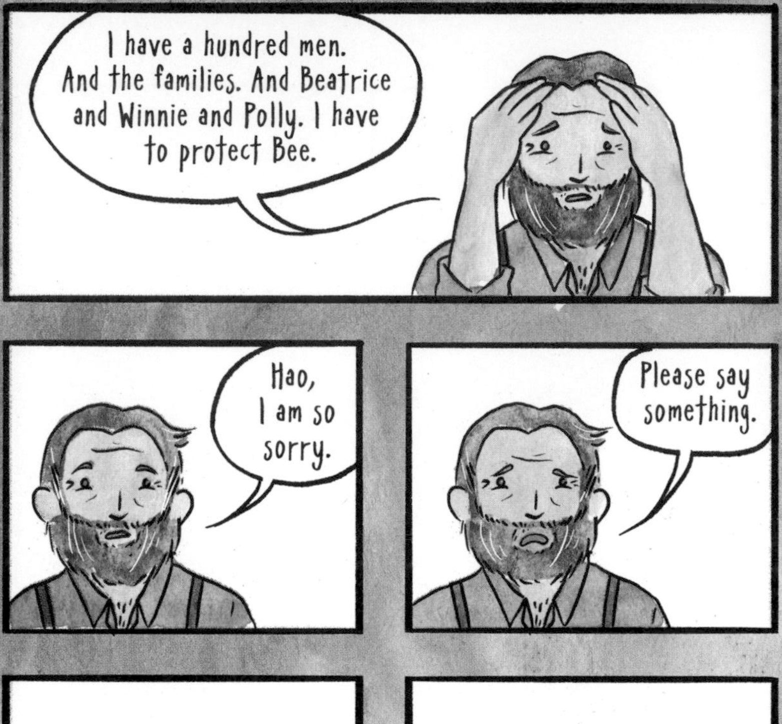
I have a hundred men. And the families. And Beatrice and Winnie and Polly. I have to protect Bee.
Hao, I am so sorry.
Please say something.
Okay, Mister Andersen.

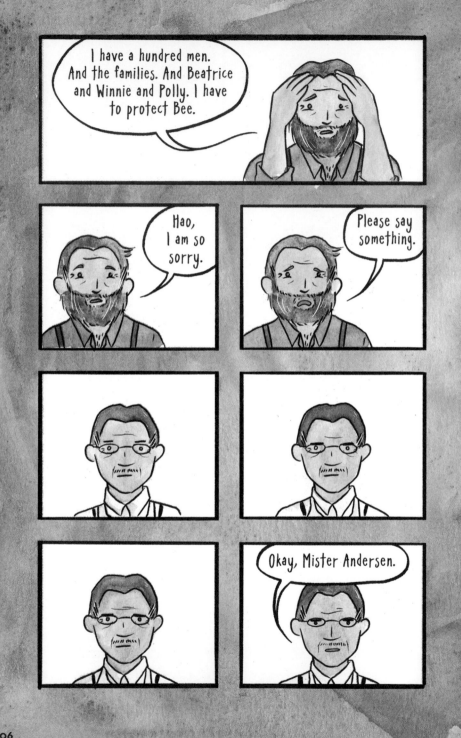

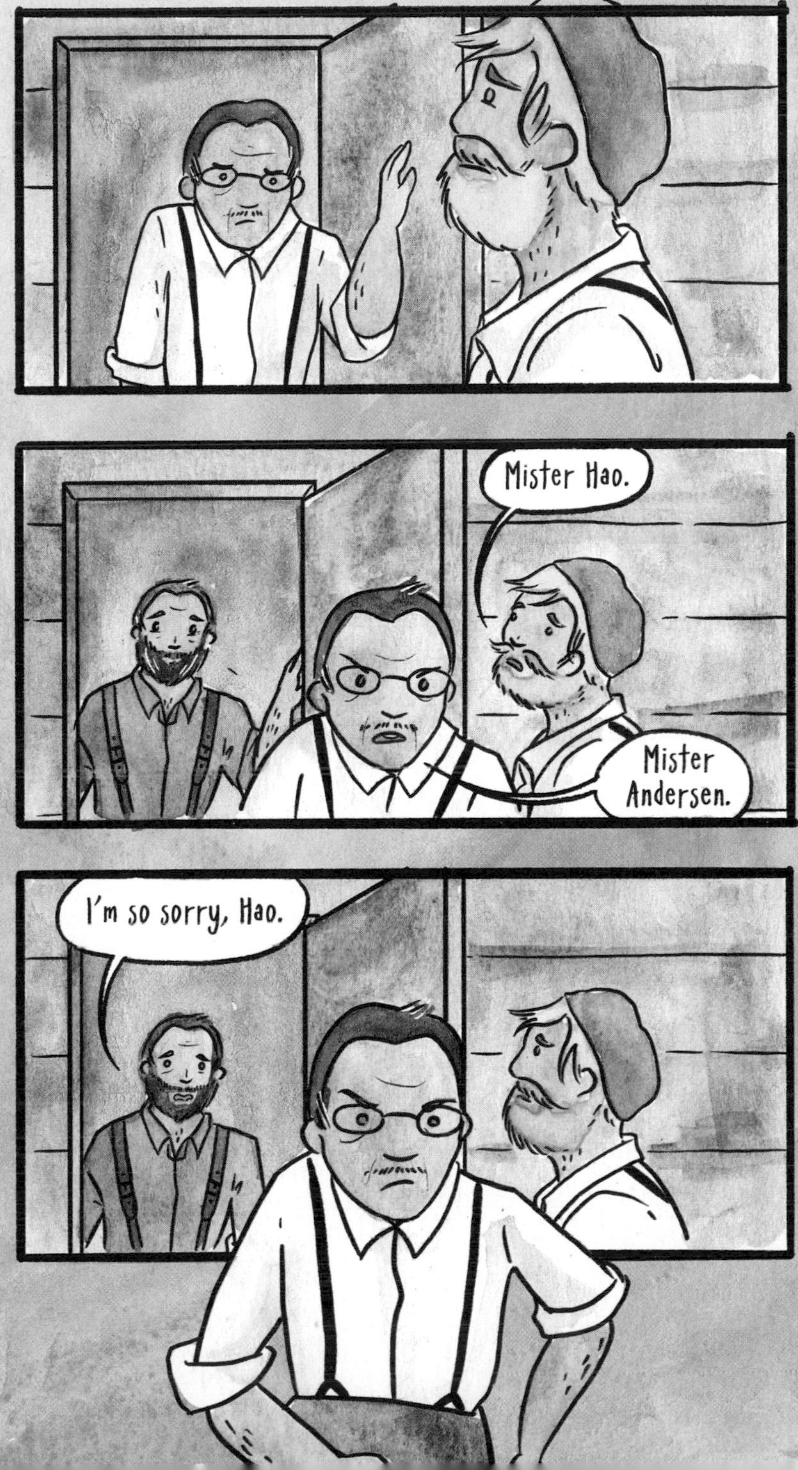
Mister Hao.
Mister Andersen.
I'm so sorry, Hao.

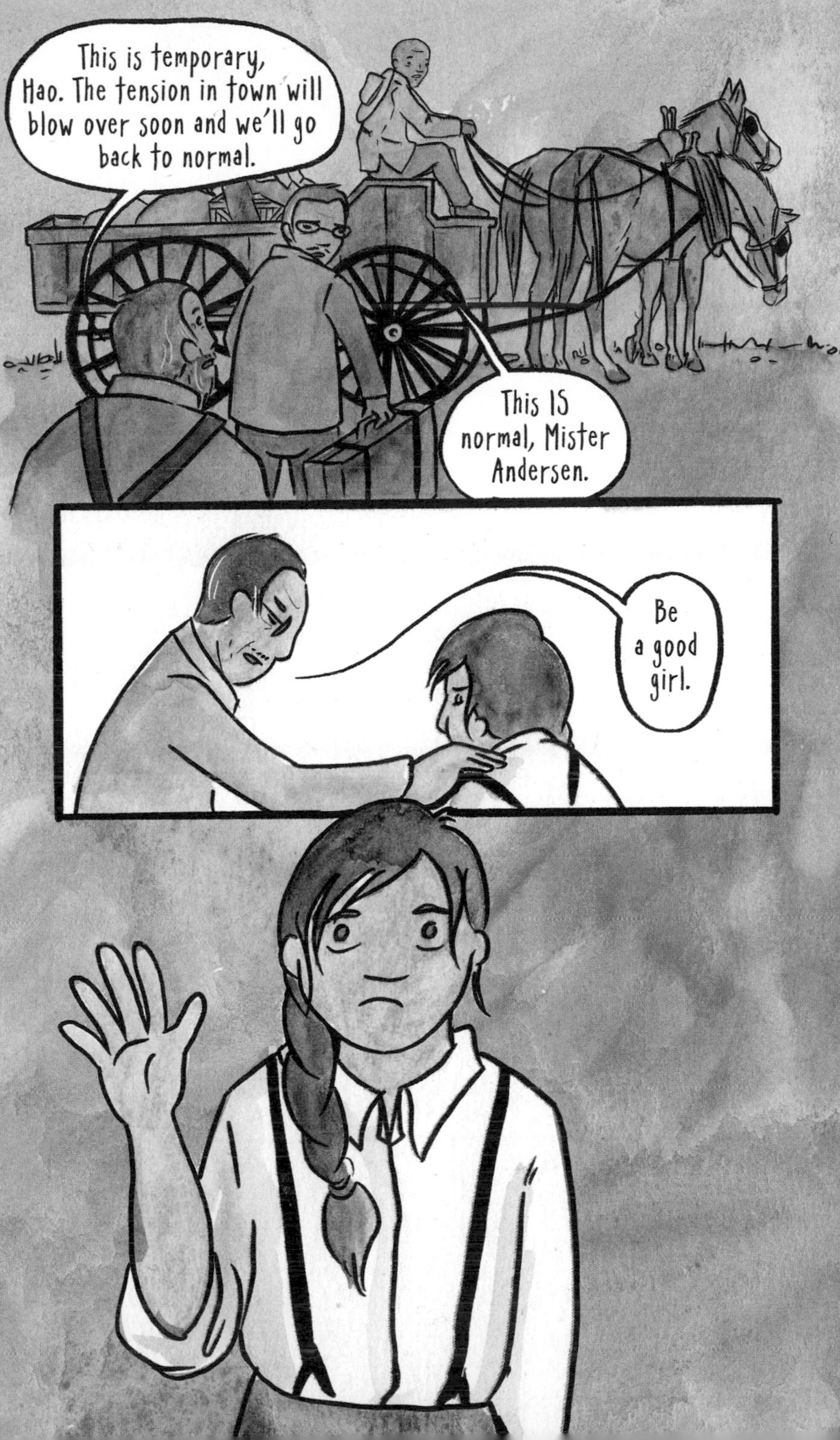
This is temporary, Hao. The tension in town will blow over soon and we'll go back to normal.
This IS normal, Mister Andersen.
Be a good girl.

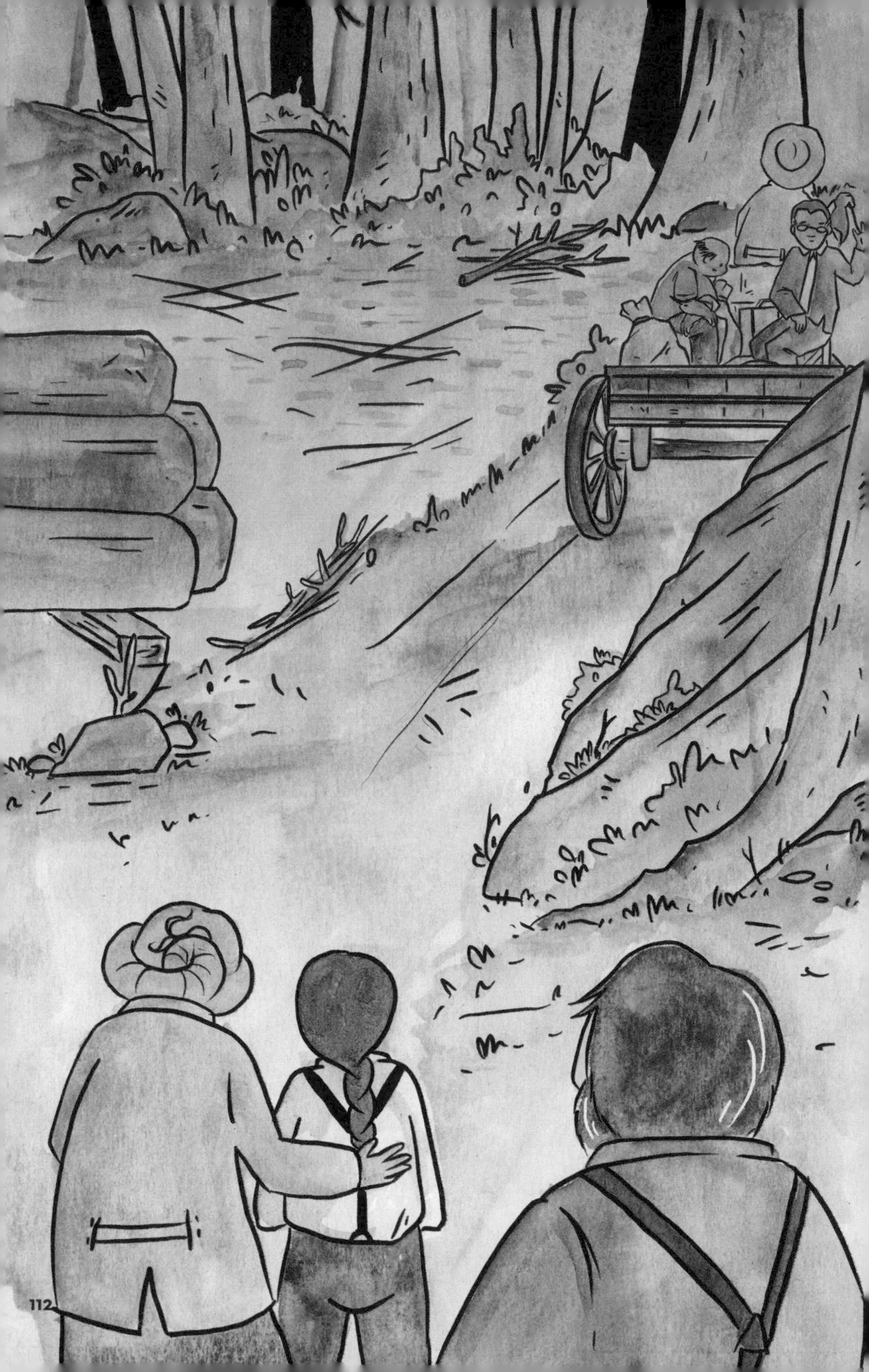

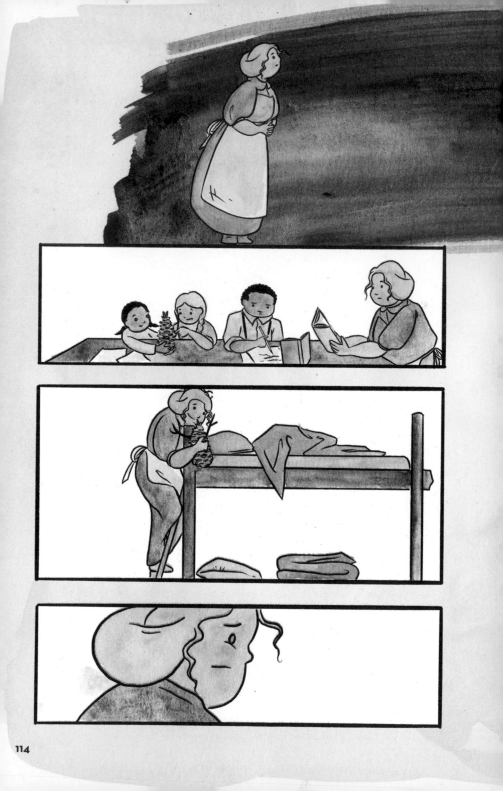

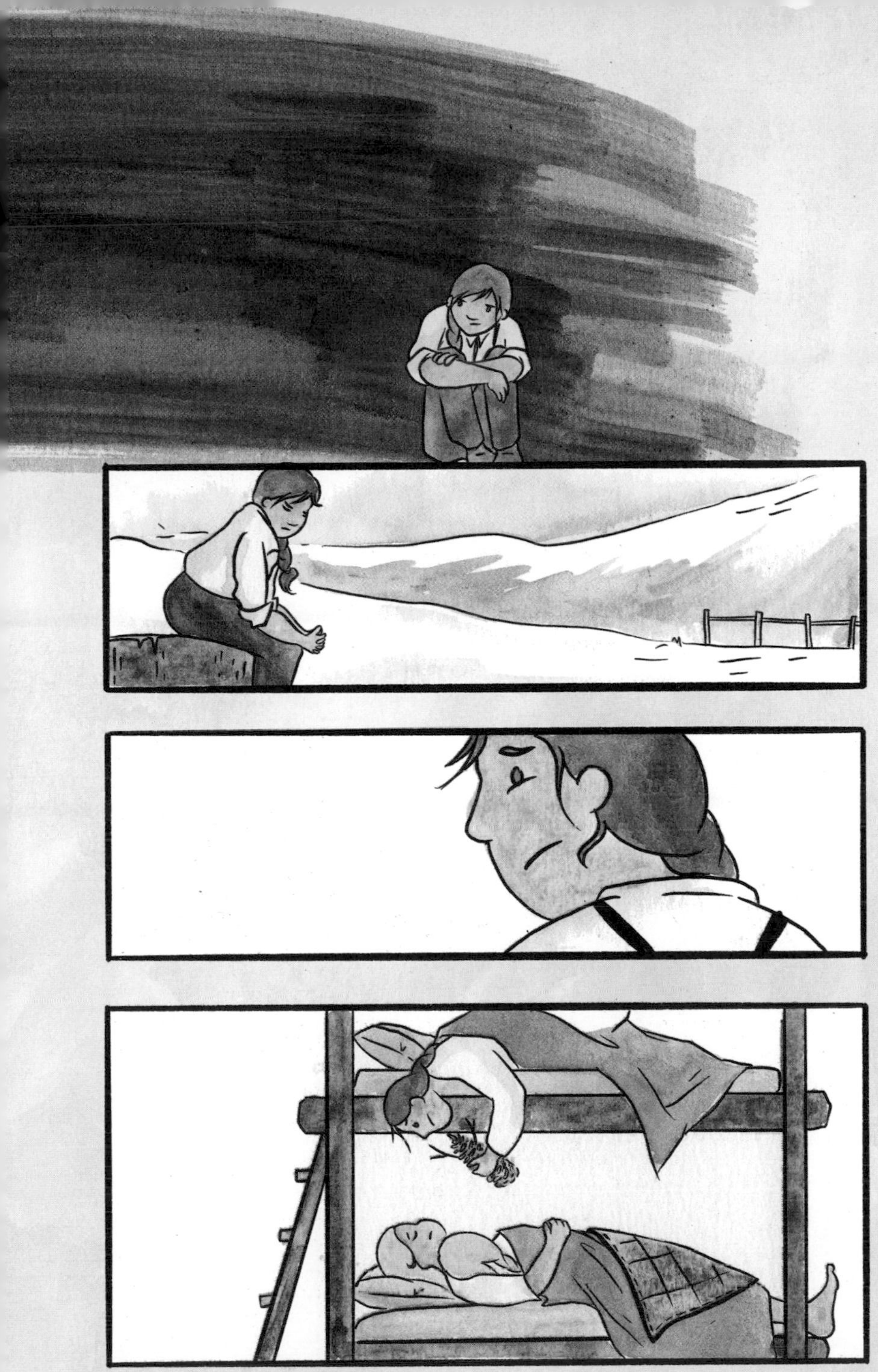

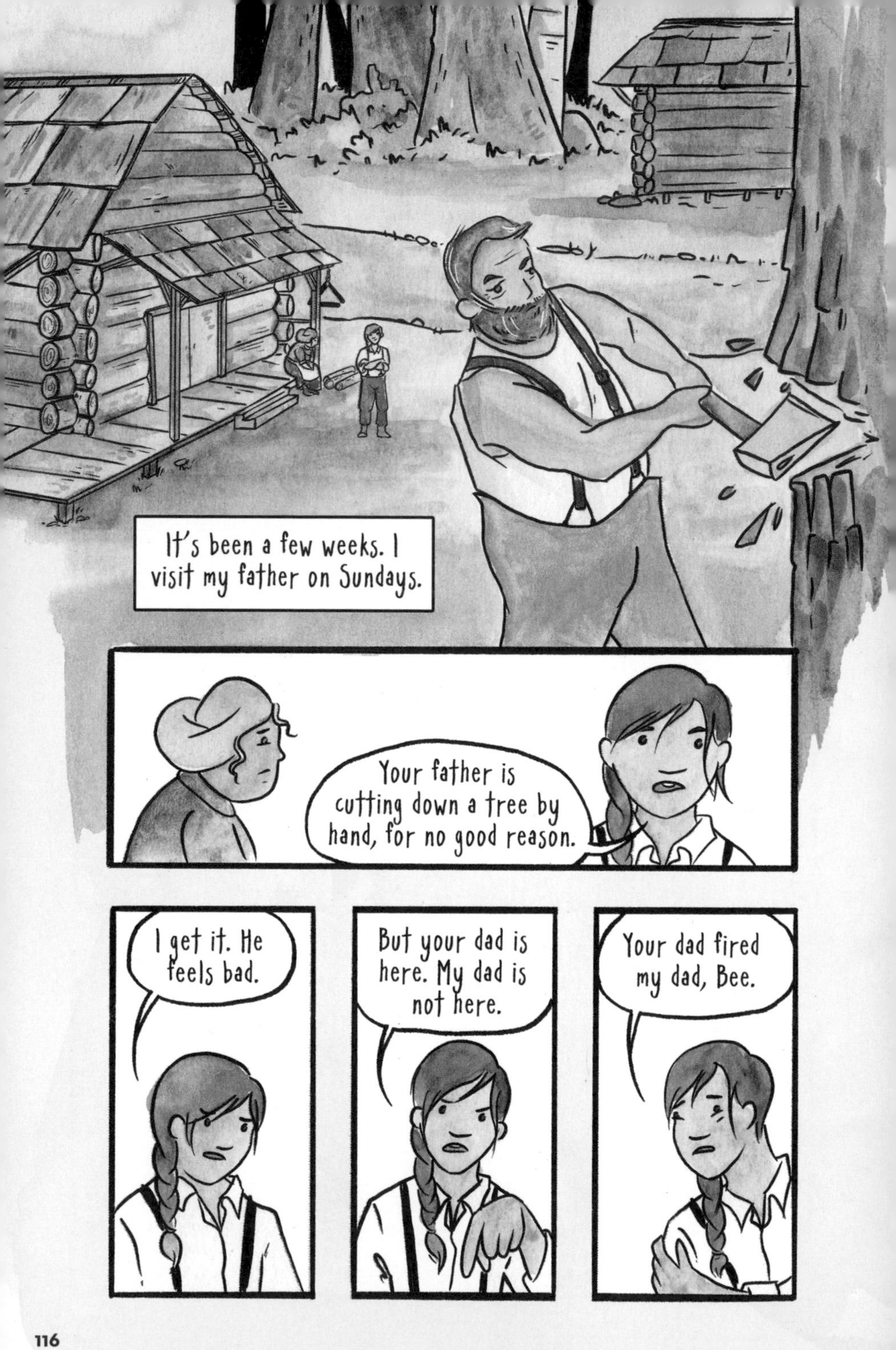
It's been a few weeks. I visit my father on Sundays.
Your father is cutting down a tree by hand, for no good reason.
I get it. He feels bad.
But your dad is here. My dad is not here.
Your dad fired my dad, Bee.

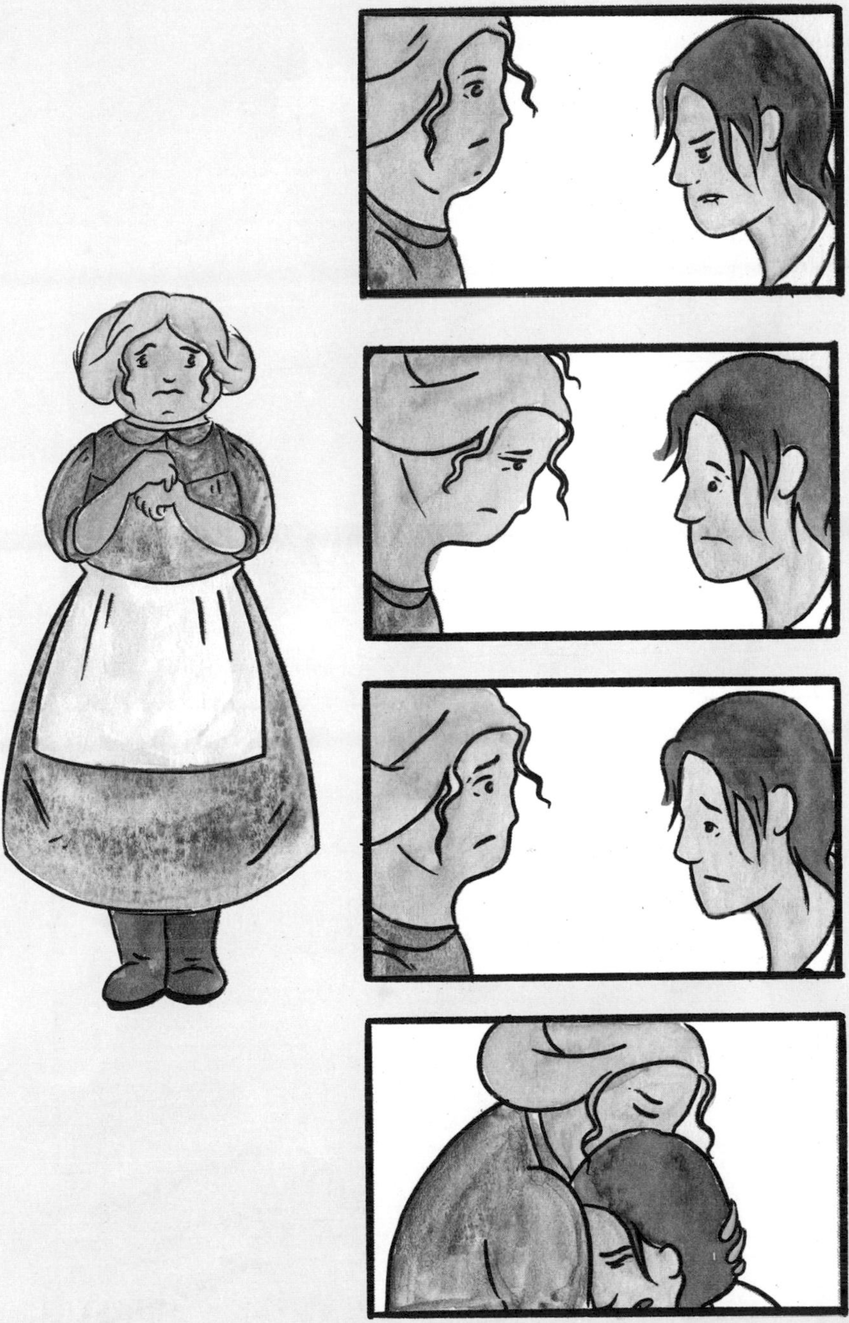

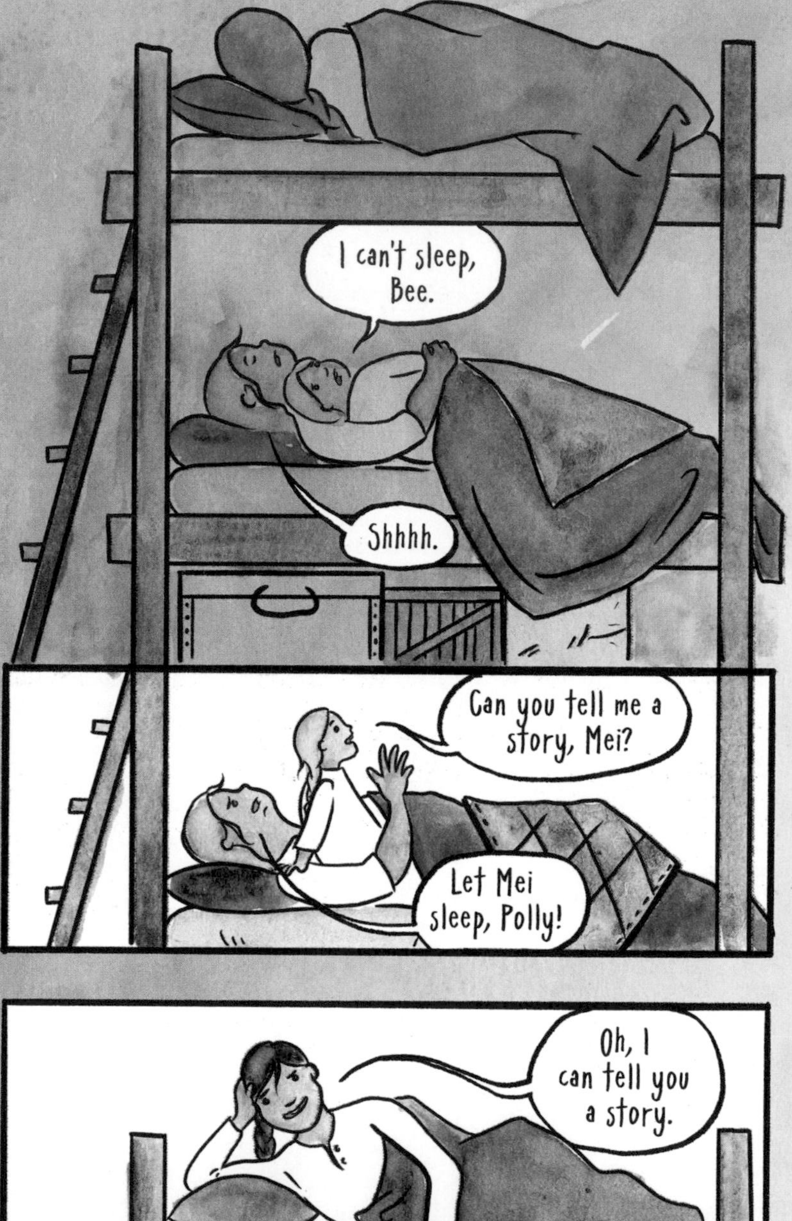
I can't sleep, Bee.
Shhhh.
Can you tell me a story, Mei?
Let Mei sleep, Polly!
Oh, I can tell you a story.

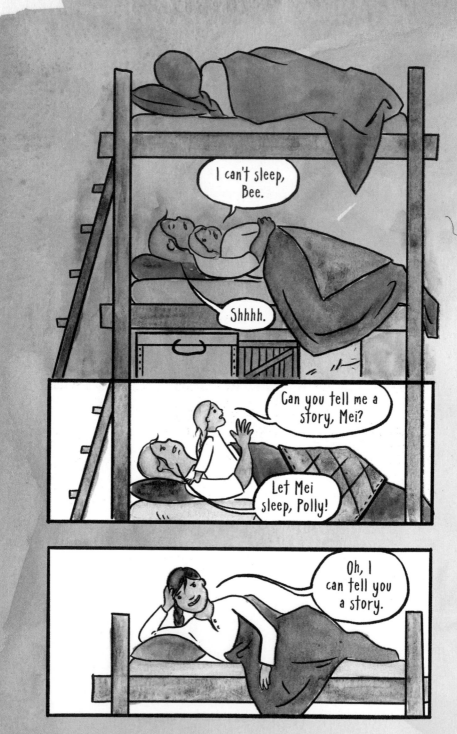

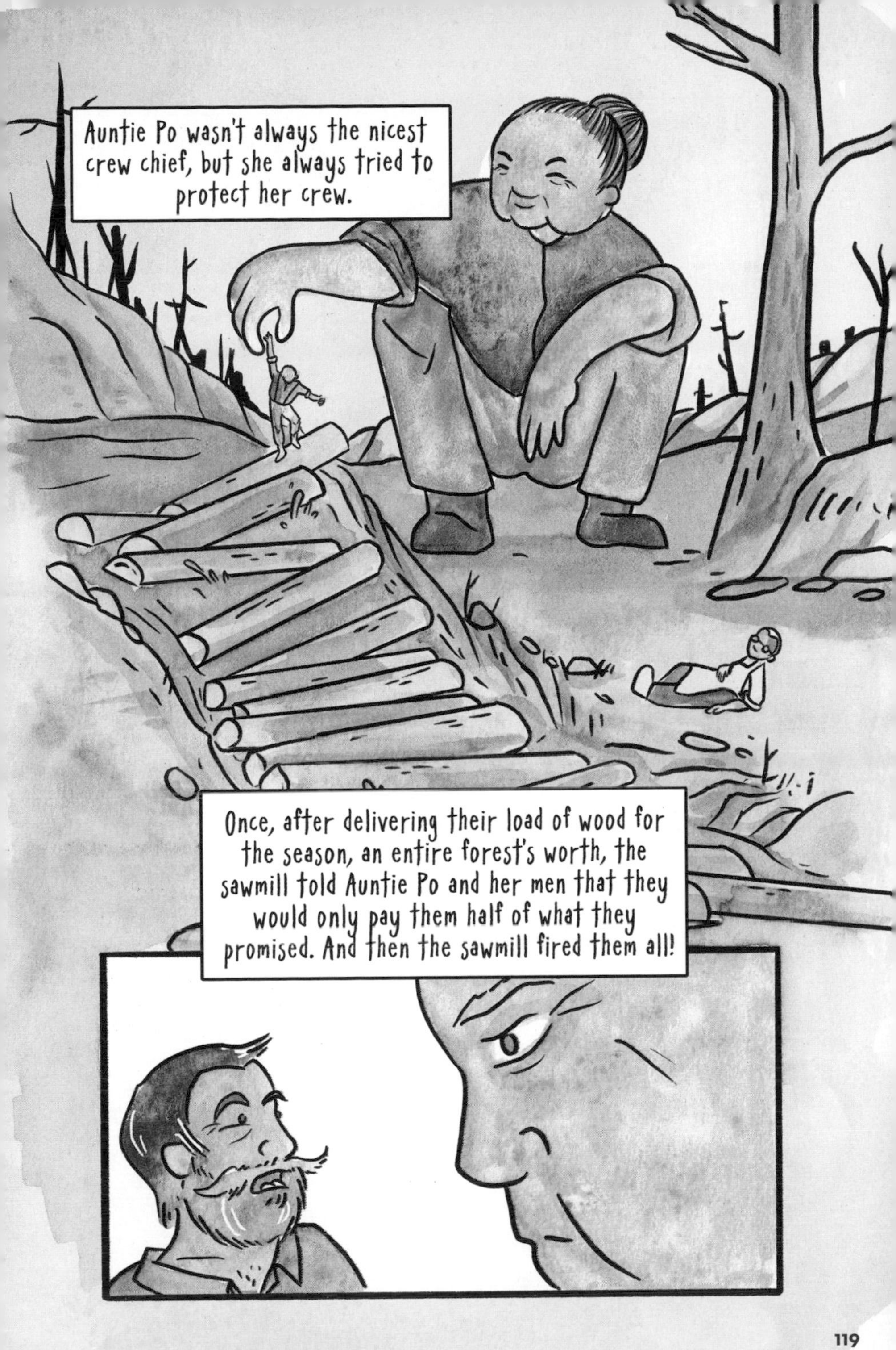
Auntie Po wasn't always the nicest crew chief, but she always tried to protect her crew.
Once, after delivering their load of wood for the season, an entire forest's worth, the sawmill told Auntie Po and her men that they would only pay them half of what they promised. And then the sawmill fired them all!

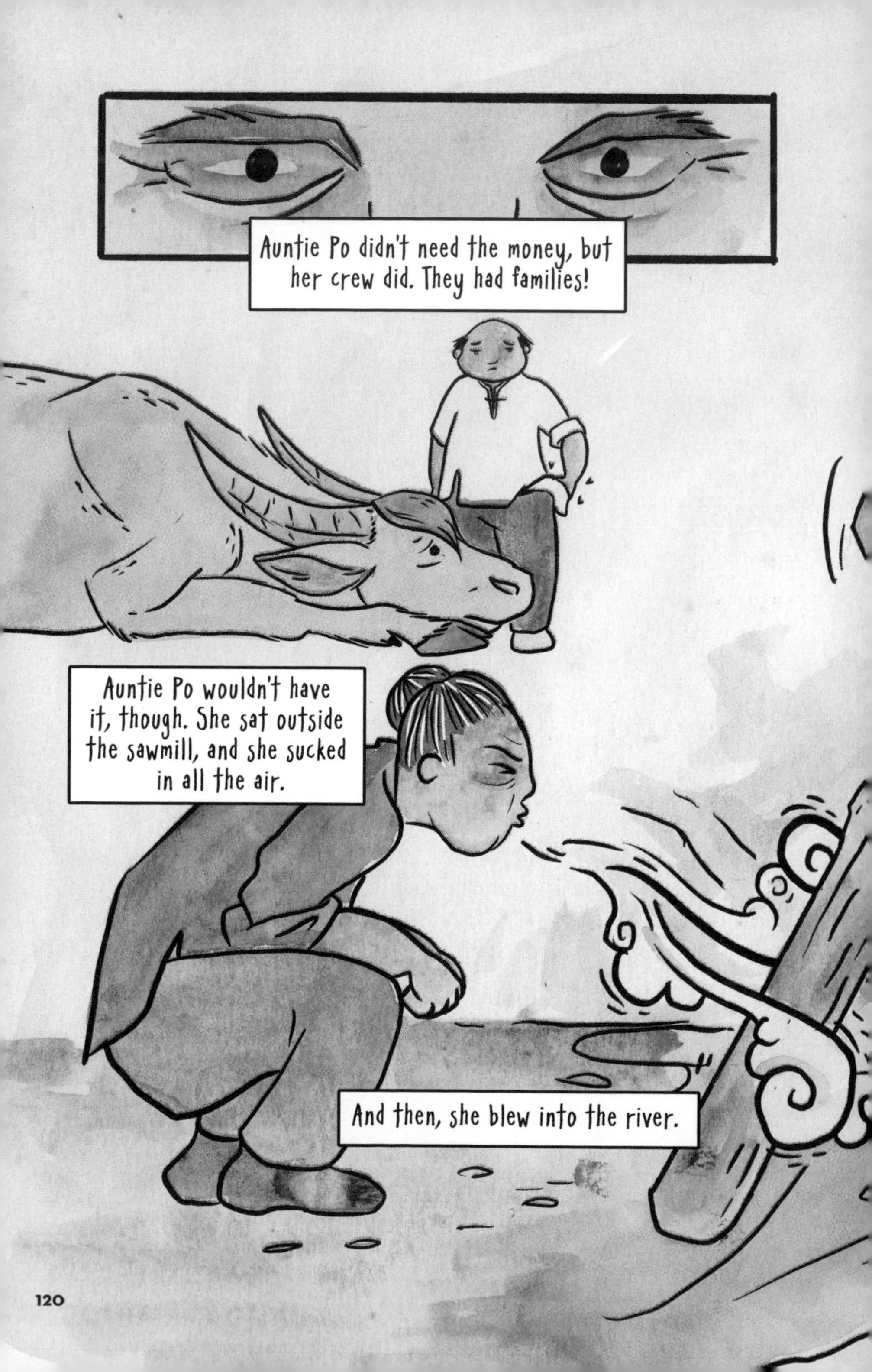
Auntie Po didn't need the money, but her crew did. They had families!
Auntie Po wouldn't have it, though. She sat outside the sawmill, and she sucked in all the air.
And then, she blew into the river.

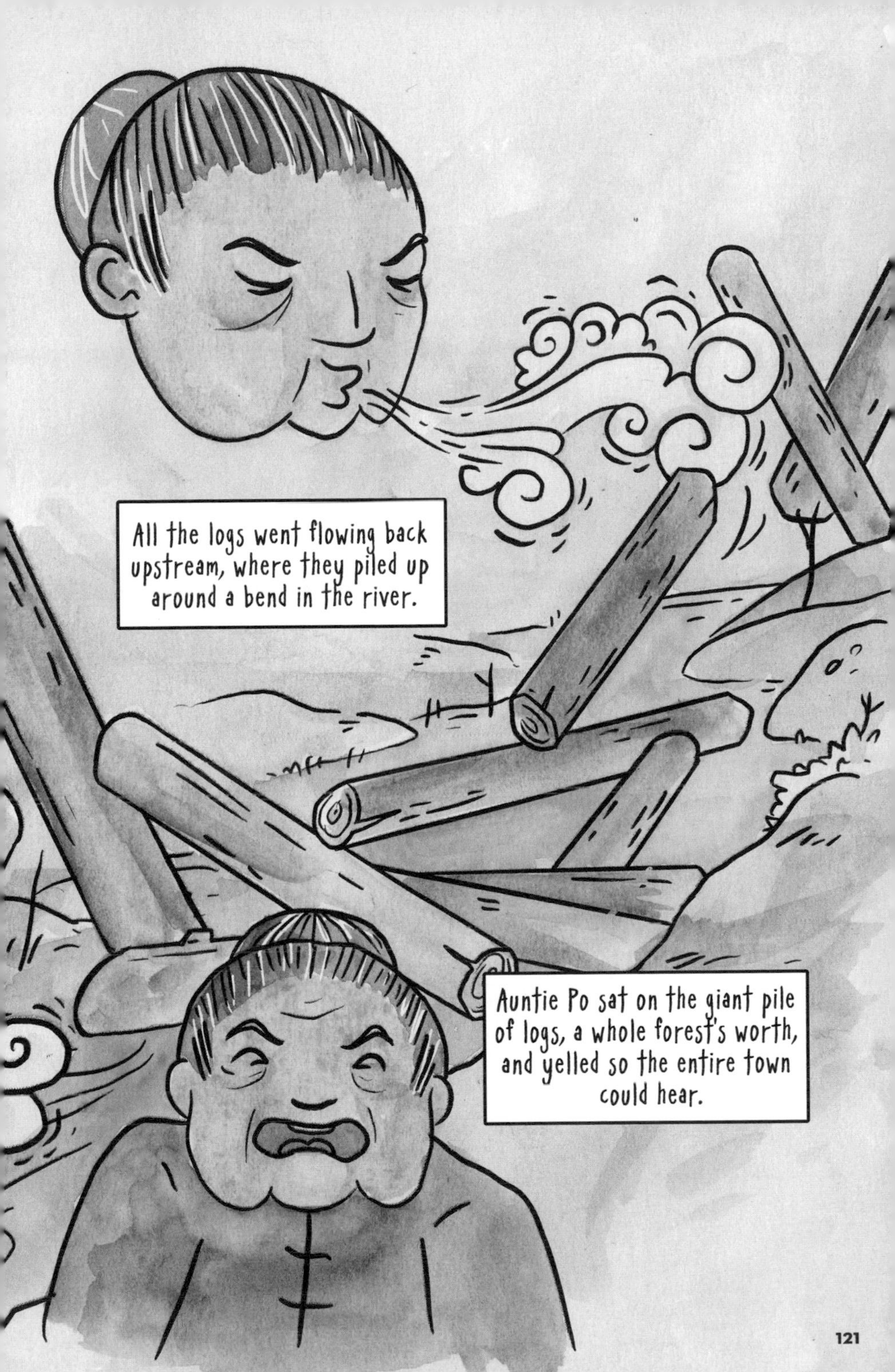
All the logs went flowing back upstream, where they piled up around a bend in the river.
Auntie Po sat on the giant pile of logs, a whole forest's worth, and yelled so the entire town could hear.

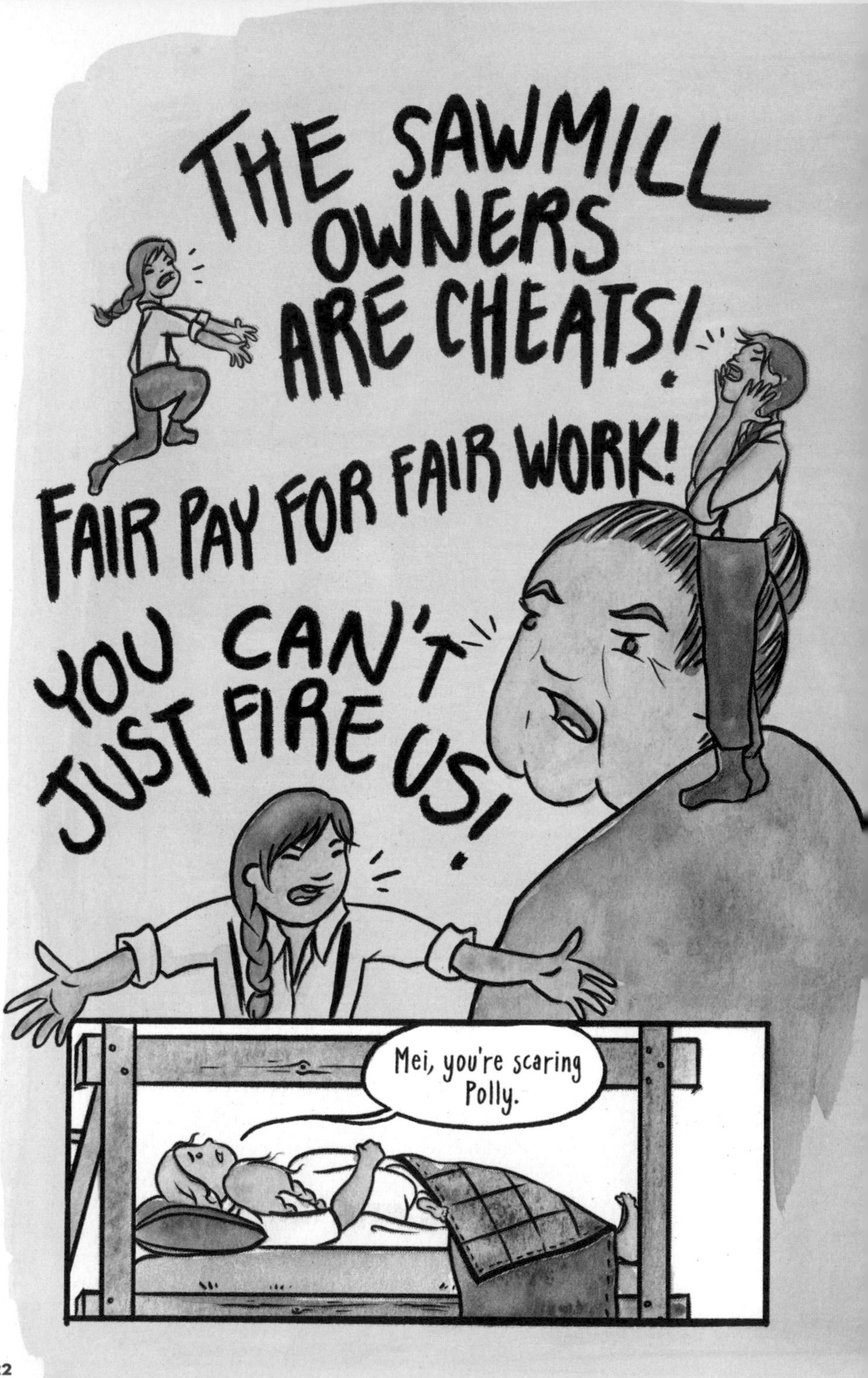
THE SAWMILL OWNERS ARE CHEATS!
FAIR PAY FOR FAIR WORK!
YOU CAN'T JUST FIRE US!
Mei, you're scaring Polly.

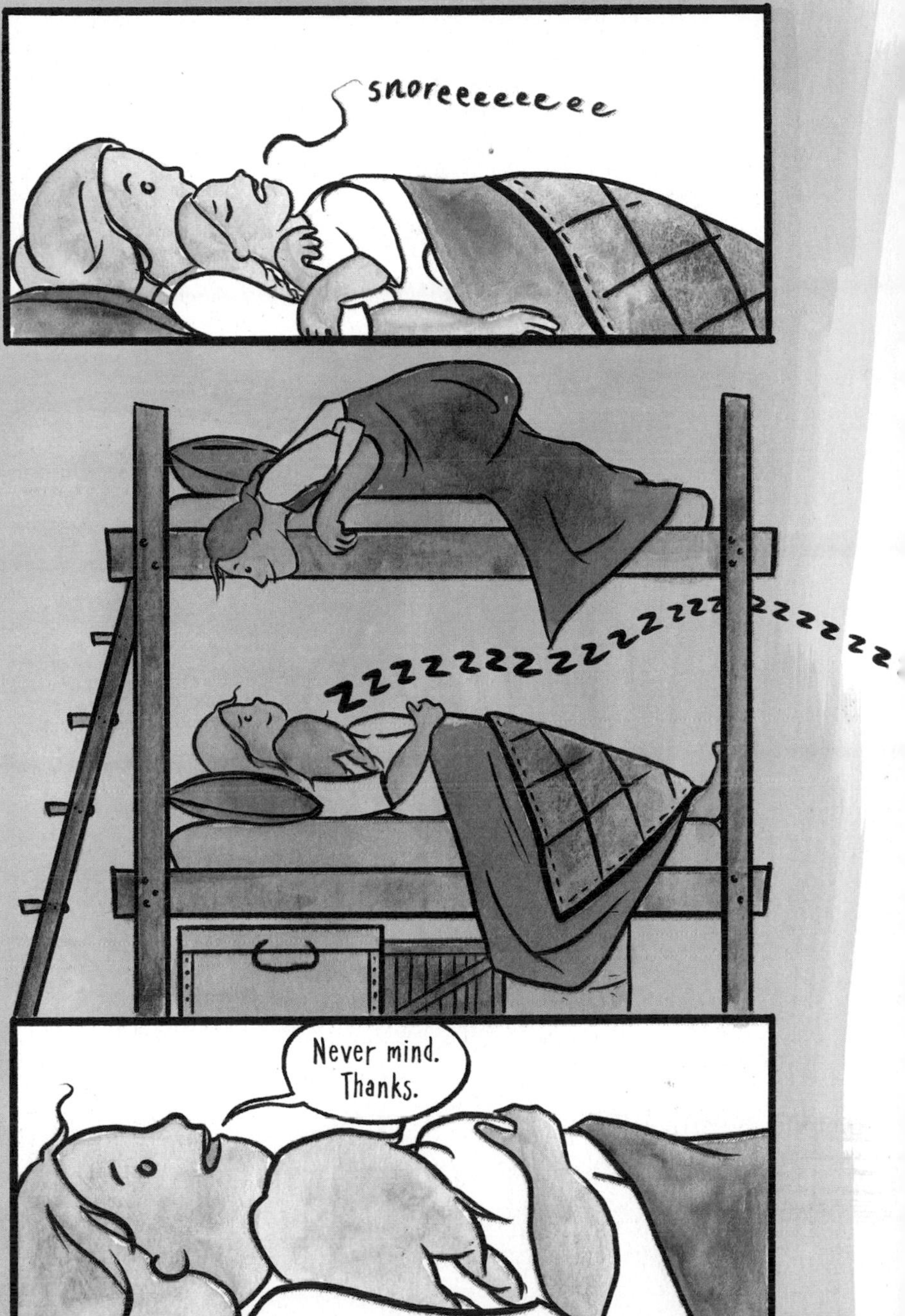
snoreeeeeeee
ZZZZZZZZZZZZZZZZZZZZZZZ
Never mind. Thanks.

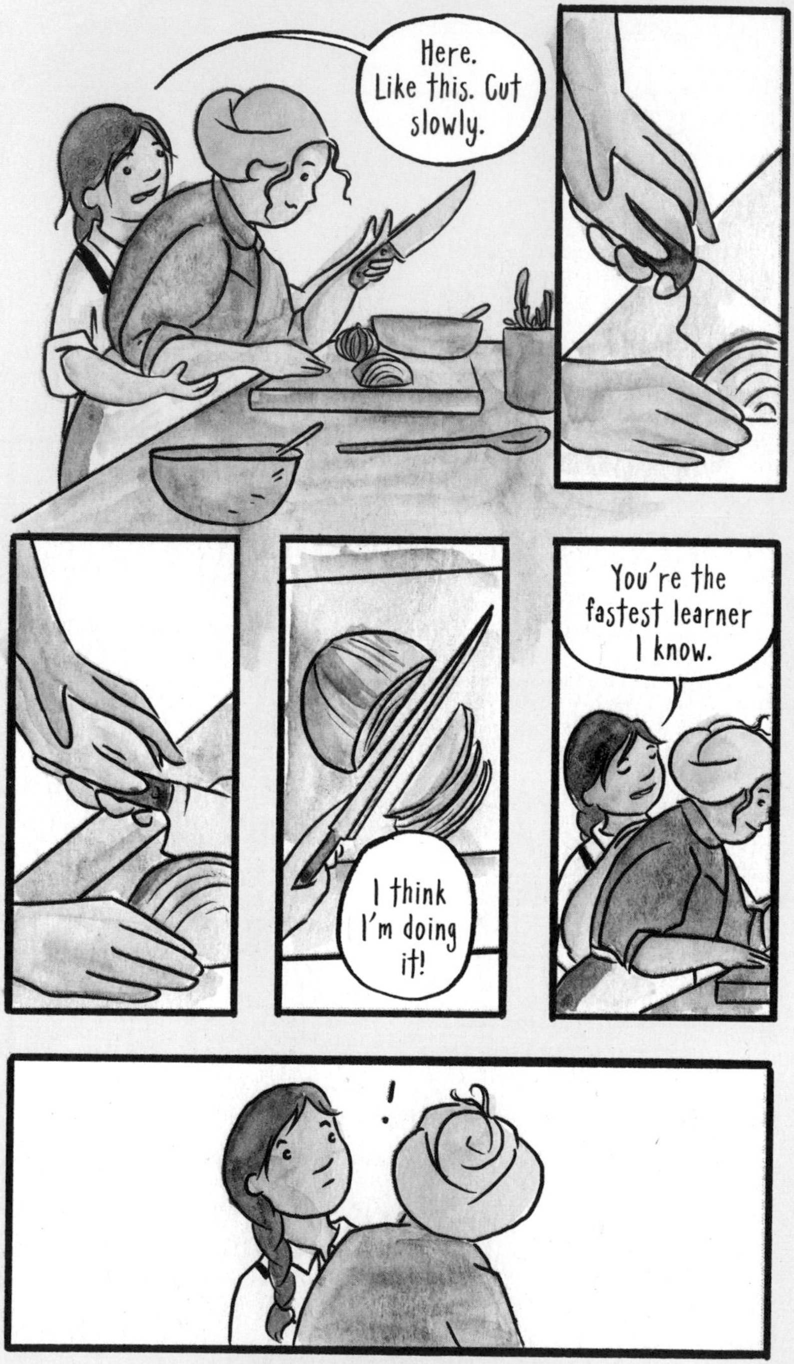
Here. Like this. Cut slowly.
I think I'm doing it!
You're the fastest learner I know.
!

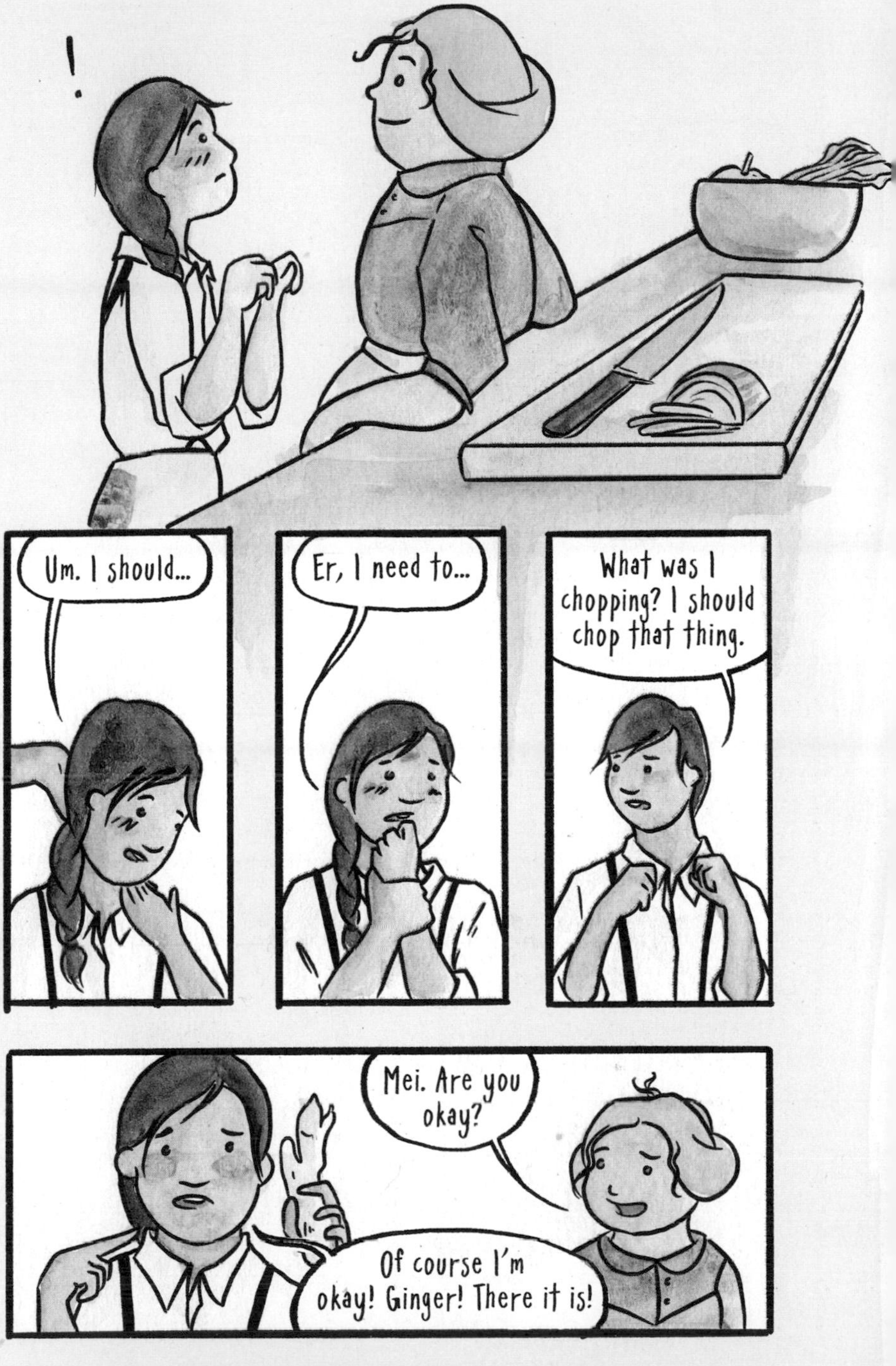
!
Um. I should...
Er, I need to...
What was I chopping? I should chop that thing.
Mei. Are you okay?
Of course I'm okay! Ginger! There it is!

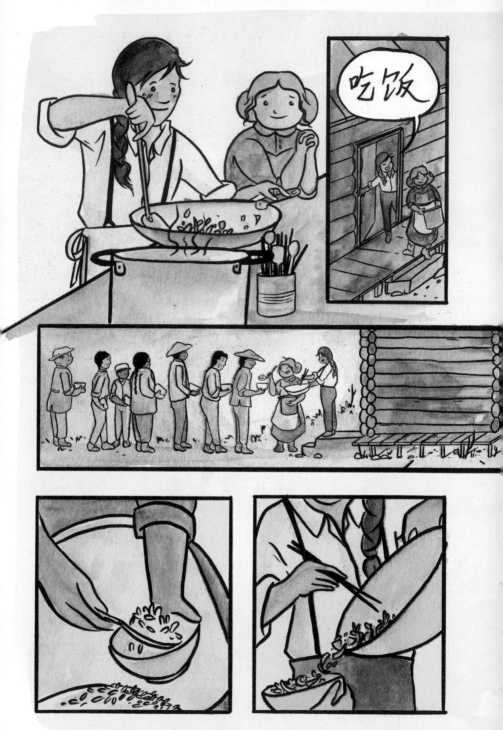

吃饭

吃饭

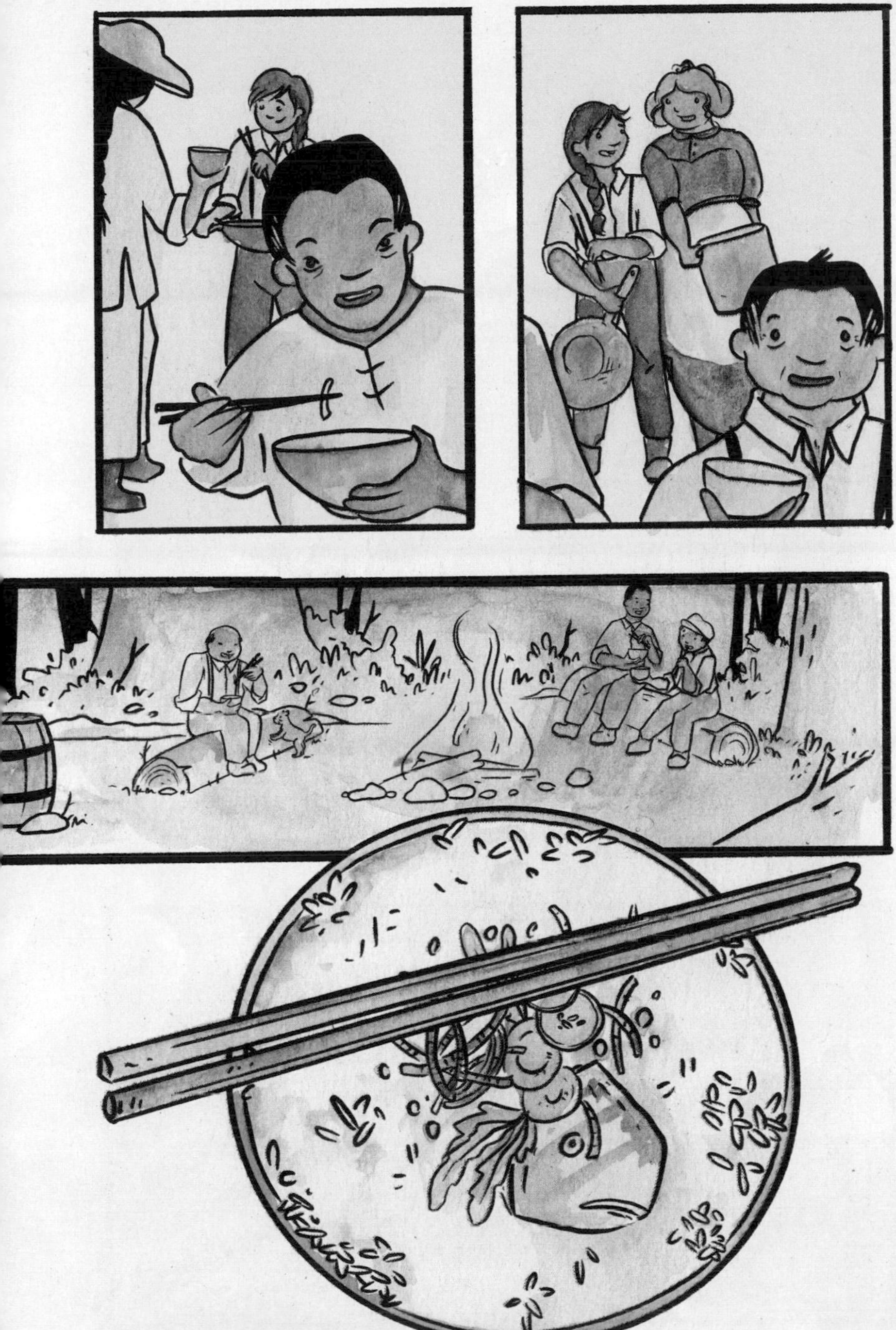

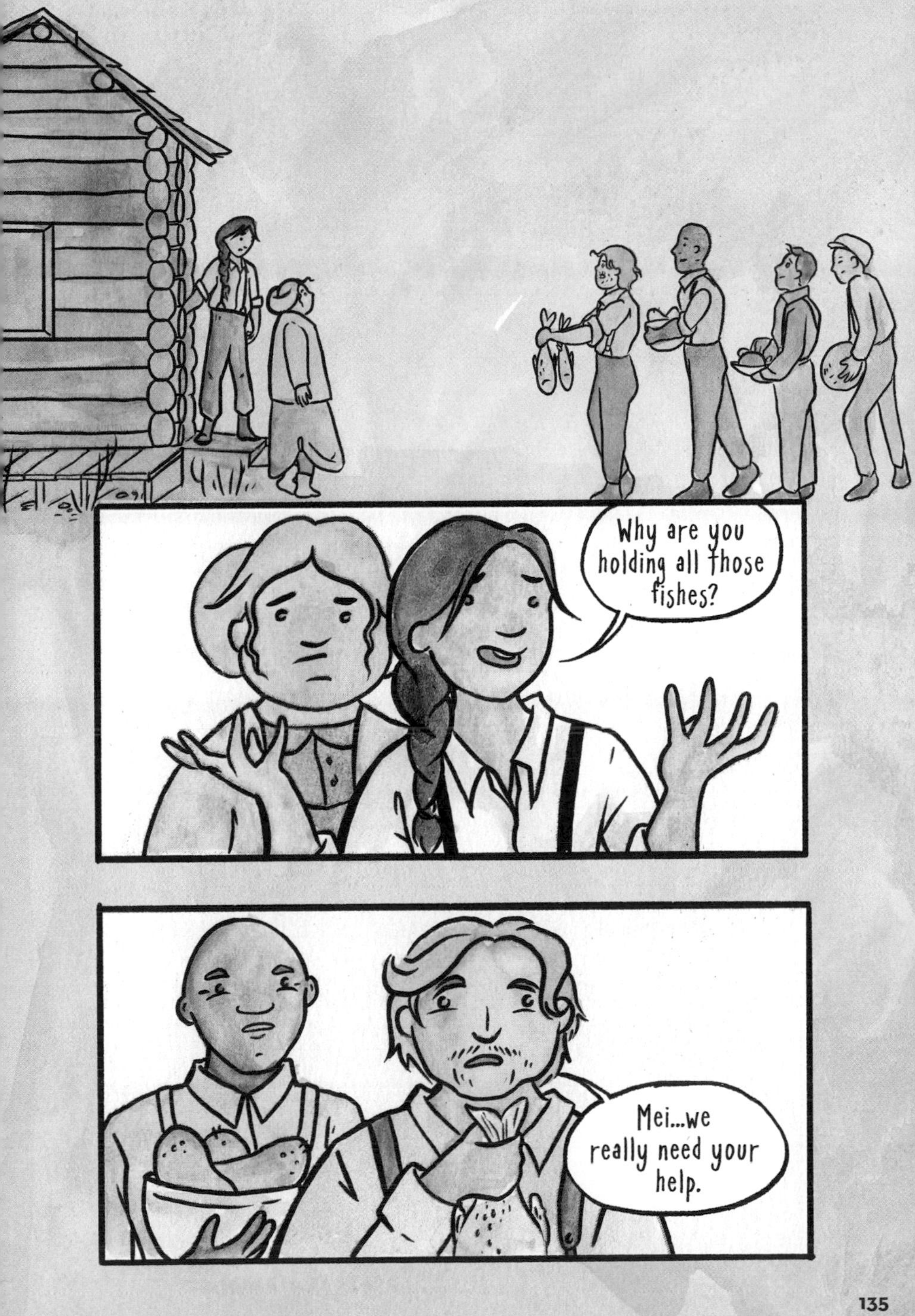
Why are you holding all those fishes?
Mei...we really need your help.

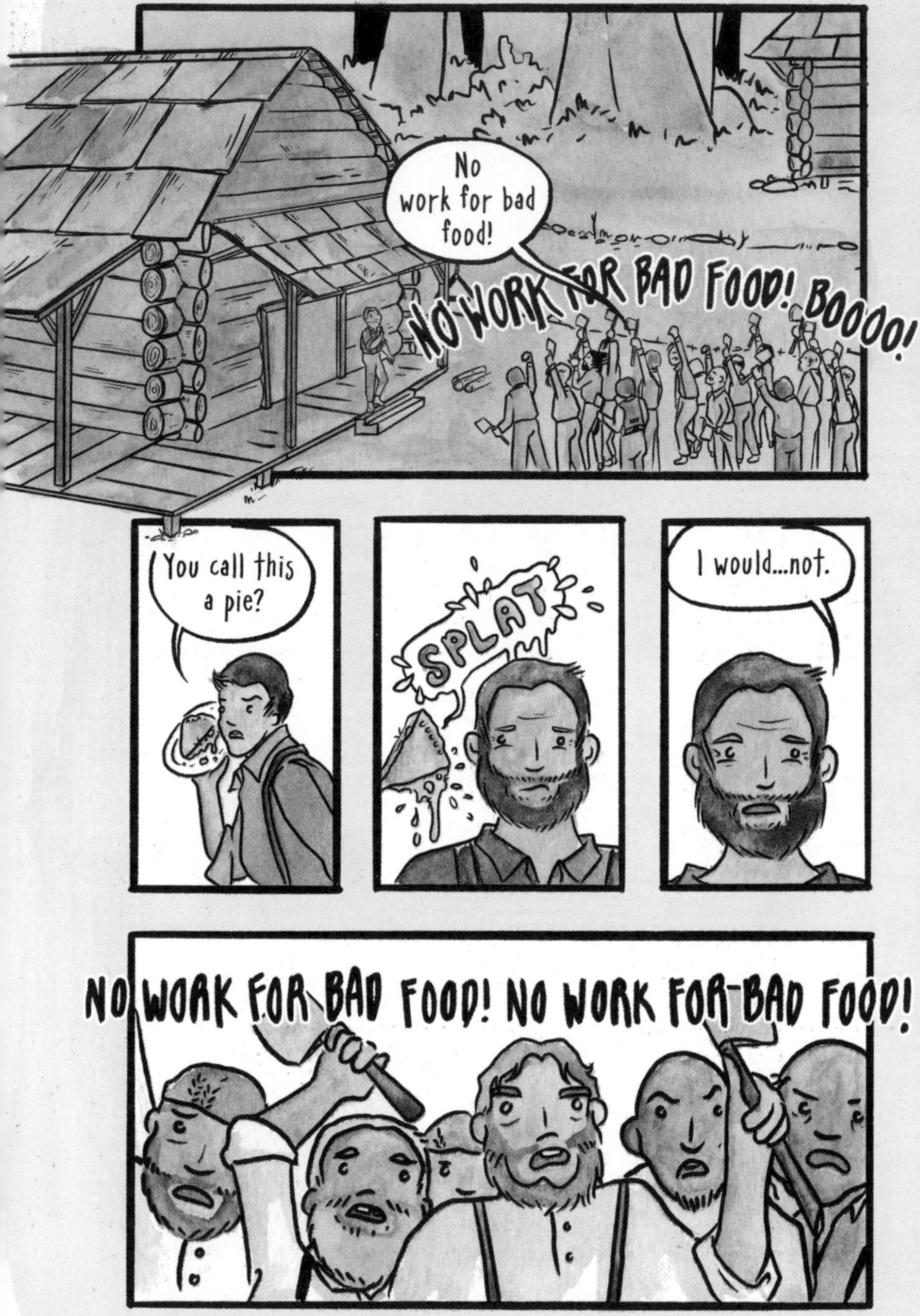
No work for bad food!
NO WORK FOR BAD FOOD! BOOOOO!
You call this a pie?
SPLAT
I would...not.
NO WORK FOR BAD FOOD! NO WORK FOR BAD FOOD!

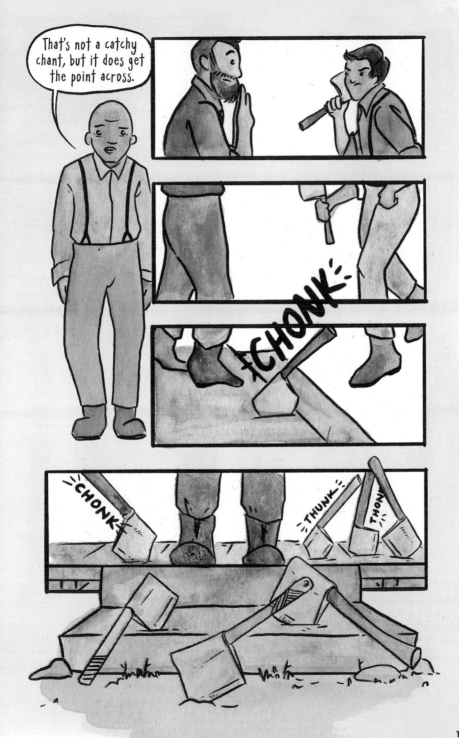

143

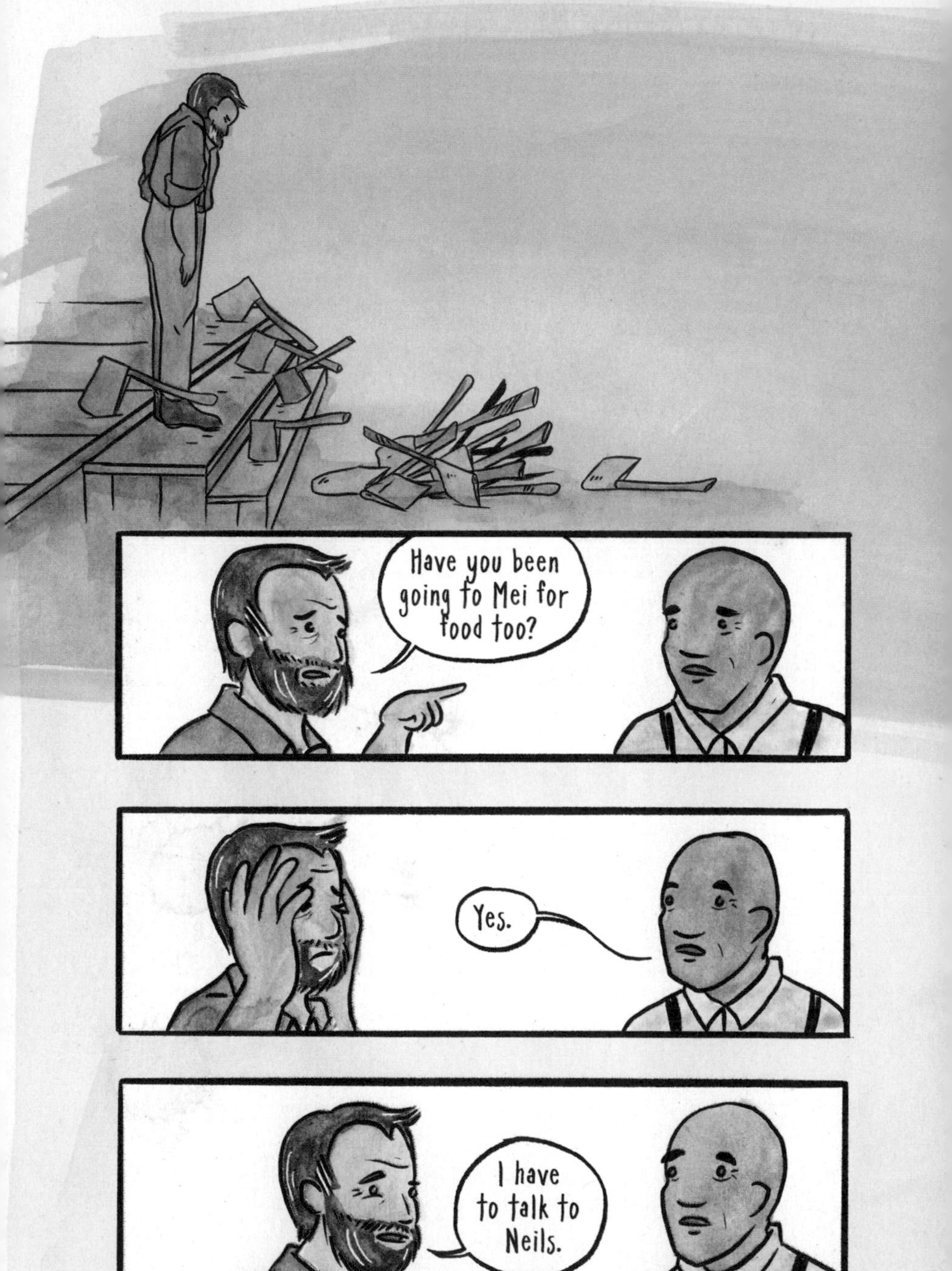

Have you been going to Mei for food too?
Yes.
I have to talk to Neils.

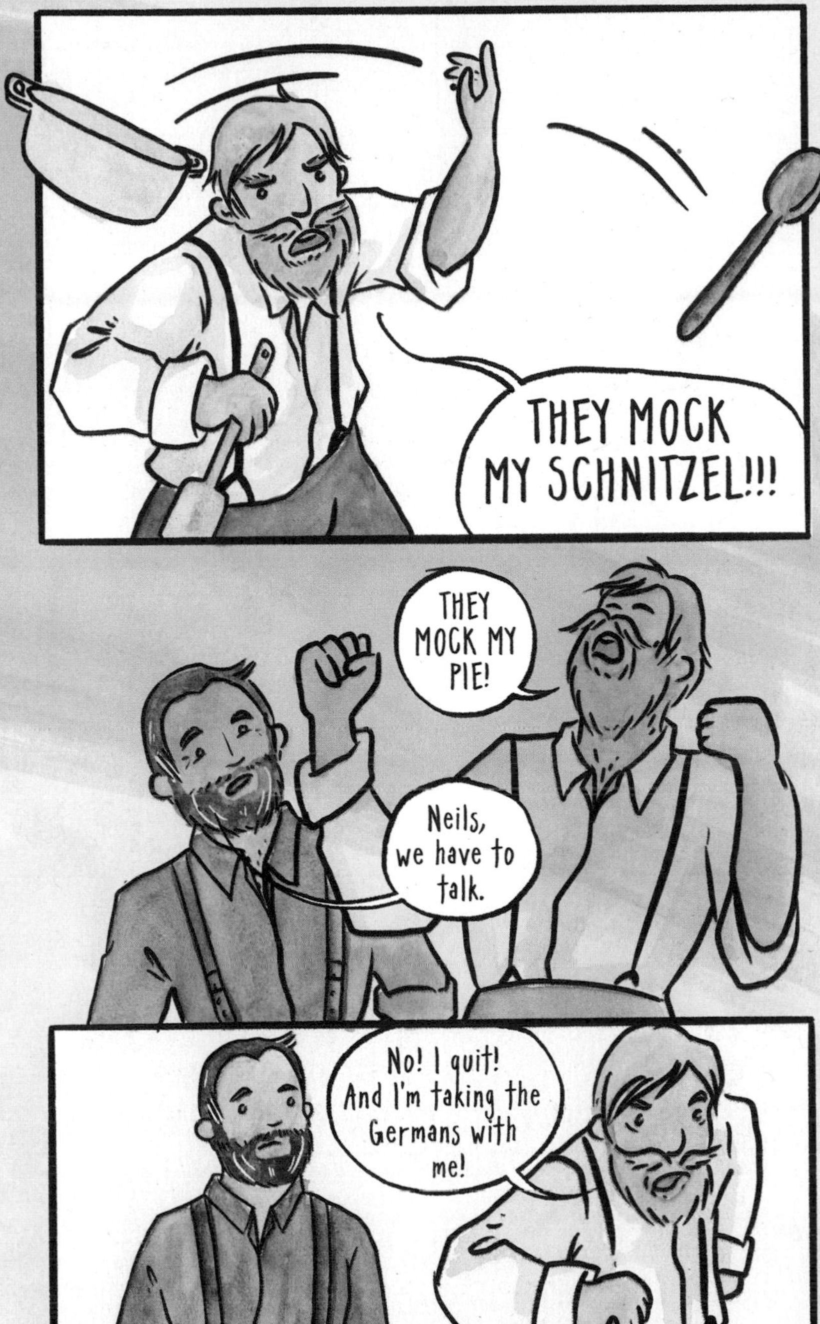
THEY MOCK MY SCHNITZEL!!!
THEY MOCK MY PIE!
Neils, we have to talk.
No! I quit! And I'm taking the Germans with me!

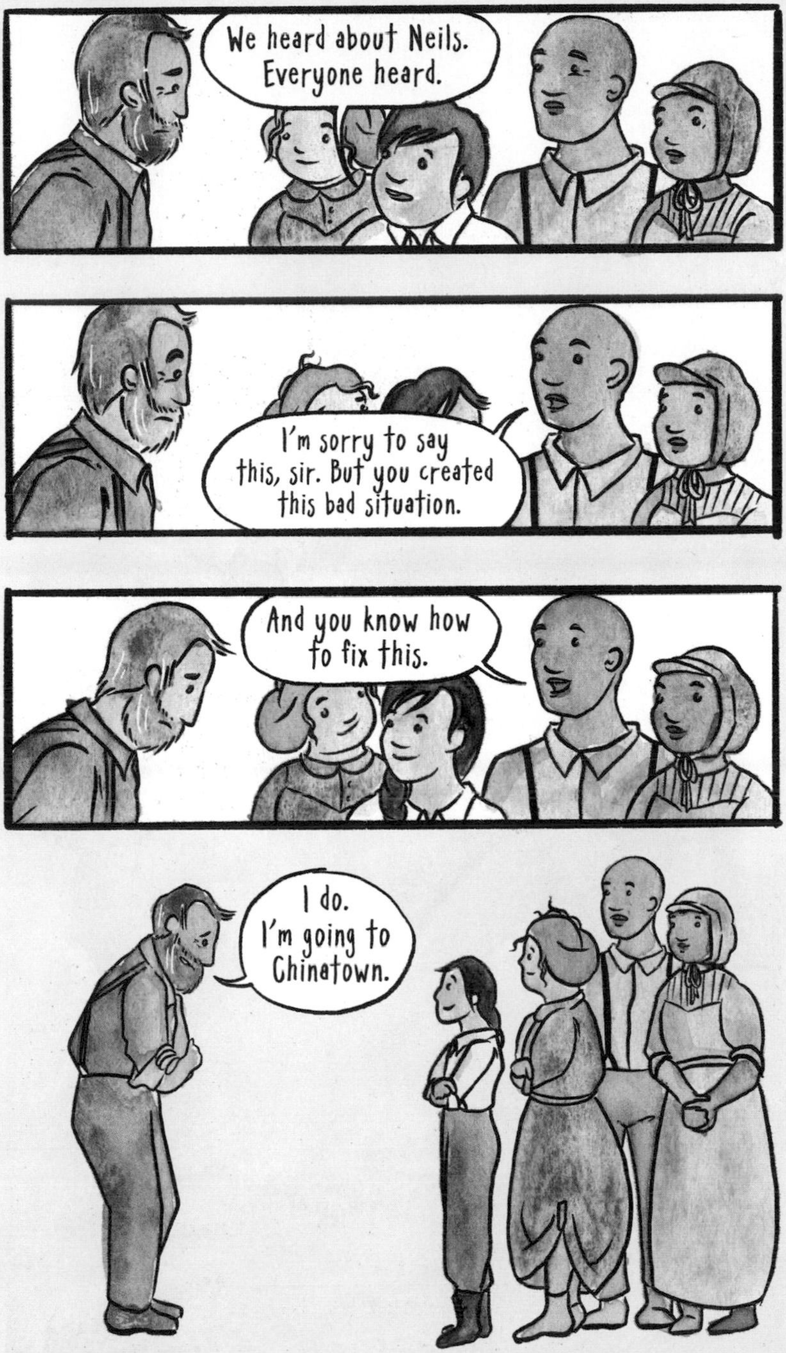
We heard about Neils. Everyone heard.
I'm sorry to say this, sir. But you created this bad situation.
And you know how to fix this.
I do. I'm going to Chinatown.

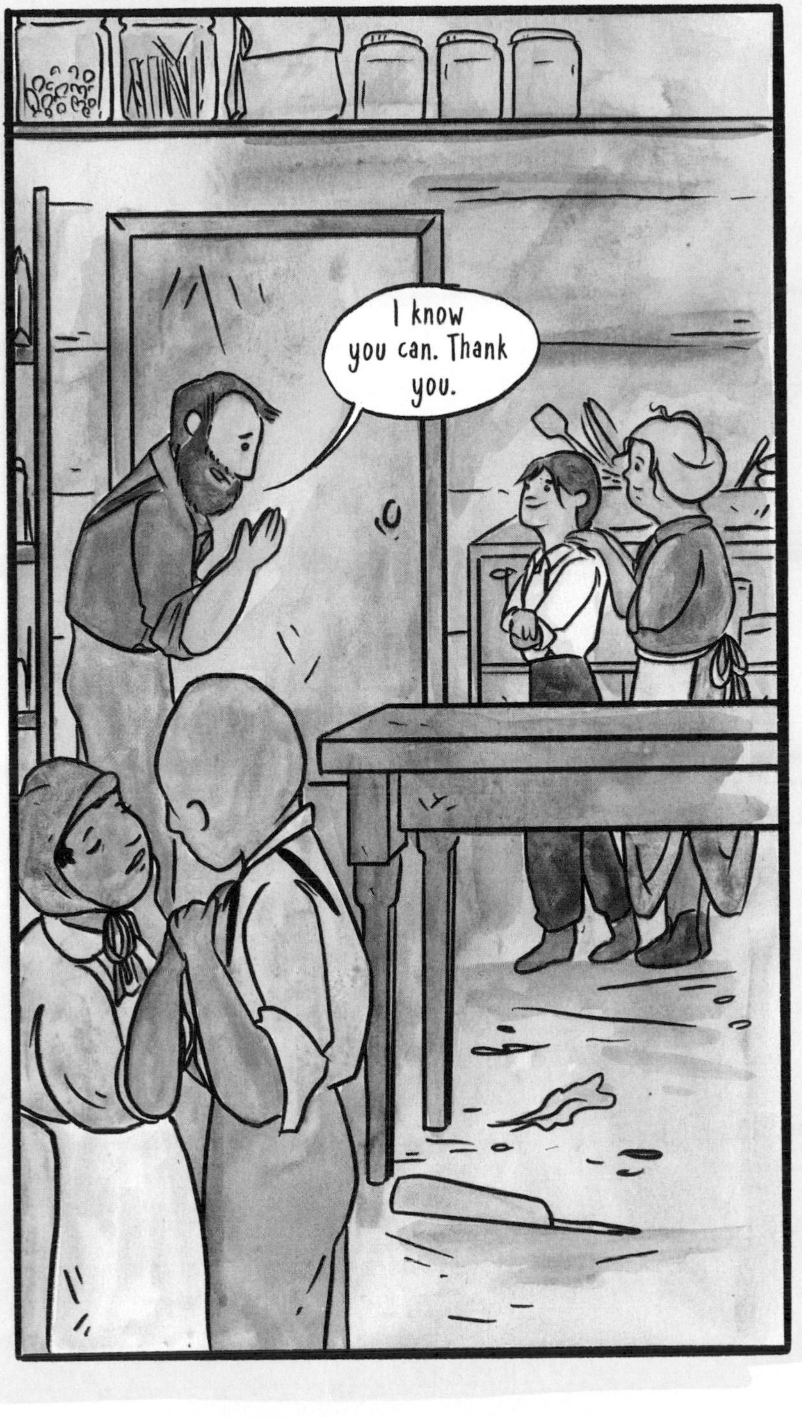
I know you can. Thank you.

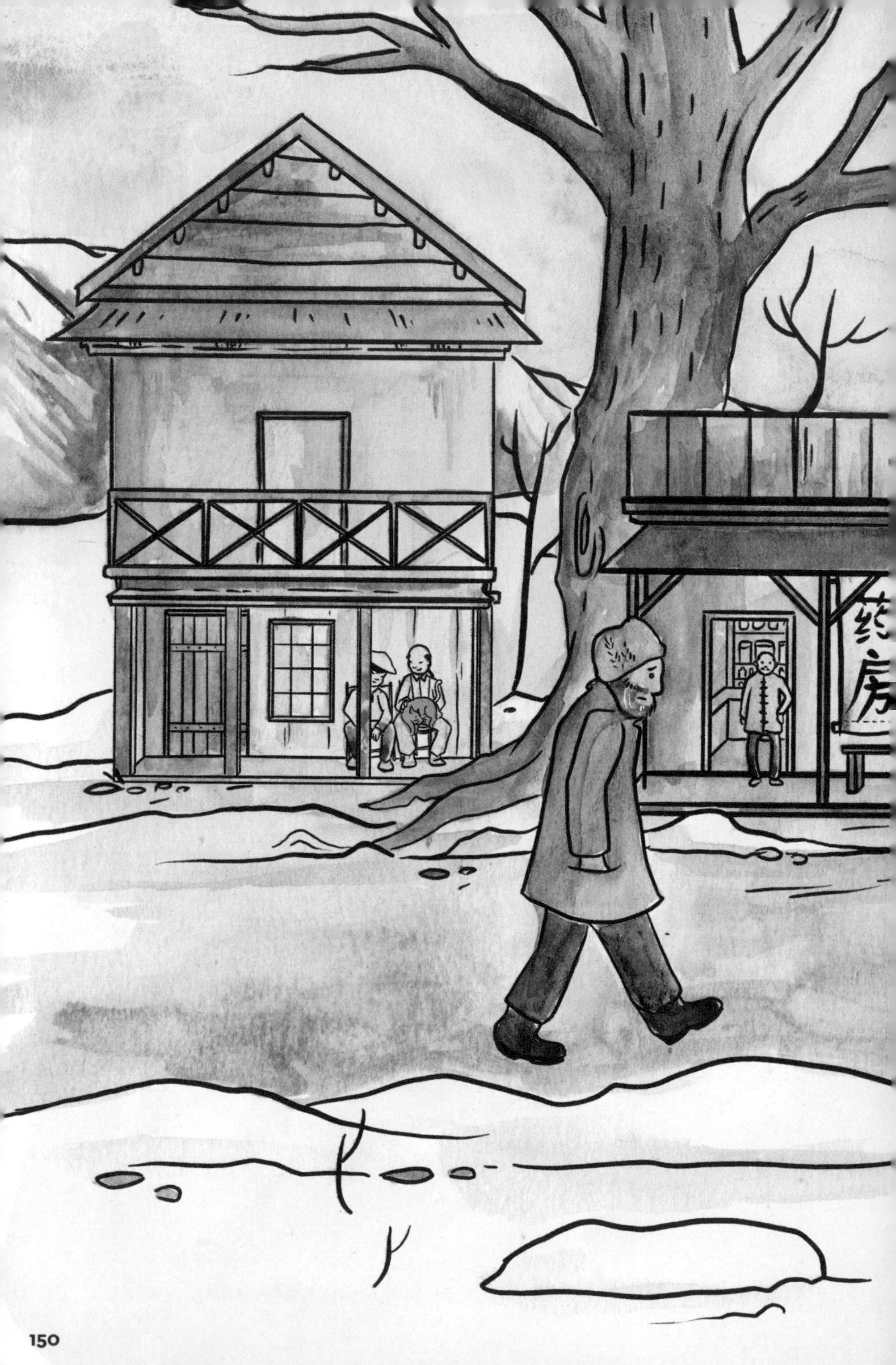
房

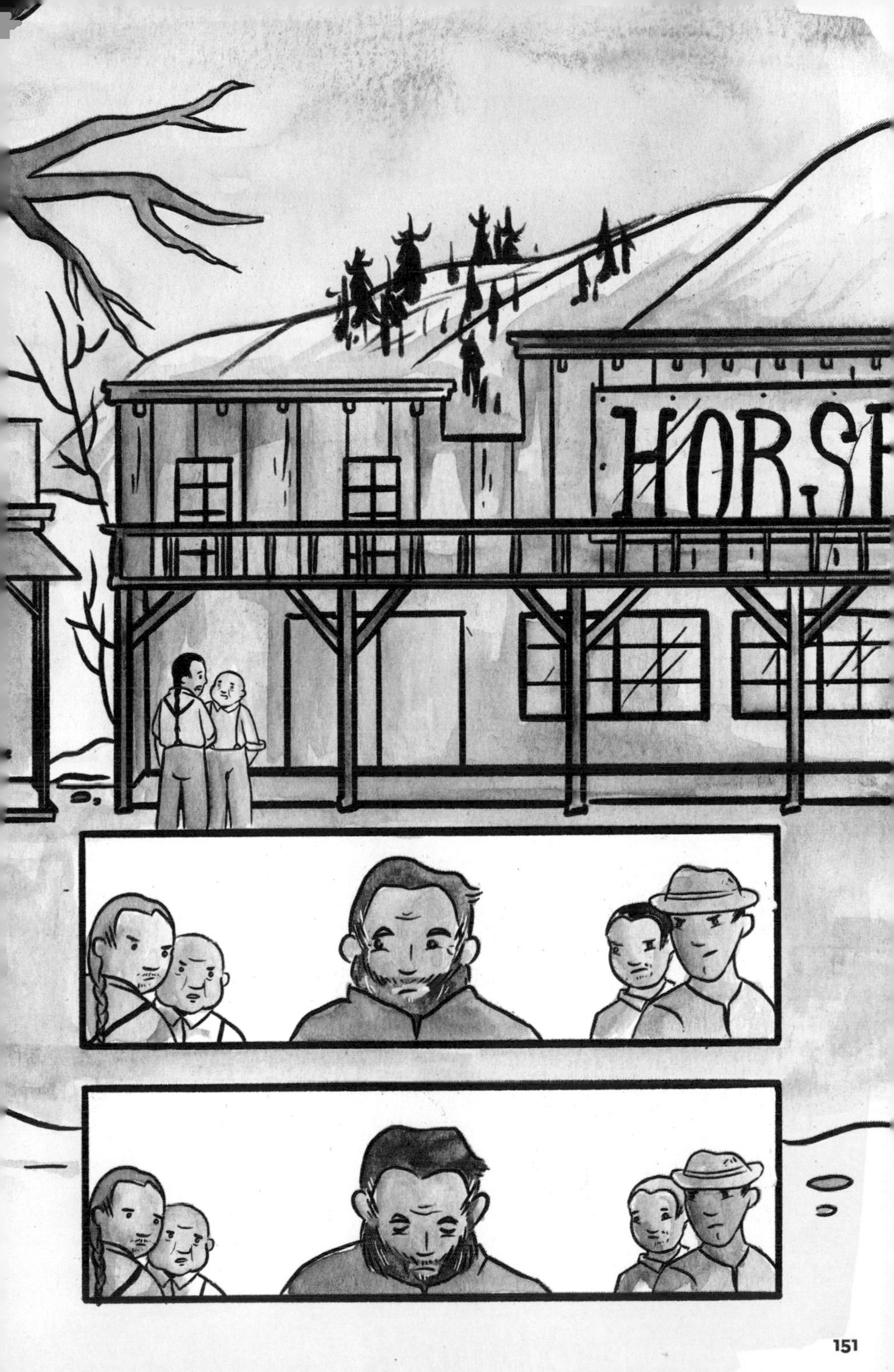
HORS

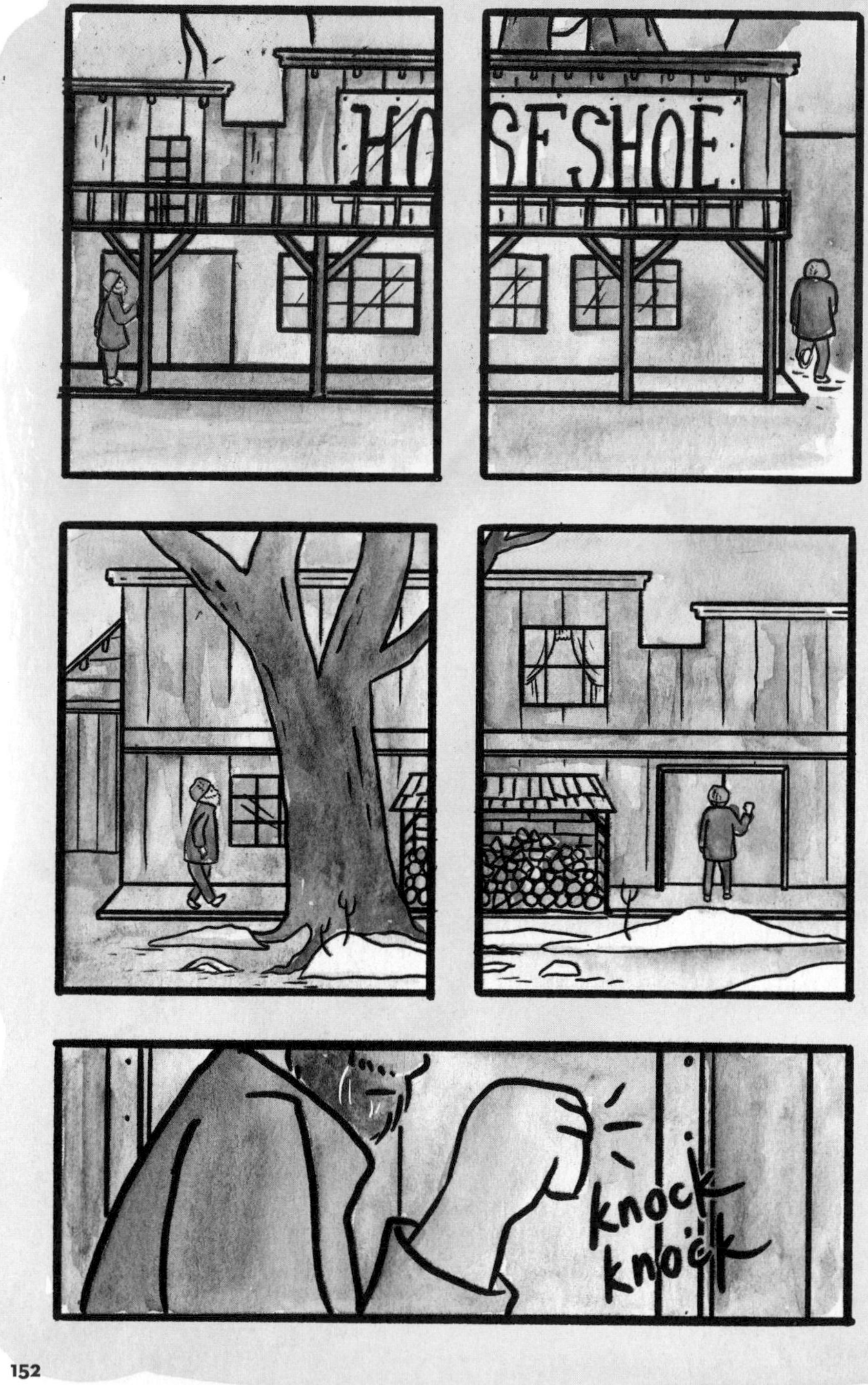
HO SESHOE
knock
knock

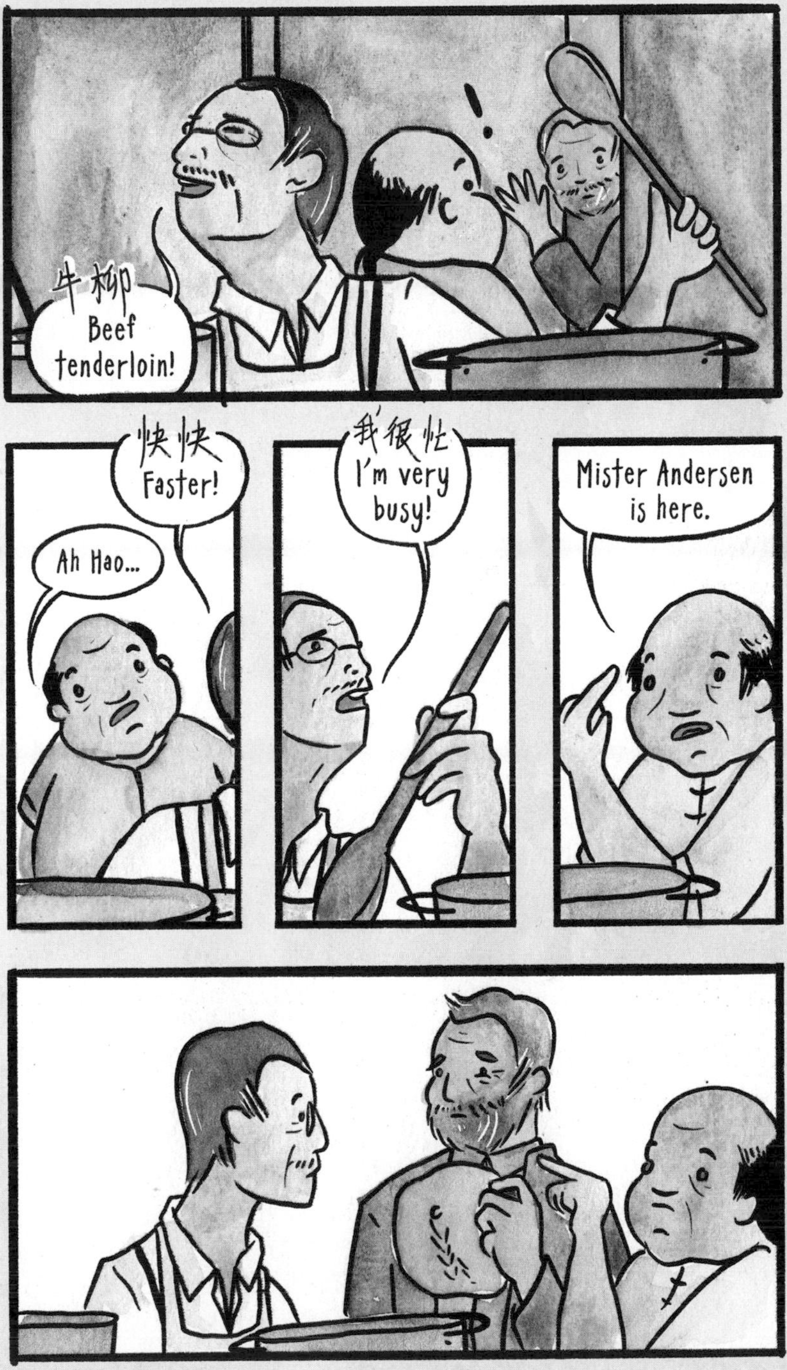

牛柳
Beef tenderloin!
快快
Faster!
Ah Hao...
我很忙
I'm very busy!
Mister Andersen is here.

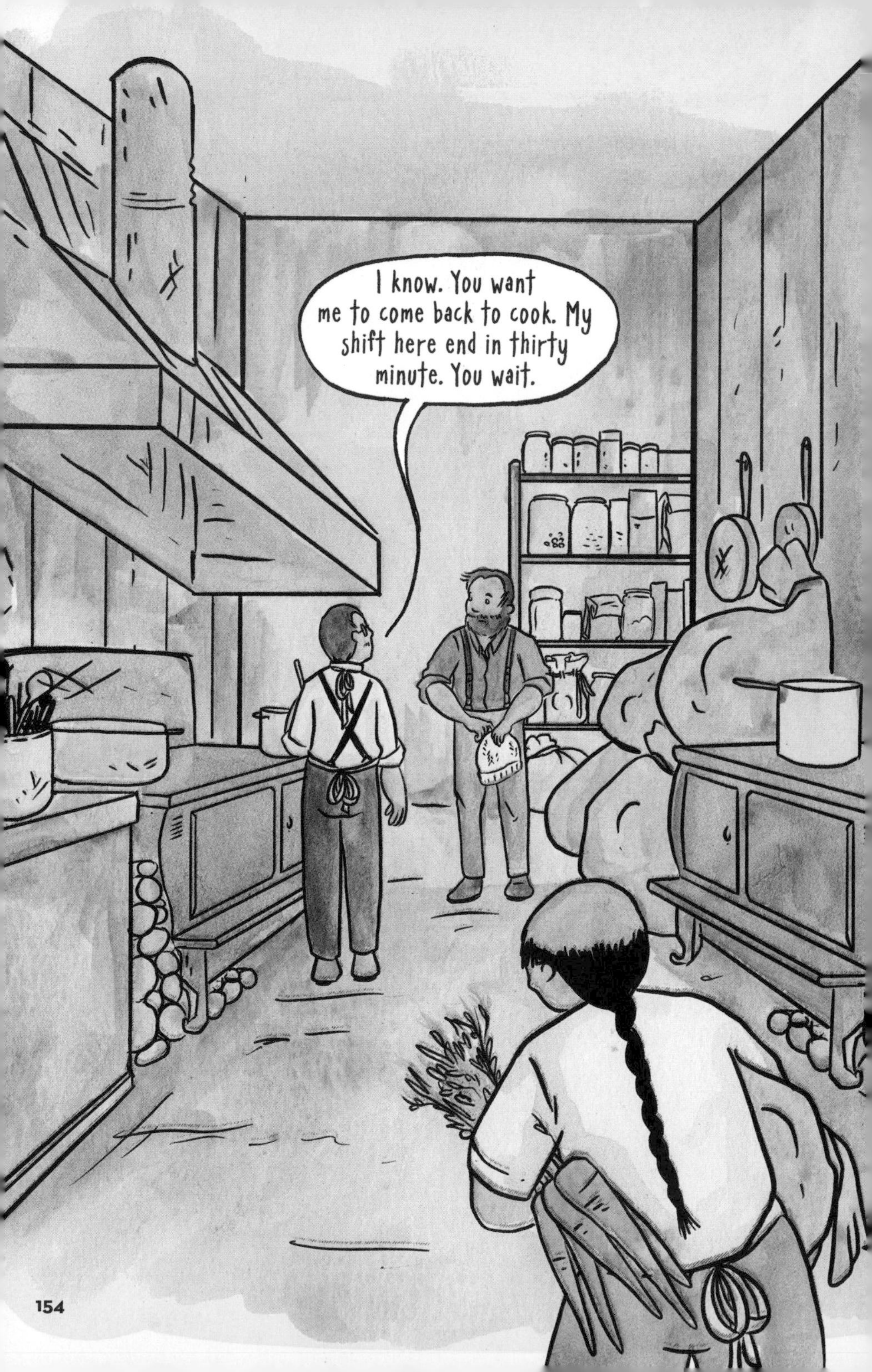
I know. You want me to come back to cook. My shift here end in thirty minute. You wait.

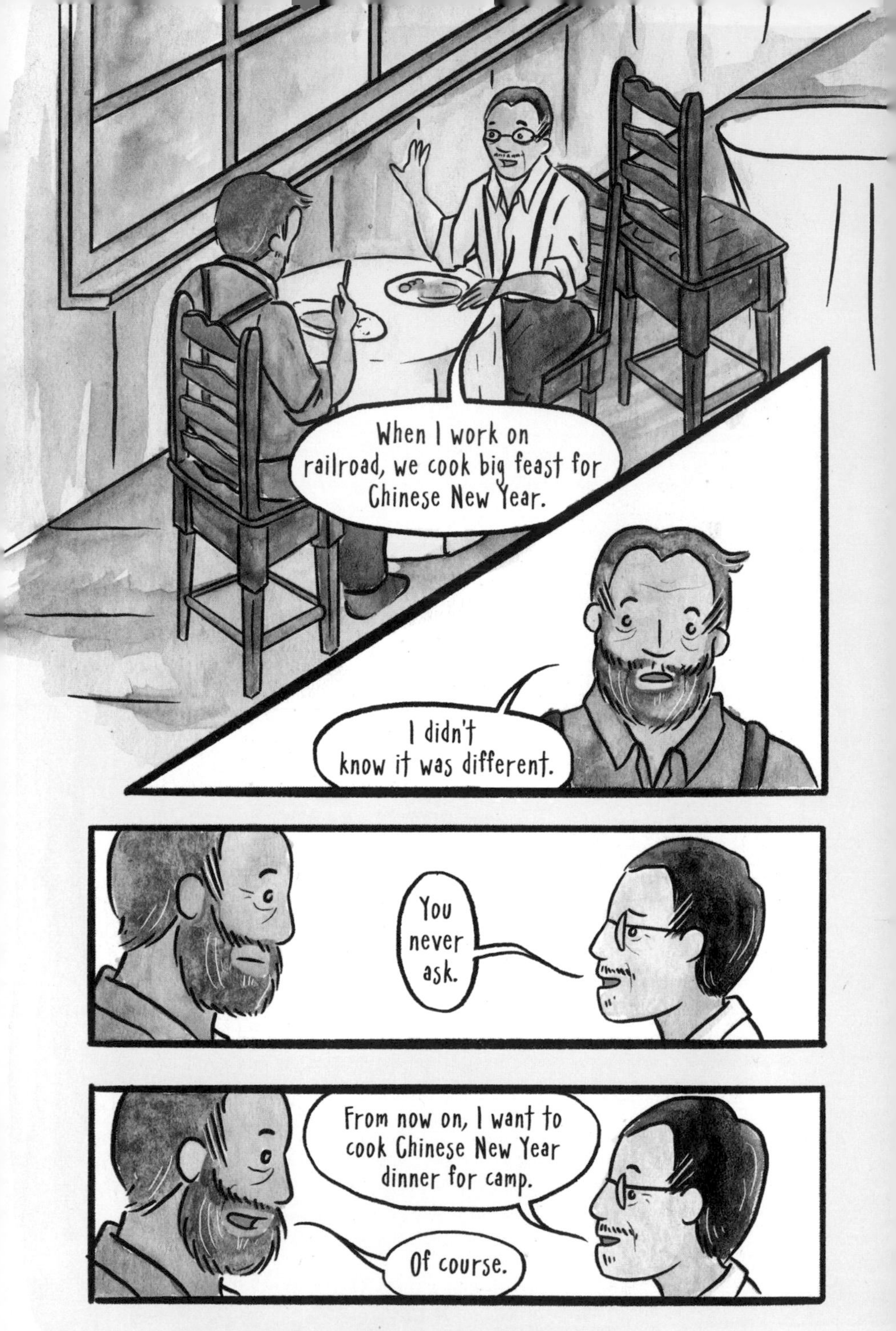

When I work on railroad, we cook big feast for Chinese New Year.
I didn't know it was different.
You never ask.
From now on, I want to cook Chinese New Year dinner for camp.
Of course.

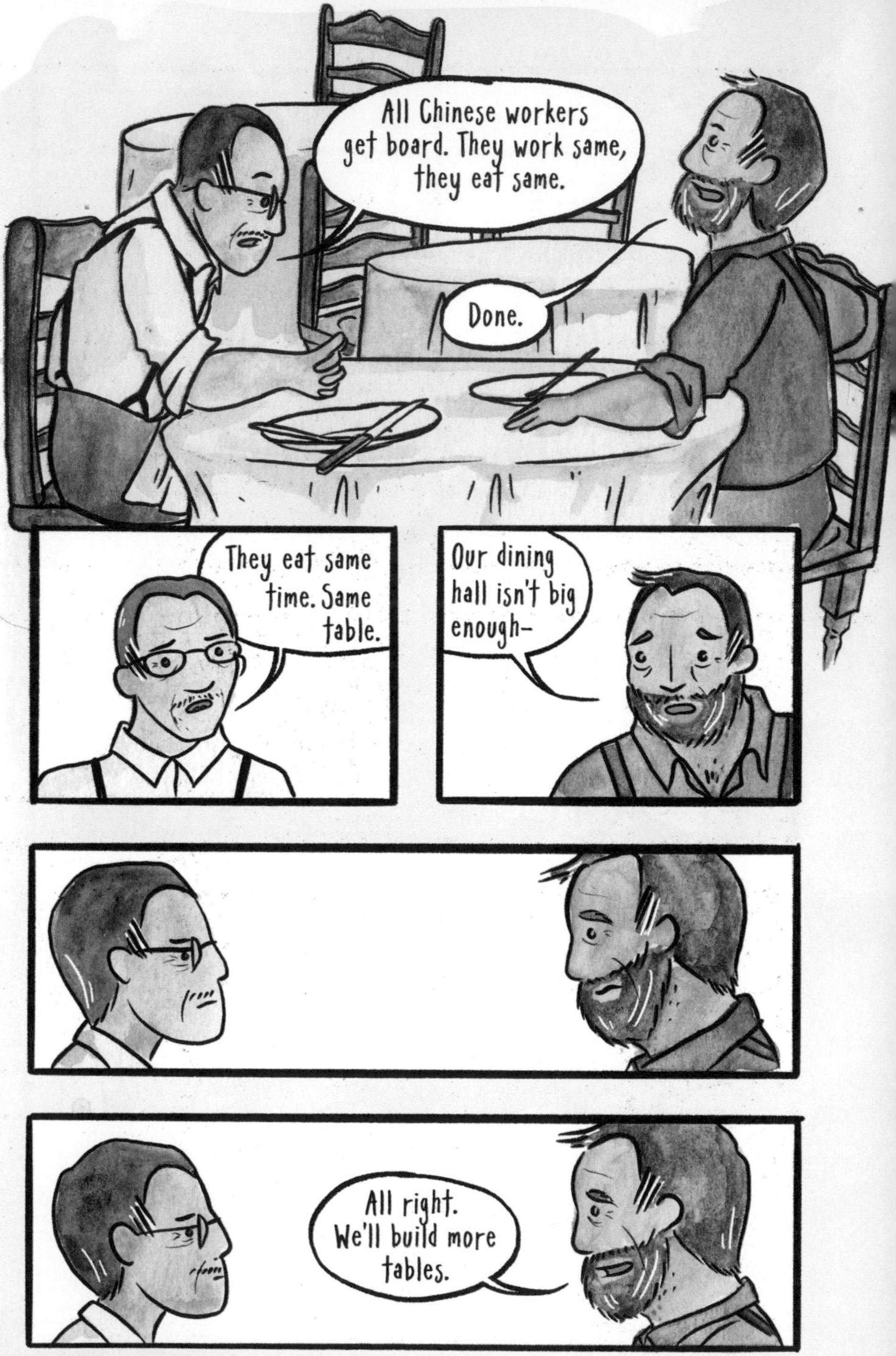
All Chinese workers get board. They work same, they eat same.
Done.
They eat same time. Same table.
Our dining hall isn't big enough–
All right. We'll build more tables.

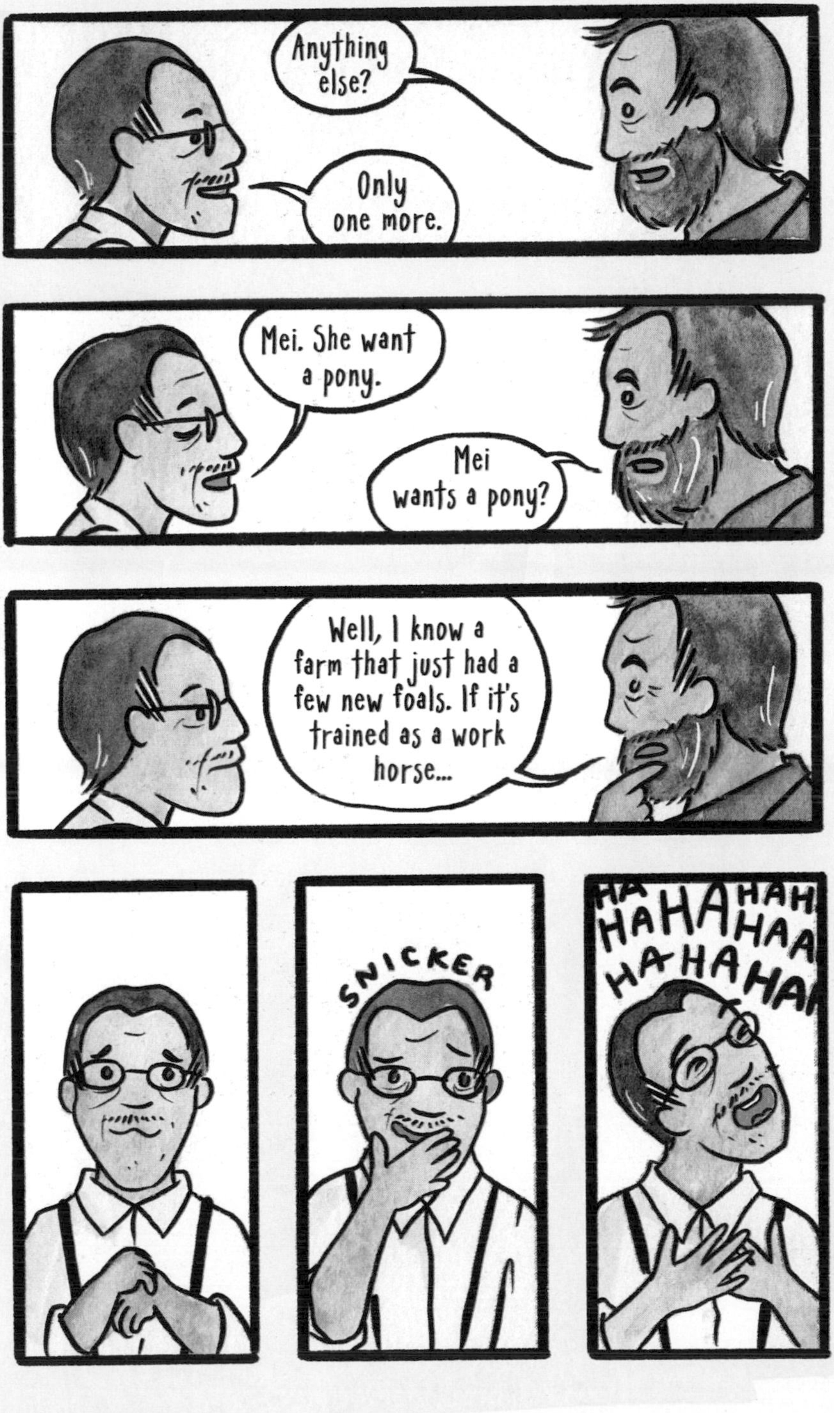
Anything else?
Only one more.
Mei. She want a pony.
Mei wants a pony?
Well, I know a farm that just had a few new foals. If it's trained as a work horse...
SNICKER
HAHAHAHAHAHAHAHAHAHAHA

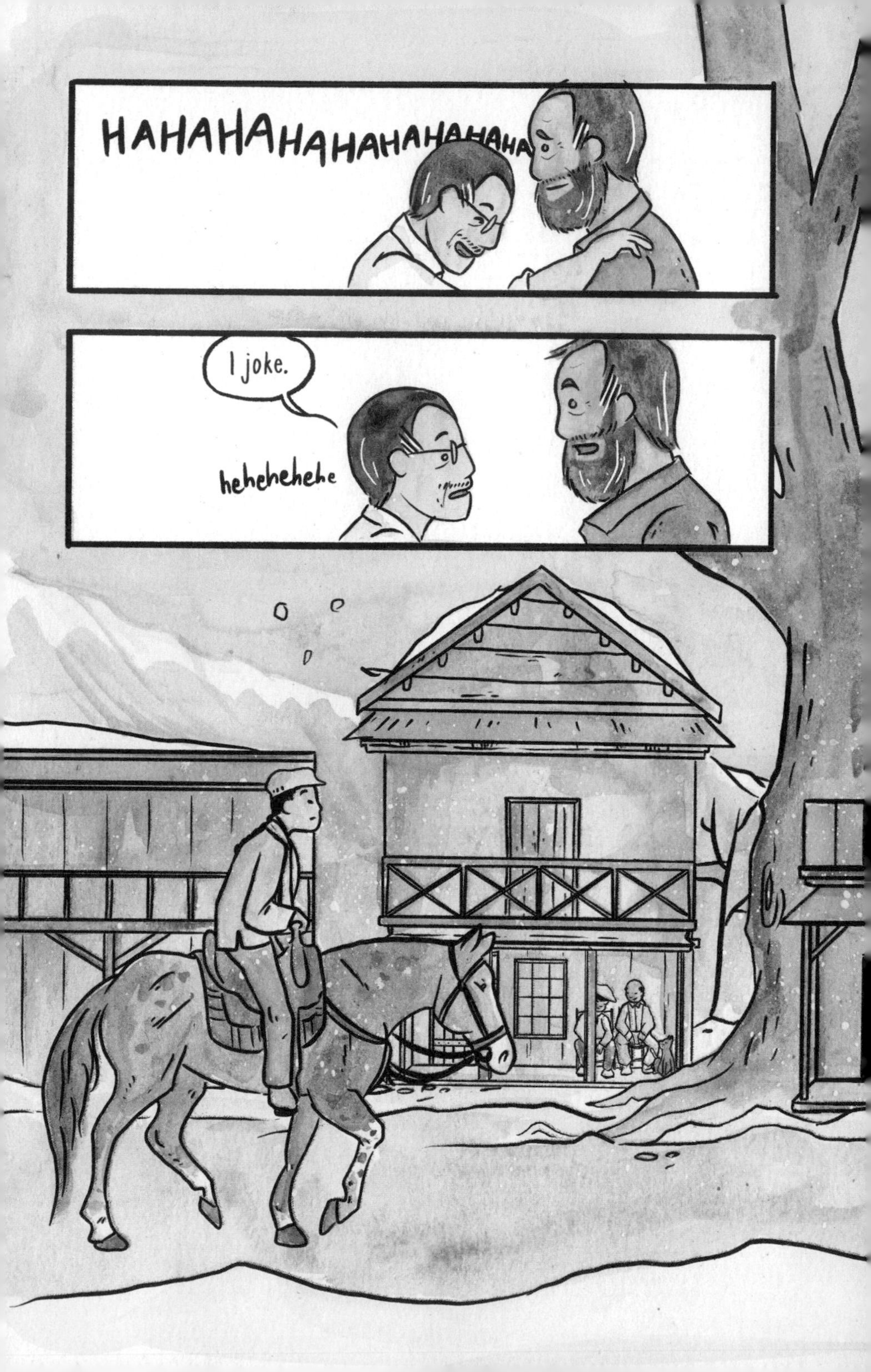
HAHAHAHAHAHAHAHAHAHA
I joke.
hehehehehe

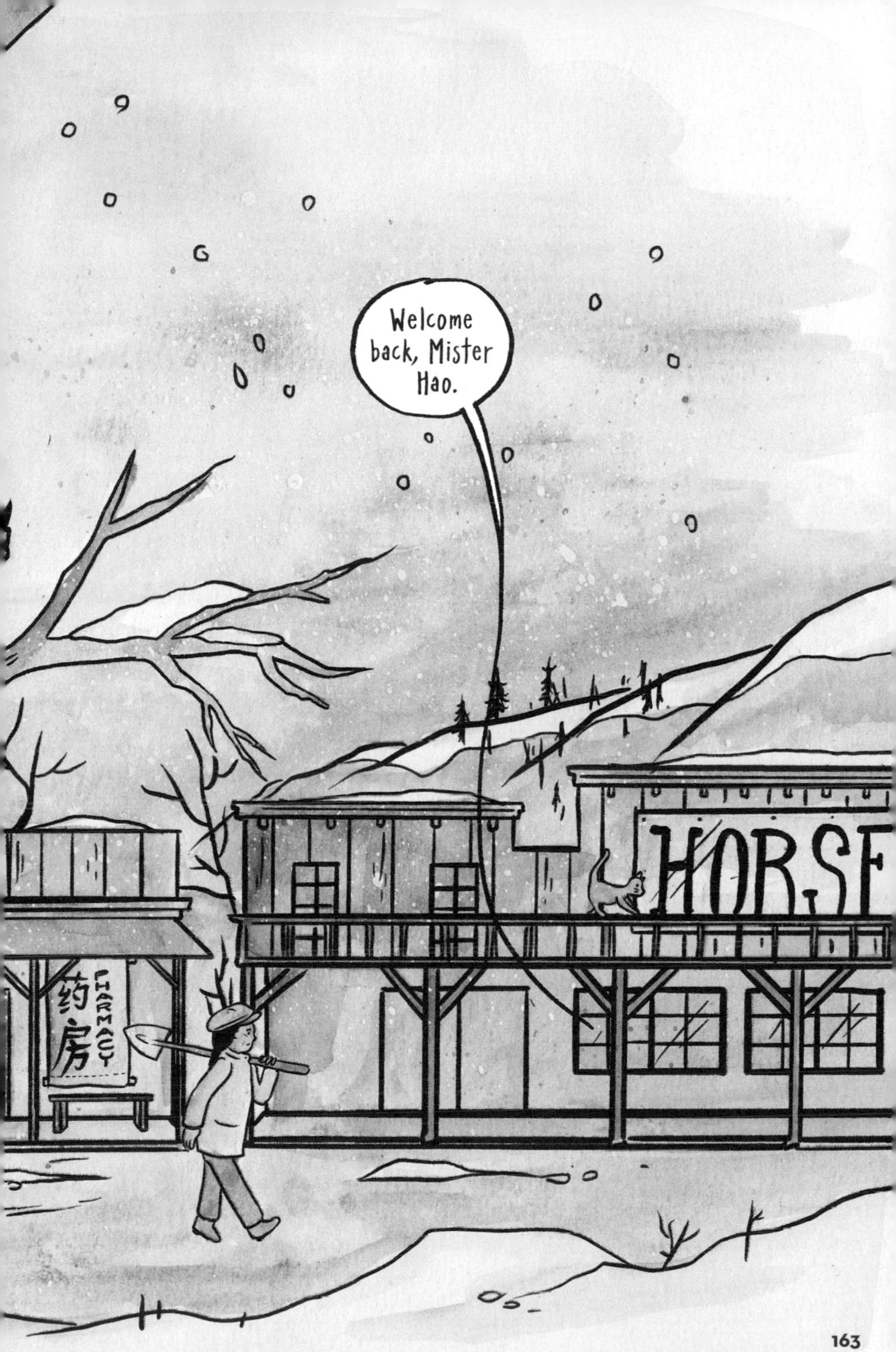
Welcome back, Mister Hao.
HORSE
药房
PHARMACY

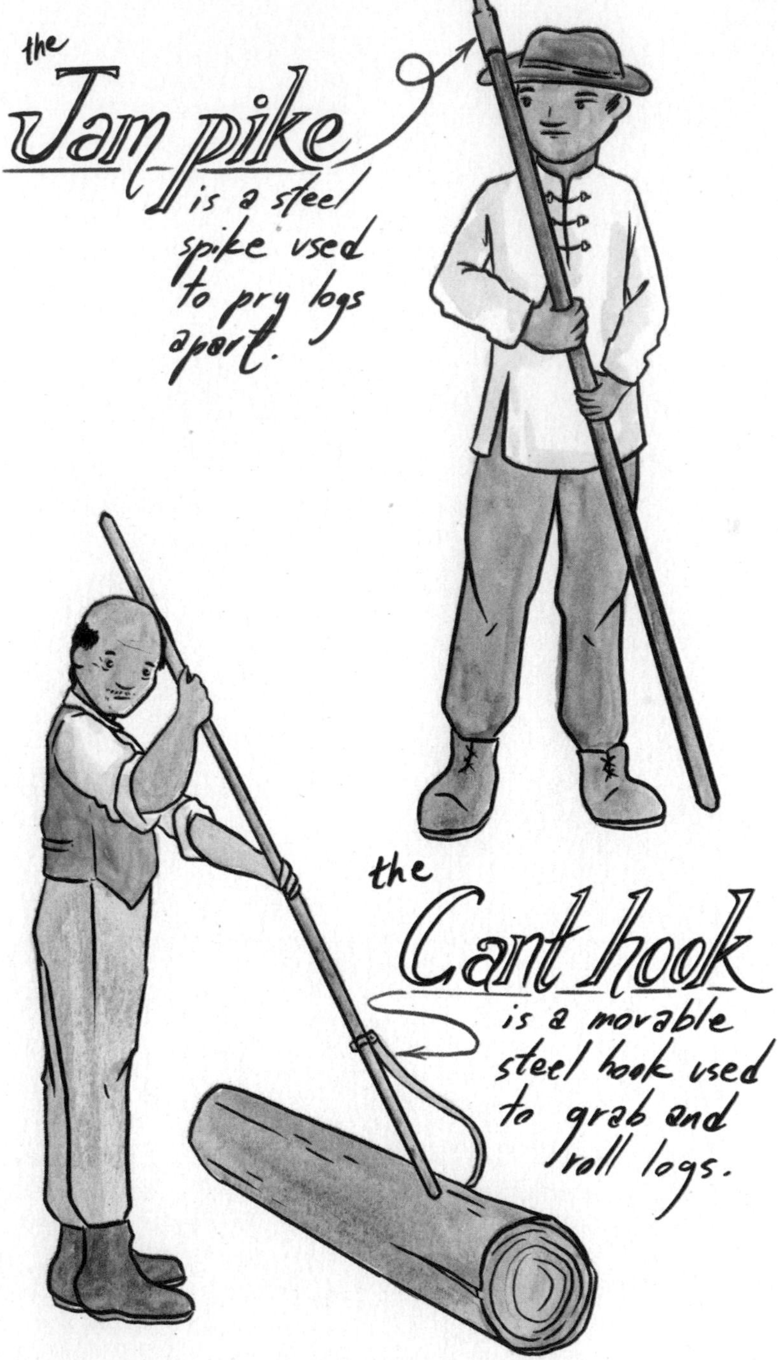
the Jam pike
is a steel spike used to pry logs apart.
the Cant hook
is a movable steel hook used to grab and roll logs.

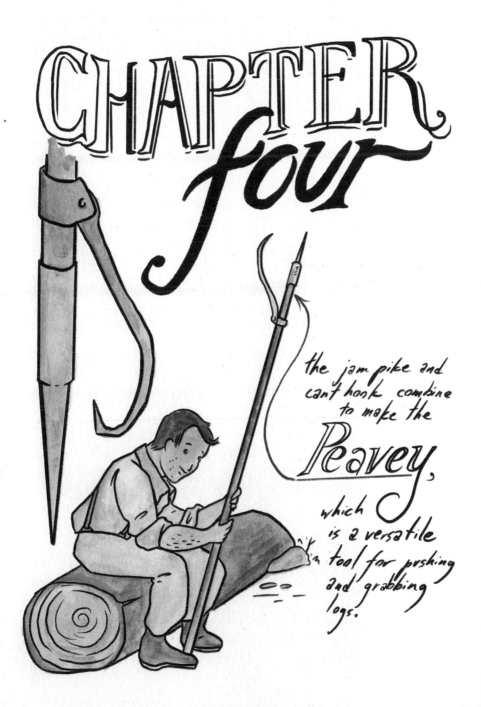

CHAPTER four

the jam pike and cant hook combine to make the

Peavey,

which is a versatile tool for pushing and grabbing logs.

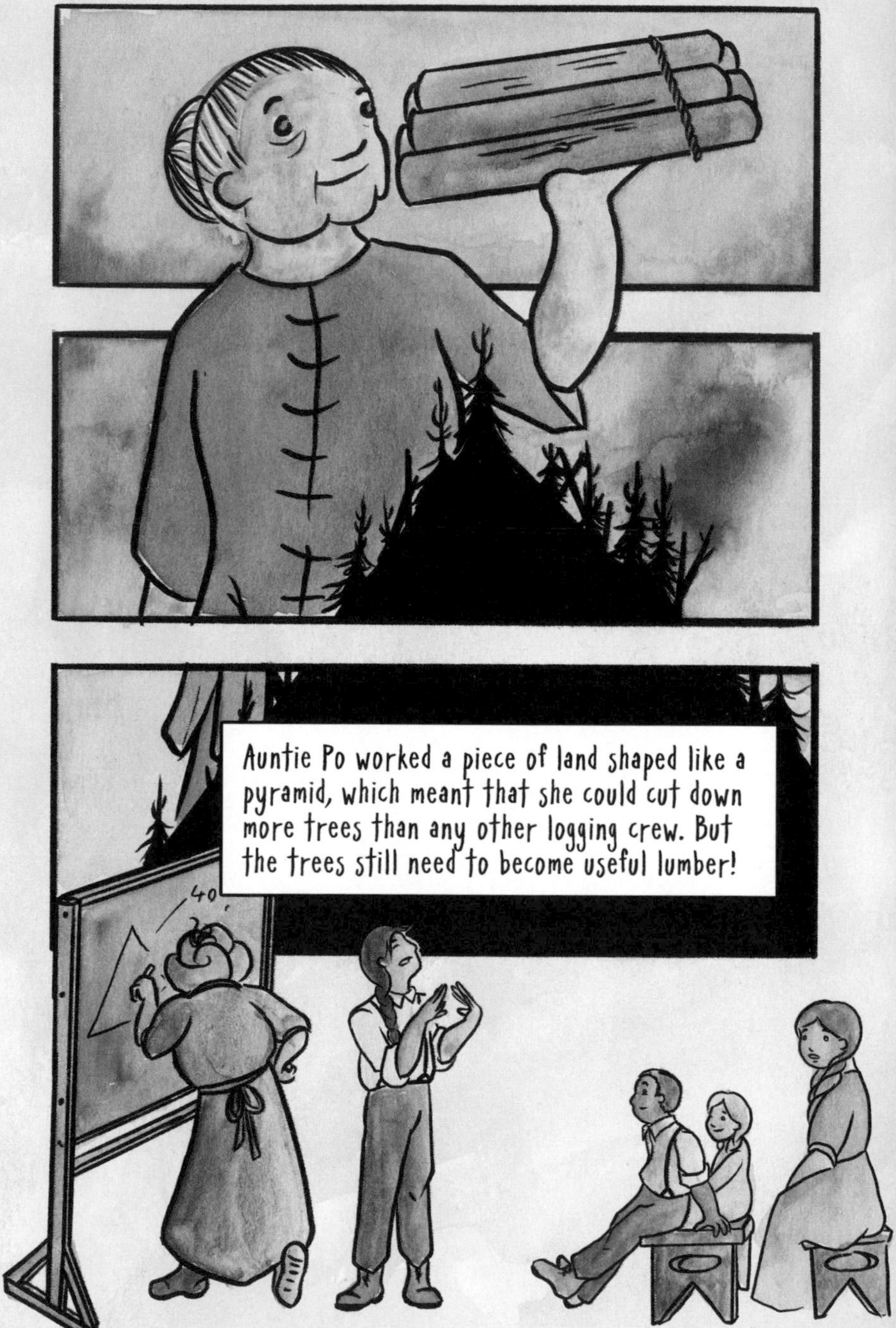
Auntie Po worked a piece of land shaped like a pyramid, which meant that she could cut down more trees than any other logging crew. But the trees still need to become useful lumber!
40

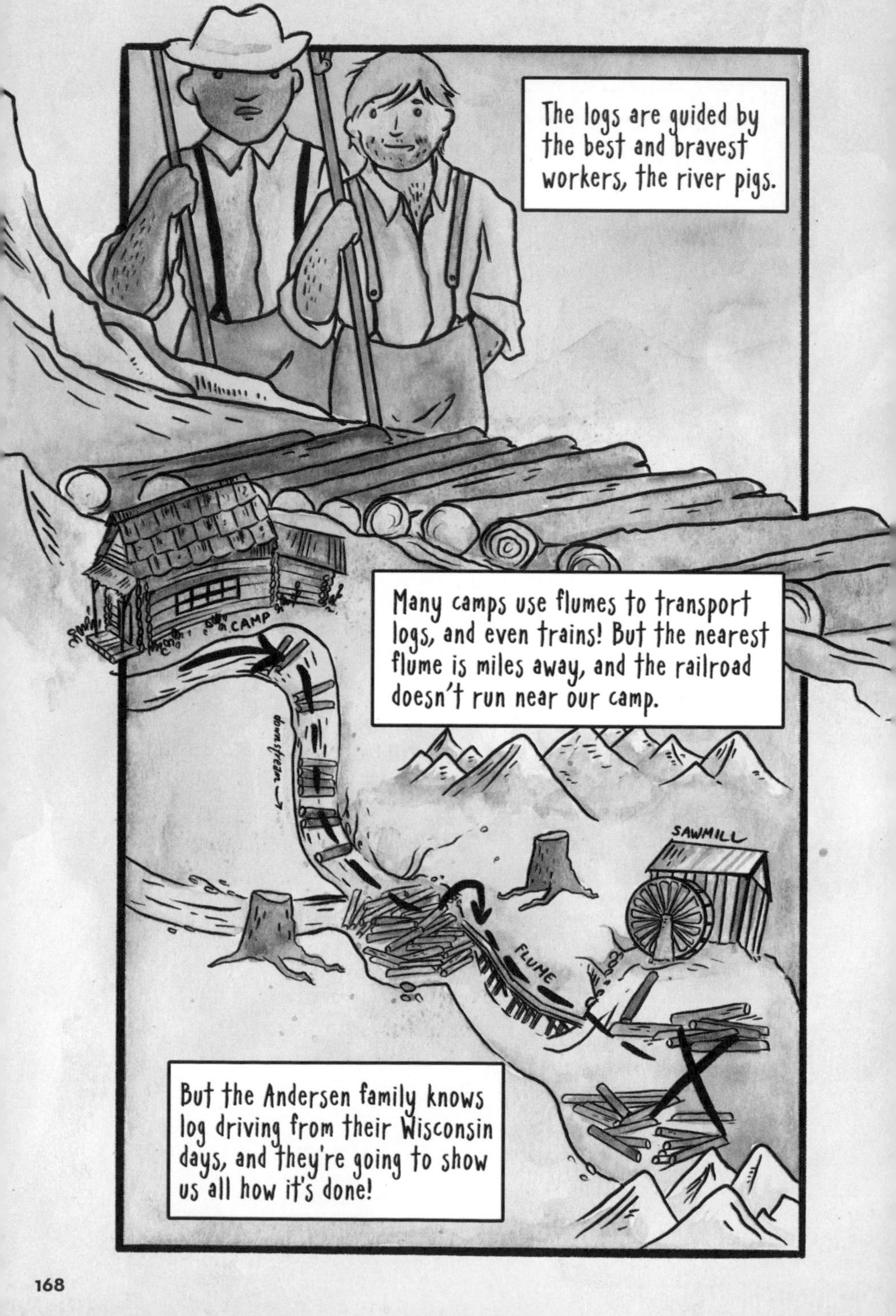
The logs are guided by the best and bravest workers, the river pigs.
Many camps use flumes to transport logs, and even trains! But the nearest flume is miles away, and the railroad doesn't run near our camp.
CAMP
downstream
SAWMILL
FLUME
But the Andersen family knows log driving from their Wisconsin days, and they're going to show us all how it's done!

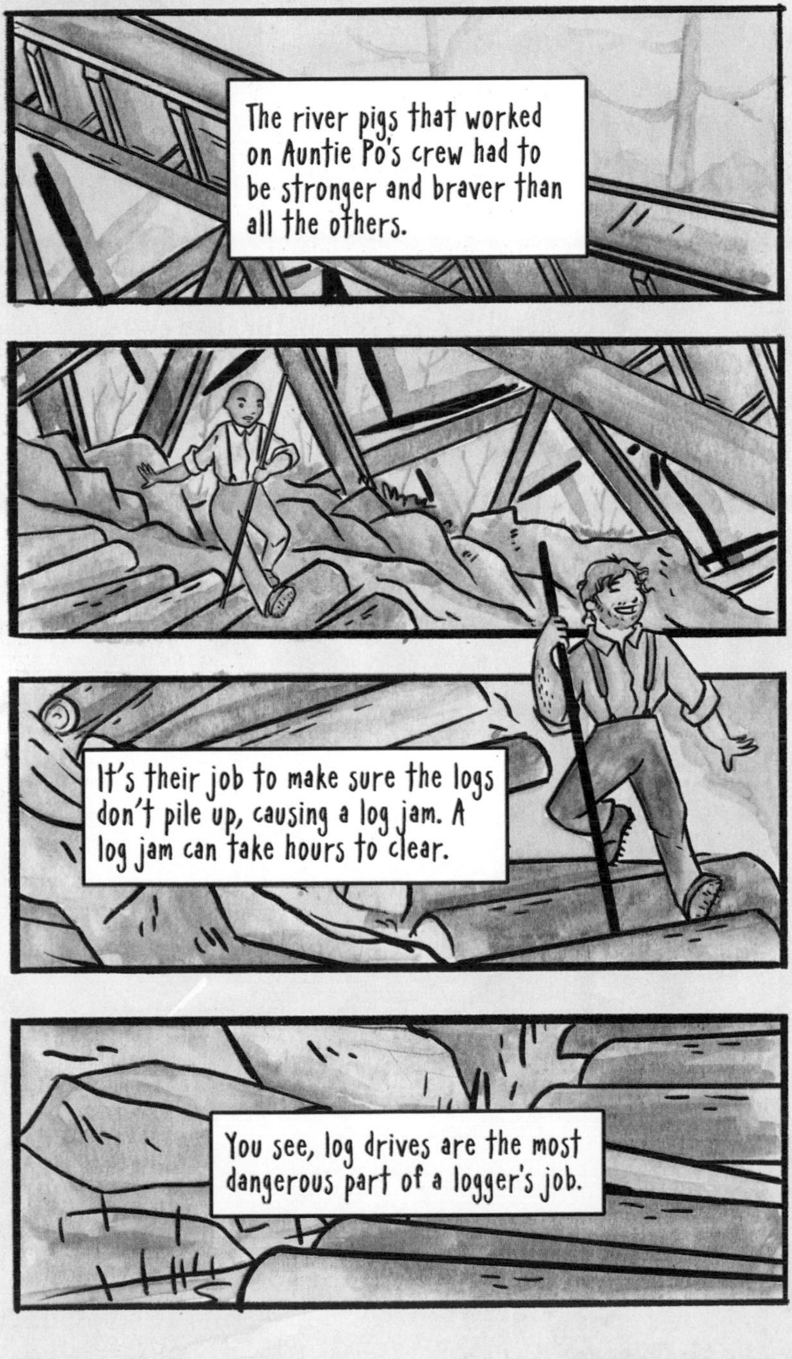
The river pigs that worked on Auntie Po's crew had to be stronger and braver than all the others.
It's their job to make sure the logs don't pile up, causing a log jam. A log jam can take hours to clear.
You see, log drives are the most dangerous part of a logger's job.

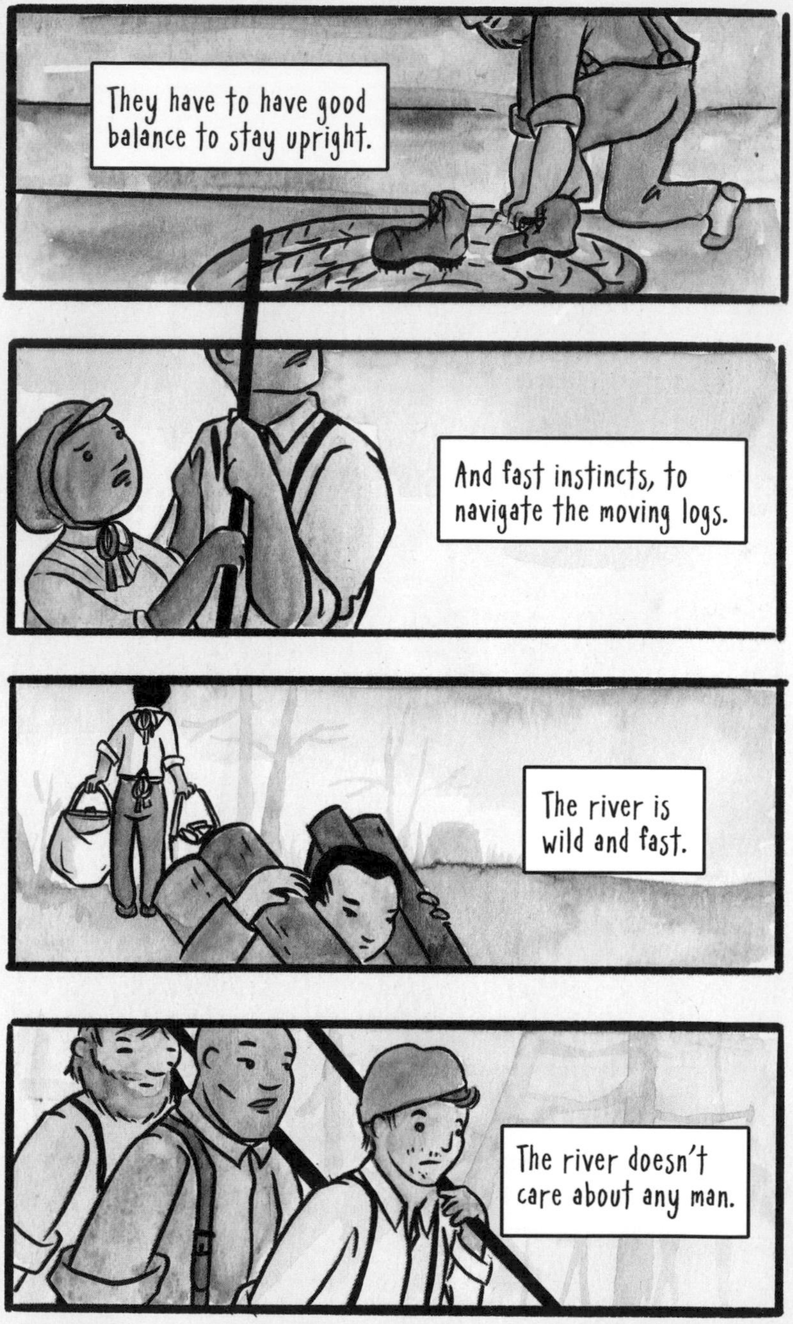
They have to have good balance to stay upright.
And fast instincts, to navigate the moving logs.
The river is wild and fast.
The river doesn't care about any man.

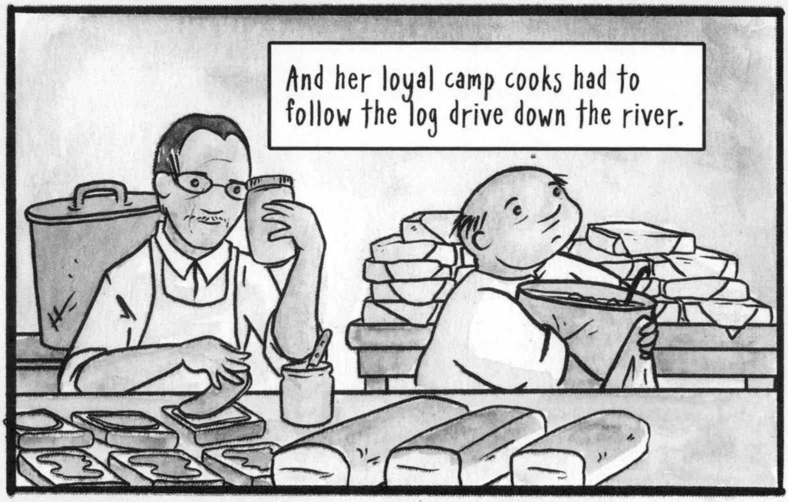
And her loyal camp cooks had to follow the log drive down the river.

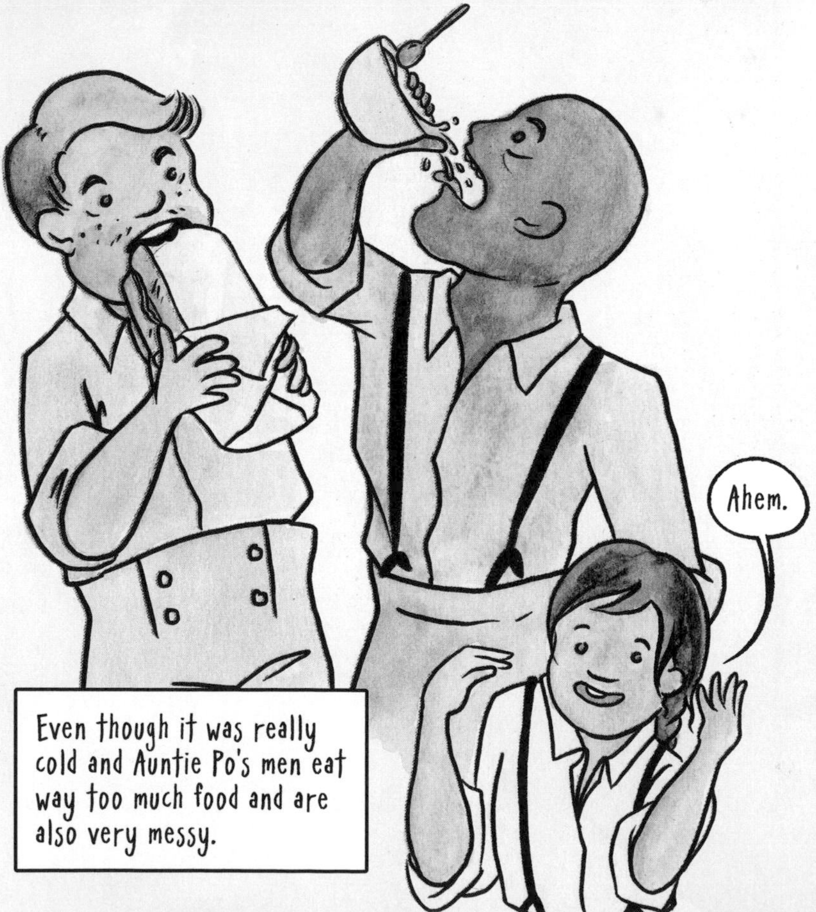
Even though it was really cold and Auntie Po's men eat way too much food and are also very messy.
Ahem.

173

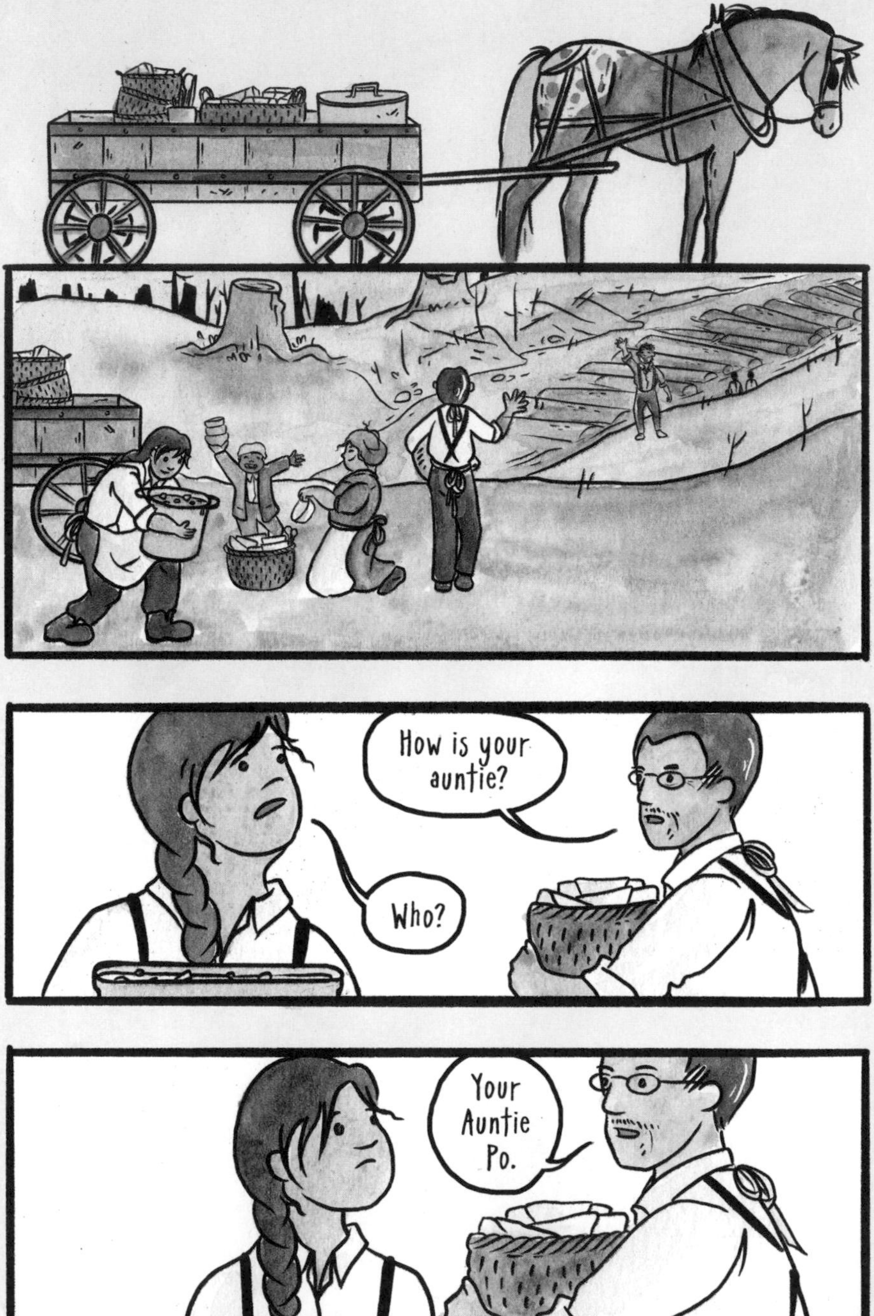
How is your auntie?
Who?
Your Auntie Po.

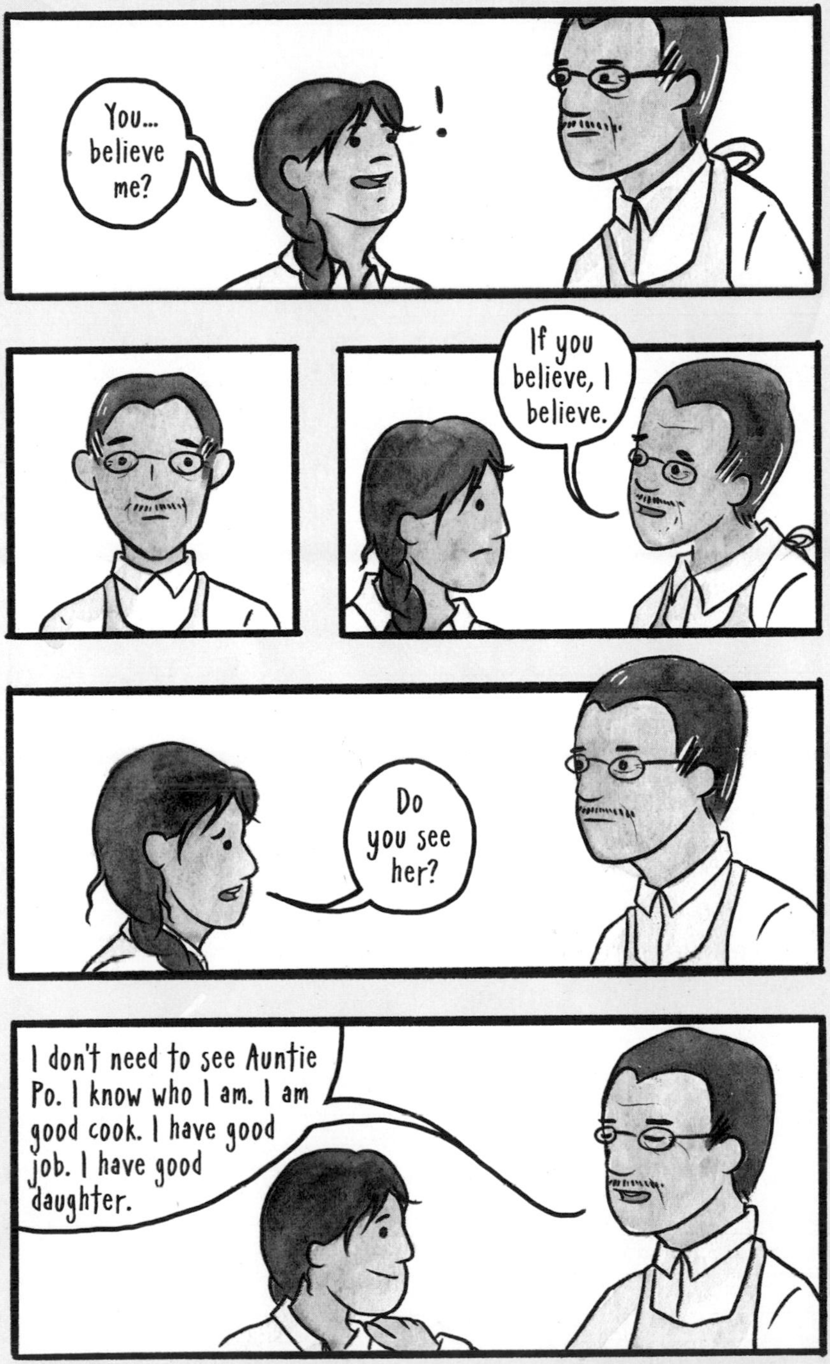
You... believe me?
!
If you believe, I believe.
Do you see her?
I don't need to see Auntie Po. I know who I am. I am good cook. I have good job. I have good daughter.

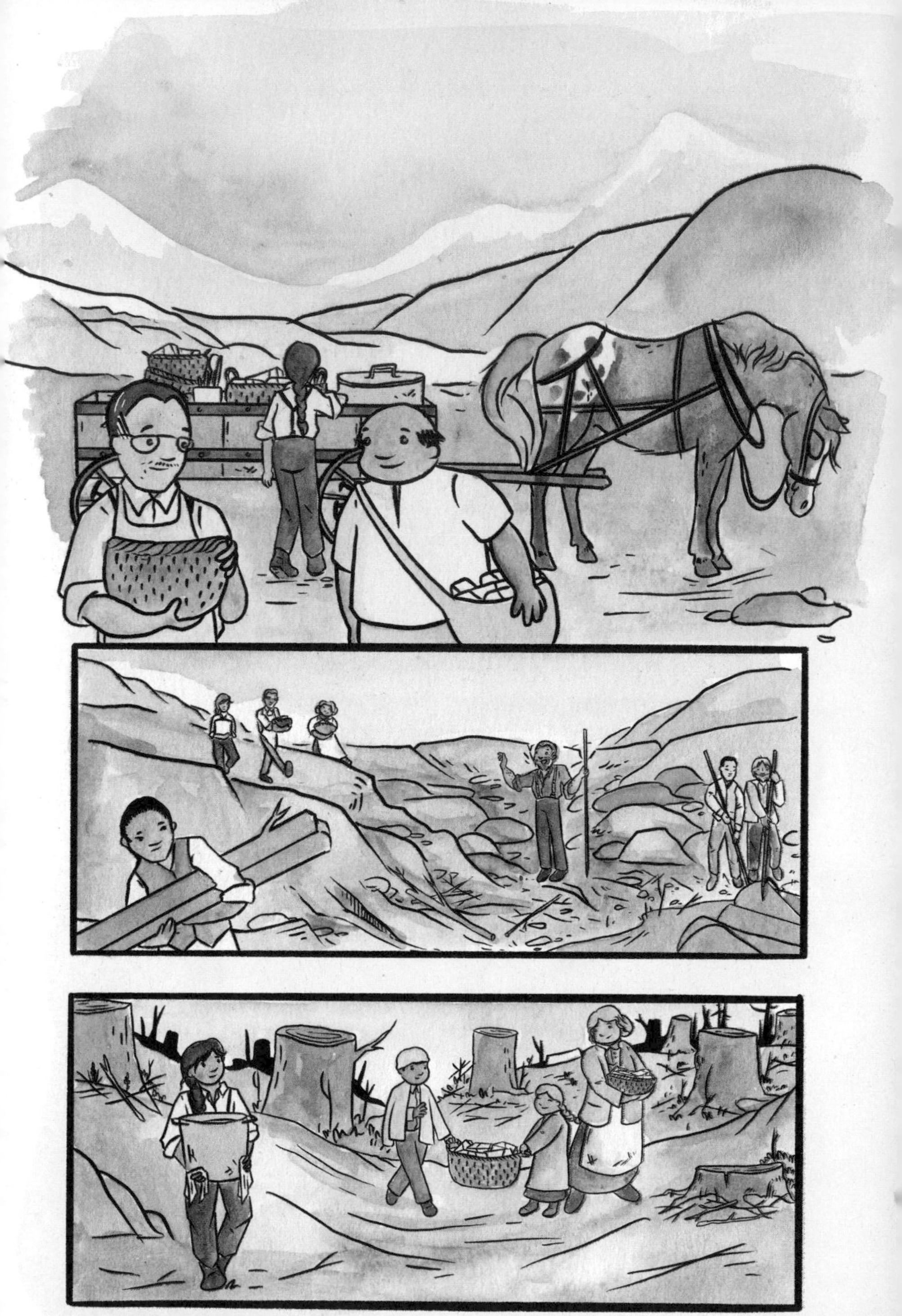

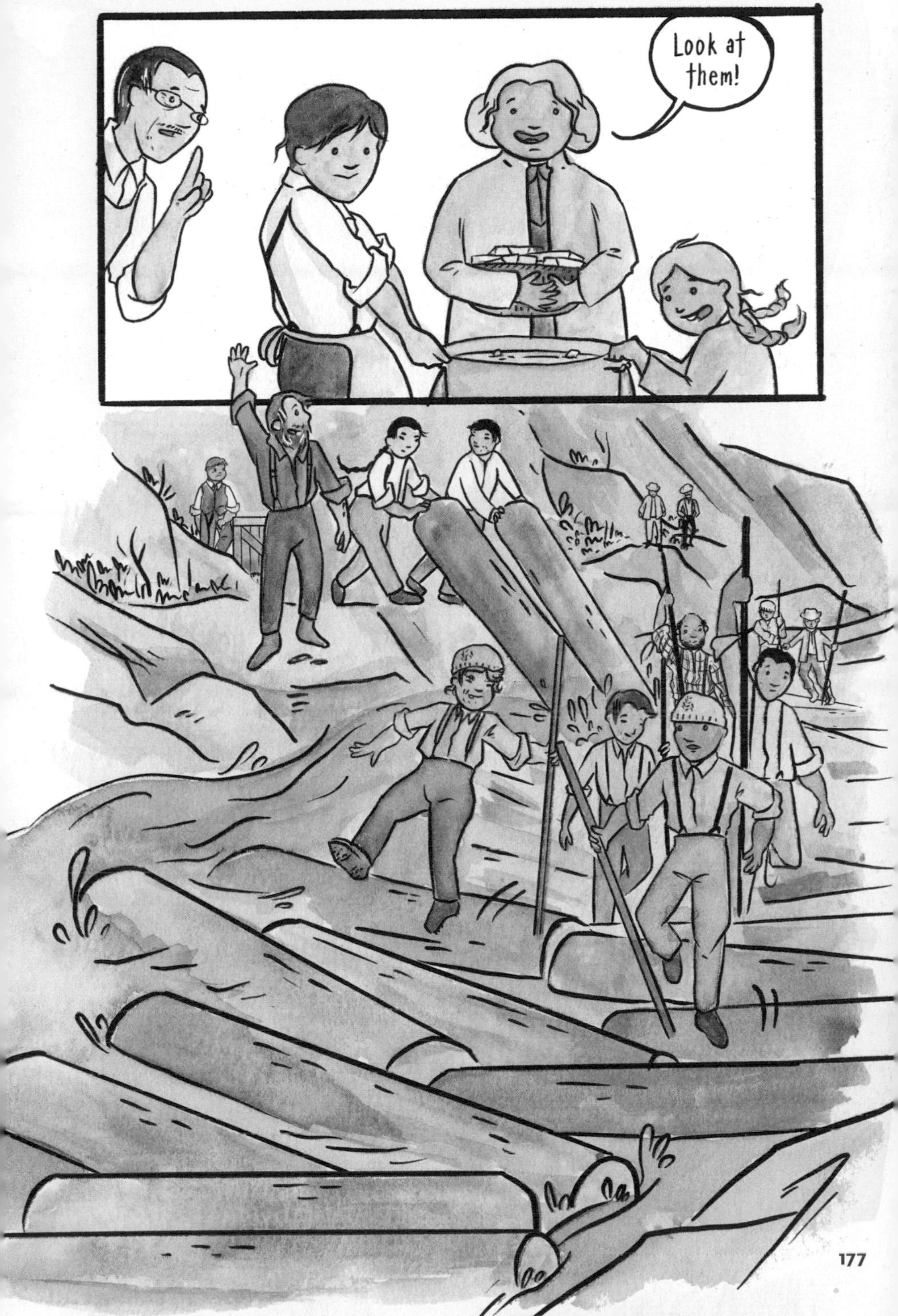
Look at them!

179

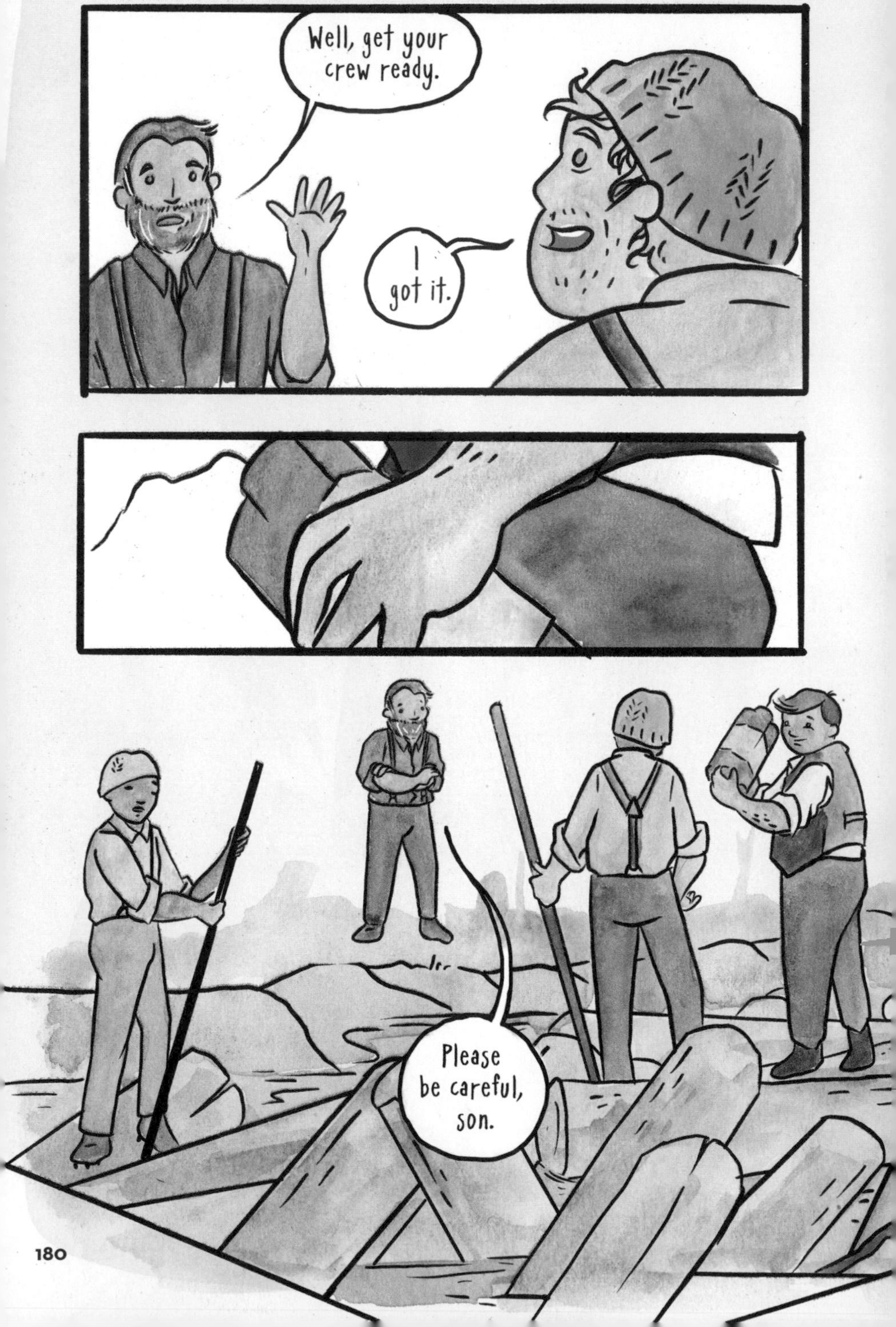
Well, get your crew ready.
I got it.
Please be careful, son.

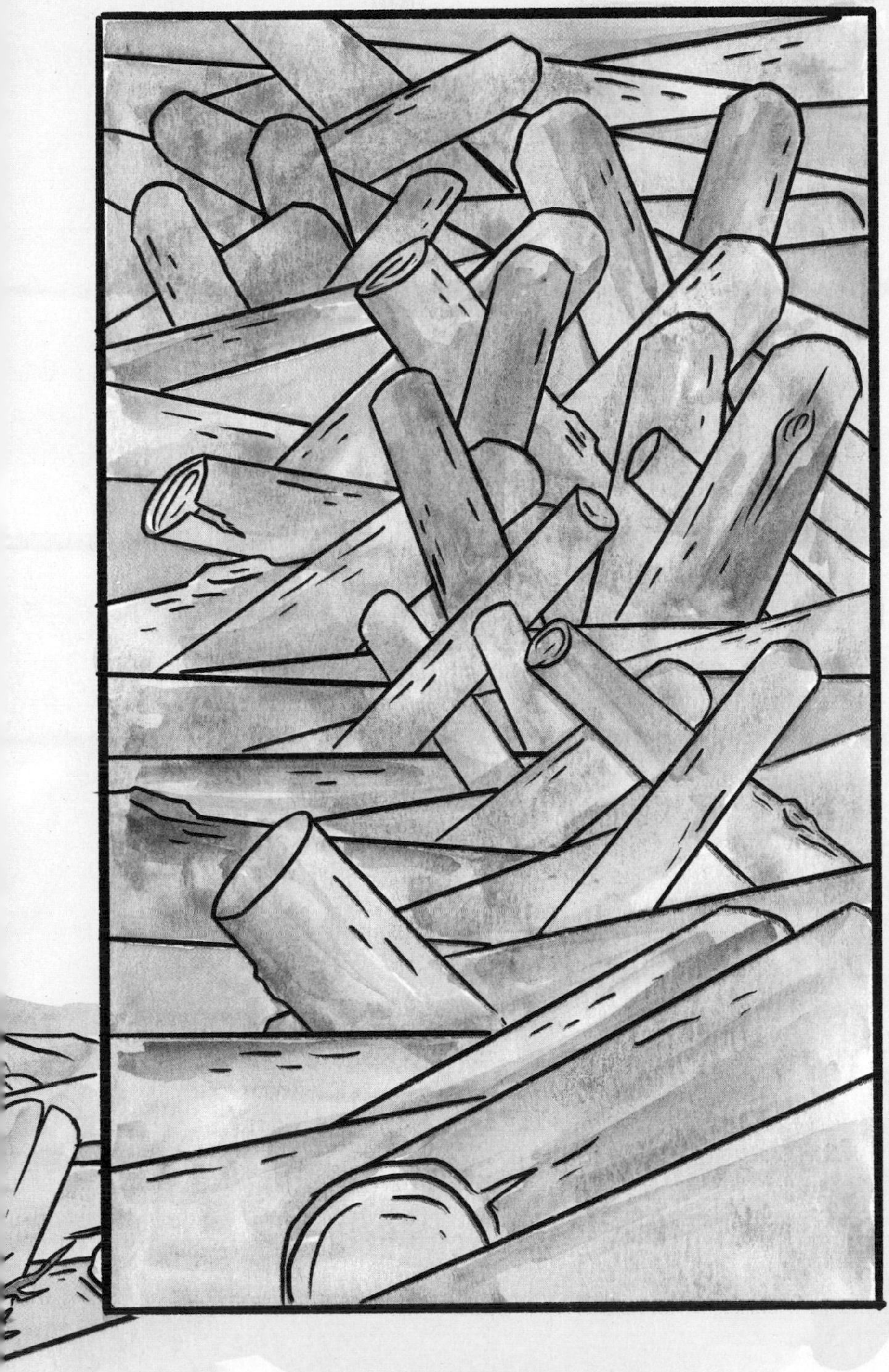

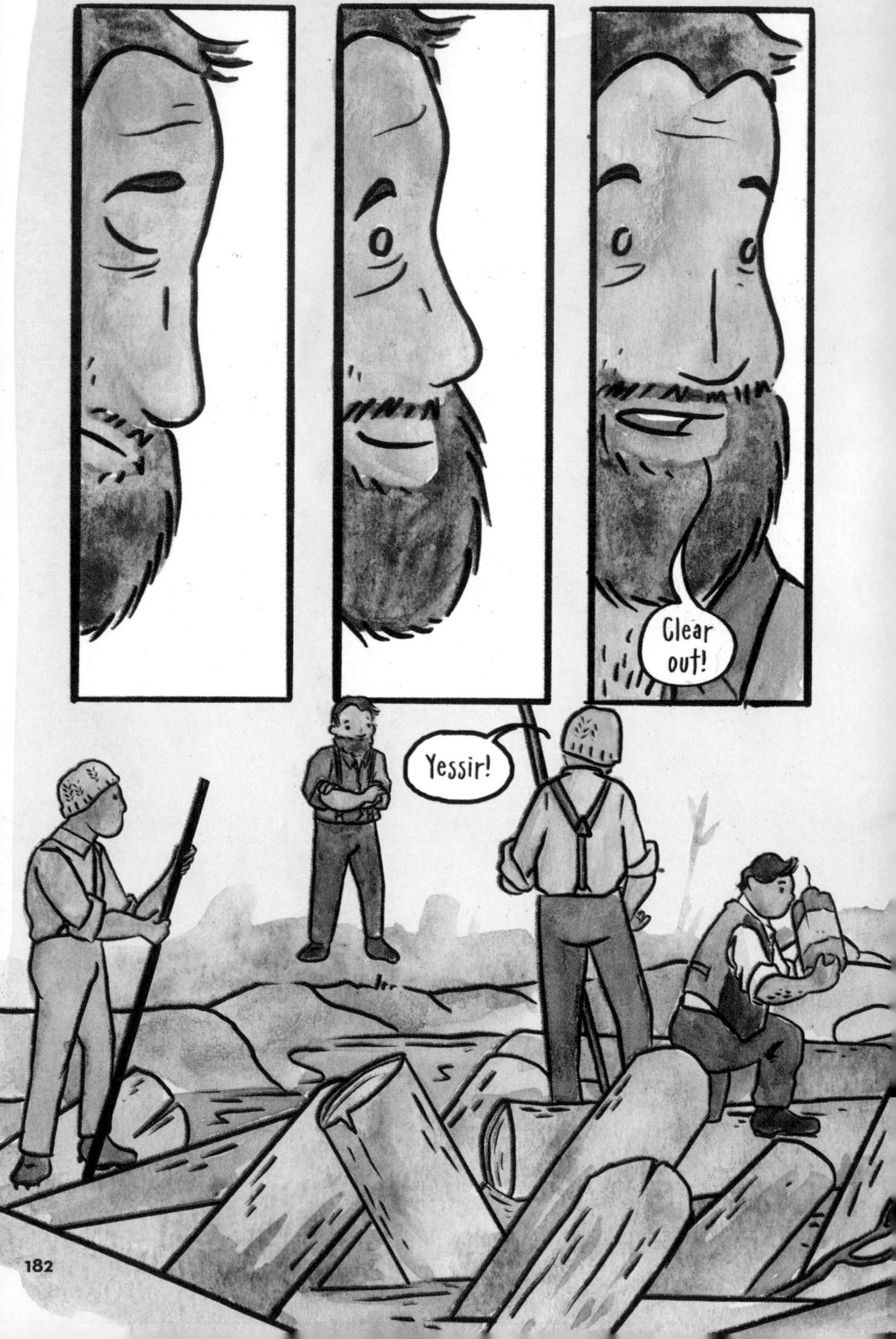
Clear out!
Yessir!

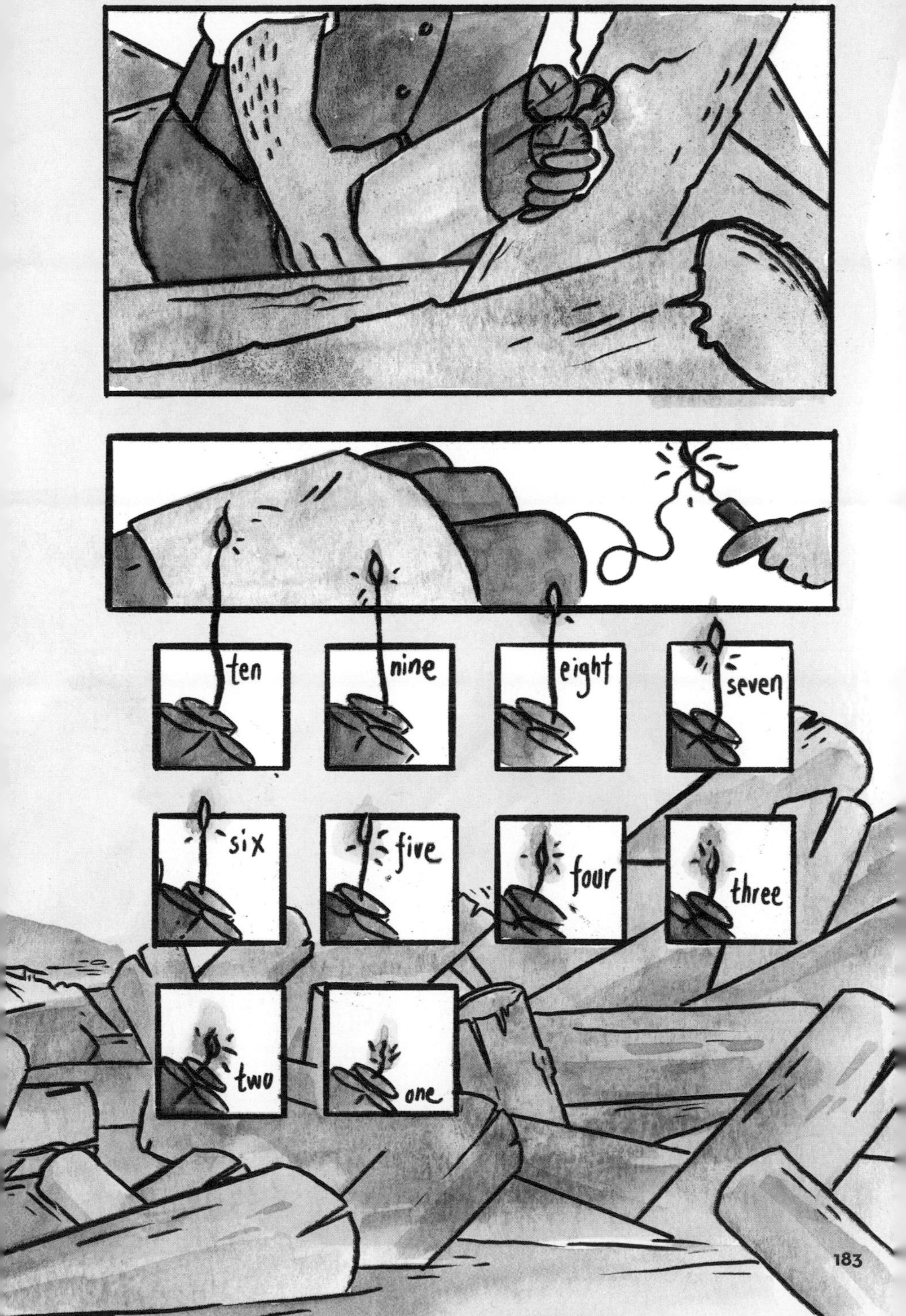

ten
nine
eight
seven
six
five
four
three
two
one

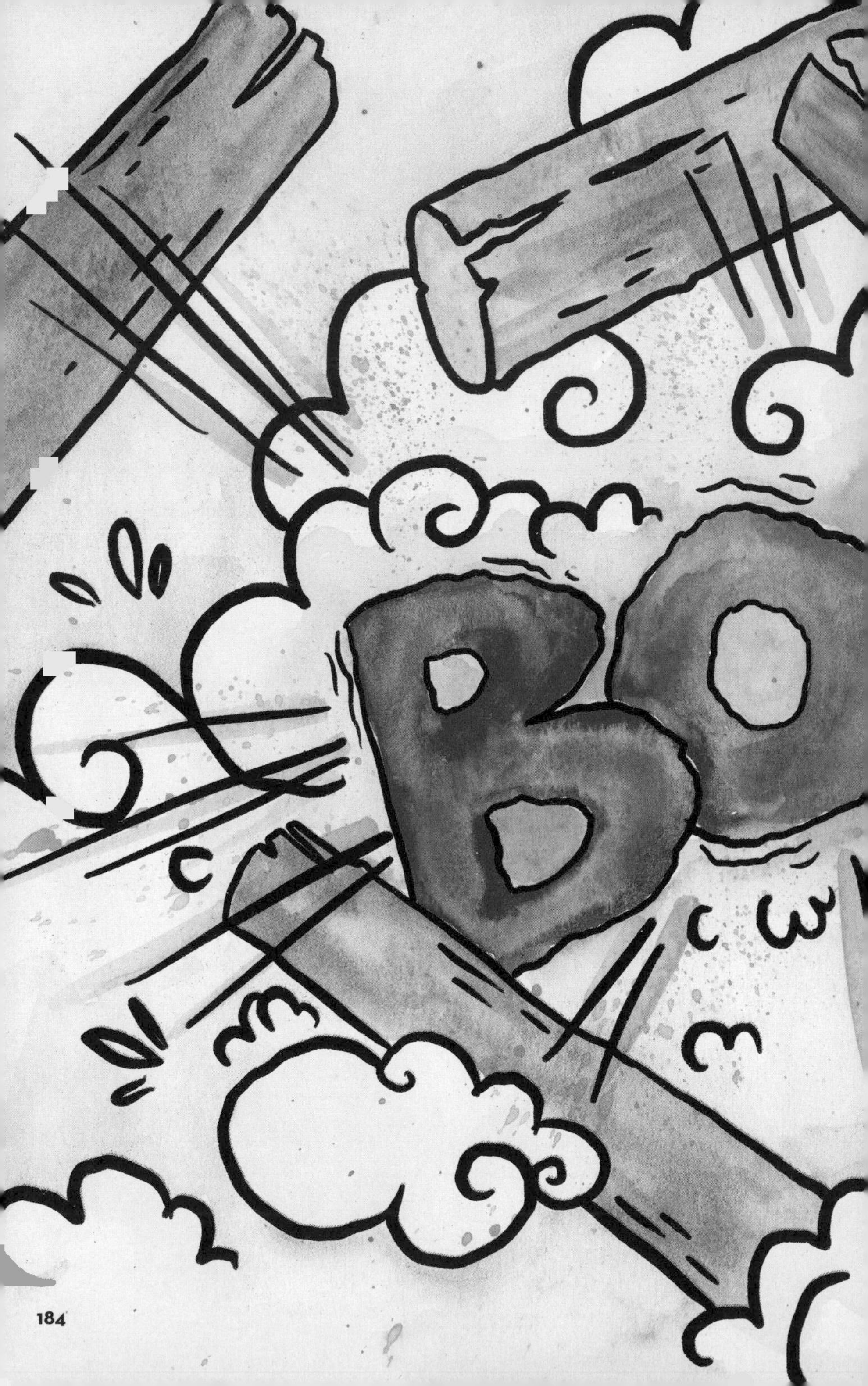
BO

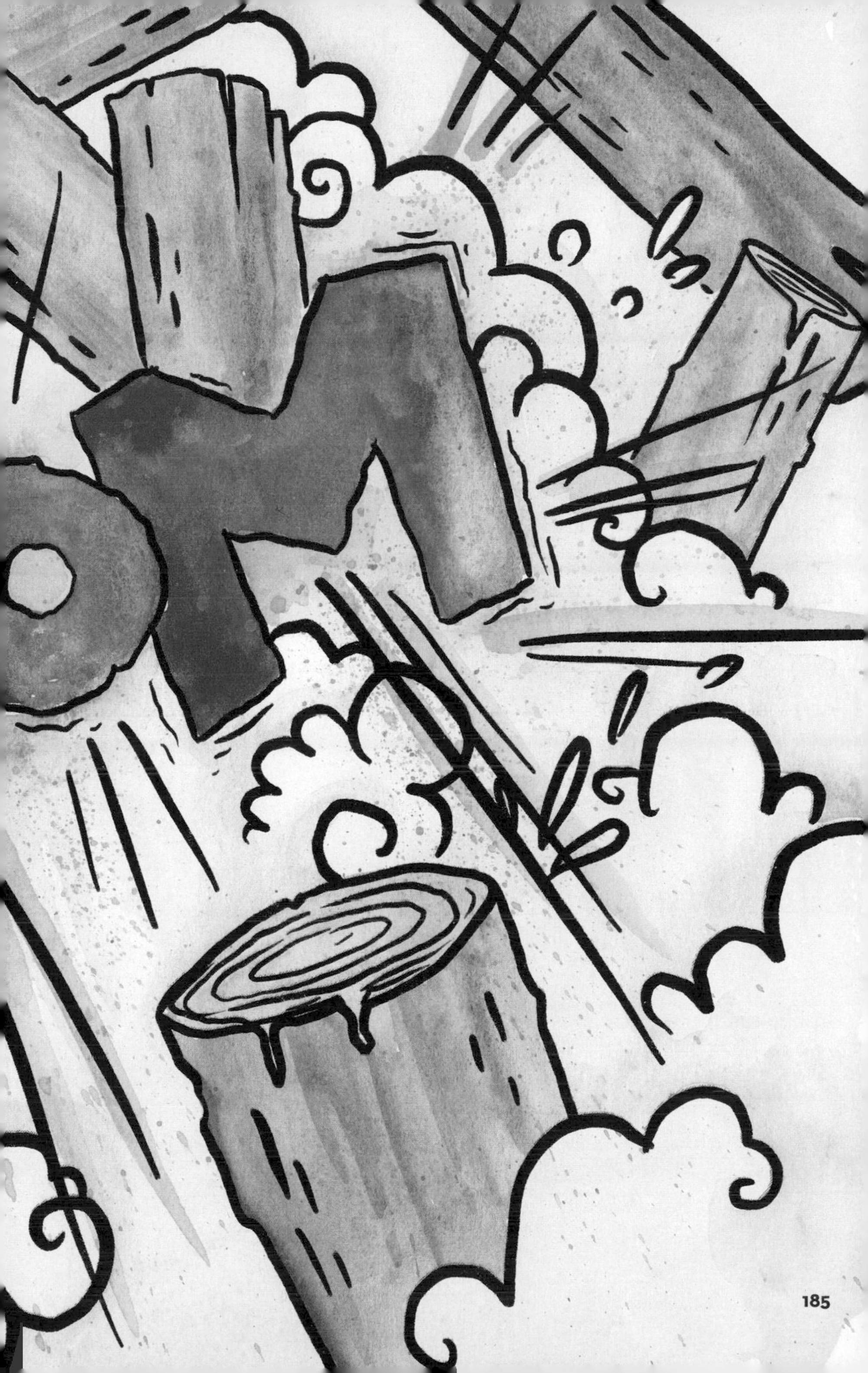

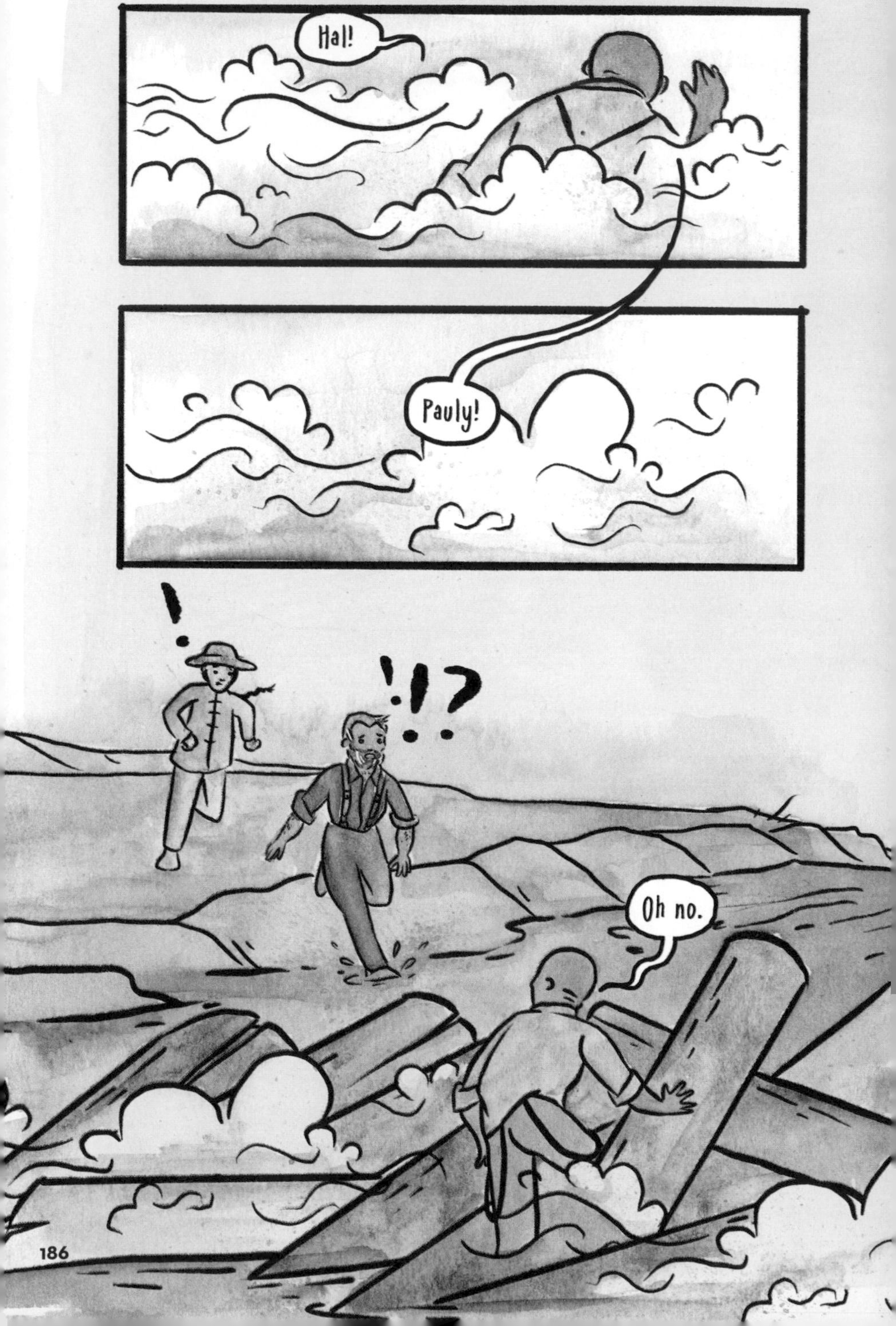
Hal!
Pauly!
!
!?
Oh no.

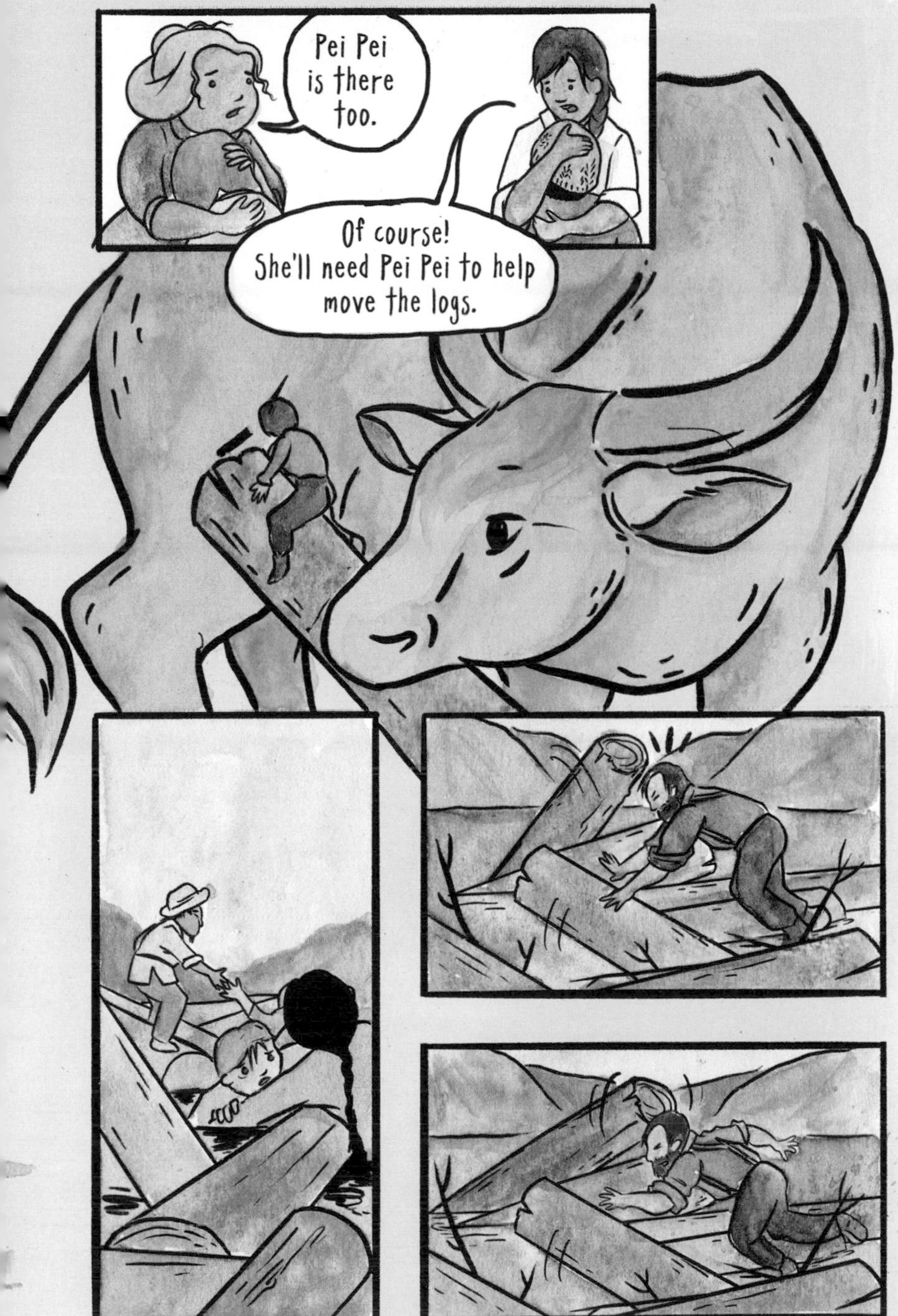
Pei Pei is there too.
Of course! She'll need Pei Pei to help move the logs.

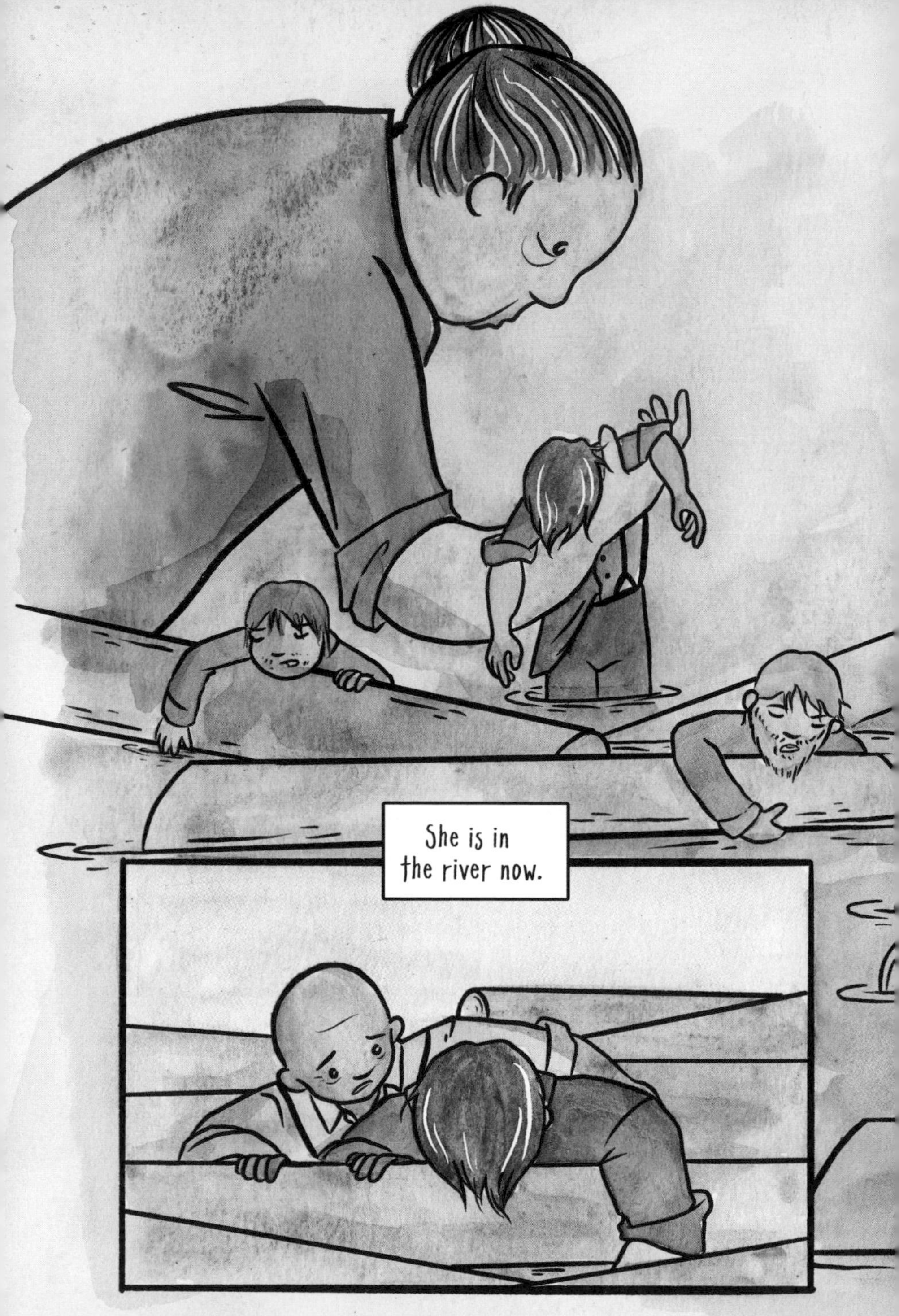
She is in the river now.

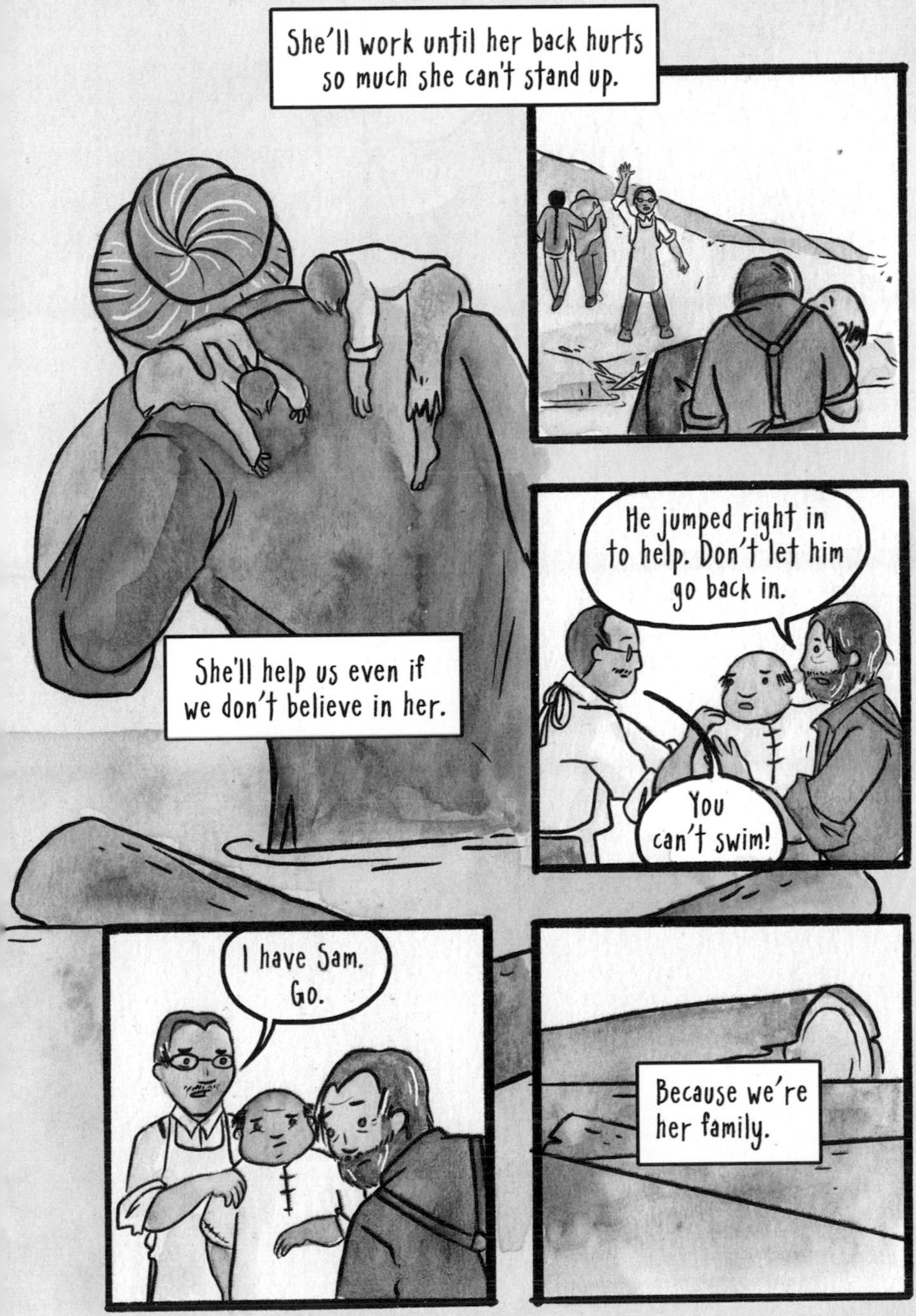
She'll work until her back hurts so much she can't stand up.
She'll help us even if we don't believe in her.
He jumped right in to help. Don't let him go back in.
You can't swim!
I have Sam. Go.
Because we're her family.

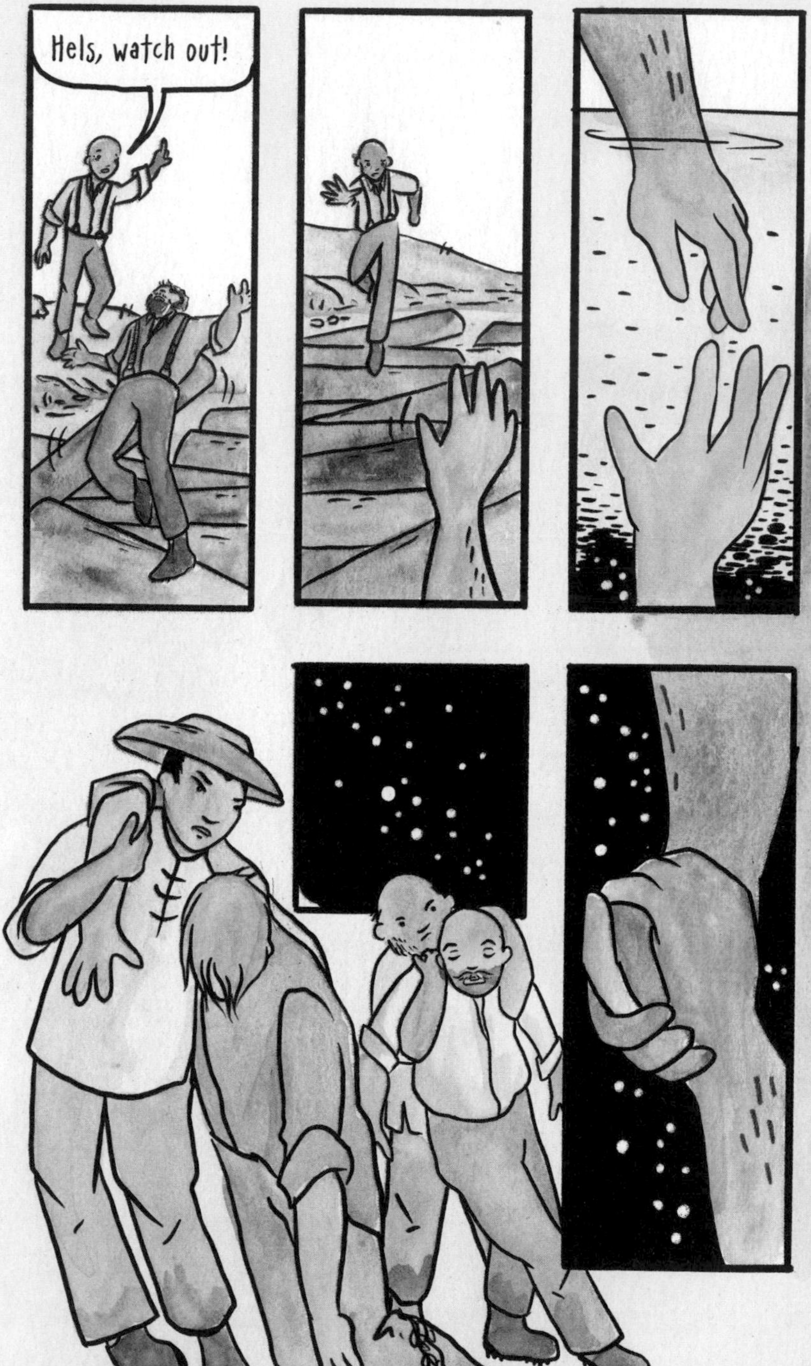
Hels, watch out!

199

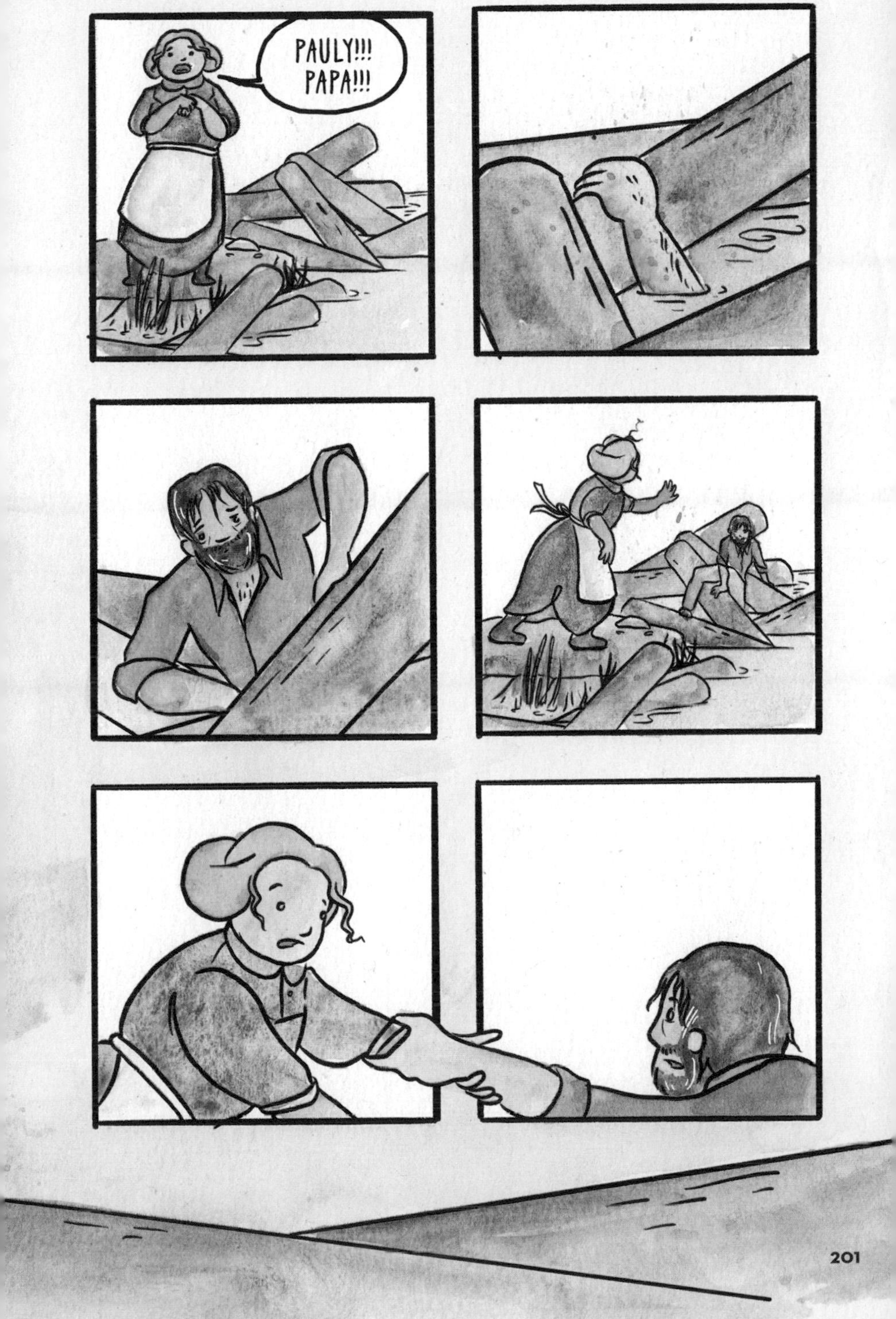
PAULY!!!
PAPA!!!

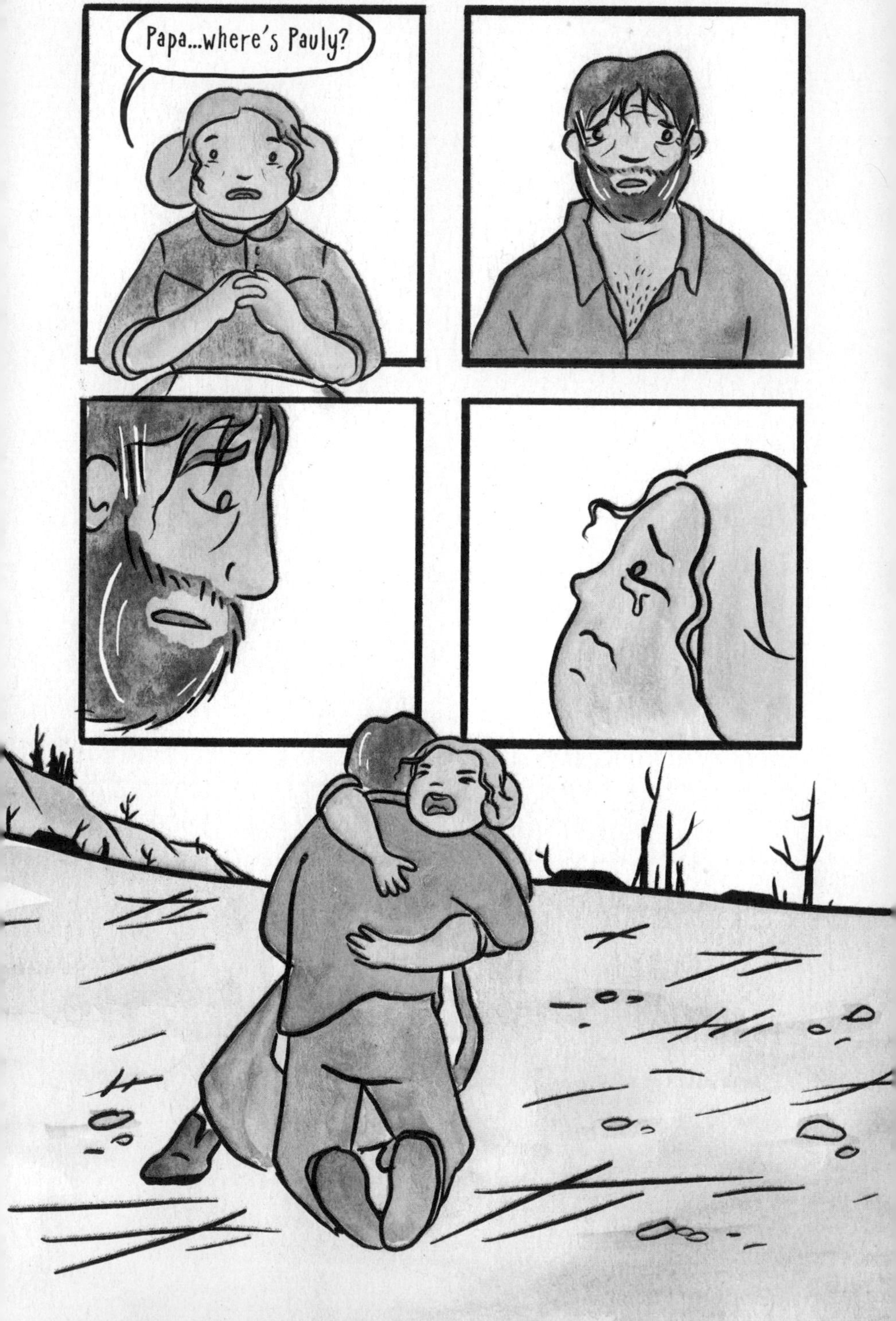
Papa...where's Pauly?

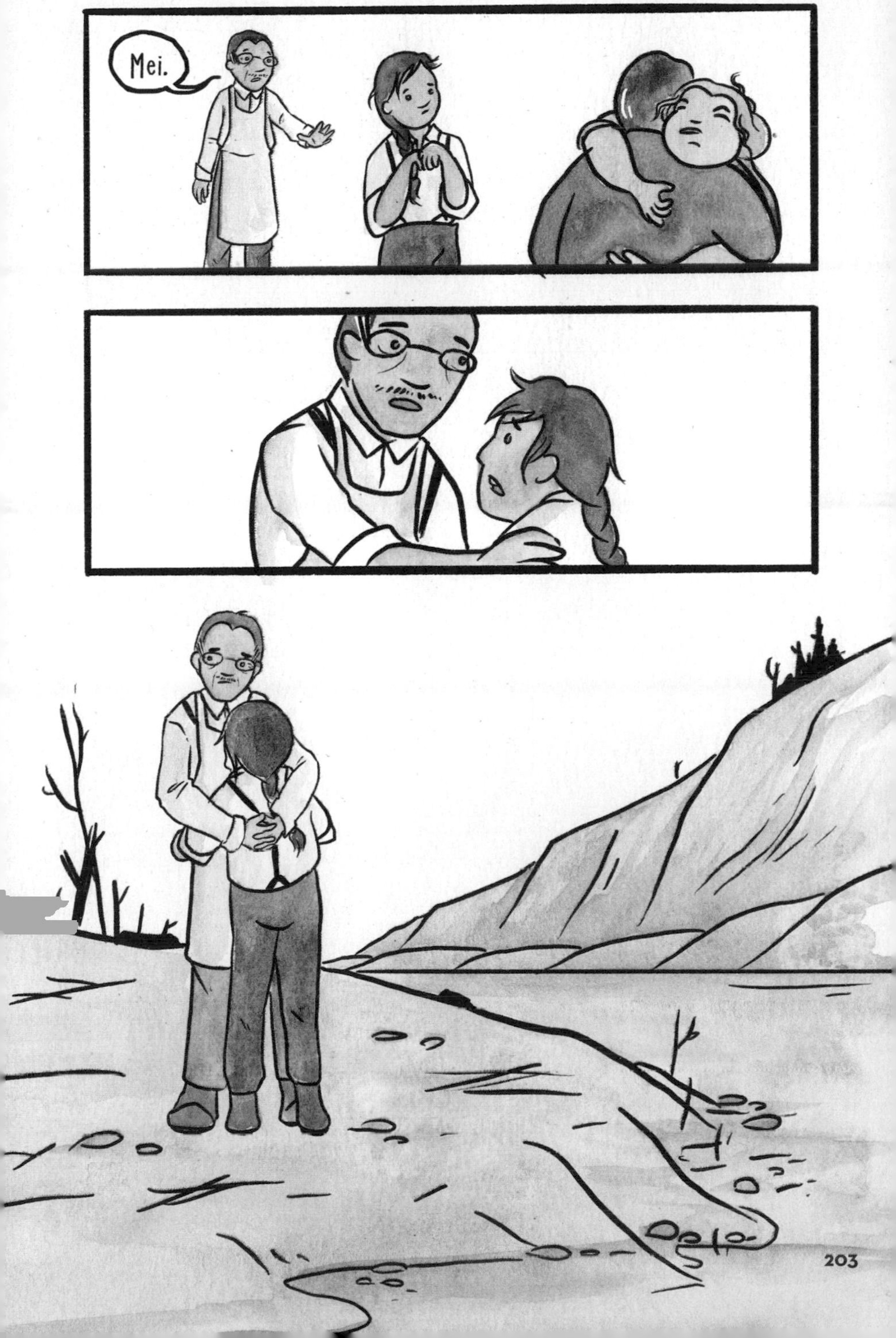
Mei.

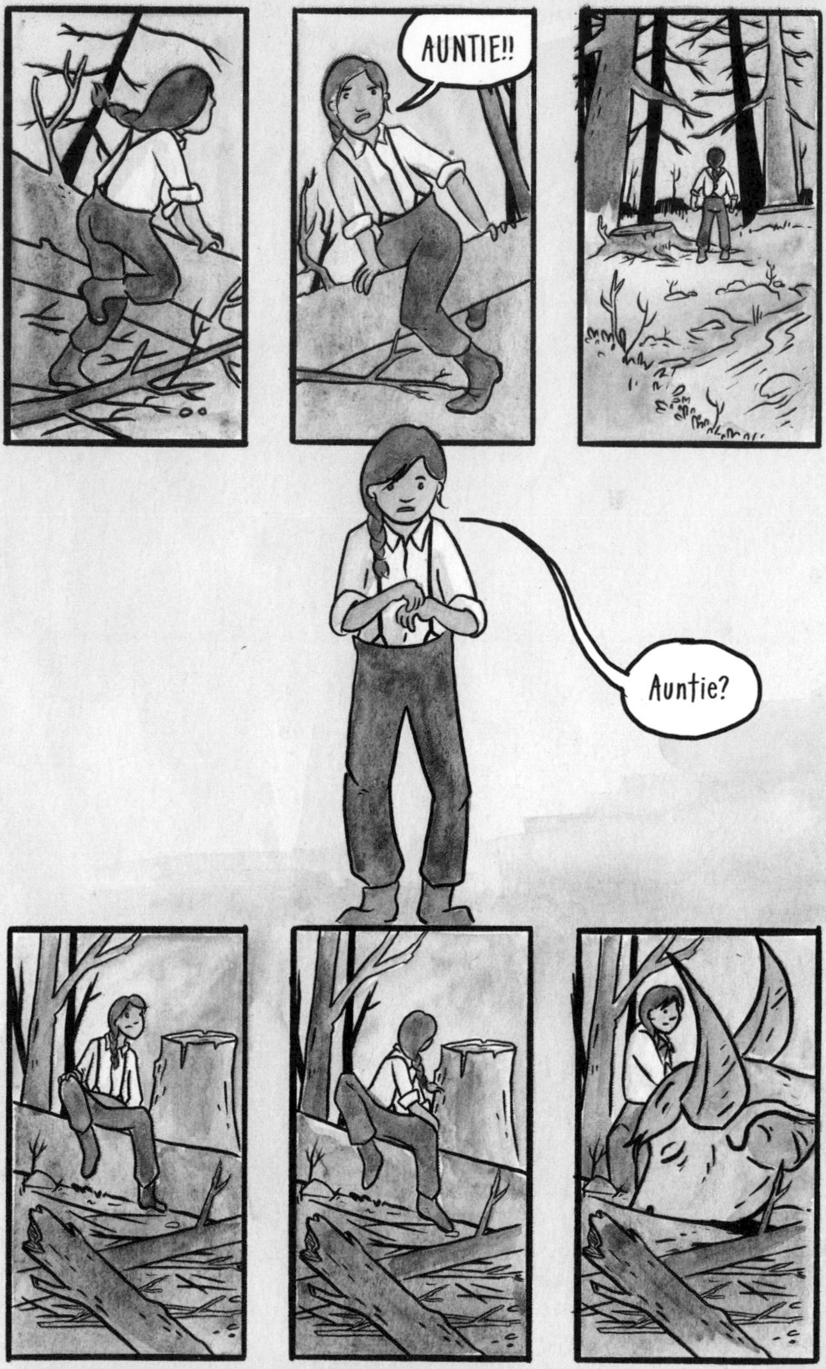
AUNTIE!!
Auntie?

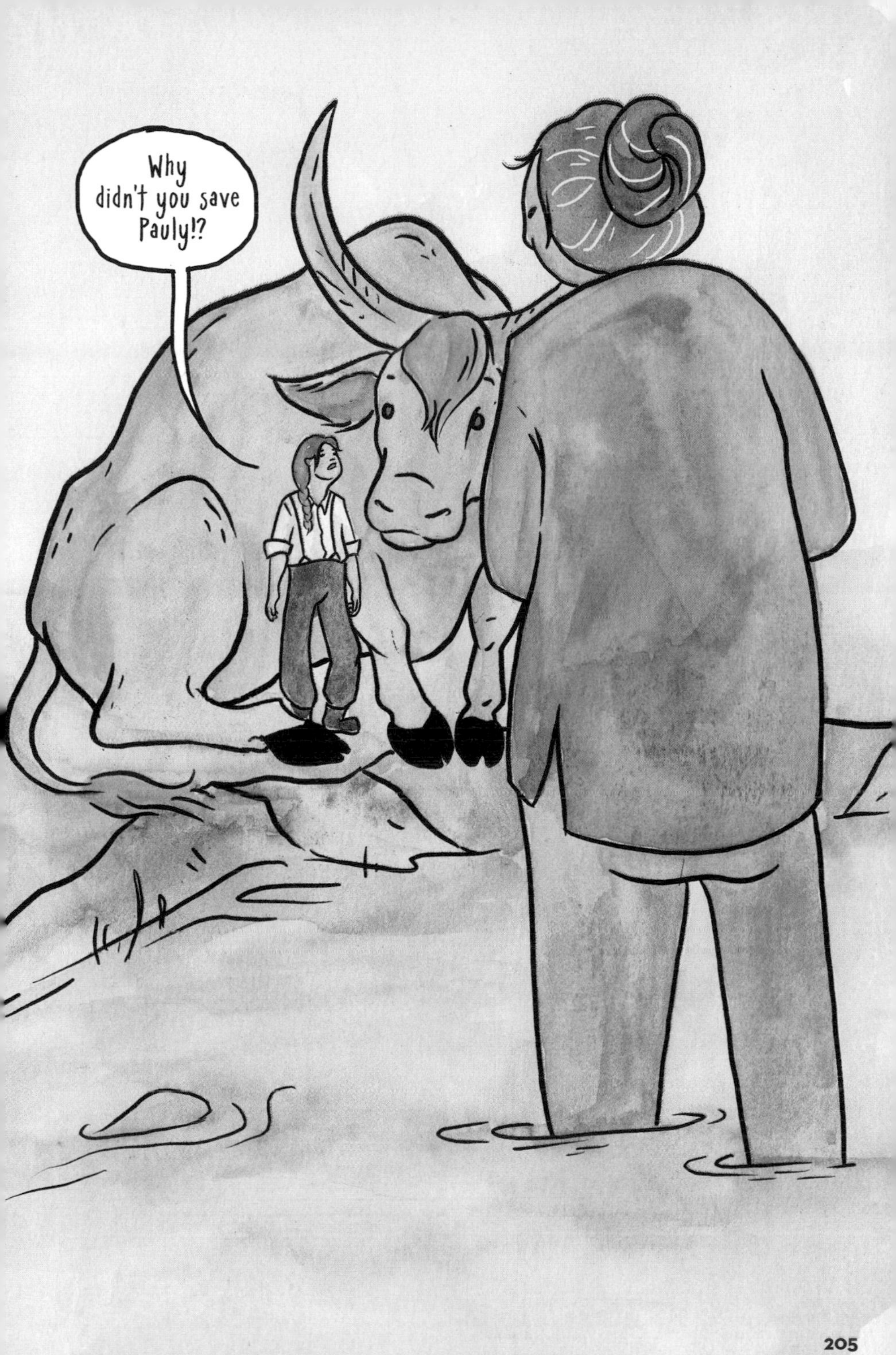
Why didn't you save Pauly!?

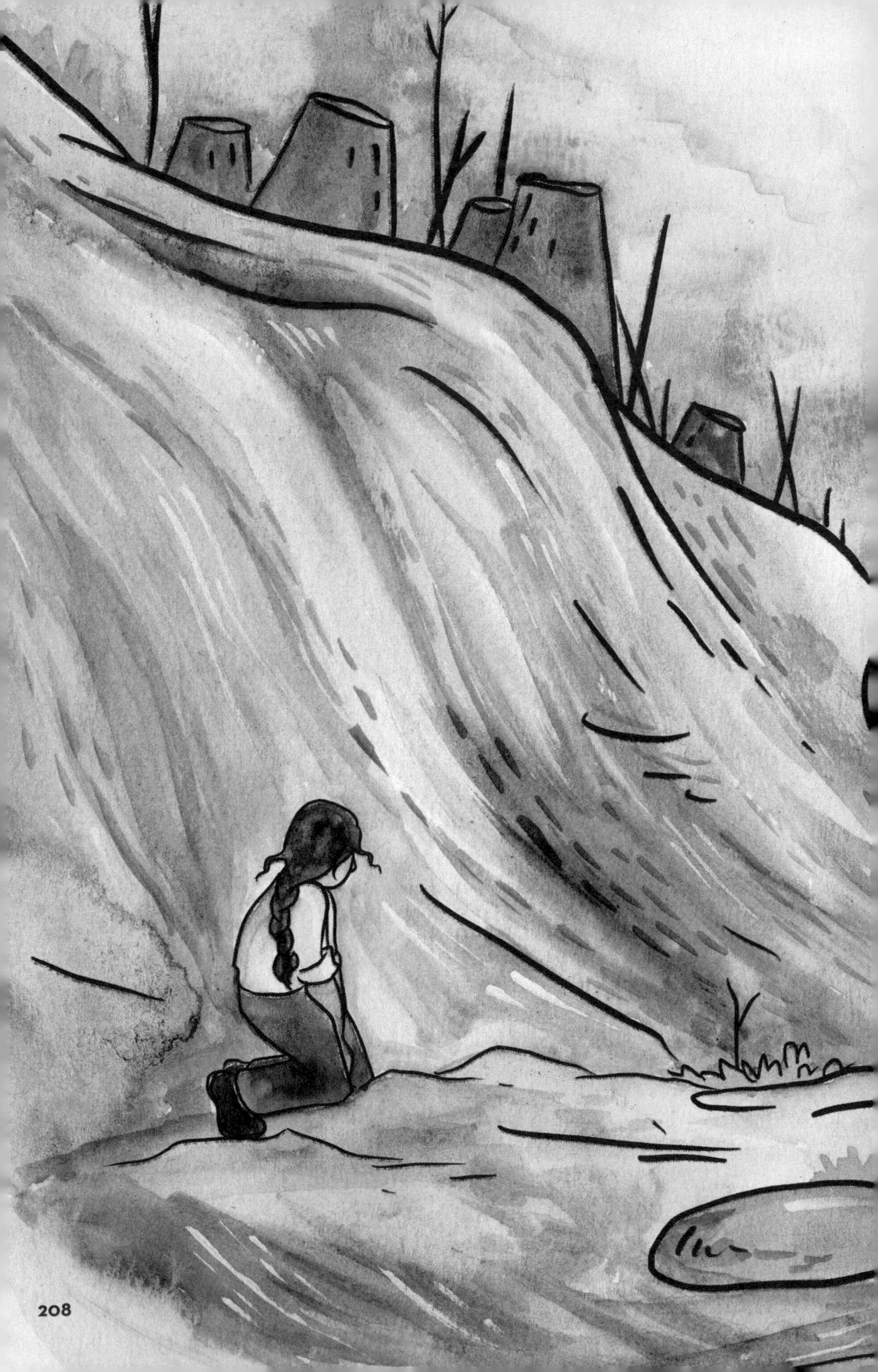

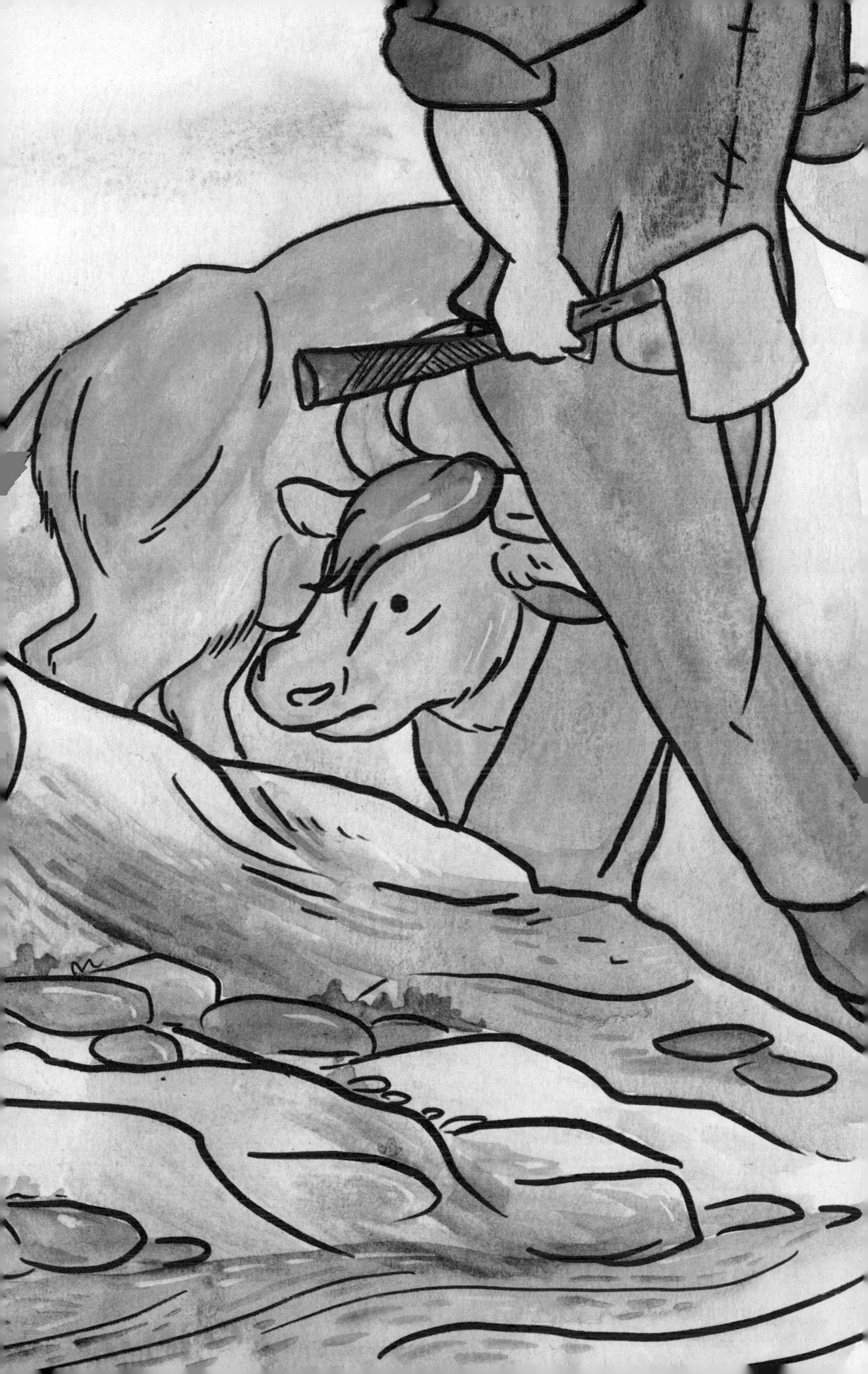

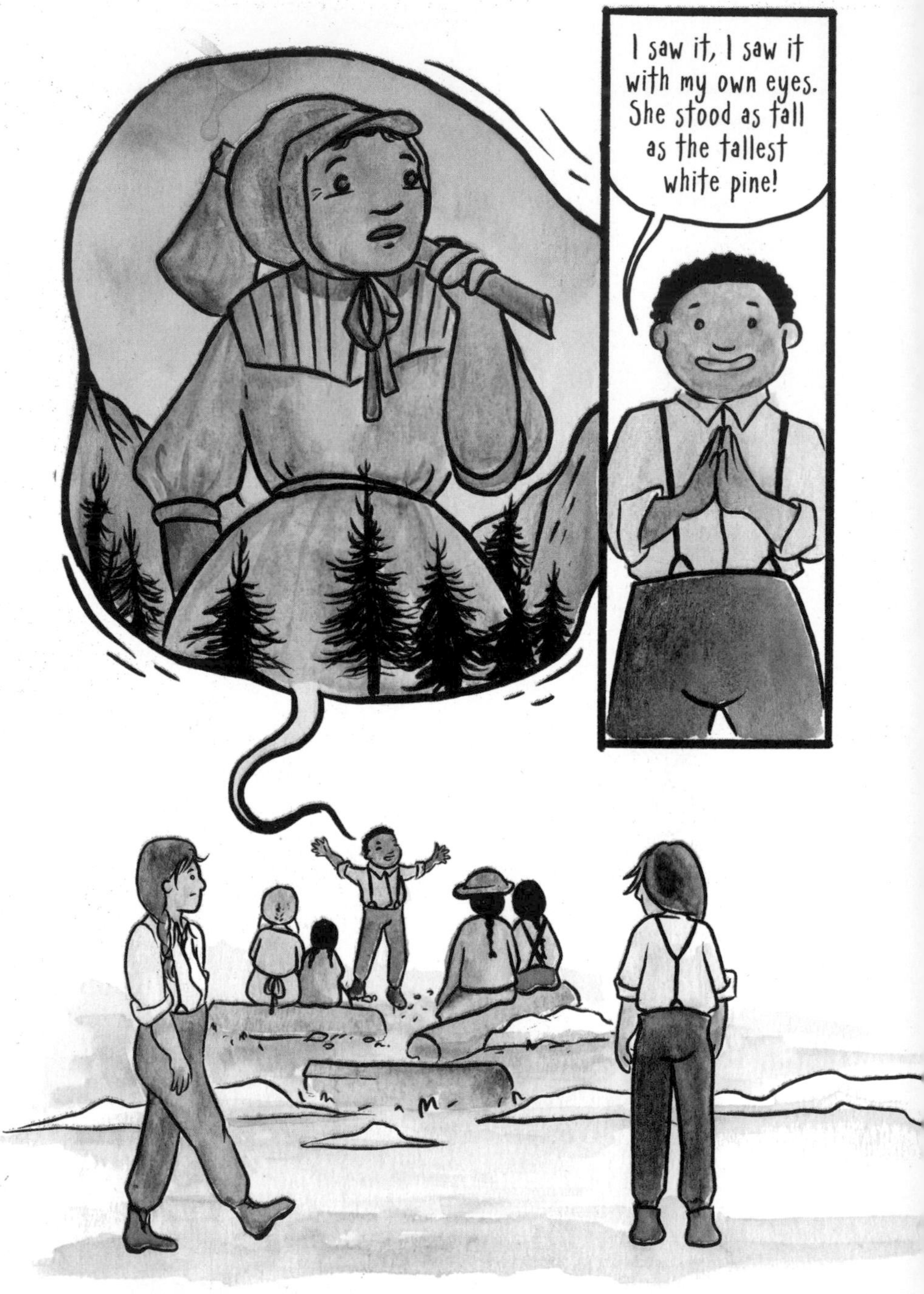
I saw it, I saw it with my own eyes. She stood as tall as the tallest white pine!

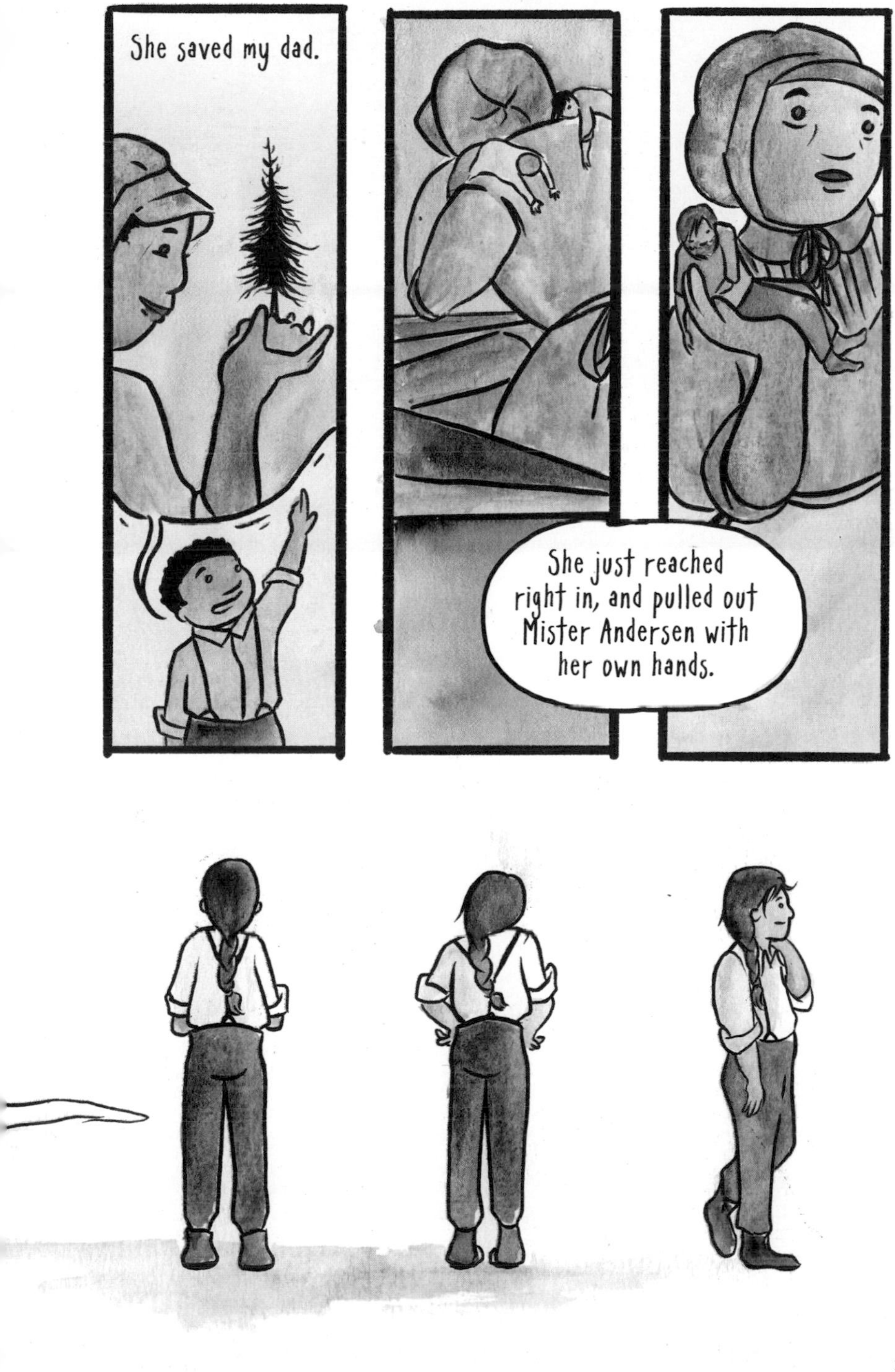
She saved my dad.
She just reached right in, and pulled out Mister Andersen with her own hands.

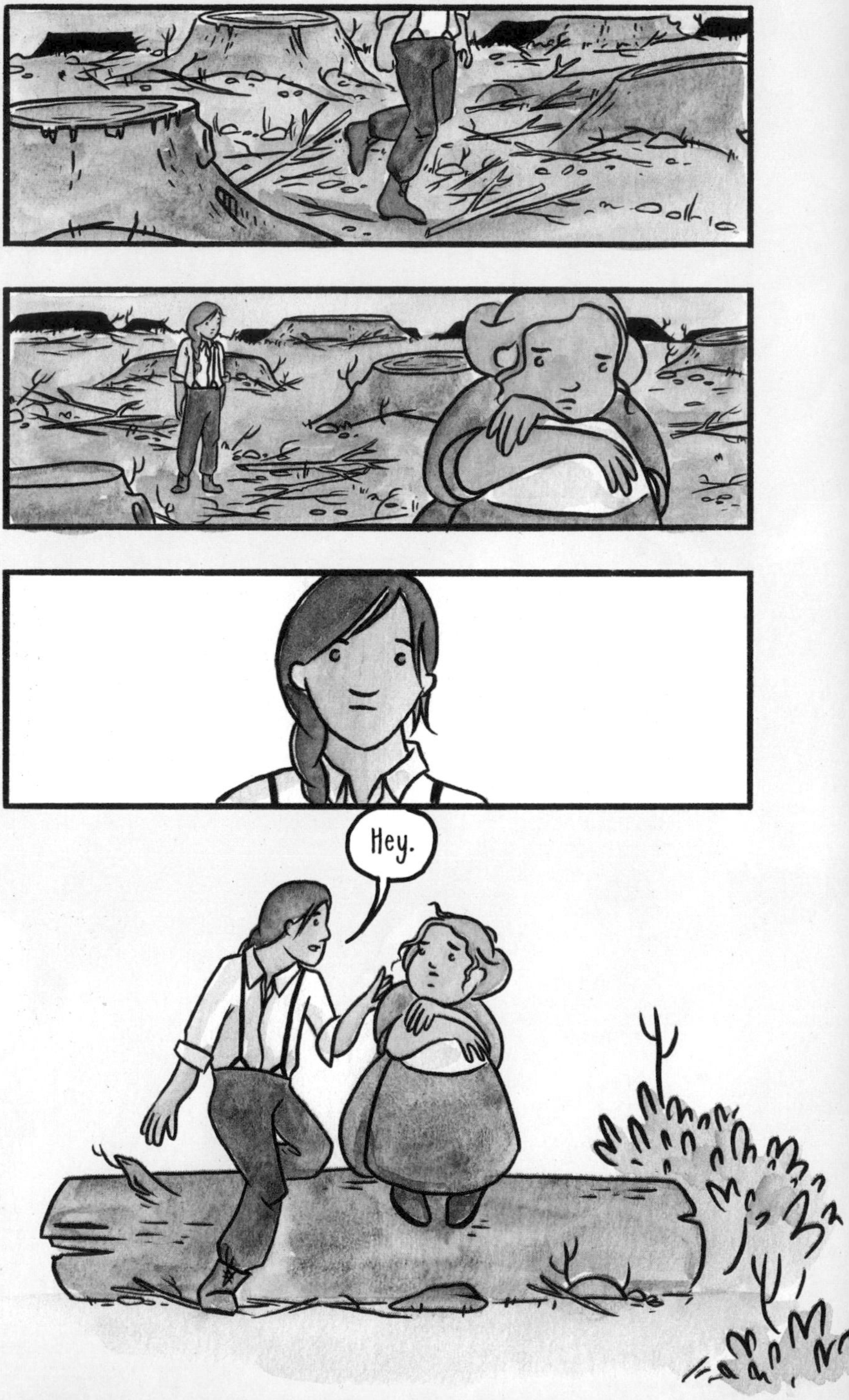
Hey.

213

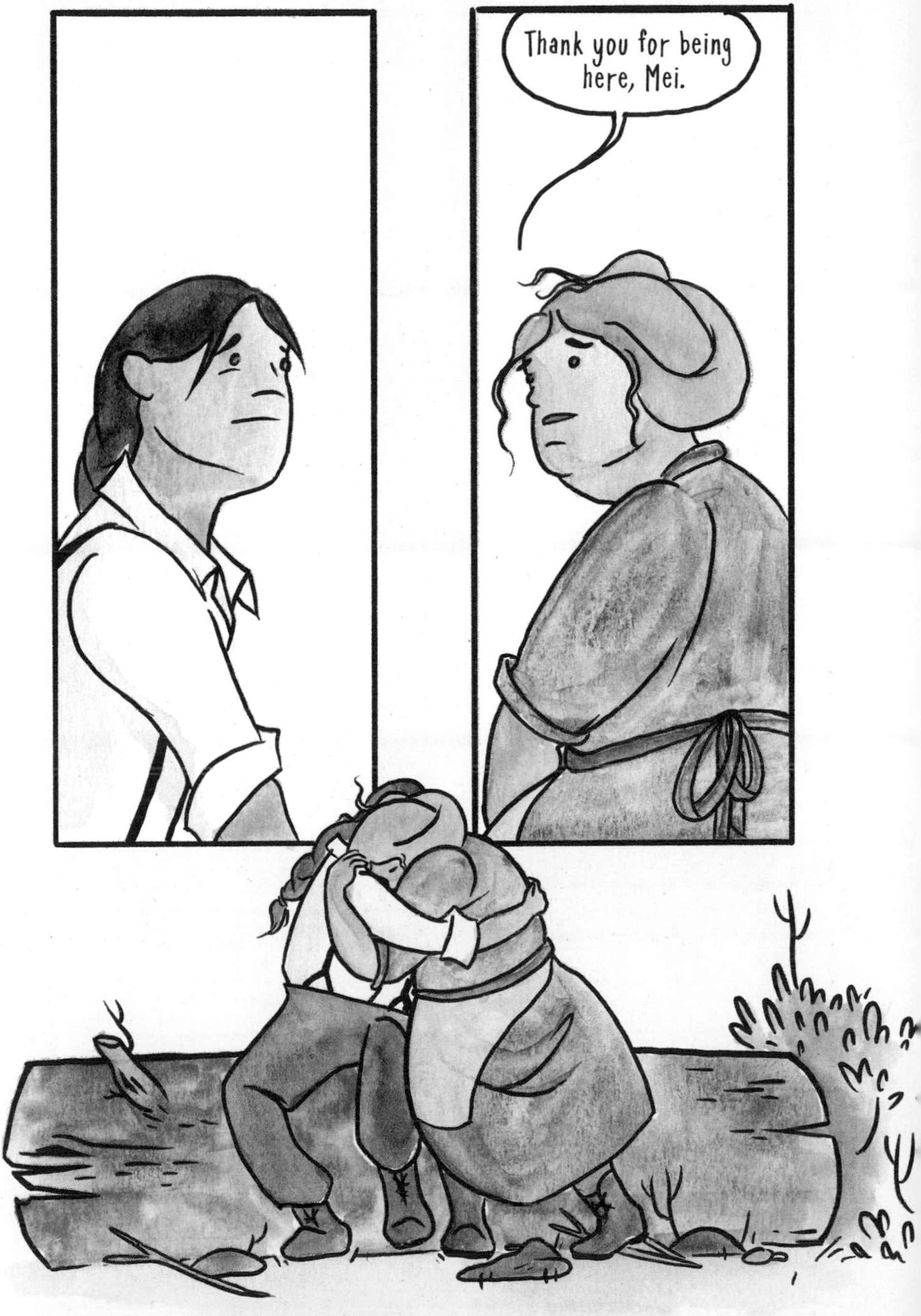
Thank you for being here, Mei.

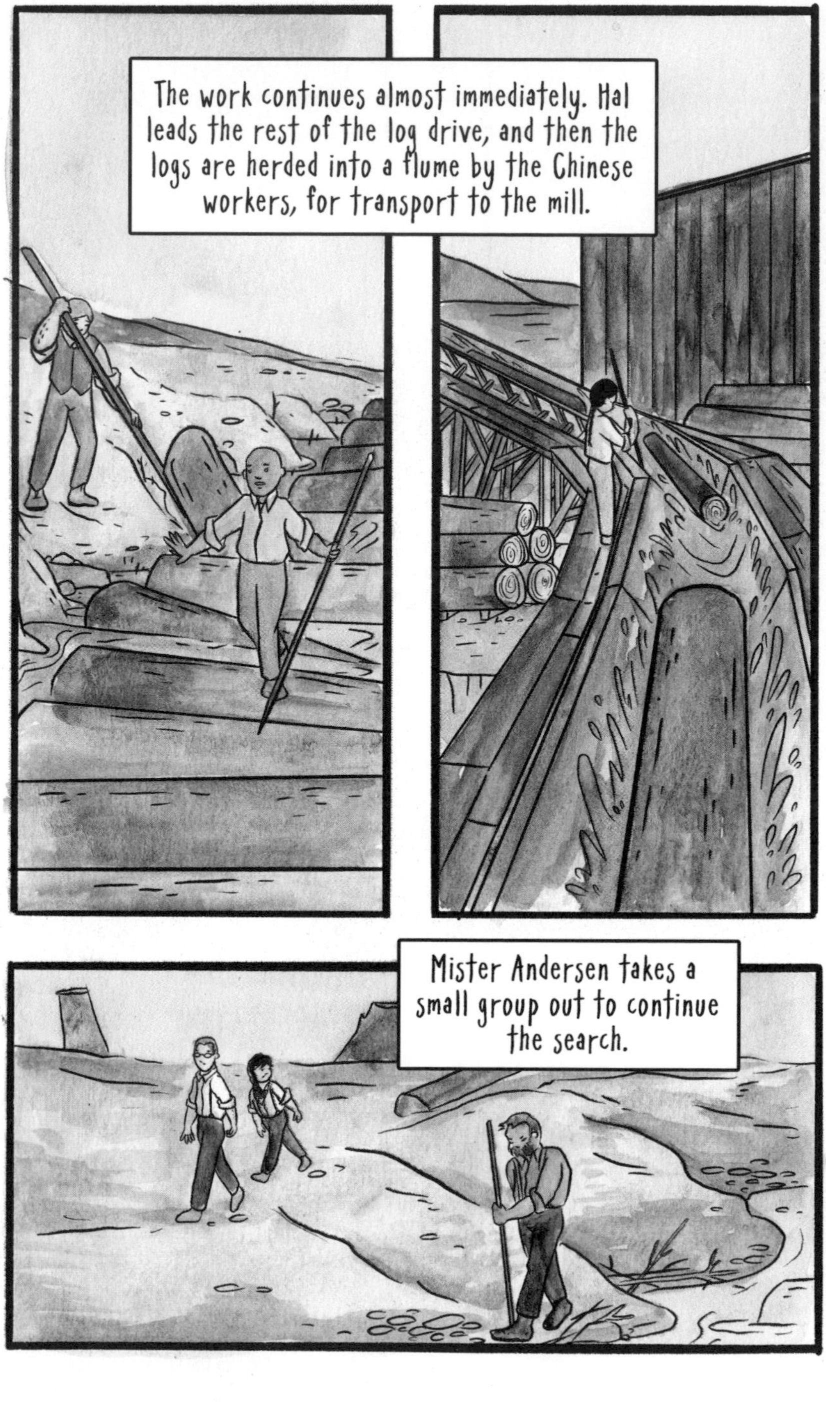
The work continues almost immediately. Hal leads the rest of the log drive, and then the logs are herded into a flume by the Chinese workers, for transport to the mill.
Mister Andersen takes a small group out to continue the search.

We find Pauly on the third day.

AUGHOWDAUWOHOHOHWHHHHUHHHH

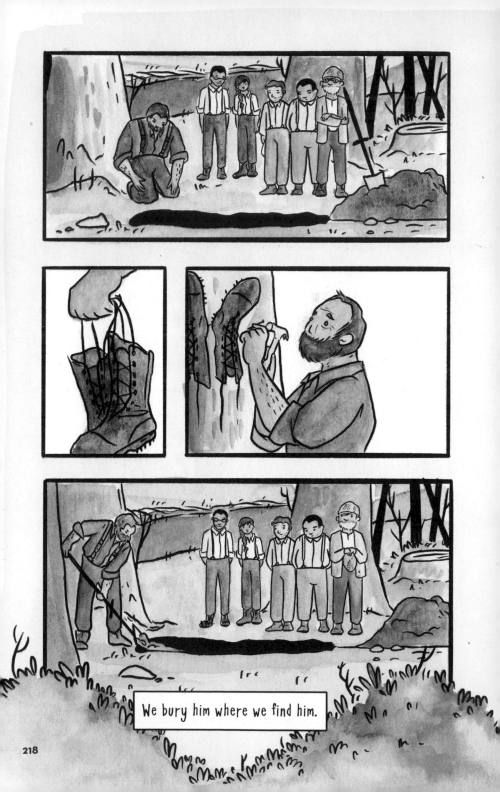

We bury him where we find him.

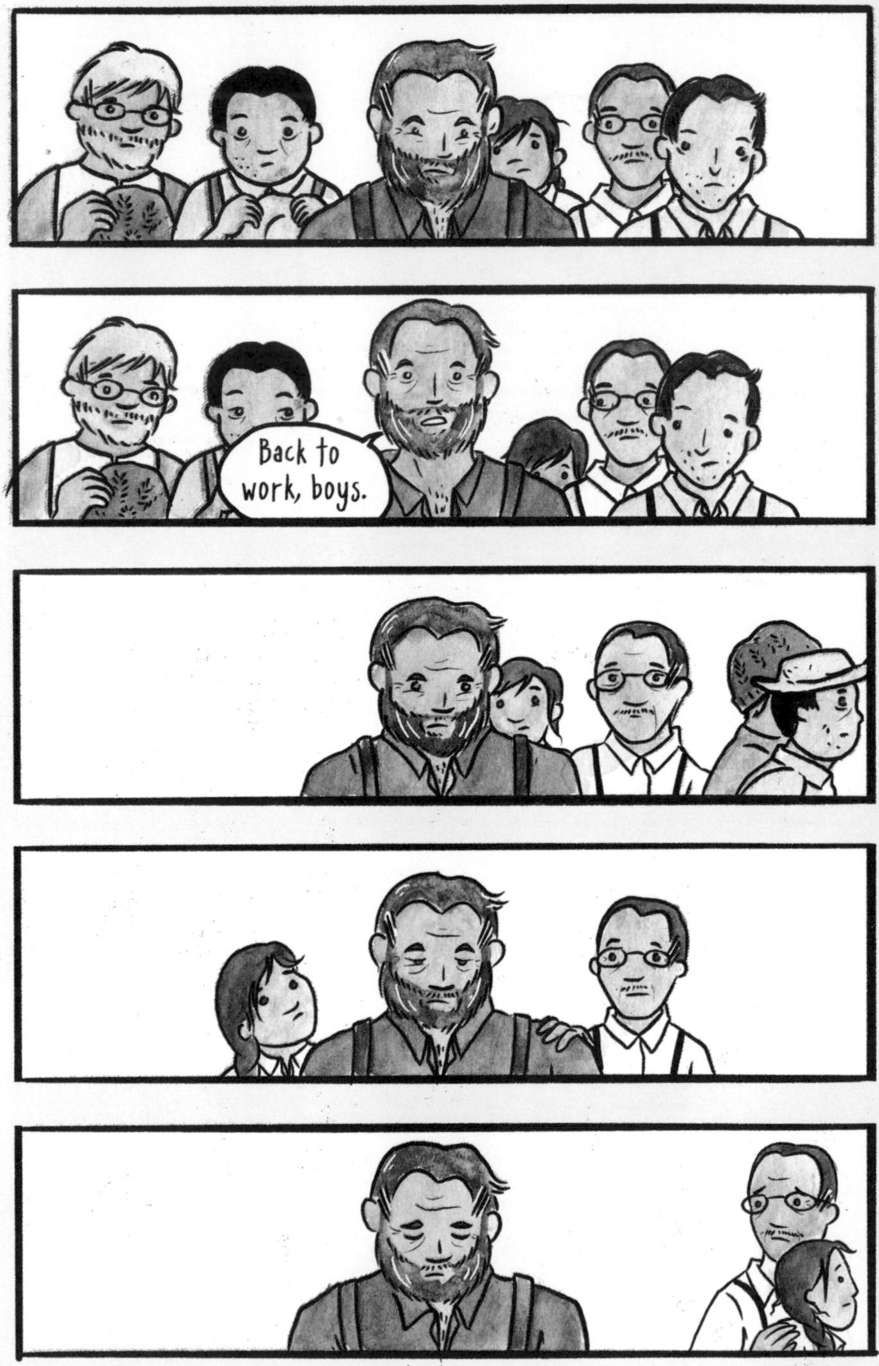
Back to work, boys.

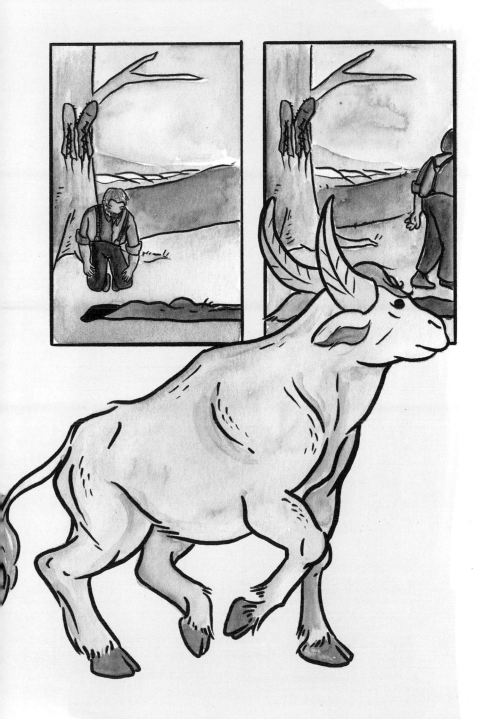

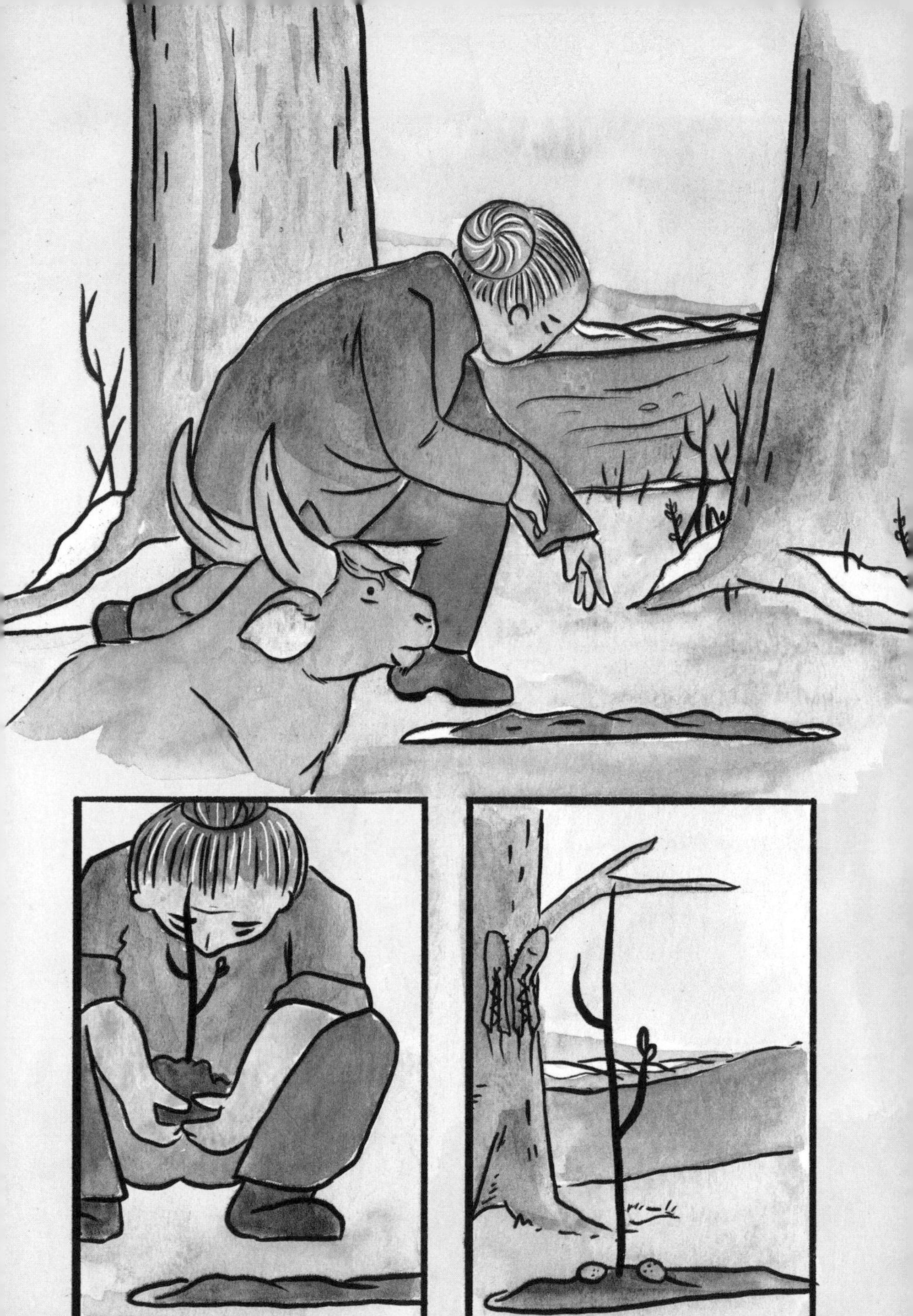

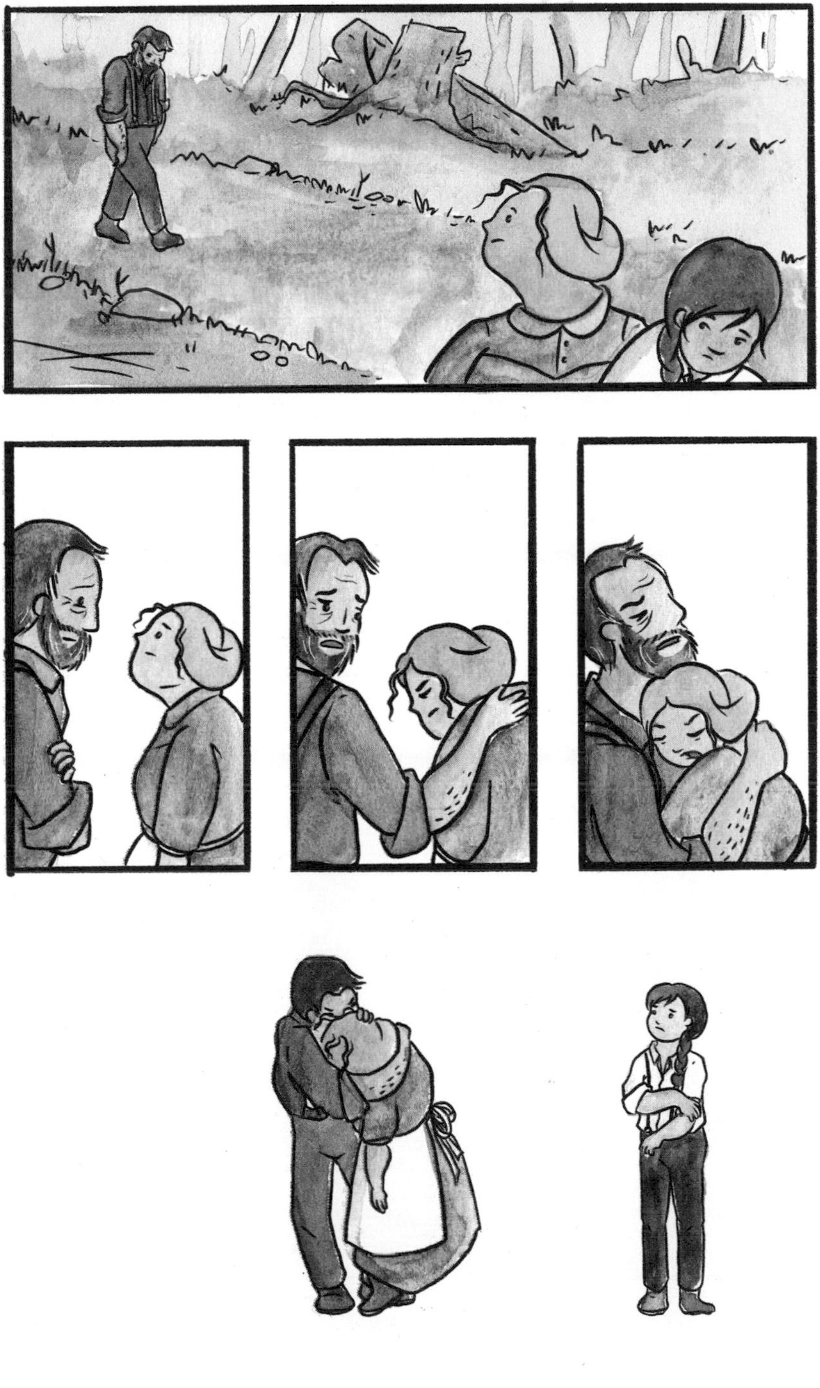

CHAPTER
five

chimney

warming cabinet

Wood stove

wood logs
are loaded
here

oven

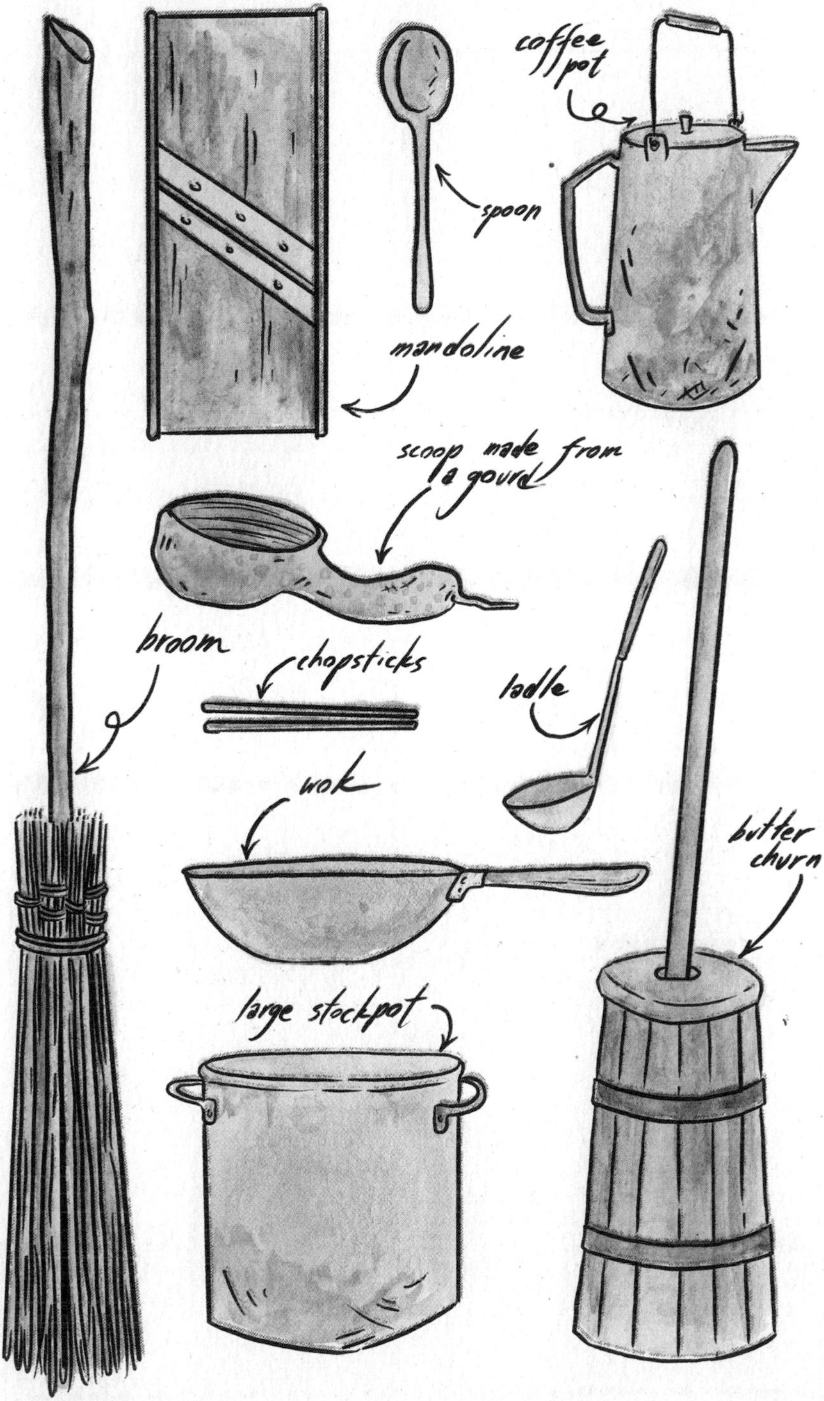
coffee pot
spoon
mandoline
scoop made from a gourd
broom
chopsticks
ladle
wok
butter churn
large stockpot

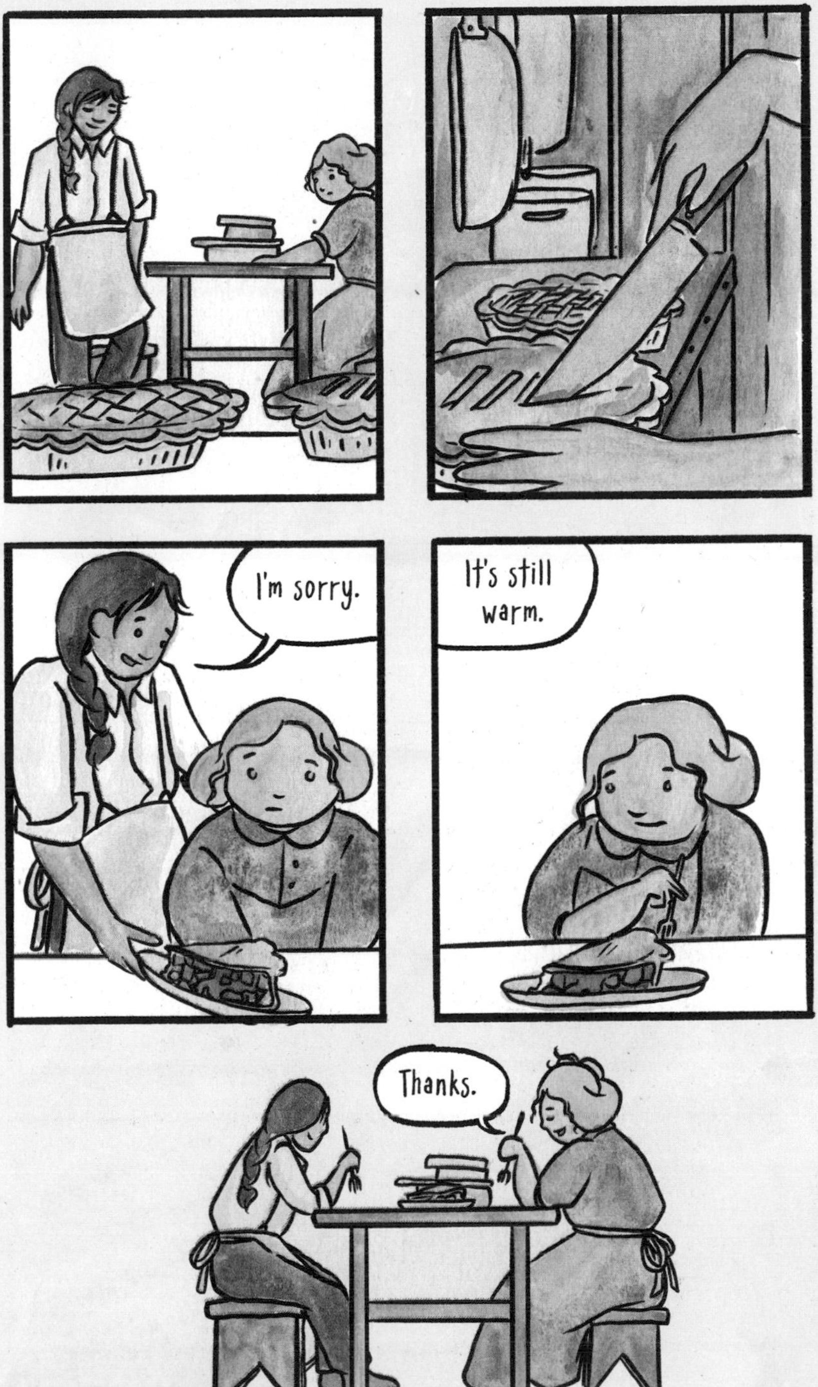
I'm sorry.
It's still warm.
Thanks.

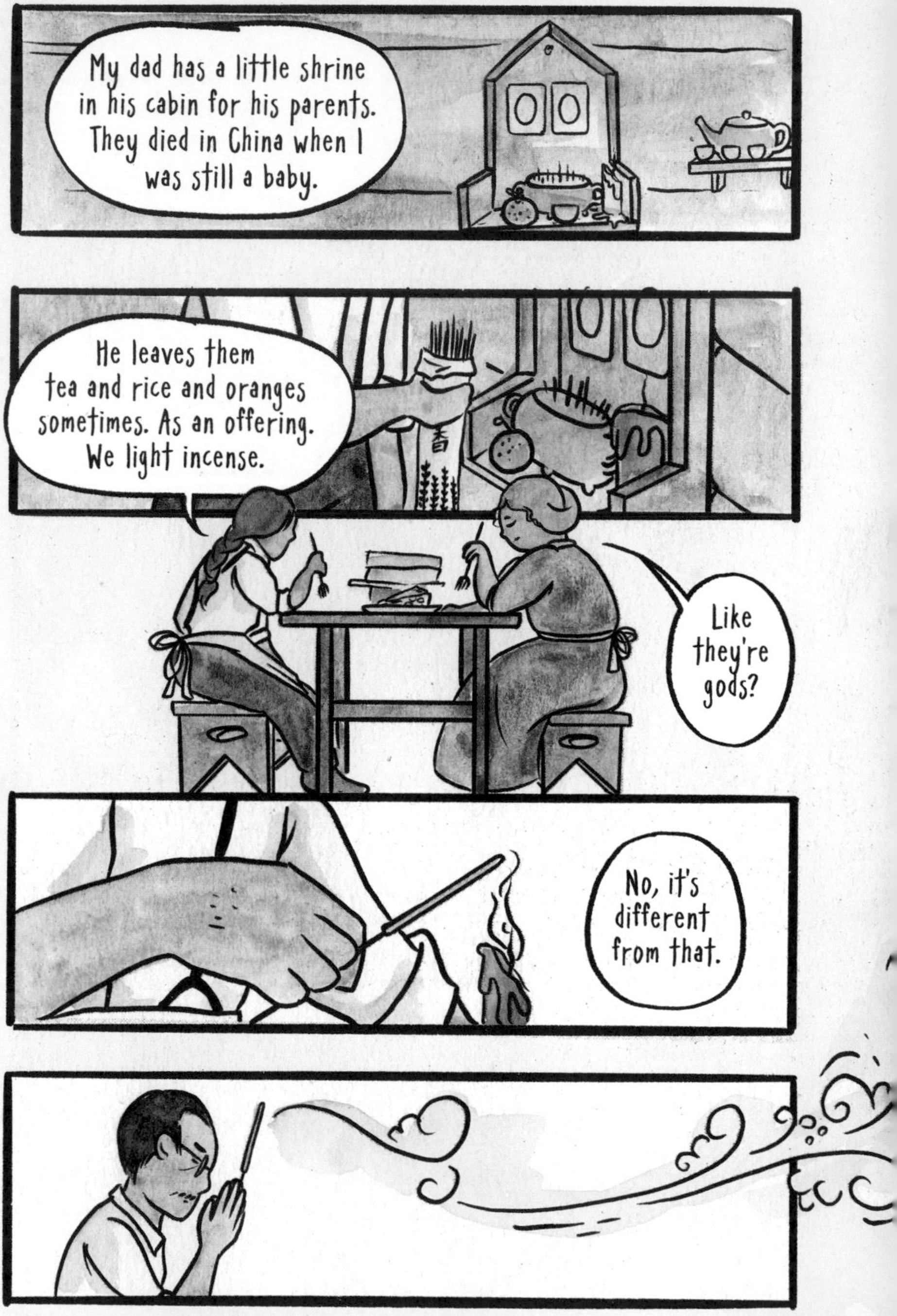
My dad has a little shrine in his cabin for his parents. They died in China when I was still a baby.
He leaves them tea and rice and oranges sometimes. As an offering. We light incense.
香
Like they're gods?
No, it's different from that.

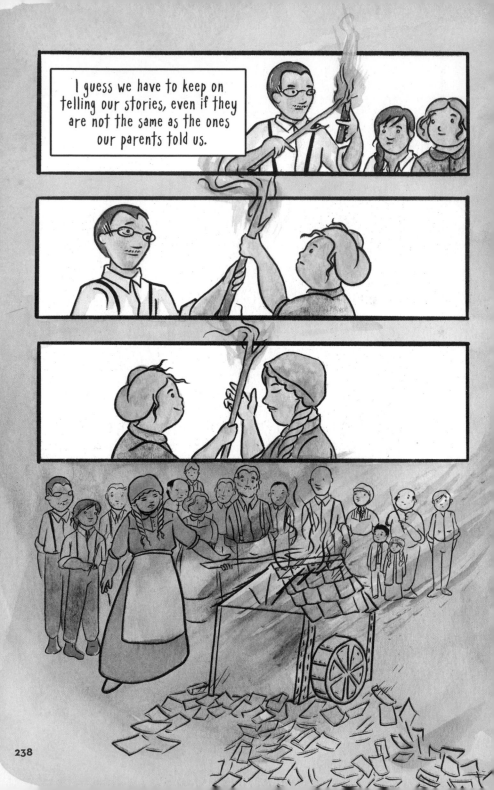

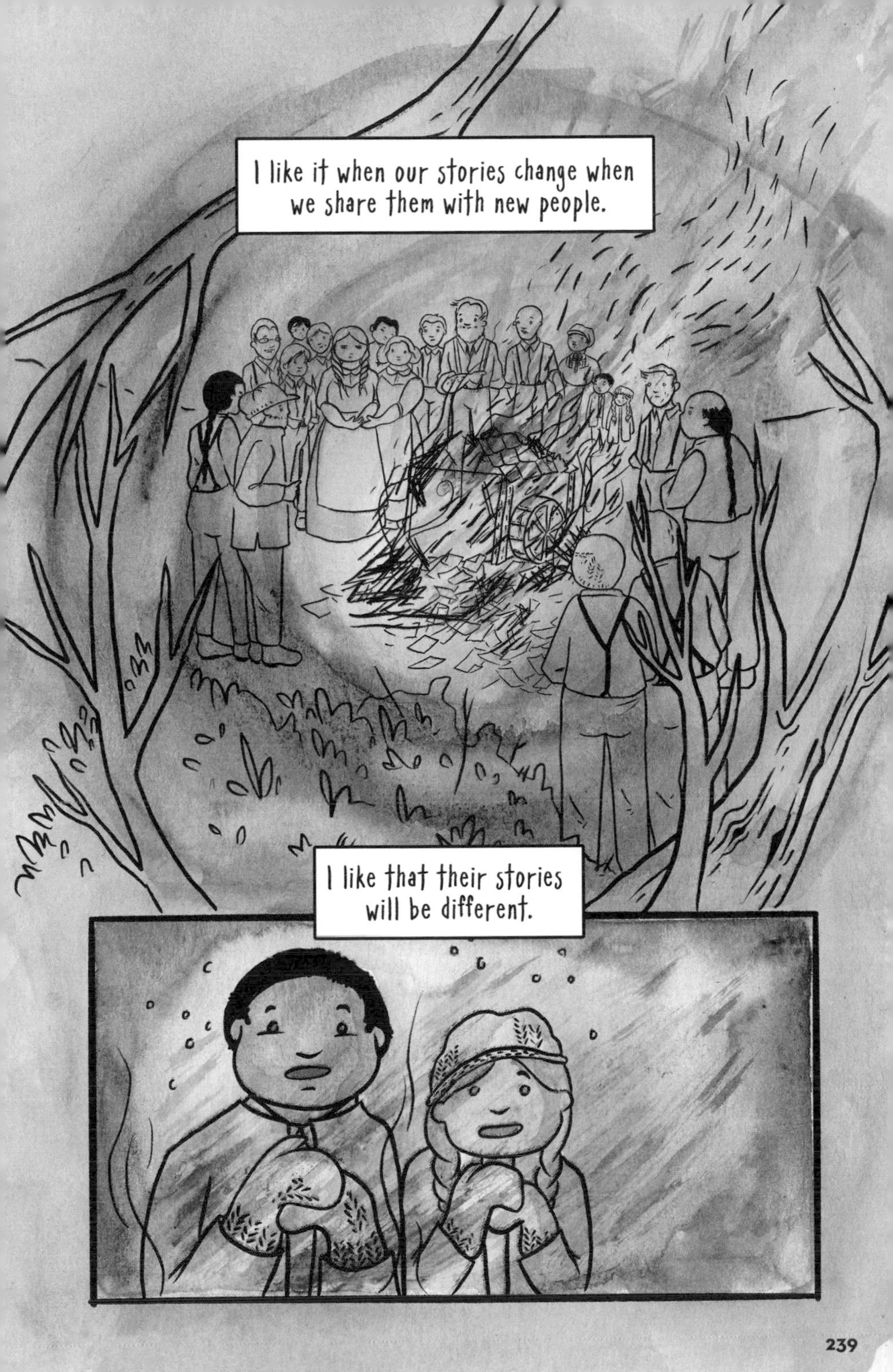
I like it when our stories change when we share them with new people.
I like that their stories will be different.

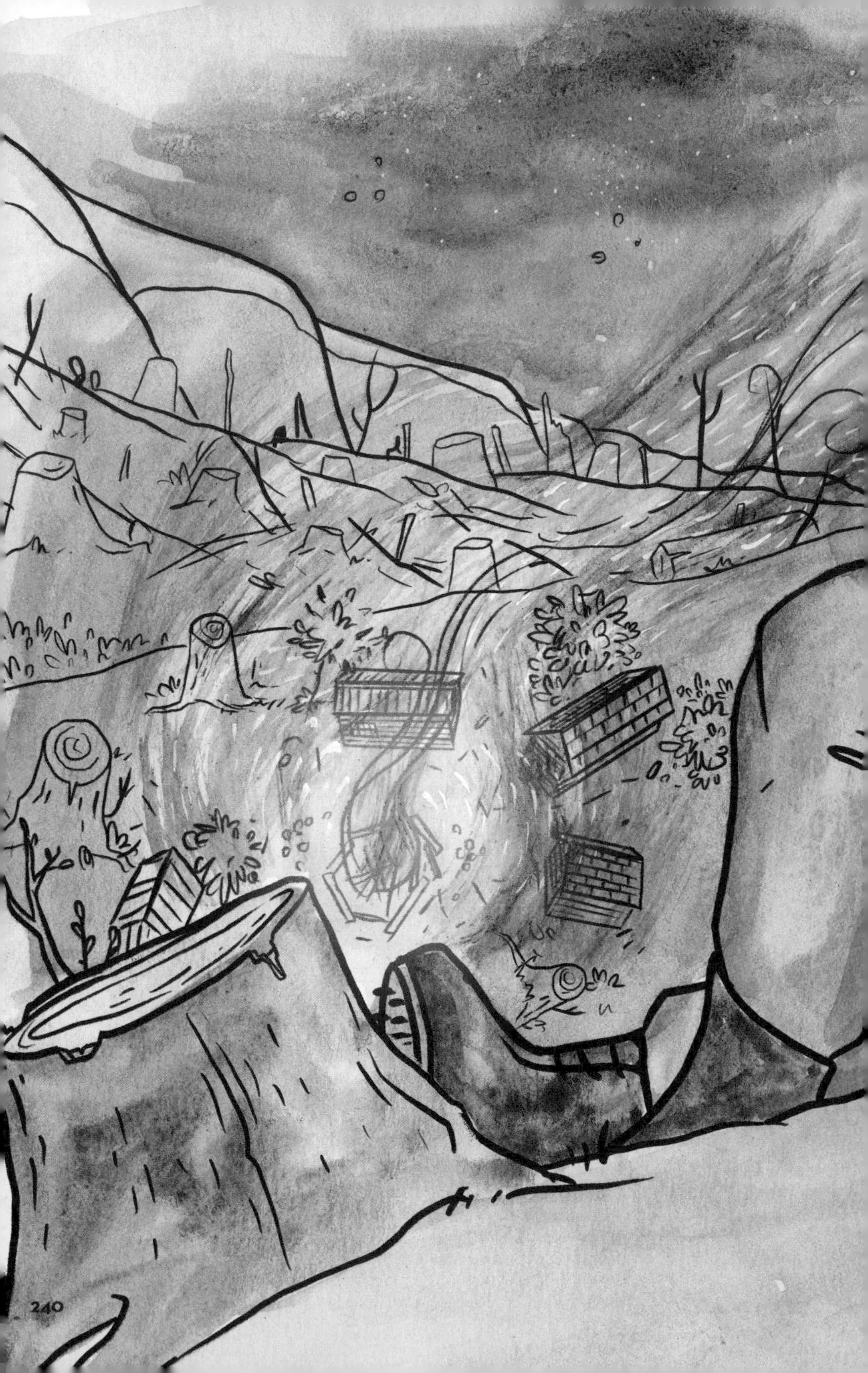

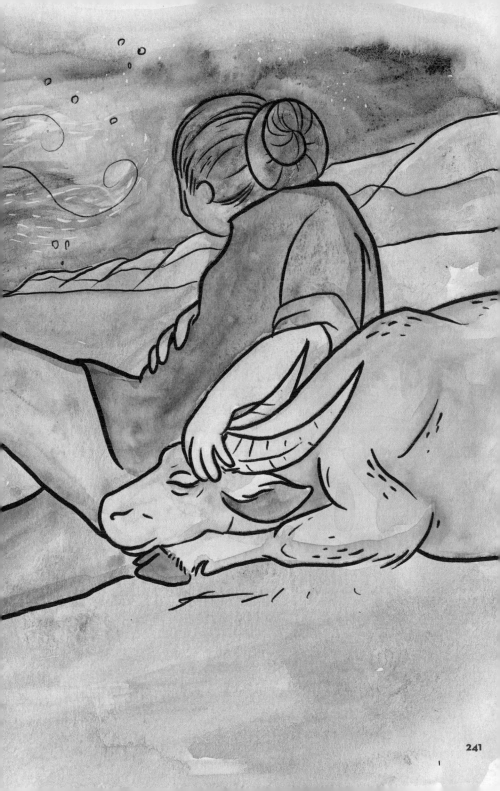

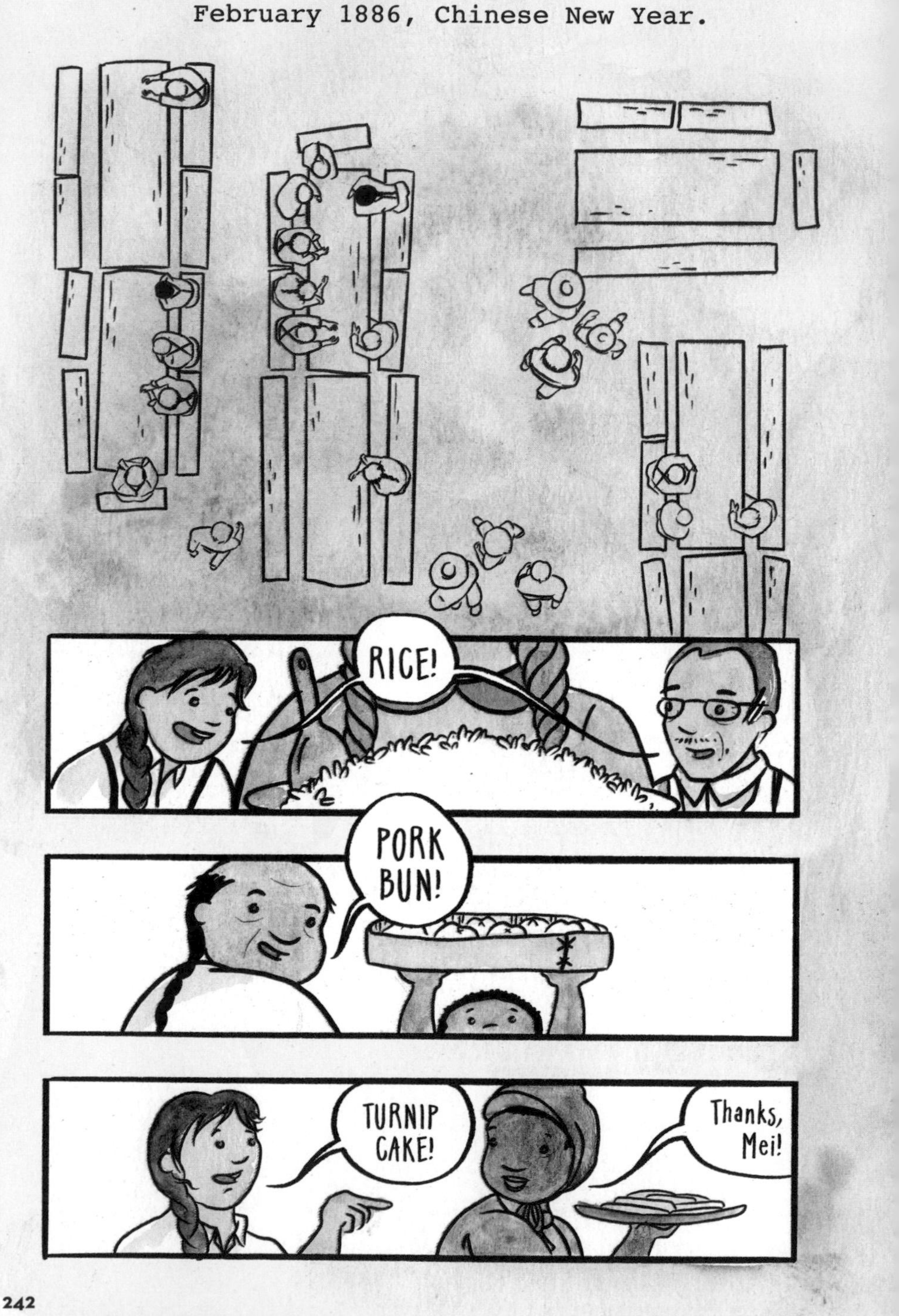
February 1886, Chinese New Year.
RICE!
PORK BUN!
TURNIP CAKE!
Thanks, Mei!

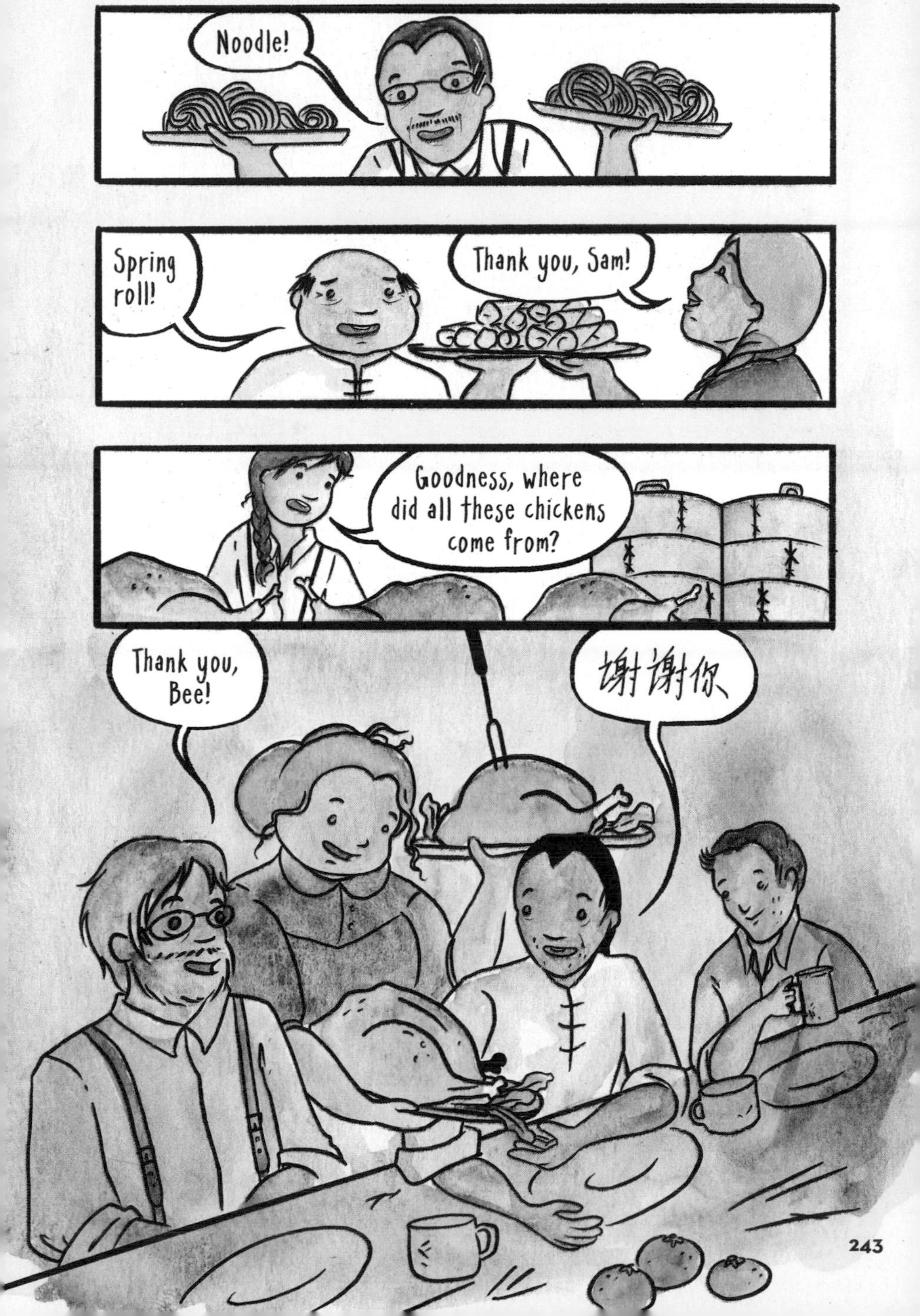
Noodle!
Spring roll!
Thank you, Sam!
Goodness, where did all these chickens come from?
Thank you, Bee!
谢谢你

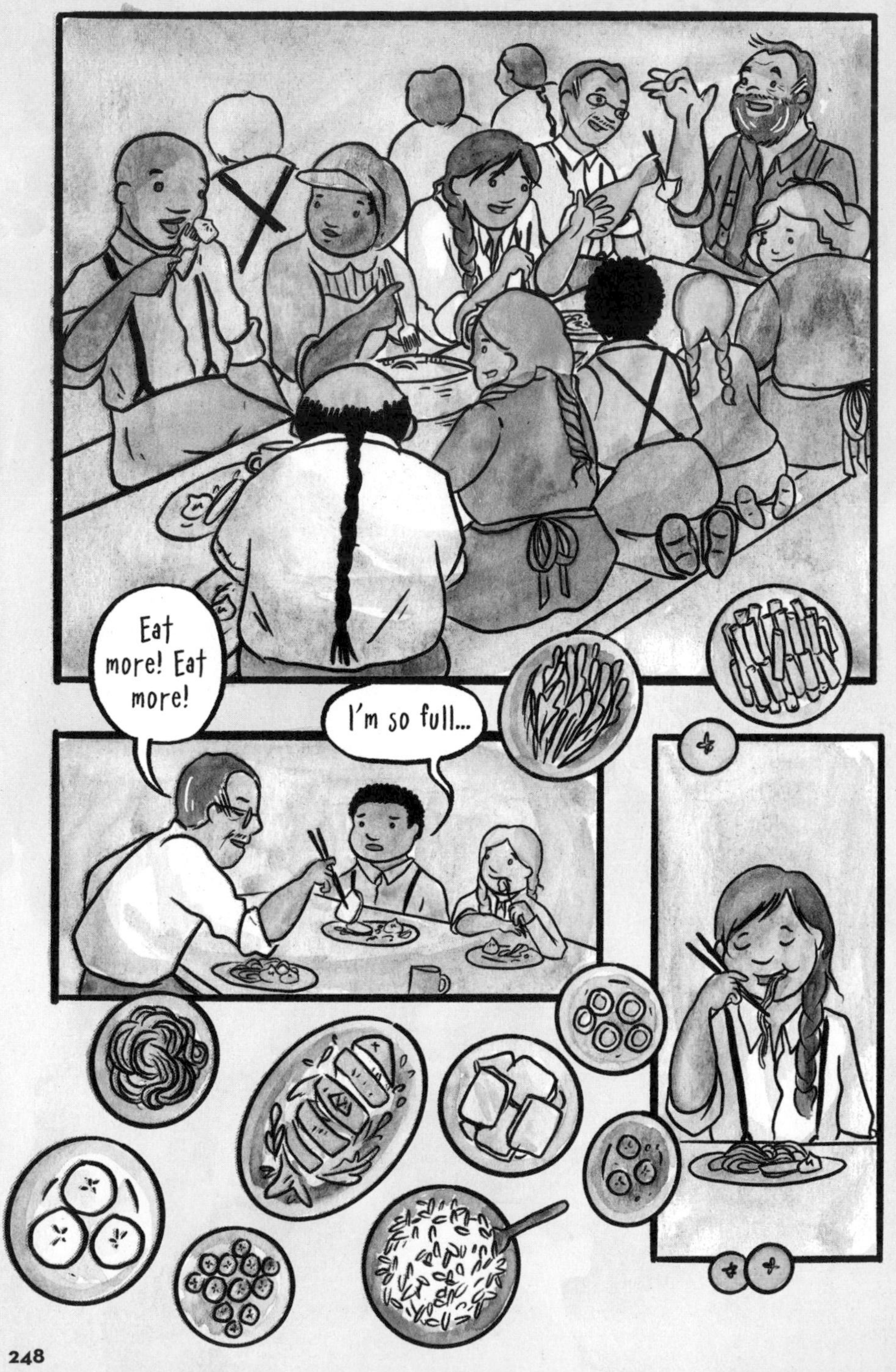
Eat more! Eat more!
I'm so full...

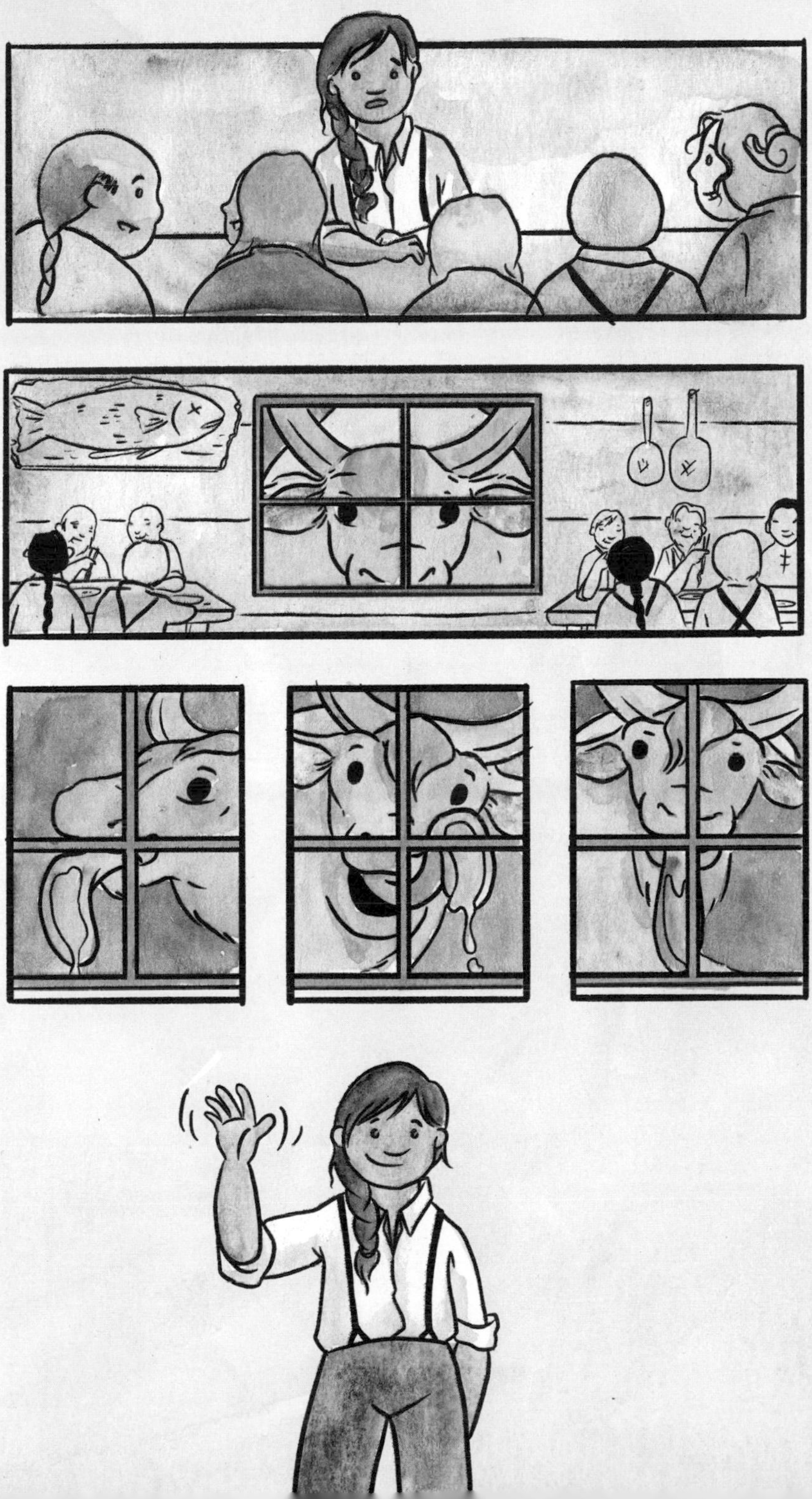

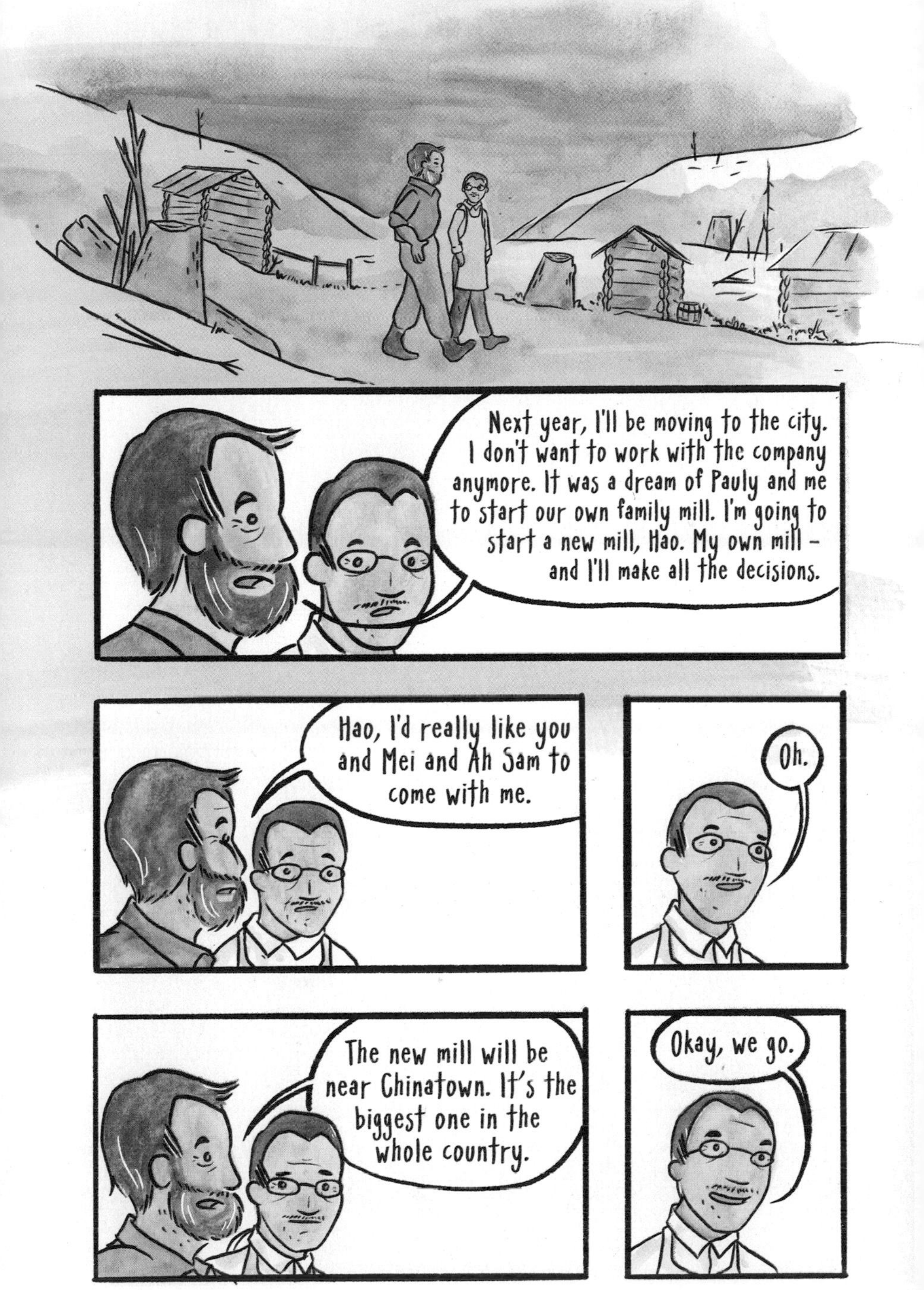
Next year, I'll be moving to the city. I don't want to work with the company anymore. It was a dream of Pauly and me to start our own family mill. I'm going to start a new mill, Hao. My own mill – and I'll make all the decisions.
Hao, I'd really like you and Mei and Ah Sam to come with me.
Oh.
The new mill will be near Chinatown. It's the biggest one in the whole country.
Okay, we go.

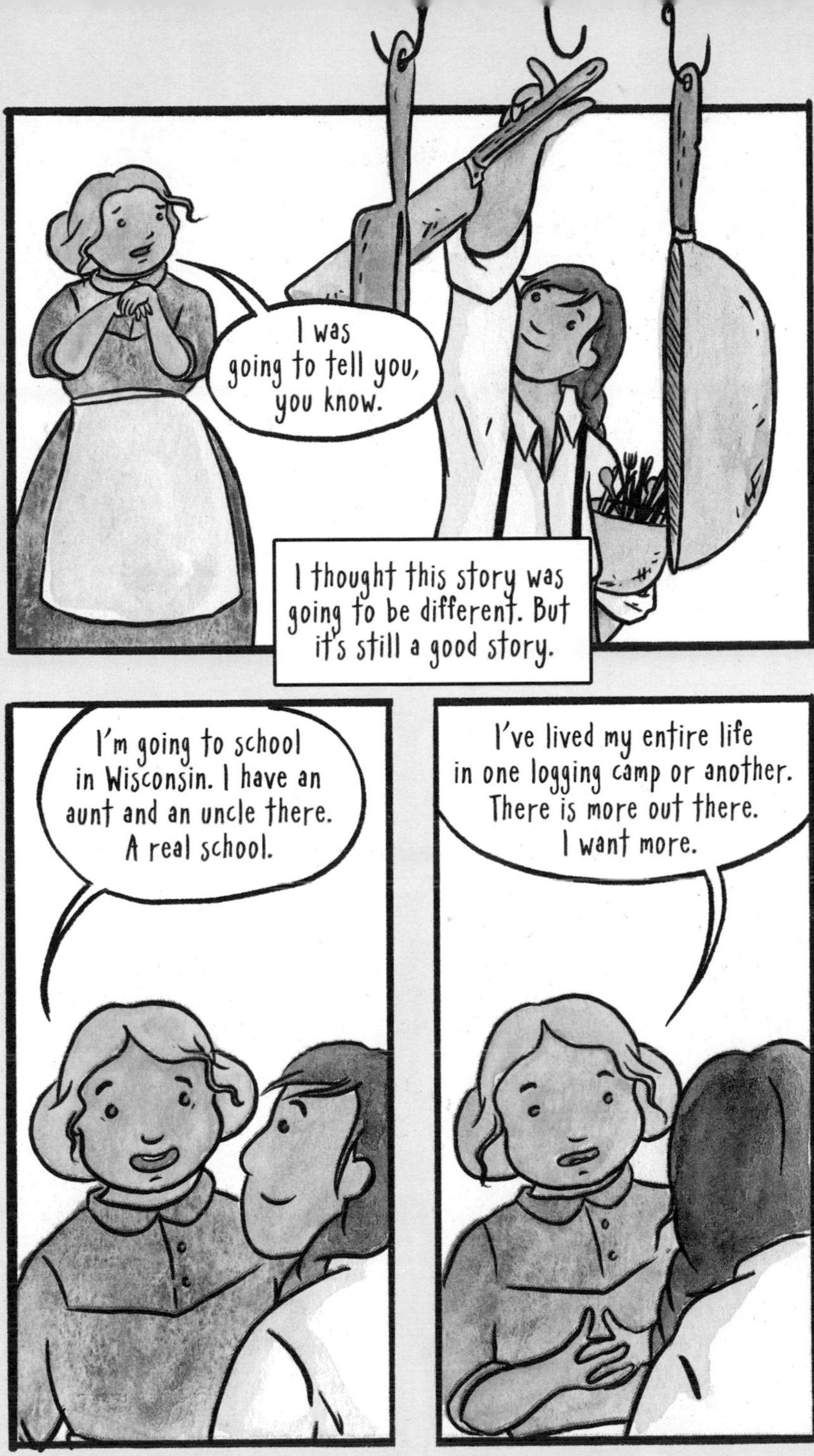
I was going to tell you, you know.
I thought this story was going to be different. But it's still a good story.
I'm going to school in Wisconsin. I have an aunt and an uncle there. A real school.
I've lived my entire life in one logging camp or another. There is more out there. I want more.

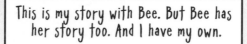

This is my story with Bee. But Bee has her story too. And I have my own.

And maybe when you graduate and marry a handsome and rich man, we can open a pie shop together.

265

What? Yeah, I want to go. I mean, it's still a few years away. Yeah, of course!
But I didn't really think -
Then I fire you.
!
No job. No more work in kitchen. We hire new cook.
Oh.

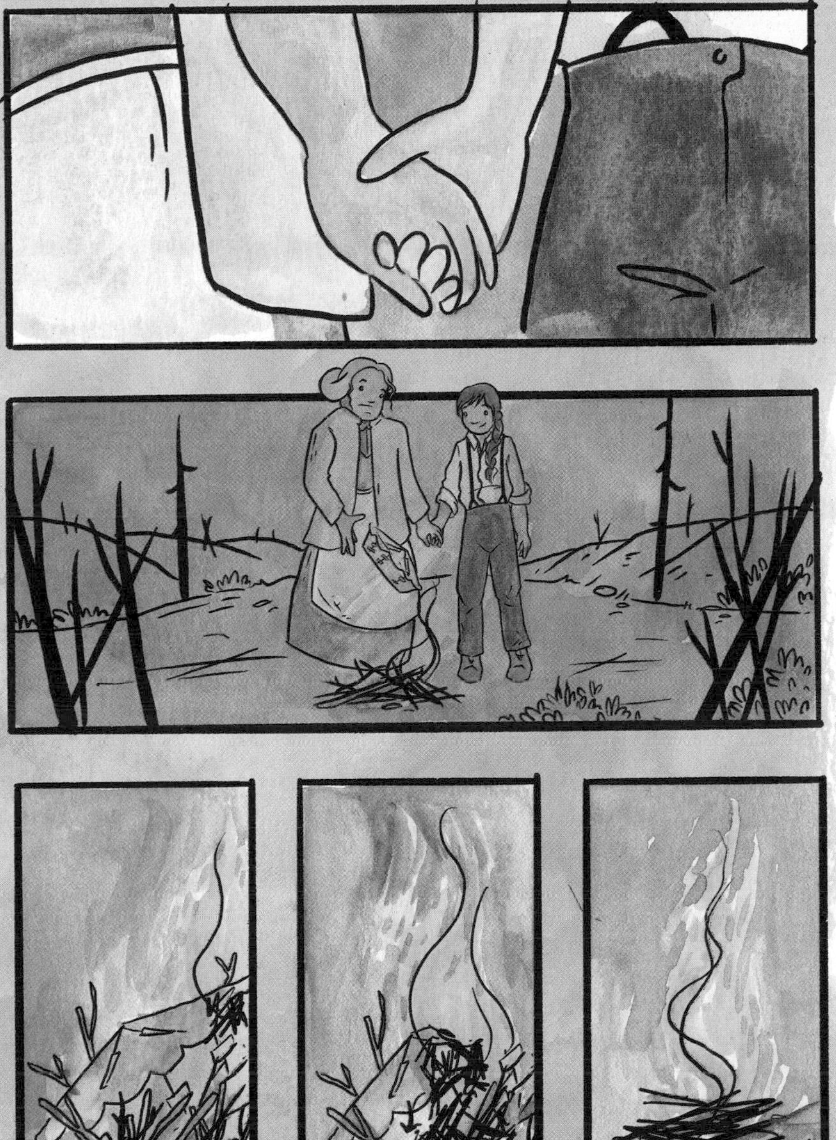

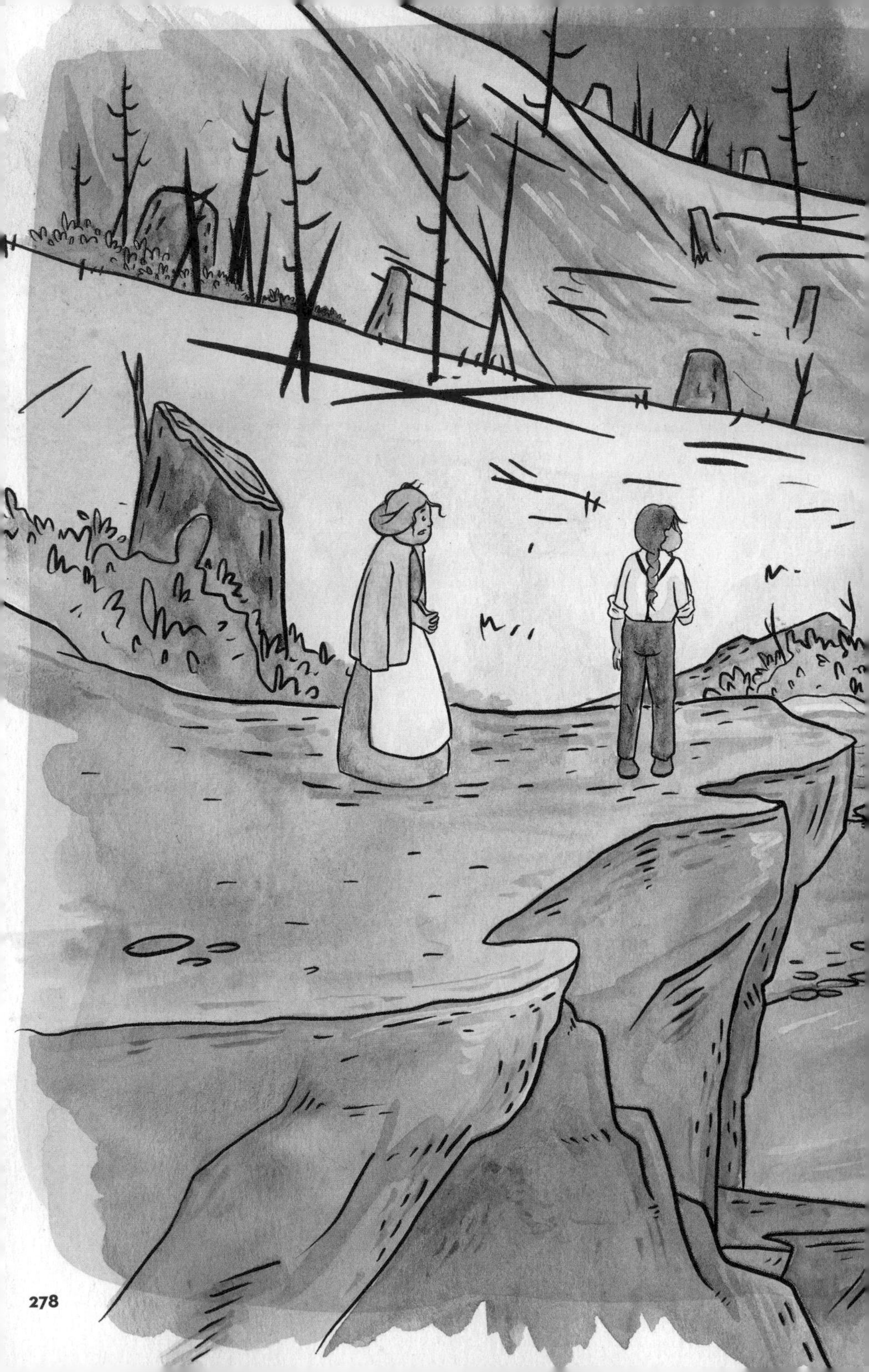

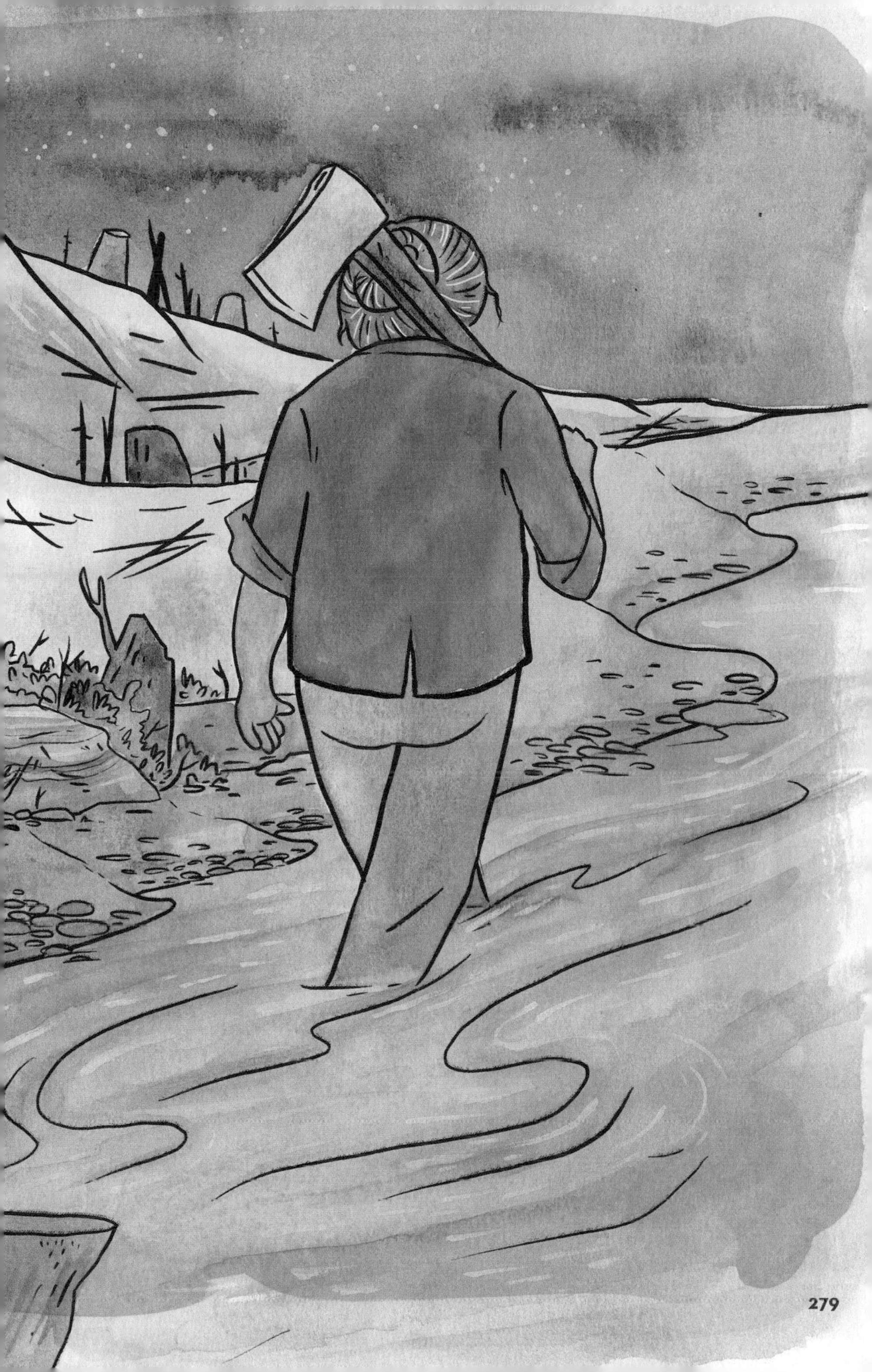

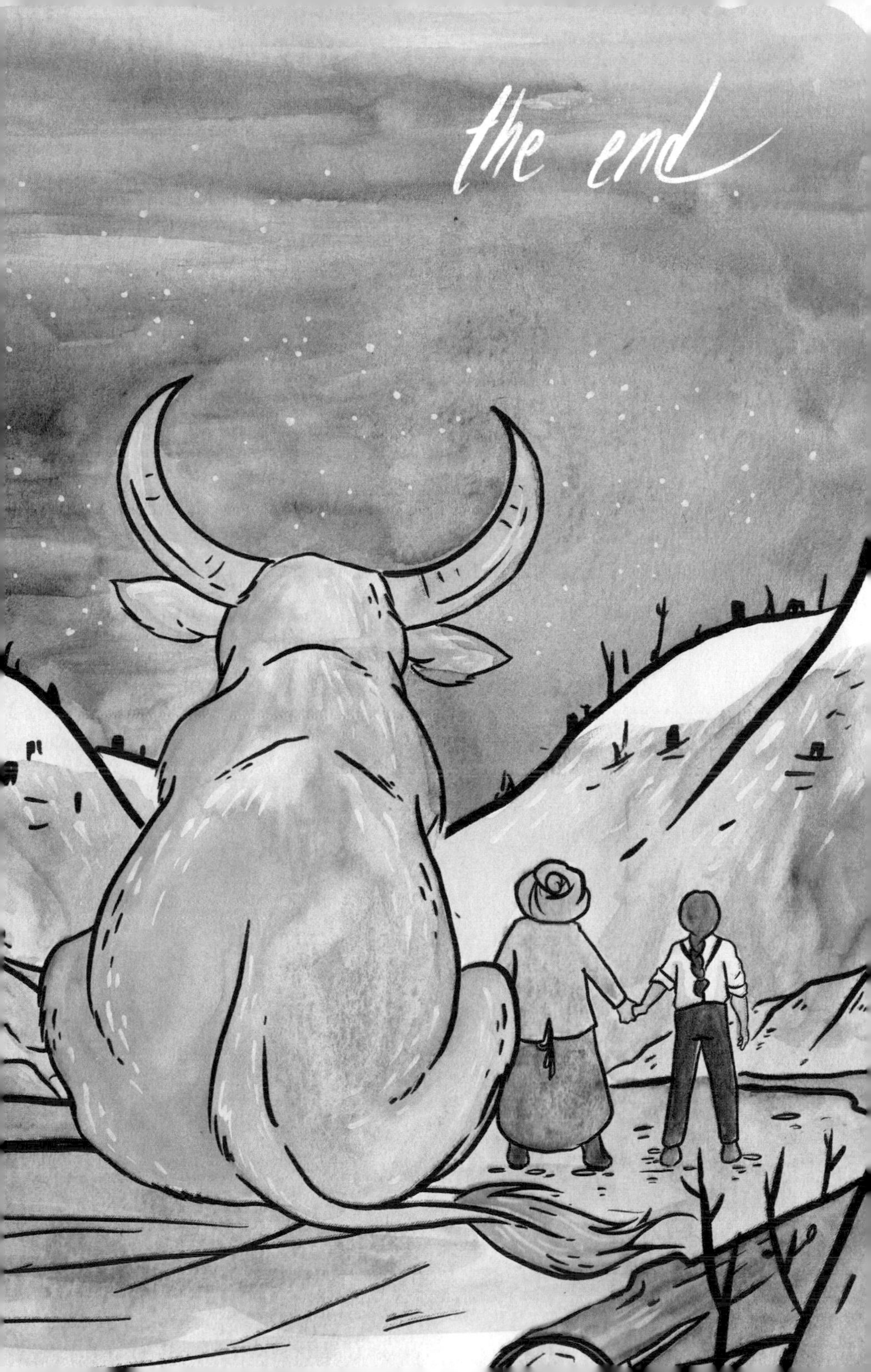
the end

AUTHOR'S NOTE:

When I wrote this book, I was hoping that it would be released in a new era of traditional publishing—one that was a vibrant landscape of stories from all kinds of marginalized voices. I sought to tell a single specific story, a story about one queer Chinese American girl contending with her place in a world that isn't catering to her needs, the tensions and friendships of a marginalized working class navigating proximity to whiteness for both the privilege and violence it confers, and a story about who gets to own a myth. I hope it is read as that specific story.

There are some omissions from this book, the most important being that there are no named Indigenous characters.

The story of Indigenous people and logging camps is complex. Many people were complicit in the erasure of Native Americans from their land, including Black people, and Chinese and European immigrants. This book was written and completed on the traditional lands of the Tongva. The Sierra Nevadas, the area where this book takes place, was historically inhabited by the Yokut, Sierra Miwok, Maidu, Mono, Northern Paiute, Southern Paiute, and Washoe, who still live in the region today. Native Americans worked in logging camps, including in the Sierra Nevadas, and some reservations also operated their own logging concerns. There is documentation of Native American logging camp foremen being valued, as they could communicate with both white people and Indigenous logger crews. There is also documentation of Native Americans being paid less than white immigrants. This is a complicated story and a story that needs nuance, and ultimately, I did not think it was my story to tell. But they were there. We were all there. This history, like all American history, is not a white story.

Researching working class Chinese in lumber camps is not easy. To that end, I am grateful to the scholars and writers whose academic sources I read. Specific details, like Ah Hao being paid more than Neils, and the small glass bottles to mark burials by train tracks, come from the research and writing done by Sue Fawn Chung (*Chinese in the Woods*) and the late Iris Chang (*The Chinese in America*), respectively. Ultimately, where I took liberties with history, I chose to do so because when our histories have been repressed and our people were not deemed worthy enough to document, I feel that we have the obligation to return ourselves to the narrative. If history failed us, fiction will have to restore us.

Thank you.

BIBLIOGRAPHY:

Aarim-Heriot, Najia, and Roger Daniels. *Chinese Immigrants, African Americans, and Racial Anxiety in the United States, 1848–82.* University of Illinois Press, 2003.

Barth, Gunther. *Bitter Strength*. Harvard University Press, 1964.

Chang, Iris. *The Chinese in America*. Penguin, 2004.

Chung, Sue Fawn. *Chinese in the Woods*. University of Illinois Press, 2015.

Chung, Sue Fawn, and Priscilla Wegars. *Chinese American Death Rituals*. AltaMira Press, 2005.

Edmonds, Michael. *Out of the Northwoods*. Wisconsin Historical Society, 2010.

Farquhar, Francis P. *History of the Sierra Nevada*. University of California Press, 2007.

Felton, Harold W. *Legends of Paul Bunyan*. University of Minnesota Press, 2008.

Shephard, Esther. *Paul Bunyan*. New York : Harcourt, Brace, 1924.

Stewart, Bernice, and Homer A. Watts. "Legends of Paul Bunyan, Lumberjack." *The Wisconsin Academy of Sciences, Arts, and Letters*, 1916.

ACKNOWLEDGMENTS:

I am honored to have finished this book in collaboration with, and the primary company of, people of color, who I never ever had to explain myself to. The Kokila team is a dream to work with—I am so grateful to Namrata Tripathi, for shaping and guiding this book with thoughtfulness and a critical eye, to Jasmin Rubero for her visual instinct and excellence, and to Sydnee Monday, Joanna Cárdenas, and Zareen Jaffery for contributing their insight and experience to the book-making process.

My agent, DongWon Song, believed in this book from the very start, and I am grateful for both his counsel and friendship.

My parents were constant cheerleaders, but also actual collaborators in reviewing drafts of my book, and giving me comments, both snarky and useful. Specifically, my mother did and advised on all the Cantonese translations in this book; and the majority of Chinese characters in the book are her own handwriting.

My husband, Jason Bender, is my bedrock, and also a solid beard drawing reference.

Heather Gilbraith, my horse friend, penciled every horse and buffalo in this book, filling in for one of my deepest inadequacies as an artist. If the horse parts still do not fit together correctly, it is entirely my fault; if they do, Heather deserves all the credit.

The book is fictional, but it was written on a fundamental anchor in academic research, specifically Sue Fawn Chung's *Chinese in the Woods* and Iris Chang's *The Chinese in America*. The former is an academic press book which I had trouble finding when I first had the seed of this book in my head; Leigh Walton, who expresses affection with research, sent me a .pdf from the NYPL ten minutes after I complained about not being able to find a hard copy.

The final stages of this book were completed in COVID-19 quarantine, between March and August 2020. For the people who helped to hold my brain together during this period—Leslie Levings, Sarah Gailey, Matthew Marco, Callie Rogers and Eron Rauch, the Monsterhearts crew, the Waywarders, the Space Gnomes, the Space Hobos, the Team DW Slack, my secret Twitter pals, the Comics Campers, the great indoor fighters—thank you; I needed you.

Finally, a thank you to the very good animals I pet while working on this book—Tinkerbell, Alma, Nacho, Precious, Henry, Rufio, Inky, Odin, Pagan, Chelsea, Ginny, and as always, my best friend Bug.